Abou

Like April in *The Continuity Girl*, Patrick is an Anglo-American. He was born to an English mother in Amarillo, Texas, but moved to the UK when his American father was stationed in Oxfordshire with the USAF in the mid-1970s. Unlike his older brother, Patrick was sent to a local rather than a base school, and very quickly went native. He eventually gained a PhD in English Literature at the Shakespeare Institute in Stratford-upon-Avon. For the past 14 years, he has taught English to secondary school children in an inner-city comprehensive in Coventry.

Long a fan of Sir Arthur Conan Doyle's Sherlock Holmes stories, Patrick contributed one of his own, 'The Doll and His Maker', to MX Publishing's *Sherlock's Home: The Empty House*, an anthology of pastiches put together to raise funds for the preservation of one of the author's former homes. As well as writing fiction, Patrick is a keen poet. He was short-listed for the Bridport Poetry Prize in 2012 and long-listed for the Fish Poetry Prize in 2013.

THE CONTINUITY GIRL

THE CONTINUITY GIRL

PATRICK KINCAID

Patrick Kincaid

Unbound

This edition first published in 2018

Unbound

6th Floor Mutual House, 70 Conduit Street, London W1S 2GF

www.unbound.com

ISBN (eBook): 978-1-911586-99-9

ISBN (Paperback): 978-1-911586-98-2

Design by Mecob

Cover image:
© iStockphoto.com/ CSA-Archive

Printed in Great Britain by Clays Ltd, St Ives Plc

MIX
Paper from
responsible sources
FSC® C018072

For Mum, who was there at the beginning.

For Eileen, who was there at the beginning

Dear Reader,

The book you are holding came about in a rather different way to most others. It was funded directly by readers through a new website: Unbound.

Unbound is the creation of three writers. We started the company because we believed there had to be a better deal for both writers and readers. On the Unbound website, authors share the ideas for the books they want to write directly with readers. If enough of you support the book by pledging for it in advance, we produce a beautifully bound special subscribers' edition and distribute a regular edition and e-book wherever books are sold, in shops and online.

This new way of publishing is actually a very old idea (Samuel Johnson funded his dictionary this way). We're just using the internet to build each writer a network of patrons. Here, at the back of this book, you'll find the names of all the people who made it happen.

Publishing in this way means readers are no longer just passive consumers of the books they buy, and authors are free to write the books they really want. They get a much fairer return too – half the profits their books generate, rather than a tiny percentage of the cover price.

If you're not yet a subscriber, we hope that you'll want to join our publishing revolution and have your name listed in one of our books in the future. To get you started, here is a £5 discount on your first pledge. Just visit unbound.com, make your pledge and type CONTINUITY18 in the promo code box when you check out.

Thank you for your support,

Dan, Justin and John
Founders, Unbound

Super Patrons

Anthony Alonzi
Clare Alonzi
Sebastian Alonzi
Spencer Anderton
Sandra Armor
Perry Asbury
Tim Atkinson
Peter Balderstone
Lyn Barton
Bob Beaupré
Alex Breeze
Iain Bruce
Emily Bryan
Fiona Wagstaff Buttler
Stephen Calcutt
James Carreras
Charlie Carter
Robbie Chandler
Liam Clark
Claire Clarke
Stuart Claw
Jonathan Coe
Dale Collett
Paul Cox
Jane Crowter
Dan Crowter
Anthony Davis
Val Davis
Shaun Delaney
John Dexter
Nicky Downes
Mike Draper

Bob Edwards
John Elliott
Oye Eneje
Tom Evershed
Kate Every
Jeanette Flannery
Elzbieta Furgalska
Paul Garbett
Judi Garland
Tom Garner
Miranda Godfrey
Majella Greene
Fiona Halpin
Rebecca Hare
Nick Harleigh-Bell
Anthony Simon Harries
Timothy Hearn
Lee Herbage
Frank Hibberd
Amanda Taylor Hobbs
Janice Holve
Tristan Hore
Kris Horne
Gyles Horner
Stacy Howe
Rob Jefferson-Brown
Margaret & Tim Jenkins
Sam Kelly
Dan Kieran
Brad Kincaid
Patricia Kincaid
Heather Kincaid
Alva Clayton Kincaid
Shannon Kincaid
Ric Kincaid
Elizabeth Klett

Paula LeLean
Mark Leonard
John Lindley
Tony Lindsell
Daniel Lloyd
John Malcolm
Katie McCann
David Mccormack
TJ McGowan
Breda Mitchell
John Mitchinson
Benjamin Moss
Kerry Moyes
Eamon Murtagh
Brian Murtagh
Arun Nagra
Patricia Orr
Louis Osborne
John Oswin
Rebekah Owens
Marcus Patterson
Laura Peak
Neil Phipps
Justin Pollard
Mark Price
Becky Price
Sandeep Purewal
Bhupinder Purewal
Curtis Riley
Steven Russell
Clare Seeley
Emily Sherriff
Elizabeth Sidwell
Michael Spencer
James Stacey
Janice Staines

Rachel Stephenson
Richard Stephenson
Anita Sullivan
Diana Sweeney
Carol Tilling
Dave Toulson
Solitaire Townsend
Colin Udall
David Valls-Russell
Jose Volcato
Charlotte Walters
Jacquie Walters
Jacquie Walters
Steve Ward
Joshua Wiffen
Jackie Williams

With grateful thanks to Alva Clayton Kincaid, who helped to make this book happen.

London, 2013

Holmes is pensive. He leans on the shoulder of the fireplace and addresses Watson directly. Madame Valladon isn't in the shot.

'We've come across this situation before,' he says.

'We have?' *Watson stops fidgeting in his borrowed kilt.* 'Where?'

Holmes moves towards the open casement of the window. Through it, we see a sliver of moonlit loch and the dim outline of mountains. 'At the ballet.'

'The ballet?'

Holmes gestures outside. 'There's a lake, and there's a castle, and there's a swan that isn't really a swan—'

David's hand is on Gemma's thigh again. Projected light glints off his glasses, but otherwise he's invisible to her. It's like he's both Holmes and Watson in the scene that's just been referenced, the one set at the ballet. He's bored and horny at the same time. He's also shattering her willing suspension of disbelief, pulling her out of the Victorian Scotland that's being shown on the screen and dropping her into a cinema in Islington in the 21st century. That's something she won't tolerate. She raps the five-fingered beast on its knuckles until it slips off the black nylon, retreating to its shadowy lair.

There's a swan that isn't really a swan, she thinks. Holmes is standing at the foot of the four-poster bed now, Madame Valladon gazing up at him from under the sheets with large, frightened eyes. *Or in this case, a monster that isn't really a monster…*

'So, there are two things everyone knows about Billy Wilder's *The Private Life of Sherlock Holmes*.'

They're sitting in the King's Head at a table too near the door, because it's a busy Thursday night and all the other tables are taken. Gemma has bought David a craft beer, as a reward for sitting through the film. She's already halfway through her glass of Merlot, gearing up to tell him her big news.

'Two things *everyone* knows?' His eyebrows have risen above the frame of his glasses, almost to his blond fringe. 'Nobody knows anything about *The Private Life of Sherlock Holmes*. I didn't know it existed before I met you.'

His Midwestern cuts through the English babble like a submersible through murky water. He's not a show-off, just loud – it took Gemma a while to figure that out. 'Okay, there are two things that Film Studies lecturers obsessed with *The Private Life of Sherlock Holmes* know about *The Private Life of Sherlock Holmes*.'

He nods, satisfied. 'And what might those two things be?'

She takes another sip of Merlot. 'First, it was a bloody difficult shoot. Actors who weren't used to Wilder's style had real problems with the number of takes and the very precise line readings and movement he required of them. It was bad enough for Christopher Lee, who was already a veteran film actor by 1969 – for others, who'd come from the stage, it was a nightmare. Poor Robert Stephens had the worst of it. He hoped that playing Sherlock Holmes for Billy Wilder would be his ticket to Hollywood. Instead, all the retakes and notes led to a massive crisis of confidence. He ended up taking an overdose, which caused a big delay and cost the production money. There was also the fiasco with the Loch Ness Monster...'

'Fiasco?' says David. 'That was the best part.'

Gemma rolls her eyes at him. 'The film had a huge budget – 10 million dollars – which bought them an appropriately huge Baker Street set. It also bought a practical prop of the Loch Ness Monster for use in your actual Loch Ness, made by Wally Veevers of *2001* fame. But on the day they tested it on the water, it sank without trace. Straight to the bottom of the loch, no hope of recovery.'

'Then what was that we saw in the movie?'

'They built another one and shot the scene in a tank at Elstree.'

David blows out his lips. 'More delays, more money, huh?'

Gemma nods. He's getting it.

'You said there were two things Billy Wilder nerds know about *The Private Life of Sherlock Holmes…?*'

'I did.' She takes another sip of wine. 'The second is that the finished movie was cut to shreds by order of the studio, and that it broke Billy Wilder's heart.'

Damp, gritty air blows over them. A group of women have entered, dressed in bright satiny stuff and strappy stilettos. It's wholly inadequate to the demands of even a mild December night, but isn't a million miles from the get-up Gemma would have chosen on similar nights, five or six years ago. They're here to pre-load on cheaper drinks, she knows, before heading to a nightclub. David gets a good eyeful of these latest arrivals – the pub's full of them – before growing self-conscious and offering Gemma a grin.

'You're incorrigible,' she says, tugging her cardigan more tightly around her.

He shrugs, as if to say, *What can you do with me?*

'Anyway,' she continues, 'the producers didn't give a toss that Wilder had won them every Oscar going with *The Apartment*, ten years before. They were just scared shitless he'd delivered a film they couldn't sell. Wilder wanted a roadshow presentation – a three-hour epic, like *Ben Hur*. But it was a format that was no longer doing the business. Nobody had gone to see *Doctor Doolittle* a couple of years earlier, which was considered comparable because it's another period piece. So, the producers ordered the film cut by a third, and whole sequences were lost, seemingly forever. It didn't save the movie, either. Audiences still stayed away and critics ignored it. Poor Robert Stephens never did become a Hollywood superstar.'

'So, what's happened now?' He's looking at her slyly. 'Something's happened, or you wouldn't be telling me all this, like it's something that would interest me.'

She beams at him. 'A bloody miracle,' she says, 'that's what.'

She fishes her iPhone out of her handbag and finds her Queen Mary account. 'Here,' she says, scooting her chair around so they can both see the screen. 'John Letterer at the BFI sent me this on Tuesday.'

It's headed simply, '*TPLOSH*':

'*Hi Gemma,*

'*I've forwarded the email from MGM Holdings, with permission. Long story short, the rumours are true! During an audit last year, a cache of missing cans was traced to the home of an old United Artists employee. (I couldn't confirm whether it was the janitor, as you speculated.) He's long gone, but his daughter rooted about in the attic and found treasure. Nothing exciting, except for one complete film.*'

'That easy?' says David.
'That easy,' Gemma says. She slides up.

'*They're a good way through the clean-up and digital transfer, and are aiming for simultaneous theatrical and DVD/Blu-ray releases next autumn. But NB: they're keen on festival screenings first!*

'*Given your established support for the film, and for Wilder's late work in general, we'd like to hand it over to you. Of course, we could show it at the LFF next October, but if there's a slot available in the summer, somewhere appropriate, that would be even better.*

'*Also, who could we interview? Mark Gatiss is scheduled to present the "old" print here in the spring, but I think we should be looking for someone involved in the original shoot for the big re-release. Would Christopher Lee be a stretch, given his age? Maybe one of the crew who's not so long in the tooth? I'll leave it to you...*'

David laughs and, as ever, it's a sight to behold. His long face creases in all the right places.
'Good, isn't it?' says Gemma.
'So, what'll we see that we didn't see tonight?'
Gemma is almost overwhelmed by the riches that lie in store. 'Well, it was always meant to be a whole casebook of stories Watson didn't think the Victorian public were ready for. So, lots of sex

and drugs.' She puts down her iPhone and counts off the items on her fingers. 'There's a prologue featuring Dr Watson's Canadian grandson. There's "The Dreadful Business of the Naked Honeymooners"—'

'That's all in the title, isn't it?'

'Pretty much. There's "The Curious Case of the Upside-Down Room", which is Watson trying to distract Holmes from his cocaine habit with an unsolvable mystery. And best of all, there's a flashback to Sherlock's student days, and a formative encounter with a hooker. In the studio cut, we've only two cases: "The Singular Affair of the Russian Ballerina" and "The Adventure of the Dumbfounded Detective", which is the one with the Loch Ness Monster in it. They're wonderful, and they make up what's always been my favourite film, but they hardly amount to a casebook. It's going to be a different movie now.' She feels an odd tugging inside her as she says it. 'Very different.'

David throws an arm around her and squeezes, a little too tightly. 'I can't imagine anything like it in my line,' he says. 'Maybe if George Lucas let Han shoot first again.' She pokes him in the ribs. 'I'm kidding.'

He's looking towards the bar now. Either he's thinking of his second pint – his beer glass is empty – or he's allowing himself to be distracted by the pre-loaders. It's perfectly possible he's doing both.

'I think this calls for another round,' he says. 'Same again?'

She watches him at the bar, and watches how the pre-loaders watch him. They're throwing him glances, muttering into their drinks, into their girlfriends' ears… He's quite a presence: a long Minnesotan Viking in hornrims and hipster tweeds, hair gelled so that it looks like it's been sculpted from yellow meerschaum. She's told him it's a bad look – that he's nearly thirty, catching up with her, and that dressing like an old man is a young man's game. But the truth is he looks just fine, and knows it.

She taps her PIN into her iPhone again, and spends some more time marvelling over John Letterer's email. Then she opens her Gmail account. There's a ping – it's Julie Crosby at the University

of Aberdeen. She feels a fluttering in her belly. The preview reads
'*Dear Dr MacDonald, Further to our conversation on Tuesday, I'd...*',
but that's all there is, and she can't open it properly now because
David's returning with the drinks.

He sits beside her again and slides the new Merlot her way.
'Okay,' he says, his hand finding her thigh, the way it did in the
cinema, 'time to talk Frightfest. *Quid pro quo*, Clarice.'

Gemma feels the damp tightening her hair as they head for Angel
Tube station. It isn't Christmassy, despite the lights in the windows and their reflections in the pavement puddles. She's actually
too warm in her overcoat. Even last February, when everyone
else in the country was enjoying real snow, Londoners had had to
make do with a few days of slush.

Just before they go underground, they pass a poster for Matthew
Bourne's *Swan Lake*, on the side of a bus shelter. The lead dancer
is wearing shaggy-feathered breeches. He's barechested, his arms
raised behind his back like wings. Gemma laughs, but keeps the
joke to herself. Talk about a swan that isn't really a swan – here's a
ballerina that isn't really a ballerina. What would Billy Wilder have
thought of that?

She doesn't bother looking at her phone on the journey
back to Whitechapel, because mostly there's no signal, and
she's forgotten a book. So, while David's reading off his Kindle
app, she's watching faces: the implacable, been-everywhere,
seen-everything faces of the capital – that great cesspool to
which Dr Watson is irresistibly drawn at the beginning of *A
Study in Scarlet*, with all the other idlers and loungers of the
Empire. Not that these are the faces of idlers and loungers, so
far as she can tell. Instead, they seem scored by experiences as
various as their origins. There are foreign books being read,
and foreign newspapers, and Gemma doesn't always recognise
the languages. Even the printed characters aren't always identifiable.

Once in the flat, she monopolises the bathroom. Then, while

David's in there after her, brushing his teeth, she opens up her laptop and reads her emails in bed.

Dear Dr MacDonald,

Further to our conversation on Tuesday, I'd like to confirm that we are interested in your ideas about the scope of the Film Studies department. Can I ask you to send a summary in writing? Then I'll get back to you and see if we can't arrange a time to discuss things. We can do that by Skype, but perhaps it would be better to try for a face-to-face, either in London or up here.

Best wishes,

Julia

Prof J. H. Crosby

School of Language, Literature, Music and Visual Culture,

University of Aberdeen

Gemma can hear the cistern filling now, and knows David will be in the bedroom within half a minute. Her sense of guilt is palpable and irritating: there's nothing to feel guilty about. But she quickly taps open a new tab and closes the old one. She types in a search: *film festivals scotland.*

'Want to watch something?' He's wearing pyjama bottoms and a T-shirt. To him, it's cold – Gemma has to have the window open even when there's frost outside. She'll take off her nightdress before she tries to sleep. '*Game of Thrones?*'

She nods. 'Nearly done here.'

There's Edinburgh, of course, and a couple of others that are instantly familiar. The Glasgow Short Film Festival, and Dead by Dawn, the Scottish version of Frightfest. She clicks to the

next page of results and scrolls down until she finds the one
she almost believes she's imagined: the Loch Ness Film Festival. She opens the link in a new tab, bookmarks it, then closes
the browser. She brings up her documents and hits the folder
labelled TPLOSH.

But then the screen tips and the keyboard slides almost from her
knees. She has to scramble to catch it.

'Or we don't have to watch anything,' says David. His hand is
on her knee again, under the duvet, and there's no nylon in its way
now.

'I said I'm nearly done.' She sighs histrionically, as though she
doesn't really mean it. 'You're like a bloody puppy.'

'Not a puppy—' he nuzzles her neck while she's trying to right
the computer, '—more like a full-grown "big Baskerville dog".'

He's putting on Clive Revill's accent, as the Imperial Russian
Ballet manager from the film, but not quite remembering the
line. While he growls in her ear, she keeps trying to scan the
list of crew on the screen. The role she's after is near the bottom, and called 'Continuity', but it wouldn't have been called
that in the summer of 1969, when the film was being made.
As befits the *Mad Men* era that hadn't quite passed, it would
have been something far more gender specific and patronising.

David's pushing the screen down now, nuzzling more deeply.
Gemma laughs, but she's also grabbing the screen, arresting its
descent. 'Let me close it properly, you loony.'

'Loony – that's right,' he growls. 'It's the moon turning me into
a monster. I'm the Wolf Man of the Baskervilles.'

She manages to hit *hibernate* and guides the fading laptop off the
bed and onto the floor. She's going to give in to the beast for now
and return to this stuff later. Why shouldn't she? He isn't really a
monster, after all.

Chapter One

For the first time since October, Jim was too warm for his army-surplus jumper. He'd put it on out of habit that morning, but now peeled it off and let it slip down the side of the van. Though snow still clung to the higher reaches in the Cairngorms to the south, and in the mountains to the north and west, here in the Great Glen it was finally spring.

He took a new exercise book out of his kitbag and folded back the cover. At the top of the first page he wrote '*L.N.R.G. member's log book, J. Outhwaite, No. 64*'. He underlined it, checked his watch, and jotted down the date and time. '*Thursday, 22-5-1969, 08:43 BST.*' Then he made a note of the location and conditions. '*Campbell Pier, Urquhart Bay. Visibility good.*'

The biro blotched, filling the second 'o' and the loop of the 'd' with black ink.

He looked up again.

From here on the quayside, standing on the roof of the van, Jim could see with his naked eye the ochre-coloured stones of the ruined castle, nearly a mile across the bay. Across the loch proper, nearly double the distance, he almost believed that he could make out individual yellow flowers in the gorse. He couldn't, not with his naked eye, but still, he had to concede that visibility was '*very good*'. He wiped the nib of the pen on his jeans and amended the note.

'Cup of tea, Jamie?'

Tessa was standing in the shade of the downy birches at the limits of the concrete landing. She'd set up the camp stove there and her hands were wrapped around a steaming mug. She was still in her duffel coat, too. Was she cold? More likely, she only wanted it for its big patch pockets. Jim could see a broken-cornered paperback sticking out of the one over her right hip.

'No ta,' said Jim. 'Had one before I came out.'

He slotted the new 35mm reel into the camera, hooking it to the sprockets. He ratcheted it in and snapped the casing shut. Then he peered down the length of the lens into the heart of the water. It looked steely blue from this angle, but that was only a reflection of the sky. Closer, it would seem black – closer still, and its true colour would appear: a deep and ruddy brown.

He felt again that pulse run through him that he'd first felt as a child, thrilling to illustrated books about dinosaurs, and thrilling further to reports that maybe – just maybe – one species persisted, confined to a lake in the British Isles. When he'd been old enough to go out alone, he'd spent secret hours looking out on Lake Windermere with his dad's field glasses, imagining that it, too, might hold secrets. That pulse had remained with him through his grammar school years, through his degree in biology at Manchester, and hadn't entirely gone when he was approached by a senior member of the LNRG while completing his master's in marine biology at Aberdeen. Three years on, and the pulse was as strong as ever. So what if the data he and his colleagues had amassed so far had pointed in other directions? It would take just one unanswerable piece of physical evidence to change the world forever...

'Good day for it, though, isn't it?' said Tessa.

Jim kept his eye on the loch. 'Depends.'

'Sorry?'

'Depends on what conditions might be considered favourable to whatever might be out there.'

'Well—' Tessa was forcing the bright tone, '—it stands to reason she'd like the sun, doesn't it?'

Jim didn't know what that meant. Or maybe he did, but didn't want to engage in the discussion it was prompting. The water's temperature couldn't have risen much since yesterday, could it? Probably, it was no more than forty degrees. How much joy would that bring to the frolicking plesiosaur of their dreams?

A hooded crow cawed nearby and the breeze raised a seashore sound in the trees.

'Well,' she said at last, 'I'm off for a stroll. See you for elevenses.'

'Right you are, Tessa.'

He didn't look around until she'd gone a good way down the

path towards Inverness. No doubt she'd find some spot where she could read the latest claptrap without being interrupted by the thinking of others.

Jim unfolded the chair and slotted it securely in its runners. He was glad to get on with the work, but as he tried to settle, he felt lonely, too. How long would it be before someone joined him? This late start was irksome, but inevitable, given last night's gathering of the junior members of the LNRG – all two of them – at the bar of the Drumnadrochit Hotel. The pints of McEwan's had given way far too early to drams of whisky, and Jim had only avoided the worst by switching to halves as soon as he could, and then to singles when they moved to shorts. But he knew that his fellow junior member would be nursing a champion hangover this morning...

There was a shudder beneath Jim's feet, followed by a fearsome creak from one of the van's back doors. He turned in time to see the lad himself stumble out onto the mossy landing in bare feet.

'Alan?' Jim couldn't believe it. 'You never slept in the van?'

Alan squinted up at him with minuscule eyes, set in a face the same colour and shape as a bowl of porridge. He was wearing the same jeans he'd had on last night, but was otherwise naked. His over-padded torso glowed pink, as though with heat.

'Morning, Jamie.' He coughed, hacked up a globule, and let it drop between his feet. 'It's better than the shed' – he meant sleeping in the van was better than in the creosoted shack, set a little way from Tessa's camp stove – 'and I would've been heaving if I'd tried the *Cally.*'

The *Cally* was the *Caledonian,* the LNRG's 22-foot cabin cruiser, riding placidly in her moorings now. Her square cabin, which gave her a wide-eyed, high-browed look, gave enough protection to the pilot even on blustery days, but Jim wouldn't have fancied trying to sleep in it. The *Cally* was chiefly valued by the group for her deck, which allowed for largely unimpeded photography off both bows and the stern. Though she belonged to the LNRG's director, Jim always thought of her as Alan's baby.

'And how are you feeling now?' Jim asked.

He was standing with his hands on his hips, drawing breath in slowly and peering out at the loch. 'Better for that view, eh?' he said, then added, 'Still shite, mind.' He patted the pockets of his jeans. 'No fags, for fuck's sake.'

Jim realised something. 'You don't have your camera, do you? You won't be able to go out. You're going to have to walk back to the farmhouse.'

'Taken care of, pal.' He'd made his way to the back of the van again, and out of view. 'Sandra's bringing it down in the Alvis. It was the deal we made when I agreed to come here for the night.'

Jim mouthed a curse. Sandra was the last thing he needed. In fact, the thought of Alan's wife arriving any minute, bearing not only the camera, but all the grudges she'd nurtured since sending her husband to this mobile dog house, was enough to make him want to abandon all that he'd planned to do here today. There wasn't a chance Jim wouldn't be caught in the crossfire, called as a character witness on one side, blamed as a co-conspirator on the other. Sandra wasn't like Tessa – terse replies and turning a deaf ear wouldn't be enough to send her packing.

'She was not pleased,' Alan was saying. The van rocked a little, and Jim supposed he was sitting in the open doorway, pulling on the rest of his clothes. 'What made us do it, eh? Crazy!'

'No idea, Alan.' Jim picked up the biro and the new log book again, and struck out all the details he'd written beneath the title. 'But we've learnt our lesson now, haven't we?'

'Oh ay,' said Alan, sounding uncannily as though he meant it. 'Never again.'

Jim put away the book and pen, then got up and started detaching the chair from its runners. Alan came around the side of the van again, whistling something familiar. He was in yesterday's shirt and shoes now, as well as the jeans.

'You're not staying?' he asked, seeing Jim busy. 'Thought you were doing Urquhart Bay all this week.'

'Change of plan,' said Jim, folding the chair. 'Thought I'd try the high road past Lewiston. I've been meaning to for a while.'

'The one with the gradient?' Alan took the chair as Jim passed it down. 'Good luck getting the Green Goddess up there.'

Jim pulled the kitbag over his shoulder and clambered down the ladder on the nearside. Alan was whistling again, and it wasn't until Jim had put the chair in the back, and had slammed the door, that he recognised the tune.

'"I'm Getting Married in the Morning"?' He said it with a sneer. 'Why on earth are you whistling that?'

'No idea, pal.' Alan ambled towards the *Cally*. Then he laughed. 'Oh ay, I do know. Remember what they were talking about at the Drum? Stanley Holloway, and all that?'

'Stanley Holloway?'

'Ay, you know – funny man, actor. "Albert and the fucking Lion."'

'I know who Stanley Holloway is,' said Jim.

'Well, it's him who sings the song in *My Fair Lady*. One of Sandra's favourites – had to sit through that, too, as well as *The Sound of Music*...'

Vaguely, Jim did remember something of the only conversation there'd been at the bar last night. He'd been paying too much attention to keeping his drinking down, and to trying to interest Alan in his new theory about migrant species, to listen properly. A group of actors were expected at the hotel in the next few days. Not just actors, either: cameramen, lighting and sound crew, costume girls, makeup artists... They would be staying at the Drum right through the summer, making a picture.

'Christ.' The import of this was only now becoming clear. 'Did they say where exactly they'd be filming?'

'Well, here.' Alan was pointing past the *Cally*, out at the loch, as though that could possibly be a film location.

'And what's it about,' Jim asked, 'this picture they're making?'

'A Sherlock Holmes flick,' said Alan. '*Sherlock Holmes in the Highlands*. I'm pretty sure that's what they said.'

They – the proprietor of the Drumnadrochit Hotel and the local sots. What could they know?

Jim picked up his jumper from where he'd let it drop. At the same moment, he heard the hectic buzz of a car coming down the lane in too low a gear. 'That's me ready,' he said. 'I'm off.'

'Good luck, pal,' said Alan, though he was the one who needed it.

Jim was reversing when he saw the white Alvis appear in his side mirror. By the time he was turned the right way, the road out of the quayside was clear. He waved at the impression of red hair and cigarette smoke, which was all he could see of Sandra through the car's windscreen.

The last time he'd come this way had been on foot, back when he'd still been figuring out the lie of the land. It hadn't seemed a good prospect at first, but when he'd got past the thicker patches of birch and hazel, and then of plantation conifers, a panorama had opened out that he'd been wanting to exploit ever since.

The incline was every bit the challenge Alan had predicted, but once over it, he drove with a smidgeon of glee in his heart. Clear of the trees, he found the passing point he remembered and parked clear of the road. On the roof again, he manipulated the camera so that it pointed downwards and off the side. He settled in the folding chair, secured now to the cross runners. Conditions remained perfect, and the sky was a cobalt slab with only some light mackerelling high up, mirrored in tremulous form on the loch below. He could still see yellow in the opposing hills, while in the deciduous forest below there was white cherry blossom.

He picked up the newspaper and flicked past some sombre stuff about the American war in Vietnam. It wasn't that he didn't care, it was just that knowing more about it didn't make any difference. There was a report on Apollo 10, and another about how the astronauts who returned from the moon would be quarantined to guard against 'space bugs'. 'Space bugs' – even Jim couldn't help thinking of Professor Quatermass...

Something tickled his vision over the top of the newspaper.

This was how it happened – an interference just bothersome enough to keep him from reading. Usually, it didn't happen so soon. He put down the newspaper and stared at the dark streak, like a wound in the water, where otherwise there was a sheen of reflected light.

A disturbance.

In the time it took him to throw the switch on the camera, look through the eyepiece and find his mark again, Jim had already gone over the half-dozen different types of disturbance that the LNRG had already catalogued. A grebe or cormorant, or some other species of displaced diving bird. A red deer crossing from the other bank – unlikely, but possible. A floating log, brought down by a burn full of meltwater. Most probably, it was the dying surge of a passing motor boat, though it would have been long dying, since there was no sign of such a vessel in the wide expanse of loch that was exposed to him. He focused on the crest of the surge.

Oh, hell.

Something black and spherical, or close to it. Smooth. Far too big for the head of a cormorant, and the wrong shape for a deer.

Go through the procedure, he told himself. *You need to go through the procedure.*

He took out the exercise book and biro and checked his watch. '*09:28, BST,*' he wrote. '*New variety of disruption.*' Then he drew a question mark. It was enormous, wasting half a page – why had he done that? He raised his binoculars, just in time to see something else break the surface near the object.

It was a hand – a human hand. And now he knew that the round object was a head, covered in a black swimming cap.

'Oh, for pity's…!'

Jim flung down the exercise book and biro, so that they ran smoothly off the roof and into a patch of gorse. When he looked through the binoculars again, the swimmer was backstroking, moving her arms like the wheels of a paddle steamer, thrashing the water white with her feet. As well as the cap, she was wearing a two-piece swimming costume with yellow flowers on it, which didn't belong anywhere but a foreign beach. Christ, she must have been freezing! He tried to get a good look at her face, but it was screwed up against sun and spray.

He got down from the roof and reached through the open driver's window.

'You bloody fool,' he cried over the sound of the horn, 'You'll get caught in the current. You'll die of bloody hypothermia…'

But there was no chance she would hear either him or the van's horn, except as things far off that had nothing to do with her. By the time he was back on the roof, she was on her front again, swimming towards the near bank. He stopped the camera. The last thing he needed was footage of some stupid bloody cow risking her life for no good reason. He'd have to wait until she was gone, and then start the process all over again.

Jim learnt early that there were two things that guided Douglas's running of the LNRG. First, there was the belief that all leadership is a kind of parenting, and that it was incumbent on him to show the same care towards the group's members that a father would show his grown-up sons. Second, and in complete accord with this, was Douglas's strict adherence to the Homeric ideals of hospitality. Since the headquarters of the LNRG also happened to be his own house, that meant making everyone feel thoroughly at home.

Jim found him in the kitchen, as usual. He was chopping onions at one end of the massive block of solid beech that served as desk and workbench, as well as dining table. After every fourth or fifth slice, he threw a bright ring to the floor, where a young pine marten – like a chocolate-brown weasel grown long as a cat, with a dirty yellow bib – was waiting to catch it in its teeth. The sharp taste made it shake its head, but it champed down and swallowed all the same.

'Ah, yes,' said Douglas, 'the film crew.'

Despite the little crease over his Roman nose, and the downward hook either end of his wide mouth, he sounded unconcerned. His mottled hair was perhaps a little more dishevelled than usual, but he was one of those older men who'd embraced the new liberties in that regard, leaving behind the short-back-and-sides tyranny that had been more-or-less absolute in his youth. He even sported surprisingly luxuriant sideburns.

'If it's true, they're going to be in our way, aren't they?' Jim said. 'It could be disastrous. I think we should get confirmation from the Drumnadrochit Hotel, and then let the university know. Surely, we can make some kind of appeal. We ought to have precedence.'

Douglas's frown had deepened. 'I don't see why they should hinder us.'

'Alan says they plan to film on the loch,' Jim insisted. 'If that's true, how will we carry out our monitoring?'

Douglas continued slicing. 'It's a big stretch of water. I'm sure it can accommodate both parties.'

'But what about the depth research? The whole point of that is we'll cover the whole loch.'

Douglas laid the knife down and scooped the chopped onion into an earthenware bowl with both hands. 'Not in one go,' he said. The pine marten leapt up him lightly, treating him the way it might treat a tree, and was on the table. 'No, Autolycus, that's not for you.' He grabbed the animal around its belly before it could reach the bowl and dropped it on the floor again. 'Look, Jamie,' he said, 'there's something I should tell you. I know about the film crew because one of their representatives has been in communication with me.'

Jim didn't quite understand. What did 'in communication' mean? A letter, telephone call, semaphore…?

'They wanted to use the quay,' Douglas said, making for the pantry now, Autolycus at his heels. He picked out four large potatoes from a sack behind the door. 'I told them I had no objection in principle, but asked for a firm date, since the quay was in continual use by the group.' Jim must have made a face, because Douglas smiled at him wryly. 'They thanked me, but I didn't hear from them again. I believe the owner of Temple Pier proved more amenable.' He put the potatoes in the sink and ran cold water over them. 'You do know what this film's about, don't you?'

Jim shrugged. 'Alan said it was a Sherlock Holmes flick.'

'Sherlock Holmes battles the Loch Ness Monster.' He took the rinsed spuds to the table and sat down again. 'Something along those lines, I believe.'

'But that makes it worse,' said Jim. 'It'll be a travesty.' As he spoke, he pictured some ill-conceived model sticking out of a tank, some anti-scientific notion of a dinosaur, with a lot of fools in tweeds and gaiters staring up at it. 'It'll lower the tone,' he said. 'It'll make what we're doing laughable. And—' last, but certainly not least, '—it could affect our funding.'

Douglas said nothing to that, which was something he was good at. He seemed to have halved the size of the first potato he'd been peeling and was moving on to the next. At his feet, Autolycus was chewing manfully on a thick piece of what had been discarded.

'As I've said, we've got precedence,' Jim persisted. 'We should apply to the council, or to the courts, try to get them shut down…'

'This is Scotland,' said Douglas, 'not the Lake District. We don't have the same laws about trespass.'

'Then we should shame them away.' Jim wasn't going to give up. 'Get the press involved. Make it clear they're standing in the way of science. At least make them consider filming somewhere else. If they really need a loch, there's plenty of them about, isn't there?'

'Perhaps you're right,' Douglas said, but there was no power behind the statement. 'What does Alan say?'

The question annoyed Jim. What did it matter what Alan said? 'I'm sure he agrees. He has as much riding on this as any of us, doesn't he?'

'Well, it's an international film company.' Douglas was slicing what remained of the potatoes into little rounds. 'They'll have some financial clout. And a film's a great thing for tourism, you know.'

Jim shrugged. 'Is it?'

'Oh, yes. Did you see *Far from the Madding Crowd*?'

Jim hadn't seen it, no.

'Well, when Tessa and I saw it, we talked about moving to Dorset straight away. Now, I don't really believe the West Country is a patch on the Highlands, but while I was watching the film, I wasn't so sure.'

A sudden flash of memory from the morning added fuel to Jim's fury. 'Christ,' he said, 'more tourists are the last thing we need. I saw some stupid bloody woman taking her life in her hands just today, swimming in the loch.'

He explained about his wasted film, and Douglas tutted. 'Dear me,' he said. 'I trust she came to no harm. Do make sure you archive it, though, and write up the report. A disturbance is a disturbance, after all.'

He was right, of course, and Jim was further troubled by the realisation that he'd almost dismissed a useful piece of data out of hand.

'But, you know,' Douglas continued, 'your view isn't likely to coincide with that of our neighbours. They'll be thinking that a Hollywood movie might be good for their businesses.'

'But it's a Sherlock Holmes picture,' said Jim, his righteous anger returning, 'not Thomas Hardy. What's the betting they'll make it something to do with the H-bomb, or Martians, or something…?'

Douglas laughed outright, and it was that great braying sound that belonged to the ruling classes. Normal people just didn't make that noise. 'I don't think that's very likely, Jamie. Have you ever read a Sherlock Holmes story?'

Jim resented the implication of illiteracy.

'Your parents or teachers were remiss if you haven't.' He was layering the potato in the pot now, over the onions and the cubes of lamb he'd prepared earlier. 'There are no radioactive monstrosities in them, I can assure you, and no little green men. They're only a bit of fun, of course, but they're good, rational Victorian fun. In fact, I think they'd be very much your cup of tea.'

And there was just enough irony, caught in the downturned hooks of his smile, to persuade Jim that he was being ragged.

Chapter Two

Jim's first sighting of the film crew was at Urquhart Castle, almost a month after he'd heard the gossip about Stanley Holloway at the Drumnadrochit Hotel.

A group of them appeared at the roadside as he rounded the bend, driving west from Lewiston. They were standing in front of the castle gate in a bored sort of way, hands on hips or folded across chests. An older man with a buzz cut, in pilot's sunglasses and a pilot's short-sleeved shirt, looked enough like a Yank to tip Jim off as to who they were. A couple of lads with shaggy hair, wearing T-shirts and jeans, looked equally bored. There was a girl, too, dressed the same way, but with shorter, more boyish hair. She was the one who looked up with excitement as the van approached and waved Jim down with a clipboard.

'Hello,' she called as Jim wound down the window, 'are you the dogs?' The accent was Scots, but not local.

'I'm not the dogs, no.'

'Oh, dear.' She maintained a strained smile as she glanced over the paper on the clipboard. 'Who are you then?'

He wanted to say, '"Albert and the Lion", who d'you think?' Instead, he said, 'Just a taxpayer going about his lawful business. Hoping not to be interrupted too much while he's doing it.'

The smile wavered. 'Sorry to have bothered you, I'm sure.'

There were strange looks on the others' faces, too. All three were looking over the top of the cab Jim was sitting in. Of course: they must have been confused by the camera. *Good*, he thought, and set off again.

When he was far enough around the curve of the hill to be lost from view, he drove into a gateway and parked up. The gate itself only led into a narrow pasture with a couple of shaggy cattle in it, but he soon found a gap in the fence and the roadside gorse that led the way he wanted to go. The children of Lewiston and Drumnadrochit liked to play 'I'm the King of Urquhart Castle' among the ruins, and less innocent games in their shadows once they were older. Jim eased past the prickles, crossed the bare field leading to the castle, then climbed the scrubby mound until he reached the edge of a low wall. There, he fell to his knees like a sniper in a crow's nest, and recced what lay below.

A score or more of people were standing amidst the broken walls or sitting on canvas chairs. There was a lot of scaffolding – wooden poles, not modern aluminium tubing. Was that a period detail? As well as the castle's tower, the white peaks of a couple of marquees cut into the grey view of the loch beyond. Nothing seemed to be happening and, even at this distance, Jim was aware of that same atmosphere of concentrated boredom he'd detected at the site's entrance. Mostly, it was men in shirtsleeves or T-shirts, but there were four who were clearly in costume. A big chap in whiskers, rigged out in Highland regalia – kilt, sporran, short jacket and glengarry cap – was standing over by a stone archway, staring at his buckled shoes. Two other men, wearing waistcoats, were sat in canvas chairs on the other side of the grassy courtyard, close to a serrated lump of wall with a paneless window in it. Both had old-style hats on: the taller and slimmer a trilby, the stouter a bowler. These were surely the Holmes and Watson of the outfit – though shouldn't the Holmes have been wearing a deerstalker? Next to the Watson, a woman in a long dress full of white and pale-green flounces was sitting under a wide-brimmed hat of her own. Jim lifted his binoculars for a better look. He didn't recognise her, either. So much for the Hollywood spectacular Pete Leith had promised. There was nobody here of Stanley Holloway's calibre…

He scanned a wider area now. A corps of middle-aged, tubby men was standing around a big mounted camera with 'Panavision' stamped on its side in stylised script. There was sound equipment, too: a microphone on a stick, with one of those furry covers on it, making it look like something Douglas would give the run of the house. Under a crumbling archway stood a man of about sixty, stouter at the waist than he was at the shoulders, wearing a short-sleeved shirt and a flat cap. Next to him was a girl, only the third Jim had seen so far. Her back was to him at first, but when she turned – looking the way her companion pointed, towards the camera – he believed for a moment that this must be the movie's real star. Surely, he had seen her in something, but he was no good at placing faces or remembering the names of people who appeared on television. Then he realised she wasn't dressed right. Her T-shirt and jeans didn't fit with the Victorian clobber the other actors were wearing, and neither did her practical pigtails and those big, modern sunglasses. He watched while she nodded at whatever the man in the cap was saying. There was something about the way she stood – resting all her weight on one leg, the way Greek statues do – that Jim was taken by. Then her companion pointed up at the sky and she took off the sunglasses.

Jim almost cor-blimeyed out loud, Sid James-style.

If he'd seen those eyes before, he would have known the where and when of it to the nearest degree and second. Even through the binoculars, which he struggled to keep steady, he knew they were a sensation. Almond-shaped and smoky, with centres as blue as the sort of equatorial seas in which he hoped one day to carry out his doctoral research... Now she strode away from the man in the cap towards the group who were seated in costume. All three stood as she approached and listened with attention to what she had to tell them, so that it seemed she had authority here. Then the one in the trilby got into a corduroy jacket, not unlike the sort of thing Jim's lecturers had worn, while the bowler hat wearer shrugged on a plain black number. The actress, meanwhile, started to play with her parasol, opening and closing it rapidly. Then they followed the girl with the knockout eyes to a bit of isolated wall with some of the scaffolding set against it, and everything went still.

The man in the flat cap raised a loudhailer to his mouth and yelled 'Go!'.

The Sherlock spoke to the Watson, too quietly for Jim to catch the words, but he supposed the furry microphone would be picking it all up. Then the Watson laced his fingers together, first at chest level and then, at the Sherlock's further instruction, down around his knees. The Sherlock put a booted foot into this cradle and hoisted himself high enough to catch hold of the wooden struts, and then began to climb. He looked over the top of the wall, past the marquees and out at the loch.

But then he turned and shouted, and it wasn't something meant for his fellow actors.

Other voices were raised now, too. The man in the flat cap cried 'Cut!' through the loudhailer, but Jim was unable to make out anything else. He was aware of another sound, though – a high-pitched buzzing, as of a boat's engine. Cast and crew were rushing towards the bankside wall, and Jim trained his binoculars on the water. Through the gaps in the crumbled masonry, he saw the *Caledonian* heading at a foolhardy rate in the direction of the castle.

Jim laughed out loud. 'Nice one, Alan.'

Arms were being waved below him, and the shouting grew louder, if no more coherent above the wind and the motor's whirr. Then the *Cally* turned as sharply as she could, just where she needed to, and a great foamy upswell threw spray the way of her remonstrators.

Jim chuckled again. 'That's the way, lad.'

'Excuse me, pal.'

It was a gruff voice, and definitely local. Jim looked up and saw he'd been joined by a giant, not only tall, but as broad as any of the stone pillars below.

'Can you tell me exactly what it is you think you're doing here?'

Jim had never seen the bar of the Drum so busy. The pall of cigarette smoke was so thick, he found himself clutching at his throat. It was what you got in a busy pub, of course, which was why Jim always avoided them. Everyone who'd been at the castle was here now, with more besides. The Sherlock and the Watson were stood at the bar in their civvies, double-lit by the bracket lamps and their reflection in the mirrors behind the optics. The Sherlock had a scarf of yellow silk knotted under his chin, and looked as though he was still in makeup. There was, at any rate, an unnatural greenish tint to his complexion, and his lips were lipstick red. His

dark sweep of hair was almost maroon. He was laughing cacoph-
onously at everything the Watson was telling him, swallowing
whole quarter pints of beer at a time. The Watson was also in an
open-neck shirt, but he didn't wear a scarf, and his skin had a more
natural pallor. Next to him, the big Highlander was leaning his
back against the bar, *sans* kilt now, but *avec* trousers, thank God.
Then there were the sound and cameramen, and the girl who'd
had the clipboard, who was smiling at something a lad with a
Sonny Bono haircut was whispering in her ear. Everyone, in fact,
seemed to be having a grand old time – relieved, Jim supposed, not
to be standing around waiting for nothing to happen. The only
people missing were the roughnecks who'd escorted him back to
his van.

Pete Leith, who was the proprietor, caught Jim's eye over the
beer pump he was handling and shot him an evil-cherub grin. *No
Stanley Holloway, though, eh?* Jim thought, nodding in response.

A shrill, fingers-in-mouth whistle made him look around.
Through the jungle mists he spotted the white flag of a bare
arm, an Embassy Filter wafting at its apex. It led him to a corner
table, as far away from their usual nook as it was possible to get.
Some longhaired strangers were occupying their favourite armchairs now, lounging beside the empty grate of the fireplace.

'Got you a pint,' said Alan, shoving it across the table to the
place next to Douglas.

'You didn't know I was coming.'

Alan shrugged. 'It wouldn't have gone to waste.'

'Where are the girls?'

'They'll be along directly,' Douglas said. 'They've gone into
Inverness.'

'Oh ay,' said Alan, 'they suddenly took to thinking their gear
wasn't quite Carnaby Street enough.'

Alan was in a T-shirt that might always have been a shapeless
rag the colour of rancid butter, but probably hadn't. Douglas was
more respectably turned out, naturally, in a sportsman's checked
shirt with rolled sleeves, but it was hardly *haute couture*. Jim himself
was dressed in the denim-shirt-and-jeans combination he

favoured as the best compromise between looking halfway presentable and putting as little thought as was possible into what he was going to wear each day.

'Alan has been telling me about his adventures,' said Douglas.

Jim harrumphed. 'Well, I saw some of them myself.'

'Get away!' Alan's little eyes widened. 'Where were you?'

'Tell me your version first.'

It was curiosity, Alan said, that had led him to the castle in the first place. 'I could see it was something to do with the picture, and I only wanted to get close enough so I could have a look through the binoculars.' But when that had proved unsatisfactory, with the ruins getting in the way all the time, he'd decided to go closer. 'There was a lassie in a frock who I thought might be worth looking at, but she was the worst for getting behind a bit of old stone. So, I took the *Cally* as near as I could.'

'That's when I spotted you,' said Jim.

'You weren't the only one. I could see they had a boat moored up, all black so you'd know it was up to no good. And then I saw everyone running over to the wall, waving their arms about. Well, it would've been impolite not to wave back, wouldn't it? Then that black boat started up and I took the *Cally* hard to starboard. Made a bit of a wave – you see that?'

'Oh, yes,' said Jim.

'But then they came after me. Hailed me down, like they were Customs and fucking Excise and I was smuggling whisky.'

'What happened then?'

Another shrug. 'They had the speed of me, so I cut off the engine and fell to my knees. "Don't shoot," I said, "for the sake of the wains and the wee woman."'

'That was probably taking things a little far,' said Douglas.

But Alan was gleeful. 'Should've seen them. This big man in a lifejacket, a fucking English bastard – no offence, Jamie – starts screaming at me to turn off the camera.'

'You were filming?'

He nodded. 'It's what we do. So I says, "I'm a scientist, and I'm not going to stop my science for nobody. This isn't fucking Russia, pal.'"

'I know the rest,' said Jim, 'because I'm pretty sure it's what happened to me. Thought you were the press, didn't they?'

He nodded. '*News of the* fucking *World*.'

'And they wanted you to hand over your film.'

'Most distressing,' said Douglas, looking fractionally more perturbed than usual.

'Ay,' said Alan. 'Claimed I was "compromising the integrity of the film set" and "potentially breaching copyright."'

'I take it you didn't give them the film?'

'I gave them nothing. Told them that what I was doing was too important. "You're the ones compromising *my* work," I said. "What work's that?" asks the English bastard, no offence, Jamie. "I'll have you know I'm looking for the Loch Ness fucking Monster."'

It had taken them a while to believe that this was something people actually did, and then they'd wanted proof that Alan was one of them. It was the same treatment Jim had received, and which he'd resolved quickly enough by showing them his Aberdeen University pass.

'You shouldnae've done that,' said Alan. 'I showed them nothing. I was minded to show them my bare arse.'

In the end, they'd had to let him go, but not without further vague threats of legal action and an ostentatious show of taking down the *Cally*'s number.

'So, Jim,' said Douglas, 'why were you at the castle?'

He told them about being mistaken for 'the dogs', and how he'd parked up and gone to have a look-see. But before he could say more, he was suddenly struck by two revelations: first, he knew why he'd found the girl with the pigtails and the spectacular eyes so familiar, and secondly, he knew she was standing right in front of him at the bar.

'That's her,' he said.

'Who?' Alan was following the trajectory of Jim's gaze. 'That's never the dolly bird in the frock.'

'No,' said Jim, 'it's the one who was swimming in the loch. Remember? The bloody idiot trying to kill herself. She was at the castle, too. Part of the crew, not one of the actors.'

Alan squinted. 'Not bad, eh?

She was on her own, smiling at others, but not actually engaged in conversation, leaning her elbows on the dark wood of the bar behind her. Jim was certain that hers was the face he'd seen under the black swimming cap, even though it had been without makeup then and those extraordinary eyes had been screwed against sun and spray.

'She is rather handsome,' said Douglas.

'A Yank, I suppose,' said Alan. 'You don't get a tan like that from standing in the Scottish rain.'

Now that he'd said it, Jim supposed he was right. In fact, it seemed abundantly clear that this was an epitome of American womanhood such as he'd only previously seen on the TV. She occupied her golden, un-British skin with an ease that was entirely at odds with the bearing of the English girls he'd grown up with. Her pigtails had given way now to a pair of sun-bleached shocks, which flowed from either side of a sharp parting and sprayed over her shoulders. She'd changed her outfit, too, replacing the T-shirt and jeans with a long frock of various pinks and purples, not unlike the sort of thing Alan's wife liked to wear, except that it suited this girl's sylph-like form much better. Hooped strings of what looked like pale-blue cowrie shells hung from her neck, matching the colour of her eyes in a very inexact way. On her feet were a pair of sandals piled with cork, giving her another couple of inches in overall length that she really didn't need...

'Hippy chick,' said Alan.

'Shouldn't think so,' said Jim. 'She's clearly had a bath in the last month. And not just in the loch.'

'Someone important, you say?' asked Douglas.

Jim shrugged. 'She was talking with the man I took to be the director, and telling the actors what to do.'

Douglas got up from the table. 'Well, she shouldn't be on her own, then, should she?'

'What are you doing?'

'I'm going to introduce myself.'

Alan was agape. 'You sleek old fox, you.'

Douglas signalled to Pete as he moved to the bar. An instant later, he was speaking to the girl, and she was looking up into his mountain crag of a face. Her smile crinkled the edges of those crystalline eyes. Then Pete's lopsided grin appeared between them, seeming to say silently what Alan had just said out loud.

'Hey, Jamie—' Alan dropped his voice to what passed for a whisper with him, '—guess what I found in the farmhouse today?'

Douglas was offering the girl a cigarette already, holding the golden packet out to her. She picked one out with her forefinger and thumb, and Jim lip-read her smiling thank you.

Alan spoke as though Jim had given an indication that he was listening. 'Only a copy of *The Spy Who Came in from the* fucking *Cold*!'

God, not this again. 'There's a lot of them about,' Jim said, watching Douglas strike a flame from his heavy Ronson lighter. The girl put all her pursed concentration into holding the end of her cigarette to it. 'It's what's called a bestseller.'

'Ay, but he doesn't read that kind of pish, does he? It's all Sir Peter Scott with him, isn't it?'

The noise had apparently become too much for Douglas, and he was bending to the girl so she could speak directly in his ear. Whatever she said made him smile, and he gave his reply straight into her ear, too. 'I'd say he's more a Robert Graves man,' Jim said. 'Greek myths, the wisdom of the ancients, that sort of thing. Or T.E. Lawrence—'

'Lawrence of fucking Arabia?' Alan slapped the tabletop. 'There you go – that's what I'm talking about. All that gallivanting around the Empire after the war, those so-called expeditions to the Himalayas…'

The girl had resumed her elbow-leaning, so that she was stretched out before Douglas, looking up at him from under her thickened lashes.

'That's not evidence,' said Jim. 'You *want* it to be true, that's all.'

Suddenly, Pete Leith's lumpen form was next to them. 'Evening, gents,' he said, placing two fresh pints on the table. 'Compliments of the big man.'

Alan's face was a picture of pasty, ovoid consternation. 'He made you bring these over?'

The lewd smile didn't falter. 'Well, he's busy yacking to the lassie, isn't he?'

The girl had turned around and was leaning forward on the bar now, making the cloth of her dress taut, delineating the curve of her hip.

'Pete, man,' Alan was saying, 'where's your self-respect? You can't go tugging the forelock to the laird these days, and especially not that one. Agent of the fucking state, I'm telling you. We were just talking about it, weren't we, Jamie...?'

Jim got up from his stool.

'Where you going?'

'Sorry, Alan, but I need to stop hearing you speak.'

He followed Douglas's path to the bar, anticipating some awkwardness when he got there. But when Douglas caught sight of him, he summoned him the rest of the way. 'We were just talking about you,' he said. 'This is James Outhwaite, of Kendal in the county of Cumbria,' he told the girl. 'Jamie, meet April Bloom, of San Francisco in the state of California.'

'Pleased to meet you,' the girl said, standing clear of the bar. Her accent was richer than Jim had thought it would be, perhaps a semitone deeper. She held out a hand, but he didn't take it.

'Do much swimming over there in San Francisco?' he asked. 'Nice bay there, I hear.'

She frowned and her smile turned quizzical. 'That would be a pretty stupid thing to do, Mr Outhwaite. They built Alcatraz there, you know, because the bay's so dangerous.'

'Well,' said Jim, 'so's Loch Ness.'

The smile vanished a moment, and then one of sly recognition took its place. 'Say, you're the paparazzo, aren't you? The one who sounded his horn at me from up on the hill. Thought I was Geneviève, huh?'

'Who?'

'Geneviève Page,' Douglas told him. 'The leading lady. She's a French actress of some repute.'

But the girl hadn't finished her accusations. 'That was you in the boat, too, I suppose, with the movie camera.'

'Not guilty on either count,' said Jim. 'I'm not a paparazzo, and I wasn't in the boat. That was my friend over there.'

But Alan had gone, leaving two empty pint glasses behind him.

'Then you were the other one – the one who gave the runner a hard time, poor girl. I hope you're thoroughly ashamed of yourself. The two of you near enough ruined the whole morning's shoot. And then the weather changed and we had to call it off.'

Douglas indulged in one of his more modest fits of laughter. It still had something of the braying quality. 'Well, you'll find the weather in the Highlands changeable, Miss Bloom. How long are you here?'

'Supposedly six weeks,' she said, 'but it's anyone's guess with Mr Wilder in charge.'

Then Douglas did a very strange thing. With a display of perhaps the worst acting imaginable, he looked at his watch and said, 'Well, Tessa will be expecting me home now. I'd better make a move.'

'I thought you said she and Sandra were meeting us here,' said Jim.

'Did I?' Douglas's show of surprise wouldn't have fooled a three-year-old. 'Well, there's the hens and the pig to feed, so I'd better be off.' It was a *non sequitur* worthy of Alan. 'See you back at the farm-house, Jamie.' He actually bowed to the Californian, but stopped short of kissing her hand. 'Lovely to meet you, Miss Bloom. I hope you enjoy your stay.'

'Well,' said the girl, when she and Jim had watched Douglas manoeuvre his way through the flamboyant crowd and out the door, 'he's a regular Rex Harrison, isn't he? Like he is in the movies, I mean, not real life.' She fixed her eyes on Jim as intently now as she had fixed them on Douglas. It was like standing in front of an arc lamp, and he almost flinched in their glare. 'So, what is it you and your friends do, if you're not gentlemen of the press?'

'Didn't Douglas tell you?'

She shook her head, then took a sip from her glass of Coke. 'Your Mr Campbell has a way of saying a lot without saying much.'

Jim could only nod at that. 'Well, we're scientists,' he said, 'conducting research in the field. By which I mean, on the loch.'

'Does that mean you're going to be disrupting us through the whole shoot?'

For a moment, he could feel the froth of rage rising in his chest. 'Let's be clear about this,' he said, 'it's your lot doing the disrupting. We were here first.'

'And possession's nine-tenths of the law, huh?' She sipped from her glass again. Was there something else in there besides Coke? 'What kind of scientists are you, anyhow? Geologists, I suppose.'

'Alan Stirling's our stone and water man,' Jim said. The anger, he noticed, had subsided remarkably quickly. 'I'm a marine biologist, but I'll do fresh water at a pinch.' Then, because he felt he had to, he reciprocated. 'And what's your part in this fiasco?'

'Me?' She picked up Douglas's cigarette from where she'd let it burn down to almost nothing in the ashtray. 'I'm the continuity girl.'

London, 2014 (I)

'Hi, Auntie Gem.'

Destiny is standing in the open door of Gemma's childhood home. She looks the spit of Gemma herself, twenty years ago: a skinny ten-year-old in a blue-and-yellow uniform, all elbows, knees and reticence, under an umbrella of reddish black frizzes. She's even performing the right chore – if the telephone rings, she'll be expected to get that, too. It feels like the sort of thing that happens in *Doctor Who* these days: loops in time, people meeting their former selves, with no ill effects.

'You coming in, then?'

Gemma risks a temporal paradox and crosses the threshold. 'You okay, darling?'

Destiny sing-songs her reply. 'Good, thanks. How are you, Auntie Gem?'

Gemma nods. 'Okay.'

She had thought this house a treasure even when she'd lived in it, though she'd also known that it was ludicrously narrow. The whole terrace had been a wreck when Dad had bought his sliver of it, forty years ago. But he'd corralled the neighbours into restoring it, using his skills as director of his own builders' firm, and now the street stands as an oasis of Victorian gentility amidst the high-rises and blocks of concrete and yellow brick.

'It's Auntie Gem, Granddad,' Destiny announces. They pass from the narrow hallway into the equally narrow room that stretches from dining area at the front to kitchen at the back.

'Hello, hen,' says Dad. He's sitting squarely in his armchair facing the front window, elbows on the wooden rests and belly straining the poppers of his sky-blue cowboy shirt. On the window sill, a 19-inch flat screen is filled with a big half-lit clock, and the *Countdown* theme is reaching its climax. 'Your mother's hanging clothes out back.'

'Nice to see you, too,' says Gemma, and makes a point of kissing his whiskery cheek.

He turns his grey eyes on her and smiles, then draws her nearer with one long arm and returns the kiss. 'How're you keeping, hen?'

'Not so bad,' she says. 'Got some news, actually.'

'That's nice.' He turns his attention back to the telly. 'As I said, your mother's in the garden.'

Destiny pulls at her sleeve. 'Come on, Auntie Gem, let's see Grandma.'

Mum's standing at a loaded clothes line strung from either end of the narrow lawn on which Gemma had romped as a ten-year-old, and had tried to catch some rays as a teenager. It's sunny today, but it's also March, and there's a bite to the breeze that tugs the line.

'It's Auntie Gem, Grandma,' Destiny announces a second time, and having fulfilled her duty, folds herself into a plastic garden chair and is instantly playing her DS.

Mum beams Gemma a smile. 'Hello, love.' She drops a blue dress into the basket at her feet and deftly deposits the pegs in the pocket of her apron. 'Come and give your mum a kiss.'

Fifteen years separate her parents' dates of birth, but sometimes it seems more like thirty. Mum's skin – the skin of Gemma's Jamaican grandparents – is more glowing than Dad's Scottish pallor has ever been. She's darker than her daughter and granddaughter, but lighter than her son. There's no telling what you'll get served out of the great genetic soup tureen.

'I wasn't expecting you today,' Mum says, returning to the unpegging. 'Everything all right?'

'Fine,' Gemma says. 'In fact, I've had some good news.'

'Oh, what about?'

She sounds interested, but Gemma knows she won't be. 'I've made contact with one of the crew from *The Private Life of Sherlock Holmes*.'

'That old film you found?'

Gemma's impressed she's remembered that much. 'It wasn't me who found it,' she says. 'And it wasn't lost – well, not completely.'

Mum's on to a pair of surprisingly pink trousers, too long in the leg to belong to anyone but Dad. 'So, who is it?' she asks, 'Some old chap, I suppose.'

'A woman, actually,' says Gemma. 'April Korzeniowski.'

Mum laughs. 'Sounds very American.'

'Well, she is. And it looks like she'll come over.'

'Come over?'

Gemma explains a little about the Loch Ness Film Festival. 'I'm going to interview her before the screening in Inverness. She was the movie's continuity supervisor, so she would've been on set the whole time, noting down what happened in each take. Frankly, even if the director were still alive, I doubt he would have more to say about what happened day to day.'

'That's lovely, dear.'

Mum's attention is taken up now with another of Dad's cowboy shirts, a silky black number embroidered with red roses. Gemma reminds herself that she's okay with this, that it's enough for her that one parent understands her enthusiasms. It's time to change the subject.

'Hey, Destiny,' she calls, 'how's your dad?'

Destiny doesn't look up from her game. 'All right, I suppose.'

Mum's bent over the basket, but her frown shows in her shoulders. 'He came for dinner last Sunday,' she says when she rises. Then she throws Gemma a 'there's-more-to-tell' look. 'Dearie,' she calls to Destiny, 'your aunt and I are going to have a cup of tea. Do you want some juice?'

'No thank you, Grandma,' Destiny replies, sing-songing again.

Gemma picks up the basket and follows her mother inside. Down the other end of that long room, the *Countdown* clock has been replaced by the strapline and bullpen backdrop of the BBC News channel. Dad seems no less mesmerised. Gemma puts the basket on the table.

'They suspended her from school for a week,' Mum says, taking the kettle to the sink.

'What?' Gemma can't believe it. 'But she's in uniform.'

'This was a couple of weeks back.' She says nothing while the water roars. 'Robbie only found out about it when he tried to pick her up from school, and they sent one of their bully boys out to ask what he was doing.'

She tells Gemma about the people the school employs to act like bouncers at the school gate. It's meant to deter drug dealers and paedophiles, but it's just as effective as a barrier to parents the school has taken against.

'They told him Destiny had been sent home for throwing a chair at a teacher. So, Robbie rang *that* woman—' Mum can never bring herself to pronounce her former daughter-in-law's name, or even admit the role she plays in her granddaughter's life, '—and she wouldn't answer the phone. He left messages, but she didn't get back to him for over a week. He was scared they'd left the country.'

'Jesus.' There's a look on Mum's face that reminds Gemma of the house rules regarding taking the Lord's name in vain. 'Sorry, Mum.' She looks through the glass in the door and thinks how peaceable Destiny looks, sitting cross-legged in that garden chair. And then she wishes, as she's wished before, that she could make more time for her niece, show her a different life... 'So, how long did this go on for?'

'Till a couple of days ago. I'm worried about him, love,' she says. 'He's a good man, I know he is. But he's so...'

Gemma guesses she's struggling for a word that isn't 'lost'. 'I know, Mum,' she says. 'He is a good man.'

Suddenly Dad's shouting at the screen. David Cameron is leaving 10 Downing Street, with a chinless aide in tow and that strange, A-shaped gathering on his forehead. Then Alex Salmond appears in a Scottish street lined with supporters, all gap-toothed smiles and well-lined *bonhomie*. He's waving with both arms, like a tricksy US president.

'Anyway,' Mum says, dropping teabags into the pot, 'enough about that. How's David?'

Gemma sits at the table now, behind the washing basket. With her back to Dad, she's effectively insulated from both of them. 'Good,' she says, making her tone light. 'He's busy organising a conference.'

'Ah,' says Mum, pouring boiling water into the pot. 'And what's that about?'

'Italian horror films of the 1970s.' Gemma knows exactly how that will sound in Mum's ears. 'I'm meeting him in a while, actually. We're going to see something at the Genesis. A late birthday present for him.'

'Oh, that's nice. And then you'll be eating out, I suppose?'

Why are you doing this? Gemma thinks. *I'm no trouble to you. I'm the perfect grown-up daughter. I'm not saddling you with childcare, or bringing around the washing, or soaking you and Dad of all your savings. I'm forging a career for myself, standing on my own feet. Why won't you be satisfied until I'm cooking and cleaning, too?* But all she says is, 'Probably.'

There's another incoherent eruption from in front of the telly. Now Nigel Farage is on the screen, gurning over a pint of beer. Mum leans over the basket. 'See if you can calm him down, dear.' She's nearly whispering, again. 'I'll bring the tea over.'

Gemma's not sure Dad notices her as she sits next to him on a dining chair. His lips are pursed, and those grey eyes seem fixed to the screen by something palpable. But then she catches sight of the shelf next to his far elbow. There's that old edition of *Halliwell's* that she pored over as a kid, and on which he sometimes seems over-reliant. Then Mark Cousins' *History of Film*, which she gave him for his 65th. Next, there's *John Wayne's America* by Garry Wills, its paper jacket torn almost top to bottom. And finally, the little BFI guide to *The Private Life of Sherlock Holmes*, with the white line down its spine that tells her exactly how often it's been read...

'So,' she says, 'I've found someone to interview.'

'Oh ay?' He hits the mute button. 'Who's that then?'

She tells him about April Korzeniowski and, because he's genuinely interested, adds some details she didn't tell Mum. About her

working for Stanley Kubrick, and on a Bond film, before moving back to the States and working for Sydney Pollack and Martin
Scorsese.

'She'll have some tales to tell, eh?'

'Hope so,' says Gemma.

But it's when she tells him about the Loch Ness Film Festival
that inspiration strikes.

'You and Mum should come,' she says. 'And Robbie and Destiny – why not? It's at the end of July. The school holidays will
have started.'

He doesn't respond at once, and then it's only with an 'Ay, hen'.

This is how it is now. Inertia hangs over Dad like a white sheet
over stored furniture. Whether he wants to do something or not is
increasingly beside the point – more pertinent is whether he'll find
it easier than staying in to watch *Pointless*...

'That's a lovely idea,' says Mum, still in the kitchen. 'Get the
London air out of our lungs. It's years since we've had a proper
holiday, Alistair.'

'Ay,' Dad says again. 'I'll give it due consideration.' Then he
flicks the sound back on and nods at the telly. 'Have you been following this pile of shite, hen?'

Half an hour later, and Gemma is running the usual gauntlet of
the Mile End Road. Pavements strewn with cartons and beverage
cups from the fried chicken shops, dark-screened Mercedes turning sharply into side roads without bothering to indicate, catcalls
from men of all colours and most creeds... Perhaps she should
worry more about this last item than she does, since many of her
students walk this way to their accommodation, but it's a long time
since she has been bothered by it personally. This is her manor,
and give or take the odd riot, or Olympic Games hysteria, she got
used to its ways a long time ago. She's more unsettled when she
gets the treatment elsewhere, in places she doesn't feel she should
be making any kind of impression.

David is standing outside the cinema dressed in exactly what a wardrobe assistant would hand out to an extra playing '2nd University Lecturer'. He's swiping at the screen of his phone.

'You're late, Dr MacDonald,' he says, pushing his hornrims back up his nose.

'By five minutes, Dr Kitch.' She tiptoes to kiss him.

'Haven't gotten tickets yet. You didn't tell me what you wanted to see.'

She'd meant to reply to his text after her lecture, but when the time came, had rushed off to Mum and Dad's instead. 'Why don't you choose?'

He plumps for Jonathan Glazer's new film, *Under the Skin*. From what she's heard, it isn't really a date movie – but then, the ordinary rules don't apply when you're a couple of Film Studies lecturers. It isn't long before Gemma is certain he's made the right choice. The opening sequence, with its nerve-tautening score and half-abstract imagery, sets up an air of menace that's maintained throughout. Scarlett Johansson's casting turns out not to be the stunt she had anticipated, but another one altogether. She's playing a man-eating alien – or perhaps something inorganic, some sort of shape-shifted AI: a monster, in any event – sent to lure ordinary blokes into her white van. But oddly, she's never looked more human. Her flesh is properly fleshy, rather than that rubber-foam material most movie flesh seems to be. And she's showing a lot of it, too – pretty much all, in fact.

But the real surprise is that she isn't even the film's star. That turns out to be Scotland – all of it. It's as though Glazer meant to strip the country barer than he strips his Hollywood leading lady. Of course, there are shots of pine-bristling mountains, their misty peaks reflected in the glassy lochs below, but before you get to them, you have to negotiate a Scotland that rarely gets screen time. The seamier streets of Glasgow, the post-industrial wastelands at its centre and edges, and the new-build estates of ticky-tacky that spill out onto the fringes of open heath. Sometimes Gemma's half-aware that the trance she's in owes as much to boredom as to rapture, but then there are scenes she knows she'll never forget. That one set on the beach, for instance, with the family, their dog and the turbulent sea, is among the most terrifying things she has seen in a cinema. She knows it will give her nightmares for weeks.

By the time she and David leave the auditorium, with the scant others who have been in there with them, she's convinced she's seen a masterpiece.

'Well,' says David, taking off his glasses and blinking, 'that's two hours of my life I'll never get back.'

For a moment, Gemma is bewildered. Then she remembers who she's with and laughs. 'Oh, it was a bit arty for you, wasn't it?'

He shrugs. 'If by "arty" you mean "boring as fuck".'

She takes his arm and gives it a squeeze. 'Well, I'll let you choose the takeaway, too. Take your time, though, yeah? No point being disappointed twice.'

They're sitting either side of the breakfast bar in the kitchenette, well into their chicken jalfrezi, when he drops the news. She stares at him over the tinfoil trays and the open necks of beer bottles.

'Chicago?' He might as well have said 'the University of the Moon'.

'Yep,' he says. ' Almost home. Just a hop to Minneapolis...'

'Wow,' she says. 'Congratulations.'

'I haven't confirmed I want it yet.' He scoops some vibrant red sauce out of a tray with a torn piece of naan. 'There's a lot to think about. It's good at Queen Mary's, you know? I feel like I've gotten some things going there. The conference, for one.'

His eyes are on the food and he seems to be putting a lot of effort into chewing. Clearly, there's something else he needs to say, and she's suddenly terrified he'll say it. He's tweaking her nerves as expertly as Jonathan Glazer did in that film.

'You've got to think about what's right for you,' she tells him.

She'd meant to indicate that they could usefully put off finishing this conversation until later, but he takes her words as a prompt to say more now. 'Well, there's your career to think about, too, I know. I'm saying this because...' He looks at her, but since he's taken off his glasses, she knows she isn't in focus. 'Well, maybe this can be an opportunity for both of us.'

She nods, but says nothing.

Is naked Scarlett Johansson the reason for the intensity of their lovemaking? Gemma suspects it's in the mix.

As always, he falls asleep first, but he seems even more content tonight than usual. Could it be that telling her his news about Chicago has removed a load from his conscience? If so, she knows what she should do to lighten her own. But he's made it far more complicated now, turned it into something momentous, when it had only been awkward before. She'd imagined a slow process in which she had persuaded him that Aberdeen was not so far away, that in time there might be room for him there, too, or at another Scottish university close enough so they could make some sort of living arrangement together that worked.

If she'd only got in first, then it would have been him making the unreasonable demands, not her...

Of course, she blamed Dad for that.

'We both ought to have a vote in this,' he told her, pointing at the screen. The coverage had moved on to something other than the independence debate, but Gemma knew that was what he was talking about. 'We're both Scottish.'

'I've never lived there,' she told him, 'and you haven't for forty years.'

'She's right, Alistair,' said Mum, placing their mugs of tea on the dining table. 'You're an old Londoner now, like me.'

'More like Sean Connery,' said Gemma, nudging Dad's shoulder, as though she could reach his sense of humour that way. 'Living it up in a foreign country while you sing *Flower of Scotland* in the shower every morning.'

He managed to laugh at that. 'Oh ay. Mistaken for the big man all the time.' But he quickly turned serious again. 'It's your friends there that make me spit.' He was gesturing at the screen again. 'Treating us like we're children who don't deserve a proper voice, who can be fobbed off with a wee pretendy parliament at Holyrood, and not one with real power.'

41

Ever since Gemma had appeared on *The Review Show* last November, talking to Kirsty Wark, he'd acted as though she were friends with everyone at the BBC. Gemma supposed it was a way to temper his pride in her, hinting at some kind of class treachery.

Now, in bed, she winces at the memory of her response.

'I'm a Film Studies lecturer, Dad, not a fucking news journalist. I've never said or written a fucking thing about Scotland.'

'Oh, Gemma, please.'

The disappointment in Mum's voice was horrible to hear, but it wasn't worse than the other thing – namely, the unmistakable sound of a ten-year-old giggling. Destiny had come in from the back garden and was standing next to her Grandma, gazing at Gemma with what was clearly a new-found admiration.

'And there,' said Dad triumphantly, 'is where the problem lies. Perhaps you could show us every so often that you do give a damn, hen?'

The worst of it was that she'd gone there to tell them about the Aberdeen job. Perhaps if she had worked up the guts to do so, it would have been easier to do it again when she'd met David. But after this spat with Dad, it became too difficult to raise the subject without making it sound like some kind of concession.

Oh, God, she thinks, and it's almost an actual prayer. *Fucking Chicago…*

Sweat is beading on her forehead, though she isn't especially warm. Through the always-open window she hears the rumble of a diesel vehicle, turning into the residents' parking below. She can't help but imagine it's a white van, driven with predatory intent by some ridiculously nubile extraterrestrial.

Tomorrow, she thinks. *Tomorrow I'll put everything right…*

Chapter Three

The little nursery-sized bedroom at the Campbell farmstead was veiled in the dullest of morning lights, but Jim still found it too bright. The Yank lass had been drinking rum-and-Cokes, and then probably just Cokes. He even thought he remembered her moving on to water at some point. But somehow, he'd been on the Bell's. Pete Leith must have urged him to it, or perhaps had simply confused him with Alan. At any rate, he'd ended up knocking back the whiskies like they were little splashes of Irn Bru at the bottom of his glass.

Two big cannon blasts rocked the bedroom door. 'Come and have your breakfast, you wee hoodlum,' Sandra thundered through the wood. 'It's greasy as fuck, so it'll do you a power of good.'

He managed to lift and rearrange his body in short bursts, until he was perched on the edge of the bed, doubled up to stop the room from spinning. In further stages, he pulled on his pyjama trousers and a vest. Then he journeyed with baby steps out of the room and into the toilet, where he let nature take its course, hugging the porcelain bowl as if it were his final comforter.

'That's right,' Sandra called through the wood again. 'Better out than in. Make room for some of Farmer Campbell's best bacon.'

What had he talked about with the girl? What had he told her? He'd been determined to say as little as possible, and had at least begun with exactly the right tone of sarcastic indignation he hoped to maintain in all his dealings with these Hollywood interlopers. She had said she was the continuity girl, but hadn't explained what that meant. Had he asked her?

In the kitchen, the fizzle and snap of frying bacon was overlaid with the tinny sound of Sandra's transistor radio. It was surprisingly enticing, that sound of cooking. Grease he'd been promised, and grease he would accept. Meanwhile, Tony Blackburn's latest offering was some idiot singing about being dizzy, which was really the last thing he needed to hear…

'There's no eggs,' Sandra told him from the range, cigarette waggling with her lips. She was wearing something new, a smock that fell to just below her knees, as white as the thick calves beneath it, decorated with red things that might have been straw-berries. 'Douglas's stretched rat had the lot. The hen house might be pine marten proof, but it isn't Alan proof. He left the eggs in the yard while he gave the pig its swill, the dunderhead. I'm told you might find them buried in the woods if you go looking. I'm leaving that up to you.'

Jim sat at the ton of hefty beech wood and watched Sandra plating the bacon. He saw that several coils of her brass-coloured hair had resisted the lacquer and had sprung free, and that she'd coloured her lips cherry red, and her eyes a shade of blue.

'Where are the others?' he asked.

'Out.' She brought over the sizzling meat and dark fried bread and laid it before him with a hint of ceremony. 'What they expect to get done in this weather, I cannot tell.' She sat beside him and poured tea into mugs from a big aluminium teapot that must once have belonged to an institution. 'Here, you'll want some sugar.'

He stopped her only after the third spoonful.

'So—' she was smiling sweetly now, and he was suddenly unnerved, '—I hear you had some luck last night?'

It took a moment to understand what she meant. 'Jesus, no,' he protested, too loudly for his own hearing. 'It was that daft cow I saw swimming in the loch. All I did was give her a piece of my mind.'

'A piece of your mind, eh?' The smile became a smirk. 'Keep a bit of it back, why don't you? You never know when it might come in useful.'

He sawed and chewed at his breakfast, finding real succour in the burn of salt on his tongue and the slither of grease in his throat.

'Alan got a call first thing,' Sandra said through her own chew-ing, 'from the police, no less.'

'What?' The same anger he'd felt when he'd begun talking with the girl welled up inside him again, only now it set his stomach gurgling.

'Oh ay. Just checking in on him, they said. The film people got in touch, apparently. But it was only Constable Allardyce, so it wasn't so bad. Should have heard Alan though: "Yes, constable. No, constable, I quite understand, constable. Oh, it definitely won't happen again, constable." And then it was all "Fucking PC Busybody, sticking his beaky nose in where it's not needed" when he'd put the phone down.'

Her laughter was cruel, and loud enough to cause Jim some jabs of pain in the region of his temples. 'They're a bloody menace,' he managed to say.

She scoffed at that. 'Not you, too.'

'No,' said Jim, 'not the police. Well, not just them. I mean the film crew. Christ only knows how long they'll be here – they don't know themselves. And we can't afford to wait for them to finish, can we? I mean, we've no idea what's happening past September.'

'Do we ever?' She slurped at her tea. 'But you know what, Jamie? It's not a film crew that's stopping you from working today.'

For a moment, he thought she was judging him, and felt an indignation that wasn't in any way sarcastic. But then a gust of wind brought the clatter of rain against the sash windows above the sink, and he saw that the light he'd thought too bright when he'd first opened his eyes was in fact too dark for any decent summer's day.

'They'll not be doing any filming in this weather,' said Sandra. 'So go ahead, knock yourself out, why don't you?' She was definitely judging him now. 'Today's just the day to dedicate to science.'

The truth was, he didn't feel like doing anything. It was an enormous effort even to wash. Though he wanted lukewarm water, a caprice of the wood burner meant that it only come out scalding, and it took all his intellect to mix in the right amount of cold. Dressing was almost as much of an ordeal, since the effort to untangle his laundered clothes from the unlaundered seemed an even more difficult conundrum than usual. Then he returned to the kitchen, filled a long glass with water at the sink and retrieved that morning's *Times* from Douglas's end of the kitchen table. He shuffled into the living room, which was satisfyingly dull, and sitting gingerly in an armchair, told himself that he didn't have to move again for at least an hour.

There was nothing in the paper about the Apollo 11 mission. He attempted to interest himself in something else – a report about American setbacks in Vietnam, a bizarre story about a British yachtsman in a round-the-world race, who'd been sending false reports on his position, and was now believed to have gone over his vessel's side…

After twenty minutes, Jim broke his promise to himself and got up again. This room contained only a portion of Douglas's library. It continued out the door and up the staircase, along the corridors of the first floor and on into the master bedroom. There were more books in the attic. No system was adhered to, and books were merely shoved wherever there was a space. This room contained hardbacks mostly, some with paper jackets, but most showing their cloth or leather bindings. *Ring of Bright Water* was next to *Tarka the Otter*, which only meant that Douglas had looked at them sometime on the same day. At least they shared a subject – nearby, a paperback copy of *Lucky Jim* was stuck in beside an old volume of Boswell's *Life of Johnson*, for no discernible reason.

He couldn't see what he wanted, so carried on out of the door.

By the staircase there were about a dozen half-sized volumes of Greek drama in green jackets, and then a little collection of John Buchan thrillers. He felt he was getting warm. Then, on the stairs, he found what he was looking for: three books by Conan Doyle. Two of them – *Sir Nigel* and *The Land of Mist* – were entirely new to him, but the third was *The Complete Sherlock Holmes Short Stories*. Its red cloth binding had been bleached pink in bygone summers, but otherwise it was in good condition. He slumped against the other books and opened it at random to 'The Adventure of the

Man with the Twisted Lip'. He squinted at the tiny print and read through his pain.

'*Isa Whitney, brother of the late Elias Whitney, D.D., Principal of the Theological College of St. George's, was much addicted to opium. The habit grew upon him, as I understand, from some foolish freak when he was at college; for having read De Quincey's description of his dreams and sensations, he had drenched his tobacco with laudanum in an attempt to produce the same effects. He found, as so many more have done, that the practice is easier to attain than to get rid of...*'

Bloody hell – the 1890s weren't so very different from the 1960s, were they?

A consternation of bells assaulted him. When he heard the front door open, he started back towards the living room, thinking it as good a place as any in which he wouldn't be disturbed.

Then Sandra was calling for him. 'Jamie, it's your new friend.'

At least the cold flags of the entrance hall felt good beneath his bare feet. Sandra was in her yellow raincoat, on her way out. She was smirking again. Under the Palladian stoop stood April Bloom, in a white mackintosh and a headscarf that must have belonged to someone else. She looked as though she had dressed up as the Queen for a bet. From her wrist hung a dripping umbrella, which must have been someone else's, too. Jim could see the rain coming down diagonally behind her, making vapour on the ground the way the bacon had made oily spit in the pan.

'I'll leave you to it, then,' said Sandra, pulling up the hood of her coat. 'Nice to meet you, Miss Bloom.' And then she was gone, leaving Jim alone with the girl.

'What can I do for you?' he asked.

'You do for *me*?' Her eyes were lamps again, dazzling even when their rims were smudged. 'You just upped and disappeared while I was in the little girls' room. I was worried about you. You were drinking that liquor like it was soda pop.'

'I'm fine,' he said, knowing he didn't look it. Then he asked what he couldn't stop himself from asking. 'How did you get here? How did you know where to come?'

'Got a ride in one of the crew's trucks. And, you know—' the smile flickered and she seemed a little embarrassed, '—you gave me the address.'

Oh, God – did I? Clearly, he had.

'You told me to come over if I ever had a spare day,' she added. 'That you'd show me the important work we're stopping you from doing. Well, we won't be doing any work today, weather like it is, so I thought this was as good a time as any to take you up on your offer. Was I wrong?'

He was aware now that she was staring at the book he was holding against his chest.

'Catching up on some reading, I see.' She tilted her head and made a show of looking at the spine. Jim had to force himself not to hide the book behind his back. 'Sherlock Holmes, huh? Now what made you pick that up, I wonder?'

'You'd better come in.' He tried it again, less abruptly. 'Please, why don't you come in?' But the repetition only made it sound mocking.

She showed no sign of offence, however, and after shaking the water from her umbrella, opening and closing it rapidly, stepped inside. 'So, this is the centre of operations for the Loch Ness Research Institute, huh?'

He took the umbrella and shoved it in a basket with some others. 'We're not called that.'

'Oh, I know.'

She began taking off her raincoat before he remembered to help her. Under it, she wore a mini-dress printed with a large-scale geometric design, in shades of green that were picked up by the jade pebbles she'd hung around her neck. White leather boots reached almost to her knees, but between their tops and the hem of the dress, a lot of golden skin was on display. She whipped off her headscarf and draped it over the coat, where Jim had hung it from a hook. Her hair was pinned into an elaborate roll, exposing a swanlike neck. All her confidence seemed to have returned with this double revelation: of his reading choice – that tangible proof that he'd been thinking of her, or at least about the picture – and of herself.

'Well, isn't this a quaint pad?' she said.

Suddenly, he was seeing it through San Franciscan eyes. The clutter of coats and wellington boots, the piles of unattended brown envelopes on the side table, the ancient Bakelite telephone with the rope cord, the tell-tale brown paw marks in caterpillar trails, crossing the flags to the kitchen... All three internal doors were frayed at their edges, revealing dark wood beneath the cream paint. Some of this was recent, made by the sharp teeth of something relatively small, but some was historic, the work of a Labrador-sized resident who'd lived and died before Jim's time here. He noticed again that acid-sweet smell, which really only belonged in an animal hutch, and was bothered by the fact that he'd grown used to it.

'Would you like some tea?' he asked, trying hard to sound sincere.

'I don't suppose you've got any coffee? The stuff at the hotel might as well be mud.'

'Only instant, I'm afraid.'

She grimaced. 'Well, I guess it'll have to be tea then.'

He made the tea without speaking, and she was silent, too, sitting at the table. Rain played a tattoo on the windows and the flat roof of the extended portion of the kitchen. The kettle took a geological age to boil.

'I won't be a tick,' he said when he'd filled the aluminium teapot, and rushed out to get rid of the Sherlock Holmes book.

He didn't go to the case he'd got it from, but climbed the stairs and shoved it in between Marcus Aurelius' *Meditations* and Albert Cohen's *Belle du Seigneur*. Since this bookcase was next to the toilet, he took the opportunity to waste some time in there, too, washing and drying his hands with infinite care afterwards. Then he returned to the kitchen and poured the tea.

'So, where's the laboratory?' she said. 'It's either in the basement or the attic, depending on whether your experiments require lightning or not. Am I right?'

'No laboratory, I'm afraid. The attic's where Douglas does his typing, and the cellar's full of fuel for the range.'

'So, what *do* you have to show me, professor?'

'A screening room,' he said.

That made her laugh. 'Oh, I was forgetting the camera on that truck of yours. Your work isn't so different from mine, is it? Okay then, Mister Scientist, take me to the movies.'

He led her up the stairs. He'd forgotten they would have to pass through the Campbells' bedroom, but made no apologies and offered no explanations. To the girl's credit, she asked nothing as they passed Tessa's dressing table, strewn with its mysterious *objets*, and the enormous marital bed, which was an upstairs equivalent to that ridiculous kitchen table, with a mattress and linen that must have been specially made for it. The blinds were down in the further room, so he reached in and switched the light on before ushering her in ahead of him.

'Well, this isn't what I expected at all,' she said.

The room struck him now, as it must have struck her, as hopelessly tiny. It was stuffed to bursting with a kitchen chair and a sofa covered in oatmeal tweed, both facing a whitewashed wall. Behind the sofa was an old Forces projector on a stand, and lining the longer walls were shelves filled with the cardboard cases that contained the film canisters. On the floor beneath them were rows of box files.

'What did you expect?' he asked.

'Something along the lines of the War Room in *Dr Strangelove*.' It was impossible to know how serious she was being.

'That's a film, is it?' Jim asked.

She narrowed her eyes at him. 'You're a kidder, aren't you? So, come on, what have you got to show me?'

He went to the shelf and after a moment picked out a case with his own handwriting on the label. 'Inverfaragaig, 19-06-1967. 08:03–08:51 BST.' He took out the canister and carefully removed the reel.

'Shall I get the light?' she asked.

'I'll do it when I'm ready, thank you.' He turned on the projector, clicked the reel into place, then hooked the end to the sprock-ets. 'Why don't you take a seat?'

She chose the sofa over the chair, as he'd known she would.

He ran the film. 'This is on the other side of the loch,' he said over the steady rattle and hum. He moved to the door and switched off the light. 'One of the first films I shot after I started here, in fact. Perhaps the most interesting.'

'Bet you're better at the *mise-en-scène* these days, huh?'

He didn't answer that. The wall was filled with a portion of the loch, but it was spoilt by a fuzzy green area near the front and to the right. Something had intruded into view and was rendered unidentifiable by a lack of focus. Probably, it was a sprig of birch or hazel. She was right, though: he didn't let that sort of thing hap-pen now.

'It was a day in spring,' he explained, 'and quite calm, as you can see.'

The surface of the loch was mostly smooth, with gentle undu-lations producing a more-or-less uniform shimmer of dark and light. Occasionally, something disturbed it – a leaf or insect, or perhaps a fish breaking the surface tension from below. Rings spread outwards and then faded. After maybe three minutes, the girl said, 'Well, this is gripping. Tell me what else you do, because it can't be this all day.'

'Watch,' he told her. 'We're nearly there.'

She yawned theatrically, hand over mouth. But then, just when he knew she would, she sat bolt upright.

'Oh,' she said.

'"Oh" indeed.'

Something had passed into the frame from the right, sticking up perpendicular from the water and showing black against the mostly white-grey surface. In its wake, also black, was a low hump, followed by two somewhat shallower humps. She half turned to him, not quite able to tear her eyes from the white wall. 'That can't be… What is it I'm looking at exactly, Mister Scien-tist?'

'Don't give it a name,' he said. 'Tell me what you think you see, piece by piece.'

She turned back. 'Well, there's a neck and a head.'

'What else?'

'A body, I suppose.'

'Necks and heads tend to have bodies, so that would make sense. Anything else?'

'Well—' she spoke very deliberately, '—I think that's a tail, sticking out at the back.'

He threw a switch on the projector. The rattling finished with a snap, and the image in front of them became fixed.

'Don't you dare keep me in suspense,' she said, turning fully towards him now. She was in shadow, of course, but her eyes glistened in reflected light. 'What the hell is it?'

'That,' Jim told her, 'is what we in the Loch Ness Research Group call—' he paused, giving the term a weight he felt it deserved, '—*an event*.'

Chapter Four

She laughed. 'The Loch Ness event, huh?'

He turned on the light, then picked out a box file from the shelf. He sat in the kitchen chair and flicked the file open. 'This is the incident form,' he said, handing it down to where she was perched on the edge of the sofa. She looked at it closely, holding it nearer her face than was normal for someone who didn't need glasses. Did she need glasses? 'I recorded the details as clearly as I could,' he told her. 'You can see that my description's not far off yours. I also noted that the object was moving at 20kph, by my estimation. Or 12.5mph, if you prefer. Nearly 11 knots. But you must remember that I'd no real way of knowing how far away it was from me, or how large it was.'

He imagined for a moment that she might have some maritime experience herself, growing up in San Francisco. He pictured her sunbathing on the deck of a yacht, sailing around the bay. He could see her father, too, or perhaps a rich boyfriend, in white trousers and a peaked cap.

'So, what did you do next?' She returned the form to him and fell back into the cushions. 'I take it you didn't send the film to the BBC, or sell it to the highest bidder.'

He almost laughed. 'Not sure how high that would go. No, I showed it to Douglas. He's the one who recruited me, the one who started all this. I'd got my degree and was almost finished with my masters when I first came out here. I didn't quite shoot that on my first day, but it wasn't long after.'

'And what did Douglas say?'

'Not a lot. "Most interesting. Now label it and put it away." Something like that.'

Jim shuffled the papers until a photograph was uppermost. It was a monochrome print of a long-billed bird in close-up. Its back was dark and its belly white. He handed it down to her. 'Seen one of these yet?'

She held it close to her face again. 'Yeah, we've got ducks in the States, believe it or not.'

'I mean this particular breed. Since you've been here.'

'Nope.' She made to hand it back. 'Haven't had time for a duck shoot.'

'It's grouse they shoot in the Highlands, and you've another couple of months until the season starts.'

She shrugged. 'Not too hot on spotting birds.'

He took the picture from her. 'This here's a red-breasted merganser,' he explained, holding it so that she could see where he was pointing. 'It's a type of sawbill. That's the duck, not the drake, so the head would be brown and the back grey. The undercarriage would be white. Sure you've seen nothing like it?'

She shrugged again. 'Of course, I'll be looking out for it now.'

He dropped the photo into the folder. 'All right, time for the next film.'

He rewound the first reel and got it back in its canister and box. He slotted it back where it belonged and took another down from the shelf. This time, the inscription was in a more slanting hand than his own, and read, '28-05-1968 on Loch, nr. Dores.'

'This was shot by my colleague, Alan Stirling,' he said, threading the new film into the projector. 'He had quite a bit more experience than me at this point.'

He turned off the lights and set the machine clattering again. The flat-bottomed V of the Great Glen appeared, its mass of grey water hemmed in by mountains that were beginning to turn from a tobacco colour to a bright green. To begin with, the image moved too much, and the viewer couldn't but feel unsteady on his feet, especially if he wasn't entirely clear of his hangover. But after a few seconds it steadied – presumably Alan had tightened the camera's mountings – and turned about, so that the near bank became visible. A red shingly beach with waves breaking against it, dotted with bigger glacial deposits of the same colour, rising to an interior dark with the trunks of deciduous native trees. But the lens was focused on something on the loch's surface, floating low in the water and moving with surprising speed. Three smaller, similar somethings were following in its wake.

'Okay,' said the girl, 'I can see that that's a duck and those are ducklings. They're going at quite a lick, aren't they?'

'For ducks and ducklings, yes,' said Jim. 'Not eleven knots, though. More like three-and-a-half. Now, watch.'

The camera – or rather, the boat – began to move away, so that the duck and its young diminished, buffeted a little by the surge. For a while they remained a duck and ducklings. Then, in an instant, the resolution vanished and they weren't four different things anymore, but a single, elongated thing instead.

'Oh,' the girl said a second time.

'What do you see now?'

She spoke like one going over her catechism: 'I see a head, and a neck, and a body, and—' she sighed, and it was almost laughter, '—and maybe a tail.' She shook her head. 'How silly.'

'Of you or me?'

Now she laughed outright. 'Well, I meant of me, but now that you mention it, O! Oz the Great and Powerful…'

He stopped the projector and switched on the light. 'Alan didn't know that he was answering my question when he shot that. It's just his job – all of our jobs – to record everything that happens on the loch.' He put the rest of the papers back into the folder and returned it to where it belonged on the shelf. 'Probably, when I shot that film, I wanted it to be something significant. But that's the wrong way to think about it. What we're looking for is disruptions to the ordinary, anything that's unexpected, but then our duty is to find if there's a way of making them *perfectly* ordinary.'

She nodded. 'Occam's razor. I know about that.'

Jim was impressed. Where had she come across that idea? 'So long as there's a mundane answer,' he said, attending to the reel of film, 'there's no need to go looking for an extraordinary one. We'll draw the well of the mundane until it's run dry.'

'Once you've eliminated the impossible—' she was leaning back in the sofa, steepling her fingers and putting on a Yank's idea of a fey English accent, '—then the remainder, however improbable, must be the answer. Or something like that.'

Again, he was surprised to hear her talk that way. 'That's one way of putting it.'

'Well, Sherlock—' she turned right around in the sofa, lifting her legs and tucking them up behind her, '—you've really taken me by surprise, I must say.'

He busied himself with the canister now. 'What did you expect, Watson? Raquel Welch in a fur bikini?'

He immediately wished he hadn't said it. Looking down at her now, he saw that the short dress had ridden up her legs, exposing more of the flesh between the skirt's hem and the top of the boots.

'Oh, I don't know,' she said, oblivious to his embarrassment. 'Something more impressive than this little room, I guess. Or maybe something less so. Depends on the way you look at it, huh?'

'Depends on your sense of the rational, I'd say.'

For a moment, the canister wouldn't fit in the box. He hadn't even seen that idiotic picture! It was the poster he remembered, that was all – the one with its star wearing that impractical and inauthentic costume. He shoved the tin against the cardboard, buckling the box's edge.

'But you know what?' she said, 'When that debonair friend of yours said you were hunting monsters, I thought he was having a joke at the expense of the dumb American. It didn't seem possible that a lot of dour Scots would go looking for brontosauruses in the middle of the 20th century.'

'I'll let you into a secret,' Jim said, shoving the box back on the shelf, making another meal of it. 'I'm not Scottish. I know you Yanks aren't good at distinguishing between British accents, but really, there isn't much similarity.'

'Oh, I know you're not Scottish. You're from Cumbria, right? Poet country. I'm not the one who got sozzled and forgot everything he did last night. Hey—' she was kneeling on the cushions now, leaning on straight arms against the back of the sofa, '—you want to know my secret?'

He was hovering by the door. 'Not really.' People didn't tell him their secrets, and on the whole, he was glad of it.

'Well, I'll tell you anyway. I'm not a Yank. Well, not only a Yank. I'm a Brit, too. In fact, I wouldn't be here if I wasn't. Union rules, don't you know?'

'I didn't.'

She got the hint and stepped back off the sofa. 'I'm a war baby,' she told him as he led her again through the Campbells' bedroom, past the gigantic nuptial bed. 'My parents met at a dance in Lowestoft. You know where that is?'

He nodded. 'East Anglia.'

'As east as you can get in England. Dad was in the Eighth Air Force,' she went on. 'You wouldn't think he was much of a military man to see him now: little white-haired guy with a pot belly who likes to tell you the same joke about twenty times. That worked for the English ladies back in the dark days, I guess. Along with the nylons and the Hershey's.'

They were descending the stairs, passing the bookshelves. Jim remembered his own mother making that old complaint about how the Yanks had been overpaid, oversexed and over here. Not that any of them would have had the opportunity to bother her much in Kendal. From what Jim could gather, her biggest wartime headaches had come from a snobbish dislike of the children evacuated to the area from Newcastle.

'Mum wouldn't have been a pushover, though,' the girl was saying – and she really did say 'Mum' instead of 'Mom'. 'Knowing her, she would've made all the running, and done it a lot more strategically than Dad would ever have been capable of. Anyway, by the end of the war, when it was time to go back to the States, I was on the way, and there was an angry Lowestoft trawlerman calling for wedding bells. Born the day after VJ Day. How about that? I'm telling you my age. Then they had to decide where to live…'

It was at this point, just as Jim was stepping off the stairs, that two distinct events occurred to interrupt the girl's story. First, a pine marten streaked across the hallway from the kitchen, at what seemed a much faster rate than eleven knots. It passed between them and shot up the stairs. Then, before April Bloom's quizzical look could turn into an actual question, a deep rumble sounded from beyond the kitchen door, exactly as if a heavy object were being moved forcibly against a stone floor.

'Burglars?' the girl said, not altogether jokingly.

Jim shrugged – he'd thought no one else was home. Had Sandra returned? No, she hadn't: there was no dripping yellow raincoat on any of the hooks. The kitchen door was only ajar enough to allow the passage of a serpentine mammal. In two strides, he was in front of it, and then swung it open.

Sandra wasn't home, but Tessa and Douglas most emphatically were.

Douglas was still in that old oilskin of his, which had no doubt done good service in the further reaches of the Empire in the years he'd spent exploring them after the war. Tessa, too, was dressed for the outdoors, in her duffel coat – but while Douglas stood with his feet planted firmly on the floor, she was lying with her back on the kitchen table. More of her bare leg was exposed than the girl had shown, when hers had been tucked behind her on the screening-room sofa. They were otherwise orientated, too, rising almost straight up on either side of her husband's substantial torso, with the toes pointed ballerina-style towards the raw beams in the ceiling.

Instantly, the two of them stopped their motion and looked the way of Jim and the girl. Both of their faces – Douglas's the right way up, Tessa's upside down – were printed with looks of mild astonishment.

'I do beg your pardon,' said Jim and carefully shut the door. There was an eternal moment when he struggled to find something to say, and he spent it looking at one of his unshod feet. Somehow, his naked toes seemed more obscene than what he'd just witnessed. 'Shall we try the living room?' he managed at last.

But the girl had returned to the stairs and was sitting on the bottom step, rocking with silent laughter. 'Oh lord,' she said, with tears in those lucent eyes, 'how I love you Brits and your stiff upper lips.'

A slit of open window allowed birdsong and rain-washed air into the living room, along with a shaft of new sunlight. A plate of doorstep sandwiches, cheese and home-made piccalilli, had been placed on the coffee table beside the aluminium teapot and some mugs. Next to these was the latest paperback Tessa was making herself read. On the cover was a colour photo of a woman gazing over her bare shoulder. It was called *The Diary of a Mad Housewife*.

'Well, it's jolly nice to meet someone involved in the filming,' Tessa said as she poured the tea. She was no longer in her duffel coat, and had changed into a pair of chastening navy-blue slacks and a white shirt, both as new as Sandra's strawberry-spangled dress. 'Do help yourself to a sandwich, Miss Bloom.'

'Thank you.' She took an unwieldy white rectangle and rested it on one knee. Jim wondered whether she'd actually eat it – the nuclear glow of the pickled cauliflower was enough to put most people off. She had a whole sofa to herself again, while both her hosts sat in armchairs. 'It's nice to meet the locals, too,' she said. 'You lived here long?'

'Quite a while, yes,' said Tessa. 'So, what exactly is it that you do?'

'I'm the continuity girl,' she replied. 'Or script girl, as Mr Wilder likes to call me.'

Jim had forgotten to ask her about that, and it felt a bit late in the day to do so now. It was a good thing Tessa was here, really. 'And what does one of those do?'

The girl had raised the sandwich almost to her mouth, but now she dropped it to her knee again. 'Well, I'm sure you know we don't shoot everything in sequence,' she told Tessa. 'We haven't gotten to the first scenes of the movie, in fact – they'll be shot at Pinewood, the studio near London. We're starting with the location shoot because it's summer and we wanted to take advantage of the good weather.'

Tessa laughed. 'So, you thought you'd come to Scotland?'

Actually, it wasn't so bad a day for it now. The sooner Douglas sorted himself out and gave the girl her promised lift back to the Drum, the sooner Jim could get on with some work…

The girl laughed along with Tessa. 'Well, if we'd wanted sun we'd have stayed in California. No, it needed to be Loch Ness because this is where the story's set. That's Mr Wilder for you, always looking for reality.'

'Mr Wilder's the director?'

She nodded. 'He's a stickler,' she said, 'and that's where I come in. I do a lot of the stickling for him. My job is to make sure it doesn't show that we're doing everything in the wrong order. It's all got to fit together in the final edit without anything giving us away.'

Tessa nodded. 'So if someone's wearing a red carnation when you're filming an indoor scene in London, he'll be wearing a red carnation when he steps outside into Inverness-shire?'

'Oh, you make it sound like any idiot could do it.' She said it half wistfully, as if she almost agreed that it was so.

'Not in the least,' said Tessa. 'Sounds like a minefield. So many things to keep an eye on at once. You must have the eyes of an eagle, Miss Bloom.'

'Well, less a minefield and more a big chart with notes all over it. Oh, and please call me April. Miss Bloom makes me sound like some kind of a gardening disaster.'

They laughed together again. Jim was beginning to feel he was surplus to requirements here. There was no reason why he shouldn't make his excuses and go and do something useful instead…

'You know what?' said April, looking his way, 'You ought to come out and see us working.'

Tessa gasped with delight. 'That would be wonderful! You'll do that, won't you, Jamie? He's our cameraman, you know.'

'Oh, I know,' said April. 'I've seen his handiwork.'

'You'd be interested to see how the professionals do it, wouldn't you?'

Jim shrugged. 'I don't work in seventy mil,' he told them, 'and I'm not trying to fool people into seeing what isn't there. Quite the opposite, in fact.'

'Still,' said Tessa, and left it at that, as if one syllable could meet the full force of his argument.

'You've really got a wrong idea about movies, you know,' said the girl. 'Or at least, the movies Mr Wilder makes. You ought to come out with us and see for yourself. I'm sure I can arrange it. You'll have to be prepared for an early start, mind...'

'Oh, that won't be a problem,' said Tessa. 'He's our early riser.'

Jim was about to object again – on what grounds he wasn't yet sure – when the door opened and Douglas's monumental head and shoulders were thrust into the room. He was back in his oilskins, if he'd ever been out of them. 'All right, Miss Bloom. I'm ready when you are.'

Dinner was testing, and not just because Jim was being asked to eat Tessa's kedgeree off a table for which one extra item had been added to its list of uses. There was some new tension between Alan and Sandra, and though they weren't speaking to one another, they wouldn't stop speaking to everyone else.

'I hope you showed our visitor a good time, today, Jamie,' Sandra said in a voice heavy with double meaning.

'The girl we met at the hotel came over while the rest of us were out,' Douglas told Alan, who'd looked at him quizzically.

'She just wanted to know about the work,' Jim told them, fishing the last piece of smoked haddock out of his plate of curried rice.

'Her name's April Bloom, would you believe,' said Douglas. 'A young person of considerable charms.'

'Considerable, yes,' said Tessa, apparently happy to know that her husband's eye had wandered that way. Of course, theoretically at least, she considered monogamy to be a tool of the patriarchy, used in men's programme of oppressing women. But Jim could never quite keep up with Tessa's ideas, or make them add up to anything meaningful.

However, he realised now that he'd got hold of the wrong end of this particular matrimonial stick. They weren't agreeing about the girl for their benefit, but for his. Jim had tried not to think about the conversation that must have taken place during that Land Rover drive to Drumnadrochit, but to no avail. He'd half convinced himself, while collating his latest notes in the screening room, that the burning sensation on his earlobes had been down to something other than the sun pouring in through the opened casements.

'Tell me this again,' said Alan, whose eyebrows were up under his blond fringe. 'You're talking about the canny lass at the Drum last night, ay? You're saying she came all the way out here looking for Jamie?'

Jim nodded. 'I told you—' he found some egg on his plate, so that it was clear Autolycus hadn't had the lot after all, '—she just wanted to know what it is we do.'

'And from what I understand,' said Sandra, sending a wicked smile Tessa and Douglas's way, 'she found that out all right.'

Tessa flushed to the roots of her mousy bob, but Douglas only roused himself to his full, seated height. 'She wasn't the least abashed,' he said, making that smile with the downturned corners. 'You're forgetting she's from San Francisco. I shouldn't wonder if she's been to Haight-Ashbury and encountered Bohemianism on a level none of us have experienced.' The smile turned enigmatic. 'At least, not for some time.'

'So, Jamie,' said Sandra, in a way that made it clear she was determined to delve deeper, 'were you really up there watching films about ducks and drakes?'

'Oh, you're making him blush now,' said Tessa, her own pallor having only just returned to normal. 'Leave the poor boy alone.'

'That's all we were doing, yes,' he told Sandra through gritted teeth. 'It was a bit of a pain, to tell you the truth. I had things to do.'

'Like recovering from a force nine hangover that you'd got drinking whisky with her last night, eh?'

'Ah, Sandra—' it was Alan coming to his aid now, speaking

directly to his wife for the first time since they'd sat down, '—why don't you give it a rest? A man's entitled to what he can get. It's a free country, or it's supposed to be. And Jamie's a free man.'

'Lucky Jamie,' said Sandra, and Jim almost expected Alan to duck under the green stare she threw him.

'But he's right.' It was Douglas speaking now, pacifically. 'It isn't fair to give Jamie the third degree. He's made a new friend, and that's always a thing to celebrate. But I tell you what, Jamie—' he spoke now as one bestowing wisdom, '—if the opportunity comes along to go and watch them filming, you really ought to take it. I, for one, would jump at the chance of meeting Geneviève Page. Did you see *Belle de Jour*?'

No, Jim hadn't seen *Belle de Jour*.

'It really is extraordinary,' said Douglas.

'Oh, yes – extraordinary,' echoed Tessa.

'Sounds a bit blue,' said Alan. 'Is it a bit blue? Is it a bluey they're shooting here on the loch? Is that what this lassie wants you to go and watch them making, Jamie?'

'Now, look—' Jim's voice was higher in pitch than he would have liked it to be, '—you're all jumping the gun. She was being polite, that's all. I'd let her see some of our footage, so she felt she had to offer something in return.'

'You mean,' said Sandra, 'that you'd shown her yours, so she had to promise to show you hers?'

Stripped of the *Carry On*-style innuendo, that was more-or-less exactly what he'd meant. 'And I stand by what I've said before,' he added. 'They've started filming now and there's no sign of them leaving anytime soon. Nobody's asked us for any advice, have they? They're not interested in reciprocation, they're just in our bloody way.'

'But how?' There was something defiant behind Tessa's tortoiseshells.

'Ay,' said Sandra, 'in what way are they a problem? It's not like they're filling the loch with flotillas. Hard to see why you're getting your knickers in a twist, to be honest.'

'She's got a point, pal.' Now Alan was joining their side. 'I mean, apart from setting the fucking police on me, they've not been so bad, eh?'

'I think an attitude of live and let live is in order.' It was Douglas, taking the role of Brutus and delivering the *coup de grâce*. 'But, as I said, if a pretty girl were to invite me along to watch her at work, I don't think I'd be able to resist. At the very least, it might contribute to a *détente*. It's certainly hard to see what harm could be done. Don't you agree, Jamie?'

Chapter Five

This really wasn't a good day for a picnic.

Though shafts of sun shot through the cumuli, making silver pools on the otherwise leaden body of Loch Meiklie, darkness covered the banks. The breeze was altogether too stiff, so that the picnic blanket had to be held down by the basket at its centre, and by a hefty cruet placed at each corner. Meanwhile, the plastic-macked picnickers themselves sat shivering nearby on canvas chairs. It was the same three Jim had seen at Urquhart Castle, three weeks ago. None of them was wearing a hat now, but when hats were required, they would have to be firmly pinned in place or tied beneath the chin with ribbon.

And it was those heavy-bottomed clouds that were making them wait.

Jim had never considered clouds the way he was being asked to consider them today. Now it was their capacity to change the frame for the moviegoer that was their chief feature. They might move great distances in no time at all, throwing distorting shadows over mountains and water, and might change their own shapes, too, flowing from one suggestive configuration into another in a matter of moments. That big cloud over the Watson's shoulder was a case in point. The last time Jim had looked, it had been an airborne plesiosaur, but now it was clearly a map of Australia.

Of course, April had warned him about the waiting. 'We need the light to be just right,' she'd said at the beginning of their magical mystery tour, when he'd first sat beside her in the back of the Land Rover with other members of the unit. 'It'll be hell trying to match the cloud cover in a different minute, let alone on a different day.'

'Why not wait for a clear day?'

'We're in Scotland, stupid.' But she'd been smiling as she said it. 'We've already wasted too much time filming uncloudy skies –

they're even more impossible to match if we have to pick up a shot later. As it is, Mr Wilder's going to be trying to do everything in single takes. Which means he'll drill us all like we're in a platoon. He's a stickler, I told you.'

'And you'll be helping him stickle. You told me that, too.'

She'd smiled the way she had at the bar in the Drum, and it might have burnt out his retinas if he hadn't looked away. 'You're learning, bud.'

They had climbed a steep and narrow road above Urquhart Bay. It had been fine for the Land Rovers, but the vans carrying the camera and other equipment had struggled, and progress had necessarily been slow. Then the crew had set up the camera in a field and had shot some soundless footage of the actors playing Holmes, Watson and the woman in the green-and-white dress cycling along a thin track, with the bay peeping at them through gaps in the coppice- and heath-covered mountains. The woman and Holmes had been on a tandem, with Watson following them on a single-seated boneshaker. At one point, serendipity – or more likely some sort of arrangement with a local farmer – had thrown a flock of sheep in their path, just as they'd passed the roofless ruins of an old croft. For a moment, the scene had seemed real: not just a group of people in shirtsleeves watching three others dressed in daft outfits pedalling a couple of antiques, but a genuine glimpse into the past.

Then everyone had got back into their 20th century motor vehicles and had driven to the main road again. They had struck out north-west, travelling for an hour and a half, passing through a country of Munros – of green and purple giants, shouldering their torsos out of the wide glens and reaching skyward – and of lochs that looked like they were made of onyx. Their destination had been Eilean Donan, a castle perhaps as old as the one at Urquhart, but which had been carefully restored so that the roofs and walls were solid and unbroken. It sat on a little island in Loch Duich – a sea loch, replete with algae-strewn tideline and pungent littoral odour – and the crew had filmed the actors cycling over the stone bridge to reach it, and then returning. It had taken less than an hour for everyone to be satisfied, and then they had got back into their vehicles and had travelled almost the whole distance back again to Loch Meiklie, where the main unit was already set up beside a picturesque bridge that crossed the pebbly mouth of the river feeding it.

Only now did it occur to Jim, sat waiting in his canvas chair, that April had invited him to watch them film on a day when they couldn't have interfered with his work on Loch Ness.

'You okay there?' She was approaching him now from where she'd been talking to the director and camera operator. Her copy of the screenplay was held tight to her chest, folded over on its bindings. He could see its sparse typescript, and her own generous annotations made in pencil. 'Not overexcited yet?'

'Not yet,' he said.

She was in mufti again, T-shirt and jeans, and he wasn't sure that it didn't suit her better than the hippy gear. She'd plaited her hair again into ropes that drooped over her shoulders. There was gooseflesh on her arms, lifting the fine hairs there.

'Reminds me of fête day,' he said.

'Of what?'

'My mother was on the parish council,' he told her, 'so had a lot to do with organising the fête at the local church. When I was little, she'd bring me along with her – well, drag me along, really. So, I got used to a lot of hanging about.'

She smiled. 'This is really that boring, huh?'

'Oh, yes.'

But in fact, his memories of those childish days weren't so painful. Mostly, he'd sat in the village hall with old issues of *The Eagle*, while the adults had done what they needed to do to feel adult. Sometimes an American comic would come in for the jumble sale, and he'd be able to get his hands on it before it was sorted and sent to the right stall. This was the time before he'd become a boy naturalist, of course, and had been allowed to go out alone with jam jars to collect frog spawn and sticklebacks. Today, he'd brought a paperback with him, but hadn't felt the impulse to pick it up yet. Something always seemed on the brink of happening, just before it didn't.

'They're going to rehearse the scene again,' April said, 'while that black cloud is in the way.' She pointed to the thing that was now making a shadow over half the loch. 'If you think you're bored, you should put yourself in the actors' shoes.'

It was true that they looked bored. Or at least, the Sherlock and the Watson did: both sat in silence, the former with his chin in his hands and his elbows on his knees, the latter glancing at the newspaper, which was an object of envy to Jim. He knew it must contain a report on the Apollo 11 launch, and though he'd heard the news bulletin before he'd come out, he was thirsty for more detail. Meanwhile, the actress was talking in an easy way to one of the crew, a girl who might have had something to do with makeup. Keeping his voice low, he made his confession to April. 'Are any of them famous? I only know that the actress was in some French film that Douglas and Tessa have seen.'

'That'll be because she's French,' said April. 'Bob and Colin are mostly stage actors, though Bob was in *The Prime of Miss Jean Brodie*. He's the art teacher who paints schoolgirls in the nude – the schoolgirls are in the nude, not him – while all the time he's got the hots for Miss Jean. They're married, by the way. I mean, in real life – Bob is Mister Maggie Smith. You know who that is, don't you?'

Jim nodded, but April wasn't fooled.

'My God, you really do live under a rock, don't you?'

Somebody called for her. The voice was distorted by the wind, but Jim recognised something Germanic in with the American.

'Better get going,' she said, 'but I guess we'll break for lunch soon. That's something to look forward to at least. The catering's terrific.'

She headed towards the actors again. The stout man in the flat cap, who had a tweed jacket on now, was standing in front of them with his hands on his hips. The Sherlock was looking up at him with complete attention, chin still resting in his hands. His expression was almost of pain, though that might have been because of the odd way he'd angled his neck. When April reached them, the man in the flat cap took her script and listened to what she had to say. Then he spoke again to the actors, and they took off their macs and returned to the picnic scene. Wardrobe girls attended to the actress, while the Sherlock and the Watson donned the same trilby and bowler hats they'd been wearing earlier. April fussed over them for a while, doing her stickling.

Then suddenly, as if a great switch had been thrown backstage, the scene was lit. The cumulus had moved on, and only a few cotton-like scuts obscured the otherwise universal blue.

'Into positions, everyone,' called the man in the flat cap through his loudhailer. There was no mistaking it: the voice was as German as it was Yank.

The actors came to life, like daisies opening for the sun. They arranged themselves on the picnic blanket just as April instructed them: the Watson sitting between the bicycles and the basket, the woman kneeling on the green-and-white flounces of her dress and the Sherlock resting on one elbow now, his tweed-clad legs stretched before him. Meanwhile, the sound men were getting into position, hanging the big microphone with its furry cover over the actors' heads. It looked like some unappetising kind of fruit on a spindly bough.

'Are you happy, Miss Bloom?' called the director.

'Happy, Mr Wilder.' She hurried to a spot behind the camera, but still distant from Jim.

The man in the cap exchanged a last word with the camera operator. 'Okay,' he cried out, 'go!'

It wasn't quite possible to hear the actors speak, but Jim got the gist of what was going on. Watson was apparently playing some sort of servant to Holmes and the woman. Jim understood enough from the three or four stories he'd read to know how wrong that was. Now he handed glasses to Holmes and the woman and filled them with champagne, or whatever was standing in for champagne. Was Holmes meant to be in a romance with this woman? Were they married? That was even more wrong. Then Watson was on his feet, a condiment pot in one hand and a spoon in the other, staring up at the bridge.

'I say there!' he called out, loud enough for Jim to hear him now, 'Good afternoon! Remember me?'

Something else could be heard, too, that sounded like a car backfiring on the road they'd turned off to get here. What would they do if the microphone picked that up, as well as the dialogue? Now the actress was shaking her parasol, opening and closing it rapidly. Holmes spoke to her, and Jim could just about make out her reply. It had something to do with a bee.

'And cut!'

The man in the flat cap was considering the sky. Another blackening cloud was rolling in. He then consulted with the camera operator.

'Break for lunch, everyone,' he barked.

'Excuse me,' Jim said, 'do you mind if I borrow your paper?'

'Not at all, young man,' said the Watson. He picked it up from where he had dropped it by his chair. 'Be my guest,' he said, handing it up. 'You following the moon mission, too?'

He was a thickset man of about forty, with a real moustache and a receding head of tightly curled hair. His smile was natural and there was a light of real interest in his eyes. Jim felt the power of personality in a way he'd never felt it before. 'I am, yes.'

'It's wonderful to have some good news in the papers for a change, isn't it?' Now that he wasn't in character, it was possible to detect something in his voice that was neither English nor Scottish. 'I supposed you've been interested in space since you were a nipper, eh? H.G. Wells and all that...'

There followed a somewhat intense exchange, in which an apparent shared interest in science and technology was the sole topic. Neither acting, film-making nor Loch Ness phenomena were touched on at all.

'Well, I won't keep you from your reading.' The actor got up and offered Jim his hand. 'I'm Colin, by the way. And you are...?'

Jim told him.

'Nice to meet you, Jim. Am I right in thinking you're April's friend?'

'She brought me here, yes.'

'Lovely girl.' Colin's smile was even more fulsome. Was there a suggestion of a wink, too? Jim couldn't be sure now it was over. 'Well, enjoy the rest of the day. Hope we don't bore you too much. God bless.'

He found April sitting with a tray on her lap. There was a matching tray in Jim's chair. Irish stew, by the look of it, with mashed potatoes and string beans. 'Stuff to line your insides with,' said April, 'as my English nan used to say. Isn't Colin a sweet man?'

'Very friendly, yes.' Jim picked up the tray and sat down.

'A gentleman. Like your Douglas.'

'Maybe,' said Jim. 'But from Northern Ireland, I think.'

Some still unsmothered sunlight shone on her bare arms, making them look like polished pine. Her eyes were hidden behind sunglasses, which diminished their power at least. He tried a forkful of the stew. It wasn't at all what he'd expected: it had a deeper, red-wine flavour, and a little onion popped against his teeth when he bit down. Was that a shallot? He'd never knowingly eaten a shallot before. Whatever it was, it was delicious. For a while he sat and ate, almost paying April no mind. In fact, the silence between them might reasonably have been described as companionable.

It was April who broke it. 'Oh, look,' she said, 'a butterfly. A Scottish butterfly – I've never seen one like that before.'

She kept her right hand still, even though she'd been about to spear a piece of meat with the fork it held. The insect had alighted on the knuckle of her thumb, and kept its wings open, sunning itself. A dusty brown, like cocoa, with a ruffled white fringe and copper-coloured eye-spots.

'You're right,' said Jim, 'it is Scottish. *Aricia artaxerxes*: the Northern Brown Argus. See those white spots, one on each wing? That's how you can tell it's the Scottish variety.'

'You know all about butterflies, too?'

She seemed about five times as impressed by this as she'd been by his demonstration of deductive reasoning back in the screening room. 'You pick this stuff up,' he said. 'I'd amaze you even more if we came across a newt.'

April put a finger to the butterfly's antennae. It turned, folding and unfolding its wings, but didn't take off. 'Say its name again.'

'Northern Brown Argus.'

'No,' she said, 'the scientific name. Or did you make that up?'

He repeated it for her.

'*Aricia artaxerxes*,' she said, working her lips around the consonants. Then she prodded the creature's abdomen with a polished nail. 'Now shoo. I've got to eat. Go brighten someone else's day.'

It obeyed her, lifting itself on those powdery membranes and making a haphazard flight up towards the birches behind them.

The threatening cloud passed and the filming started again. The camera was placed behind Holmes, Watson and the woman, and a group of actors playing monks could be seen walking in line over the bridge, their faces obscured by their pointed cowls. Watson waved to them and repeated his previous line. This was done a number of times, and the actor – Colin – played each as exuberantly as its predecessor. Then the camera was removed to the bridge itself, so that the scene could be shot several more times from that position, too.

Jim turned his attention to the newspaper. The launch had gone more or less to schedule. Lift-off had occurred at 13.32 GMT and orbit achieved eleven minutes later. Another three hours and they'd performed the lunar slingshot manoeuvre, sending the module in the direction of its destination, which it would reach in a further five days. It was extraordinarily thrilling, and Jim wished there was someone he could discuss it with. But Colin, who was the only obvious candidate, was deep in conversation with one of the crew now. Not the director, but someone who looked almost as important: a tall, long-chinned man about the same age as Douglas, in a grey worsted jacket fastened by the higher of the two buttons. He was peering down at the actor as he spoke, through clear plastic frames that rested on a prominent nose. Close by, the Sherlock actor was poring over his script, which he'd spread open at his feet.

Jim got up and went for a wander. The trees nearest the bank were the usual birch and alder and, behind them, along the road, there were green fronds of bracken and purple spears of willowherb. He strolled to the other side of the road that the bridge carried over the water, to where the monks had been sitting while awaiting their cue. He couldn't help but notice a script lying unattended on one of the chairs – could it really belong to one of the monks? As far as he could tell, none of them had any lines…

When Jim and April had first set out in the Land Rover that morning, she'd caught him eyeing her own, annotated script, and had flashed those eyes at him in a way that had almost put him in mind of Sandra. 'Hands off,' she'd said. 'I'd be sent straight to the Hollywood gulag if I let a civilian in on our secrets. A lot more than my job's worth, I'm telling you.'

He looked around now to make sure no one was watching. Attention seemed pretty squarely fixed on what was happening up on the bridge. With all the nonchalance he could muster, he dropped Colin's newspaper on top of the script and picked it up again. The script came neatly with it.

'Hey, we're all done here.'

Her hand was on his arm, and he looked up from his novel to find her perched beside him again.

'You set to go, or do you need to finish that last paragraph?'

The sun had been dipping while he'd been absorbed in the book, and the further promontory was turned into a black andiron with yellow-orange flame behind them. He guessed he'd been squinting at print that had been virtually unreadable for about twenty minutes. But now he wanted to ask April about his other reading – *i.e.*, about that script he'd returned with even more stealth than he'd used to obtain it.

'Mind you,' April said as they walked together to the Land Rover, 'we'll only be setting up this time tomorrow, ready to shoot in the golden hour. You can treat it like a full-night shoot, but you get to see the scenery. It doesn't last long, so you've got to get it right first time. Or wait a couple of hours until dawn. We'll be back at Urquhart Castle for that.'

Jim almost said, *I know.*

On the short drive back, he was even more conscious of her proximity than he'd been on the drive out. Probably, that was only an effect of the faded light: the less he could see, the more they seemed alone together, though in fact they were with the same three lads and one girl who'd been with them from the beginning of the day. April's denim-clad knee seemed to transmit a heat to his own. He scoured his brain for something pleasant and meaningless to say, but wanted to ask her about the things in that script, too…

'And there was me thinking you didn't dig movies,' she said, breaking into his reverie. 'You know I worked on that one, too, don't you?'

For a moment, he thought he'd been rumbled, and was almost relieved. 'I just glanced at it,' he said. But then he knew she wasn't talking about the script, but the novel that lay between them, which had fused into the Land Rover's shadows. He picked it up now and the white wheel on its cover appeared again in the orange light.

'Mr Kubrick's another stickler,' she told him. 'Some would say even worse than Mr Wilder, but I'd call it a tie. He's just as funny in his own way, too.'

'You worked on *2001*?'

The light flashed off her teeth. 'That's your kind of movie, huh? Science fiction for actual scientists. How many times you seen it?'

He shrugged. 'I haven't,' he said. 'Not yet.'

'You're kidding me?' It was as though he'd claimed he couldn't swim, or drive, or ride a bike. 'When's the last time you went to a movie theatre?'

He gave it some thought. He knew he'd seen *Dracula* – the remake, the one in colour – in a requisitioned lecture hall in Manchester, put on by some student society or other. But no, he'd seen something since then, too, on a date. 'A Beatles picture, I think,' he said. 'Definitely not my choice.'

'You don't like the Beatles, either, huh?'

He shrugged again. If he was going to be damned, he might as well be damned completely.

The conversation lapsed again, and in the silence, he tried to formulate one of the overwhelming questions he'd wanted to ask since reading the script. But the more she became a silhouette, the harder it was to speak to her. The silence became progressively drowsy, something encouraged as much by the pulse of the engine as by the gloaming.

At the Drumnadrochit Hotel, two of the lads and the girl got out straight away. April leant over the front passenger seat and spoke to the remaining lad. 'You okay to take this one home, bud?' There was an affirmative grunt and the Land Rover made its final leg with just the two of them sat in the back. By the time they got to the farmhouse, it was almost dusk. Light shone only from behind the curtains of the kitchen and from the bulb in the front stoop. With the Land Rover's motor idling, April saw him to the door.

'Well, I hope you found the day enlightening, Mister Scientist.'

'Oh, very.' What else could he say?

'We might be working for a dream factory,' she added, 'but that doesn't make it any less of a drudge day to day. And we aren't really interfering with anything you do, are we?'

It was hard to think of a more obvious point of entry for him, but all he managed was, 'Perhaps not.' Something else was happening here, working against what he considered to be his primary interests. 'I enjoyed it,' he said, and it was only the truth.

They stopped just short of the stoop, and by its dim light he saw her face lifted towards his own. The touch of her lips on his cheek was almost too delicate. 'Happy monster-hunting, Jamie.'

'Jim,' he said as she dropped back on her heels.

'Excuse me?'

'I'm Jim, not Jamie.' He pointed at the door. 'They just decided to call me that, I never told them to. Never told them not to, mind. But back home, I'm Jim.'

The expansive smile returned, and even when only half lit, it nearly overwhelmed him. 'Well, good night, Jim.'

She tripped back to the Land Rover with all his questions unasked. He realised then that he had no reliable way of contacting her: just the number of the hotel, where she barely ever was. He might have been able to say what he needed to say more easily over the phone. When the Land Rover was lost behind the trees, he opened the door with the intention of heading straight for his bedroom. But the door to the kitchen was open, and he couldn't avoid passing it. As he did so, four sets of eyes skewered him – five if you counted Autolycus, who at that moment was standing on his hind legs in the middle of the table.

'So, Jamie Outhwaite,' said Sandra, pulling out a chair. Her eyes were burning in their kohl borders as brutally as the low sun had burned behind that spit of land at Loch Meiklie. 'Come and tell us all about it. And if you're thinking of leaving anything out, think again. I'll only find out, and then you'll wish you'd come clean in the first place.'

London, 2014 (II)

Re: TPLOSH
  From: Gemma MacDonald
  To: April Korzeniowski
  5 April 2014 GMT: 11:04

Dear April,

Thank you for your reply!

Not to worry about the delay. You should see my inbox! I've plenty to get on with while I'm waiting for your messages. But I must admit, yours are the ones I'm happiest to receive.

Very pleased to hear that you and your daughter will be in London next month. I've been an admirer of Maisie's work since LOST EMPIRES, along with everyone else who has a love for the Golden Age of Hollywood. I hope I get to meet her too! And of course, it will be wonderful to talk to you in person rather than via a screen.

I think there's a good chance that we will indeed be asked to contribute a commentary track to the DVD. This is more likely now because the release date has been bumped to October. Still awaiting confirmation, but it looks as though we'll be able to record it in the Studio at BFI Southbank. It might even be possible to get it done and dusted during your visit next month if you're free to do it.

No other questions for now. I haven't seen the new/old cut either, but am planning to do so this week. The DVD arrived by Special Delivery this morning, and I keep checking to make sure it's still in my handbag! As you know, the version Billy Wilder hated is my favourite film, so I've very mixed feelings about this one. Not all 'director's cuts' are triumphs. Of course, I've seen the cobbled together version – the one with the audio-only segments and the film-only segments – but that was more tantalising than anything.

I'll be in touch as soon as I have anything new to tell you.

Looking forward to meeting you!

Best wishes,

Gemma

Dr G. MacDonald, Department of Film and Television Studies

Gemma clicks the send button and the message is tossed into the ether, to be retrieved and read at some point on a device now lying on a coffee table in some plush villa, set on a crag high above the Californian coastline. Then she clicks the other tab she's got open. The timber-clad lodge might not be the stone or pebbledashed idyll she'd hoped for, but at least the red-stained exterior speaks of the outdoors. Meanwhile, the inside looks well-appointed enough to please both Mum and David. The photo the owners have provided of a view from one of the bedroom windows is more pleasant than spectacular, but there are also some nice shots of Loch Ness at twilight, and of the not-too-distant Cairngorms, which more than make up for it. And then there's the clincher: the two spacious double bedrooms.

Suddenly, Gemma's anxious. It's far too easy to visualise what it will be like to have Dad and David circling each other for a whole week, rather than the customary couple of hours. They'll be like two monarchs of the glen, antlers always at the ready, though never actually deployed. David will ask a lot of earnest questions about Dad's life of honest toil at the Glasgow dockyards, and then as the owner of a builder's business in the East End. Dad will spin an equal number of half-arsed or fanciful answers. And then he'll start on his string of bad jokes: the hideous puns and borderline racist banter, the sort of crap he used to test Gemma's white boyfriends with, whenever she was brave enough to bring one of them home with her from school. And when David laughs at them dutifully, as he'll feel bound to do, he'll only be adding salt to the wound of their mutual contempt and their self-loathing...

Oh God, she thinks. *Am I really ready for all that?*

She knows she's only being her usual pessimistic self, and tries to shine a more positive light on things. Perhaps they'll change their attitudes after a week in each other's company. Perhaps they will learn that they've more in common than they ever thought possible. Or perhaps Dad won't come at all, which seems the most likely outcome, given his reluctance to do anything these days.

In some ways, she prefers her contingency plan. Robbie and Destiny would certainly benefit from some time together and away from Destiny's mother. Of course, they would have to offer something substantial in exchange, and they'd be lucky if it fell far short of poor Robbie's addled head on a platter. But almost anything would be worth it to see Destiny in the Highlands: the Tower Hamlets girl with a prospect of mountains behind her, stretching away for miles...

The knock at the door makes Gemma jump. She's left it ajar so that her students know she's in and willing to see them. She manages to click the lodge away, so that the email page is uppermost as her head of department thrusts his firebrand head into the room. 'Busy, Dr Mac?'

'Not if it's you, Anthony,' she says. 'Come in.'

He looks magnificent in a new navy-blue three-piece that sets off his mane of yellowing red hair. It's so unlike the casual or tweedy stuff he usually wears that Gemma assumes it's another sign of Aran's beneficial influence on him. Civil partnership has made a new man of him – goodness knows what will happen if they decide to get married. 'Have you heard back from *Screen* yet?' he asks her.

He means the article she sent them on the symbiotic relationship between British theatre and film in the late 1960s. 'They're keen,' she says. 'There's a couple of style issues, but they're going to run it once that's been sorted.'

'Great,' he says. Then he plunges his hands into his pockets and turns thoughtful. *Bet it's luxurious in there*, Gemma thinks. 'Well, that leads to my next question,' he says. 'I'd like to try for a book. Maybe a conference, too, but definitely a book.'

But they're always trying for a book. It's what everybody does.

'I'm talking about an expansion of your article,' he continues, 'perhaps focusing on Olivier's National, or the Royal Court, or both. Something comparative, in any case. Bring in our colleagues in Theatre Studies. Kitchen sink and the *avant-garde* versus British neo-realism. Take it up to the advent of Heritage Cinema. Show the fault lines. Commerce versus intellectualism, versus social function. What do you think?'

Gemma hears herself going, 'Hmmmm.'

'I'm being reductionist, I know,' he says. 'It needs thinking through. But there's something there, isn't there?'

'Of course,' she says, and means it. 'Sorry, I'm a little preoccupied.'

Actually, what she's preoccupied by now is the thought of Robert Stephens and Colin Blakeley on stage for Peter Shaffer's *Royal Hunt of the Sun*, and then stepping in front of the camera five years later for *The Private Life of Sherlock Holmes*. She's perfectly capable of making everything to do with her own magnificent obsession. But she's also thinking something else: *Don't ask me to commit to anything, Anthony. Not now.*

He's leaning over one of the armchairs with yellow foam spilling out of splits in its lime green vinyl covering, peering at the framed poster of *Witness for the Prosecution*. Charles Laughton has been unjustly reduced to a background figure, and Tyrone Power and Marlene Dietrich are presented as the movie's stars. They feature twice, in fact: first, respectively, in the O and the zero of the hyperbolic tagline—'ONCE IN 50 YEARS SUSPENSE LIKE THIS!'—and then again in the panel beneath, where they're reclined and snogging. Marlene's half-million-dollar Lloyd's-of-London-insured left leg predominates. In the white margin at the bottom, the fading signatures of all three actors are just about readable.

'I take it this is *bona fide*?'

'An eBay special,' she says. 'God knows what David really paid for it, but he told me it was a tenner.'

'You never know.'

He's looking at the *Avanti!* poster now. Jack Lemmon and Juliet Mills are on one side of a bathroom door, and the rest of the cast are on the other, all in full 1970s-style caricature. That's one she picked up herself. Or rather, it was given her by a Brummie projectionist from a stack of others in the back of his booth.

'Why did you...?' he begins, then stops himself.

She does a Sherlock, though, and reads his mind. 'Why did I get into Billy Wilder?' She doesn't add, *with my background?*

'Well, he's a particular kind of film-maker, isn't he?' He's still inspecting the poster. 'Very formal. What's the first one you saw?'

'*Some Like It Hot*,' she tells him. 'With my dad. A Sunday night, I think, though I'd have to check the schedules to be sure.' Then, to let him off the hook, 'I know what you mean, though. Wilder's not usually someone you get into as a kid. He's a grown-up, and makes films for grown-ups. Mostly grown-up men at that, though not entirely...'

'Go on,' he says, turning her way now. 'What was it about *Some Like It Hot* that you liked?'

'Well, it's different with that one, isn't it?' She says it like it's obvious. 'It's Wilder and his latest co-writer, I.A.L. Diamond, hitting their comic stride. There's funny in it for adults, but there's funny in it for kids, too. Dad and I just laughed together like drains. And I can't tell you how much I loved Marilyn. Not sure I was aware of her before that. She was probably an early crush, if I'm honest.' She answers his next unasked question, too. 'I was about eight, I guess.'

'What about the Sherlock Holmes film?' says Anthony. 'It's pretty obscure, isn't it? I'm old enough to have been sentient when it was released, but it completely passed me by. I was only vaguely aware of it by the time I met you. It has a certain queer cachet now, of course, but I'm not so sure about that. To my mind, there's too much of the Dick Emerys in that scene with the ballet dancers...'

'Yes,' says Gemma, and doesn't add that she still laughs every time she watches it. 'Things would have been different if Wilder had got his way. He wanted an unambiguously gay Sherlock, but Adrian Conan Doyle – Sir Arthur's son – wouldn't have it. I'm pretty sure *Private Life* was the second Billy Wilder film I saw, and my first Sherlock Holmes film. I loved Colin Blakely's performance – it's got this frenetic energy, and comic timing worthy of Jack Lemmon. And then there's Robert Stephens...'

'Another crush?'

She shrugs. 'Maybe – but it's more than that, too. It's such a sad performance, and I'm not saying that with hindsight. Of course, I know now about all his problems off-set, but I swear I saw it on screen that first time. Well, I've written about this, haven't I? Wilder reputedly cast him because he looked like he could be easily hurt. He was right: he could be.'

There's another knock at the door and a doughy face, fringed with pink fronds, appears around its edge. 'Oh, sorry—' a nervous breath of laughter—'should I come back later?'

'No, no,' says Anthony. 'I won't stand between Dr MacDonald and her *crème de la crème*. Thank you, Gemma.'

For the rest of the day, Gemma is irritated by the posters. Not just by them, either: the general clutter of the office seems an affront to her. The mix of library and bought books on the shelves, the muddle of undergraduate and postgraduate work in the in-tray, the ridiculous tally of unread emails blinking at her from the screen of the PC...

There's a ping from her iPhone just as she's shutting down the computer. A text from David, who's been at the British Library all day. '*Walking back to Kings Cross,*' it reads. '*You got food or should I pick something up?*' It's as annoying as the clutter, but it's something else, too. Enervating, perhaps. She scrolls up and quickly finds three texts that are almost identical, with smiley emoticons attached to each of them. Fuck – is this what they've become? Maybe it's what life past thirty is like for everyone, and there's no way of avoiding it. While the PC screen is fading from blue to black, she taps out a new message on her phone.

'*Sorry had text from Robbie. He's got Destiny for the night but needs babysitter for couple of hours. Will eat at his. Xxx.*'

She looks at it for a while, her thumb hovering over 'send'. It's such a bloody great lie, easily the biggest she's ever told him. Will she be able to bear up under examination? She starts to delete it, but when she's got rid of the kisses, changes her mind and sends it anyway.

She picks up her bag, checking again that the plain DVD case is still nestled inside it. The only way to make the lie believable is to make it at least partly true…

Neither sibling appears to have fallen far from the tree, but in fact the relationship between their current addresses and their parents' home tells a misleading tale. Gemma lived in Cambridge for three years, of course, and then in Sheffield for a further four. Robbie has lived as far away as Manchester. But now they all live on a line that skims the Mile End Road, with Mum and Dad in Bow, Gemma in Whitechapel and Robbie about halfway between them, in Stepney.

'This is a surprise,' he says on the doorstep.

He doesn't look surprised, though. His eyes are as wide as they get these days, which means they're half shut. You'd think he was stoned, except that the pupils act normally beneath the heavy lids. He's in his work clothes still: cargo pants and the company sweatshirt. Only his feet have been relieved of their mandatory steel-capped coverings.

'Glad to see you, too,' she says, walking past him and into the flat. It's not kept badly, and the building's quite solid. It's just a shame about the shared stairwell. Something toxic has been burnt there in the last couple of hours, and she's pretty sure it's human shit that she had to step over on the way up.

'I'm not working nights this week,' he tells her. 'Early shift, though. Four till two.'

Gemma goes into the sitting room and flops on the sofa. 'Did you pick up Destiny from school?'

'Yeah.'

'No problems?'

'Nah.' It seems he'll only be talking in monosyllables, but then he adds, 'Just back from taking her home. We watched some cartoons. It was cool.'

He leaves the room. Gemma curses her bad timing.

'Want a beer?' He's in the kitchen now, talking through the hatch.

'Go on, then. You eaten?'

'Nah,' he says again, out of view. 'Why?'

'Thought I might join you. I can ring for a pizza, if you like.'

'Aren't you eating with David?'

There's a tone to the disembodied voice that's a little like Mum's when she asks about David. 'He's busy.' It's another lie – but then, she's been lying to her big brother since at least 1987.

'I've defrosted some of Mum's stew,' he says, appearing at the hatch again, placing an open bottle of Grolsch on the sill.

'Oh, go on then,' she says.

They eat in the kitchen, drinking a second bottle of beer each, and she brings him up to date on the Loch Ness Film Festival. Then she mentions the lodge.

'The one I'm looking at accommodates five,' she says. 'There are two rooms with double beds, and there's a sofa bed in one of them, too. Of course, I can always find something bigger, so we could all go. David and me, Mum and Dad, you and Destiny…'

'No, no, Gem, don't do that,' he says, frowning. 'You're not made of money.'

I'm made of more of it than you are, she thinks, which is both true and mean. 'Well, my first thought was to invite Mum and Dad,' she tells him. 'It's years since they've been to Scotland and it would be good for them to get out and about together. Mum's got her job, of course, but Dad doesn't seem to do anything anymore.'

Robbie rolls his eyes. 'Well, that's true.'

'But then I thought of Destiny. She's never been to Scotland, has she?'

'What?' he says, 'And you think she needs to get in touch with her tartan heritage? Are we taking her to Jamaica, too, making a round trip?'

Gemma's suddenly ten again herself, blinking at a brand of sunshine you can't buy in the UK. There's a lick of heat on her bare arms and bare legs, and dust squeezes in between her toes. A sliver of yearning enters her heart, but it's not as sweetly painful as the yearning she feels for Scotland...

'What's going on, Gem?'

She looks up from the chicken and pepper on her plate. It's hard to tell in the light provided by the spots under the cabinets, but she thinks his eyes are a little brighter now. 'What do you mean?' she asks.

'I mean this is weird. You coming here on the off-chance of seeing Destiny. Really? I know you're fond of her and everything, but you've never done it before. So, what's going on?'

She has no choice but to tell him. In part, it's compensation, not only for the lie she told him earlier, but for the one she's told David. She tells him about Chicago first, and when that's sunk in, moves on to Aberdeen.

'Woah!' Robbie says, 'And you're the one who's supposed to be good at this shit. Fucking hell.'

She laughs, but not in a good way. 'Don't think Mum or Dad would agree with you on that. They're not David's biggest fans.'

Robbie pushes his plate away. 'Well, you got to expect that from Dad,' he says. 'But it's different with Mum. She's just wondering, that's all.'

'Wondering?'

He shakes his head, as though she's being spectacularly dense. 'Look, I don't think it mattered to her when you moved in together. She's modern enough to think that's a good idea even. I mean, she can't think what I did was better. But it's been a while now, hasn't it? She's old fashioned, Gem – you know that. She thinks he should've done something by now.'

'Well, he has, hasn't he? He's asked me to leave the country with him.'

'That's not what I'm talking about.' He looks slyly at her now. 'Mum's thinking he needs to put a ring on it.'

Is that a shudder she feels? An actual fucking shudder at the mere thought? Now she feels exposed: she can't hide the sheer selfishness of her position, or her professional pride, or her wish to be completely in control of her own fate. 'I don't want to go to America and do nothing,' she says.

'And you've told your boss about Aberdeen, right?'

She turns sly herself now, shifting her eyes so that her brother is in their periphery.

'Bloody hell, Gem, what's got into you? You used to be able to make a decision.'

'And I will make one, when I need to.'

Despite Aberdeen's hectoring, she knows they don't need an answer until September. It's already understood that David will go out to Chicago without her, and that she'll join him once she's... Well, that's where she always finds something urgent to do, which means she can put off the rest of the conversation for another time. Like never...

'I don't want to think about it tonight,' she tells Robbie now. 'I don't really want to think about anything. Except...'

'What?'

Her handbag is at her feet, and she dips into it and picks out the slim plastic case. 'This,' she says, placing it on the table. 'Delivered today. All the way from Hollywood.'

'That's the Sherlock Holmes flick you think's so fantastic?'

She nods. 'Want to watch it with me?'

'When's David expecting you?'

She shrugs. 'Whenever. He'll be fine. He'll only be watching some crap on Netflix.' She opens the case and looks at the plain disc with its stencilled title. 'It's long, mind – really long. I guess you'll be wanting some sleep if you've got an early shift.'

'Nah,' he says, 'it's cool. But shouldn't you watch it with Dad? He likes that shit. I'd rather torrent the latest *Transformers*, as you well know.'

She shakes her head, and this time it's a show of how deeply concerned she is. 'Well, in that case it's my job as a doctor of film to save you from yourself. And yes,' she adds, anticipating his next question, 'I will have another beer, thank you.'

Chapter Six

The Loch Ness Research Group,
Yew Tree Farm,
Arbendrain Road,
nr. Drumnadrochit
Inverness-shire.

Mr. B. Wilder,
c/o The Drumnadrochit Hotel,
Drumnadrochit,
Inverness-shire.17th July, 1969

Dear Sir,

I am writing with regard to your current motion picture production, <u>The Private Life of Sherlock Holmes</u>. On the 16th July, I spent a day observing your crew at work in Inverness-shire and Kyle of Lochalsh, at the invitation of one of your employees. During the course of the day, I stumbled across an unattended copy of your screenplay, and was able to read a portion of it before returning it to its owner unobserved. I can assure you that nobody in your employ assisted me in doing this. However, given what I now know of your intentions, I feel it my duty to comment on some points where you are currently at fault regarding the nature of Loch Ness phenomena.

First, some words about my own credentials. I am a research assistant working with the Loch Ness Research Group (hereafter the L.N.R.G.), a body affiliated to the Departments of Biology and Geology at the University

of Aberdeen. The L.N.R.G. was founded in 1964
by its current director, Dr. Douglas Campbell,
and Mr. Stewart McAllister with just two aims:

(1.) to investigate all reported sightings
of unidentified fauna in and around the body
of Loch Ness, and all unexplained disturbances
to the surface of the Loch

(2.) to make a study of the entire body of
Loch Ness using visual recording equipment,
sonar, and any new methods which might arise,
in order to gather a corpus of data against
which new theories regarding reported phenomena might be thoroughly tested.

To these ends, it has been important to
establish a clear record of reported phenomena
prior to the period of our current investiga-
tions. We have thus accumulated a considerable
archive of documentary material and are well-
versed in the history of the Loch.

At the risk of appearing bold, I offer
these observations, which may be of some use
to you.

(1.) You state near the beginning of your
screen-play that the story is set in 1887.
However, the term "Loch Ness Monster", which
you employ throughout, did not enter popular
usage before 1933. A "monster" was first mentioned in the 2nd May edition of <u>The Inverness
Courier</u>, in a report stating that a Mr. and
Mrs. Mackay had seen something resembling a
whale swimming in the Loch some three-quarters
of a mile off Abriachan pier. The full term
"Loch Ness Monster" was only employed by the
paper ten days later. The phrase became further established the following August, after a
Mr. and Mrs. George Spicer, an English couple

holidaying in the Highlands, claimed to have
seen a large, sauropod-like creature emerge
from the wood on the northern bank of the Loch
and cross the road in front of their car.
After this story was widely publicized, a
local resident, Dr. D. Mackenzie, came forward
to say that he had seen a similar creature
moving across the surface of the Loch in 1871.
Despite this claim, however, there is no
record of a general hysteria regarding a "Loch
Ness Monster" in the Late-Victorian period,
such as you depict in your screen-play.

(2.) If you must look to local supersti-
tion, then you could do worse than consider
the folkloric "kelpie" or "water horse". This
fabulous animal incorporates physiological
features of an equine nature, such as a mane
and a horse's head, with the fins of aquatic
creatures such as fish or dolphins, and sometimes the tail of a serpent. Stories of such
animals can be found elsewhere in the British
Isles, where they are often depicted as sea-
dwellers. In Scotland, however, they have
tended to be confined to rivers and inland
lochs. Whether fear of such creatures might
reasonably be supposed to have resided in the
breasts of adult Victorians is again a matter
open to conjecture. It seems more likely that
the "kelpie" only appeared in stories told to
children in order to keep them in bed at
night. Perhaps the gravedigger who warns Sherlock Holmes to stay clear of the Loch is meant
to be employing sarcasm; but is it credible
that someone as adroit as Mr. Holmes is supposed to have been wouldn't recognize the performance for what it is?

(3.) If you are committed to anachronism, and since you intend to show that your "Loch Ness Monster" is in fact the instrument of an act of subterfuge being perpetrated by the British Government upon the German, then may I suggest incorporating elements of the one verified hoax on record? In 1933, "The Daily Mail" employed a Mr. Marmaduke Wetherell (a famous big-game hunter) to seek out, and presumably kill, the sauropod-like creature described by Mr. and Mrs. Spicer. In December of that year, he alerted his employers to the discovery of tracks on the banks of Loch Ness which appeared to have been made by an enormous amphibian. However, researchers from the Natural History Museum were soon able to establish that these tracks had been made not by the feet of a dinosaur, but by those of a modern hippopotamus. Not only that, but each print appeared to belong to the same foot, and it was eventually established that Mr. Wetherell had created the effect using a hunting trophy that had been fashioned into an ashtray.

I hope that you will take this letter in the spirit of friendly collaboration in which it is written. As I have already indicated, we at the L.N.R.G. are happy to share all data that we have so far gathered, and had you approached us from the start, it is possible that you would have saved yourself from some costly errors. Even now, I am more than willing to offer assistance. I only request that you give the L.N.R.G. full acknowledgement in your finished picture.

In conclusion, may I ask that you attempt

to see things from our point of view? We are a
small and dedicated group of scientists who
wish only to uncover the truth about the geological and biological composition of Loch
Ness; but we are constantly battling those
forces of trivialization and wilful ignorance
which so often predominate in our current age.
I would ask you to decide on which side of
this particular battle line you intend to
stand.
    Yours faithfully,
    James Outhwaite, BSc., M.Sc., F.M.B.A.
    (signed)

Jim posted the letter early. He walked straight past the hotel, where
he might have delivered it by hand, over the bridge into the village and slotted it into the pillar box by the Post Office. Instantly,
his doubts returned. He'd scrapped many pages trying to reach the
right register, had tried to purge it of a priggish tone while making it clear that he meant what he was saying.

Also, he hoped he hadn't done April a bad turn.

It had been drizzling when he'd set out, so he'd put on his green
waterproof. Now he walked under an opal sky, with only some
white feathers of cirrus in it. Blackbird and yellowhammer song
filled the air. He was just turning onto the track to the farm when
he was nearly run over by the Alvis.

'Sorry, pal.' Alan's voice billowed from the open driver's window along with his tobacco smoke. 'That's what happens when
you're wearing fucking camouflage.' He leant over and got the
passenger door open. 'Get in. It's about time you got yourself some
sea legs.'

'I've got them already,' said Jim. 'I'm a marine biologist, remember. And the loch's not the sea.'

'There you go with your facts.' Alan tossed the end of his fag
into the wet bracken growing up around a gatepost. 'Get in any-

way.' From under the driver's seat he retrieved a mostly full flask of Bell's. 'We can have ourselves a boys' outing.'

'Jesus,' said Jim, but he got in anyway.

The car was ridiculous. Sandra had said it looked like a white hearse when Alan had first rolled up in it, over a year ago, but it was more like the actual coffin on wheels. Even when it had been new, a decade and a half ago, it could only have been of any use ferrying people along the straight roads between London and the South Coast. Driving it in the Highlands was like trying to walk through a maze wearing a tea chest.

At the quayside, the wind was fresher and its turbulence made little white curls in the water. Alan jumped onto the *Cally* straight-away, making her strain at her moorings. He started up the engine while Jim was still trying to board her.

'Where's the camera?' he asked. Then he saw the bunched tarpaulin in the cabin, looking exactly like an inept attempt at hiding something of great value. 'You didn't leave it here overnight, did you?'

'It's still here, isn't it?'

'Did you even bring any film?'

'Of course I did.' But he had to hook the boat to the bollard again and hop ashore to fetch the canister from out of the Alvis's boot.

When he was back aboard, they headed across the loch. Alan hugged the boat's wheel with one arm while fumbling the flask from the pocket of his windcheater. The boat veered to port and Jim had to grab hold of the wheel himself. 'Thanks, pal,' said Alan, and got the cap off the bottle.

'What's got into you?'

'Nothing's got into *me*.' He gave the last word a bitter emphasis. He stoppered the flask again and gingerly placed it at his feet. It fell over immediately and slid across the deck to portside. He made no attempt to follow it. 'Just fancied a bit of time away from the others,' he said. 'Out of the sisterhood's hair, and out of reach of Harry fucking Palmer's hundred-yard stare.' He took a flattened pack of Embassy Filters from his jeans pocket. 'Wanted to breathe some fresh air,' he said, lighting a cigarette.

'Fresh air?'

'It's a fucking metaphor, pal.' He flicked the spent match into the loch.

'But you get away from them every day,' said Jim. 'Every time you take the boat out.'

Alan glanced at him with swollen eyes. They were often that way in the mornings, but today they resembled nothing so much as a couple of poached eggs on barely browned toast. Jim suspected that what he was doing now was dosing himself with the hair of the dog that had bitten him last night. Christ, he was probably still pissed as a lord – as a bloody duke! When they were well away from the bank, almost in the centre of the loch, Alan cut the engine and retrieved the bottle from where it had slid.

'Right then,' said Jim, 'are we going to do some filming?'

'Wait a minute, pal.' He sat on the portside bench and took a swig. 'Let's have a bit of conversation first.' He patted the slats next to him, the way Sandra had patted the kitchen chair ahead of her interrogation last night. Jim shivered at the memory.

'I don't see why we can't run the camera and have a conversation at the same time,' he said.

But that wasn't what happened. Instead, they did nothing. For a few minutes, the only sound to be heard came from the water sloshing the boat's hull and the wind whipping up the tarpaulin that had covered the camera, making it pop and moan. There was the faint buzz of another engine, too, and Jim looked towards Urquhart Castle to see another boat skimming the water. It had a red stripe along its hull, so that even at this distance it was easily identifiable.

'Okay,' he said, when the awkwardness had become too much, 'that was a great conversation, thank you. Now, shall we get started?'

Alan refused to move. 'What's it all about, Jamie?'

Jim tried to laugh that off. 'It's a bit early for the meaning of life, Cilla.'

Alan shook his head. 'It's fucking late is what it is, pal.'

It was only now that Jim realised something must have happened. He knew that Alan and Sandra didn't always get along, but their disputes never normally lasted more than a day. That tension he'd noticed at the kitchen table a couple of weeks ago had only persisted until the next morning, for instance. If anything, since then, Sandra had seemed more doting towards her husband than usual, making the kind of eyes at him that she usually reserved for George Harrison's TV appearances. Something must have occurred since.

God, thought Jim, *what is he going to tell me?*

Jim hadn't had to deal with a friend's girlfriend problems since he'd left Manchester, and didn't relish doing it again. He'd lost a whole night that last time, talking that other friend down from the wizard idea of going for a midnight skinny dip in the Ship Canal. Of course, it wasn't a girlfriend problem Alan had – it was a *wife* problem. That could only mean a proportionate increase in the scale of Jim's duties.

'How old are you, Jamie?'

Jim wasn't expecting that. 'Remember that birthday cake we ate in February with the 25 candles on it?'

'I think so.'

'That was mine.'

Alan drew some more on his cigarette. 'It's okay for you. I bet you never missed it.'

'Missed what?'

He puffed again. 'Not being not grown up.'

What the hell was he talking about?

'Creeps up on you, you ken? I mean, all of this—' he spread his arms wide, seeming to encompass the width of the boat, the body of the loch and the whole of the known universe, '—all of this is great while it lasts. But it doesnae fucking last, does it?'

The other boat was striking out from the castle now, cutting straight across the loch to the west of them. Its buzzing grew louder, until it sounded like a slow and steady bee. The surge it made was white at first, but then turned black, so that it might have been mistaken for the dorsal ridge of some submerged animal. There was a 35mm camera mounted in the stern.

Jim bit the bullet. 'Look, is there anything I need to know?'

Alan looked hurt. '*Need*, Jamie?'

'I mean—' he was trying to pick the right words again, as he'd done in the letter. But different right words, obviously, '—is there any practical way I can help?'

'Don't put yourself out, pal,' Alan said.

'Is it money?'

That drew a morose cackle. 'You could say that.'

'Then have you talked to Douglas?'

Alan gasped, as if in horror. He stood, kicking the bottle of Bell's across the deck again, and grabbed the edge of the cabin roof. 'No, I've not talked to Douglas.' He was yelling now. 'He's not made of the stuff, you know? Just because he talks like Prince fucking Philip doesn't mean he owns the fucking Crown Jewels.'

The other boat was tracing a wide curve, as if it meant to cut them off. Except, of course, that it wasn't possible to cut them off, because they weren't moving. The buzzing sounded angry now, like the *Cally* herself had sounded when she'd been ruining the Hollywood crew's filming that time, but the figure Jim saw at the wheel looked entirely serene. His pink face was lifted to the sky and his cap of blond hair was being lifted by the wind in a way that must have felt pleasant. When he was near enough, no more than forty feet away, he waved an arm slowly and deliberately in the *Cally's* direction.

'Ahoy, there, Masters Stirling and Outhwaite,' he called in a burring, Edinburgh accent. 'Lovely day for it, eh, lads?'

Both Jim and Alan waved back, smiling, but didn't say a word. Then the boat passed them, heading in the direction of Dores.

'Stewart fucking McAllister,' said Alan. He took another swig of whisky. 'Wanker.'

'Indeed,' said Jim, and took the bottle when it was offered him.

They did do some filming at last, but not much and to little purpose. At noon, Alan said, 'Fuck it, let's get to the Drum while the bar's still open.'

'Is that a good idea?'

But Jim knew deep down that good ideas weren't on the agenda today. 'We'll grab a couple of sandwiches,' said Alan. 'Or are we not allowed to fucking eat now?'

It was quarter-to by the time they walked into the hotel. The bar was empty save for Jock Inness and Harry Sullivan, the usual old men in tweeds who could be seen propping up the bar in every rural drinking establishment in the British Isles. Jim wondered if they had been in here that last time, too, lost from sight amidst the kaftans and printed paisley. 'How you doing, lads?' Alan called to them, and they answered him as convivially—'Not so bad, Alan. How's yourself?'—whilst completely ignoring his Sassenach companion.

Pete Leith looked up from his copy of *The Inverness Courier* with a face like Quasimodo's beholding Esmerelda. Nothing romantic on his mind, of course: just the prospect of some coins in the till and the chance for a gossip. 'Afternoon, gents,' he said, already drawing the first pint. 'Early for you, eh?'

He meant Jim. 'Come for a spot of lunch,' said Alan. 'Better make us some sandwiches, I suppose.'

When Pete had gone to the kitchen, Alan led the way to the fireside. 'Wonder he hasn't strained a muscle, smiling like that. Doesn't make his face any better, does it?'

Jim shook his head. 'A hotel full for the whole summer. That'll be enough to keep him smiling until Christmas.'

'Oh ay,' said Alan. 'It's like Aviemore here after a good snowfall.'

Something about that thought made Alan withdraw into himself again. He was looking into his beer the way he'd been looking into the loch.

'What is it now?' asked Jim.

'Well, Aviemore has skiing,' he said, 'and the whole town's geared up for it. What does Drumnadrochit have?'

Jim shrugged. 'Water-skiing?'

Alan flicked him the Vs. 'You should be doing Jimmy Tarbuck's fucking job, pal.'

Pete brought the sandwiches over and tossed a couple of packets of Golden Wonder on the table, too. 'On the house, gents.'

Alan pantomimed surprise, dropping his jaw to his chest. 'A whole shilling's worth of crisps? You sure you're all right there, Pete?'

'Well, if you don't want 'em...'

But Alan nabbed a packet before Pete's corned-beef hand could retrieve them. He squeezed it until the seal popped, then took out a wad of crisps and stuffed them in his mouth.

Pete drew up a stool. 'I'll tell you what, though,' he said, 'it's been a revelation. When the Yanks have been out for the day – and they'll get a lot done with the weather like this, and come back with a real thirst and a wish to celebrate a bit, you ken? – well, I can barely keep up. I've had to take on more staff. Usually, there's not enough for me to do on my own. And another thing...' His voice took a further dip, and Jim couldn't help leaning in. 'You know what they say about movie stars, don't you? The way they behave away from the cameras?'

'Oh ay,' said Alan, splattering yellowy debris. 'They're all secret poofters.'

A shadow of impatience passed over Pete's face, which was a rare thing to see. 'I'm talking about Richard Burton, Oliver Reed, Peter O'Toole...'

'I said secret, didn't I?'

Pete shook his head. 'They like a drink – that's what I meant.' He craned his neck, and looked behind Alan to the door of the reception. He must have known nobody could come in here without being noticed. 'Well, I'll tell you,' he said, turning back, 'that Mr Stephens could give all of 'em a run for their money.'

'Which one's he?' asked Alan.

'Sherlock Holmes,' said Jim. 'He's a big deal in the theatre, I'm told.'

Pete nodded. 'Well, he's been the last one to go up to his room on more than a few nights.' His lips quivered with illicit information. 'Having a bad time of it, so he is.'

'Missing his movie-star wife, I believe.'

Pete looked both surprised and disappointed. 'You know about that?'

Jim shrugged.

'A wife and a wain,' Pete said. 'It's breaking his heart having to be away from them. And that director's giving him hell, too.'

'Mr Wilder,' said Jim. 'A stickler.'

Pete looked stricken. 'Who's telling you all this?'

'Ah, well,' said Alan, grinning, 'you might think you've got sources, but Jamie here's courting one of the top people on the picture.'

Jim shook his head. Neither end of that sentence was true.

'Oh ay,' said Pete, and he was grinning, too – one of those hideous things that was all on one side of his face. 'You mean Miss Bloom.'

'You were telling us about your actor friend,' said Jim. 'And about Mr Wilder.'

The leer was gone. 'A martinet,' he said. 'A little Caesar. "I've reason to believe I'm rather good, old boy"—' It wasn't a bad approximation of the somewhat effete voice Jim had heard between takes, though there was still a bit of Scots in it, '—"Sir Laurence Olivier has been kind enough to commend my work in the past. But with Mr Wilder, I feel quite incapable." He rehearses them within an inch of their lives, first one way, then a couple of dozen others. And when they film it, if it isn't exactly what they've rehearsed, he'll stop and make them start again. It's bad for everyone, but poor Mr Stephens is in every scene, so he gets it worst.'

Jim remembered the actor's morose attitude while sitting in the canvas chair, pondering his copy of the script. But that had changed when the camera had started rolling, and then he'd seemed to exude an absolute confidence.

'I'll say this for him, though,' Pete added, the leer returning to his face, 'I don't think he's beyond finding a bit of comfort where he can get it, if you see my drift. He's got an eye that roves around a room.'

'Oh ay,' said Alan. 'Seeking out that French dolly bird, I don't doubt.'

Pete shook his head. 'I'd say it's more Jamie's lass he's interested in. I've seen them leaning into one another standing at the bar, like they're sharing a secret, you ken? And it's just about the only time he cracks a smile. Well, if that's the way he's headed, you cannot blame him, can you?'

'Certainly not,' said Alan, and his tone was one of admiration.

But Jim could and did blame him, even while acknowledging that he'd absolutely no right to pass such judgements. The truth was that he was experiencing all sorts of emotions these days that on the whole he would rather he wasn't. Alongside his current prudery, for instance, he felt a keen frustration at how easily he was allowing Pete and Alan to string him along. And above all, there was that powerful desire to be out of their bumptious company altogether, and in that of another person...

'They're Hollywood types,' he managed to say. 'They're always flirting with each other, aren't they? Famous for it.'

'Oh ay,' said Alan, smirking in the most infuriating way possible, 'you keep telling yourself that, pal. And while you're doing it, you can purchase another couple of pints. What d'you say?'

Chapter Seven

It was a sign of the unstructured nature of life at the Campbells' farm that you could breakfast on eggs fresh from the hen house and home-cured bacon on a Thursday morning, and find yourself slurping up cornflakes the following Saturday. This was what Jim had been reduced to when he heard the phone ring.

'It's for you,' said Tessa, coming into the kitchen from the hall-way. 'Your young lady, I think.'

There was so much in that statement to contest that Jim didn't know where to begin. Instead, he got up and left the kitchen.

'Jim Outhwaite.'

'Sure it's not Benedict Arnold?'

'I beg your pardon?' There was an entirely unwarranted indignation in his voice. Alan and Pete's airy nothings from yesterday had clearly remained with him.

'You know exactly what I mean, mister.' That 'mister' couldn't have been altogether serious, could it? 'I nearly got into a lot of trouble because of you. I know it wasn't my script you got a hold of, because I never let it out of my sight. But you were my guest, so I had to take some of the blame. Clearly, it was you I should have kept my eye on.'

There was a letter with Jim's name on it lying on the phone-table. He bunched the receiver under his chin and picked it up.

'You still there, bud?'

'Sorry,' said Jim. The address was typed, the postmark local. He sat in the chair and slit the envelope open with a finger. 'And sorry about the script. It was just there, I didn't go looking for it. And you had aroused my...'

It was a reply from the director, Mr Wilder, consisting of just a few lines of type. It wasn't on anything official, just Drumnadrochit Hotel notepaper.

'Aroused your what exactly?'

'Sorry,' Jim said again. 'My curiosity. I wanted to know more about your picture. And quite frankly, I'm glad I found out. But I'm sorry, too, of course.'

'Sorry and glad at the same time, huh?' He could almost hear her shaking her head, those sun-bleached pigtails swaying as she did so. 'For a scientist, you're not very rational, are you?'

'*Dear Mr Outhwaite,*' Jim read. '*Thank you for your correspondence of July 17th. Please rest assured that my colleagues and I are wholly aware that we make stuff up. Kindest regards, B.W.*'

'Earth to Jim, come in Jim…'

'I'm really very sorry,' he said, missing the correct note of sincerity by about a semi-quaver. 'I didn't mean to get you into trouble. You weren't given too hard a time, were you?'

There was a PS: '*If you care to see our own Loch Ness Monster, I'm sure your contact can arrange for you to be present when she launches.*'

'He's mentioned you,' Jim said.

'Who's mentioned me? How am I mentioned?'

He explained about the letter and then read it out to her. She laughed down the line.

'Well, whether you get an invite or not is going to depend on how you behave yourself tomorrow night.'

'What's happening tomorrow night?'

'Oh, a little thing where a couple of NASA astronauts are going to take a stroll on the moon.'

She explained that she was going to watch TV coverage of the moon landing at a party that was going to last all night, if it had to.

'It will have to,' he told her.

'Anyway,' she said, 'I was told to bring anyone along I cared to, so I thought of you.'

'Is it at the hotel?' He asked it as tersely as he could.

No, it wasn't at the hotel. A London friend of April's was hosting it, someone involved in theatrical 'happenings' called Victoria, whose family owned a house out towards Balnain. This Victoria was travelling up with a contingent of other London arty types specially to throw a moon party for her dear friend April, who was so excited about it all.

'I didn't know you were interested in the moon landing.'

'Well, we're learning new things about each other all the time, aren't we?' she said. 'Like who's a sneak-thief, for instance. We'll be filming late at Urquhart Castle,' she added, 'but we'll finish just before it's really dark.'

'Golden hour,' said Jim.

'So, you do listen to me sometimes, huh?' He could hear the smile in her voice now. 'I'll go to Victoria's as soon as I'm free, but I'll tell them to expect you any time.'

There wasn't a chance he was going to be there when she wasn't. The sun would be setting at about ten – he'd check the newspaper to make sure – and it would take her at least twenty minutes to say her goodbyes and get to the house. Better say half an hour. Best yet, forty minutes. He had already scanned the *Radio Times* and knew that some preliminary prattling was scheduled for a quarter to nine, but that the real coverage wouldn't begin until half-past eleven.

'If you're being British and worrying about being there with a lot of strangers,' she said, responding to his lack of a response, 'you won't be. Colin will be there. He was asking about you, by the way.'

'What about Mr Stephens,' Jim asked, 'will he be there, too?'

'Bob?' She sounded surprised. 'I don't know. It depends what kind of mood he's in, I guess. He will have been filming, but Colin's got the night off. I'm pretty sure Geneviève will be there, though. That's got to be an incentive, right?'

Douglas had come into the kitchen through the back door, from the sty and the chicken house. He and Tessa were standing very close to each other near the pantry, and moved almost imperceptibly apart as Jim entered. *Jesus,* Jim thought: *are they always at it?*

'Good news?' Douglas asked in his utterly ingenuous way.

'Well, I don't know.' Jim took his seat at the table again. 'I've been invited to a party.' The cornflakes had cleaved together in his bowl. 'To watch the moon landing.'

'Just you and Miss Bloom?' asked Tessa.

Wearily, Jim explained what April had explained to him.

'Goodness,' said Tessa, 'that sounds fun.'

'I suspect there'll be some names there,' said Douglas. 'The hostess is a Victoria, you say? She didn't mention a surname?'

Jim shook his head. He was going to have to pour himself another breakfast.

'Well,' said Tessa, 'that'll diminish our own little moon party, won't it?'

Something inside of Jim leapt at this glimmer of a get-out: he needn't go through the ordeal of April's party if he didn't want to. 'You had plans?'

Tessa laughed in her shy, closed-mouth way. 'No plans, no. Douglas is going to run a cable down from the aerial through the living room window. We'll set up the telly in there.'

That wasn't going to be a good enough excuse. Jim got up and tipped the lumped cornflakes into the bin under the sink, then fetched himself some more from the box in the cupboard. By the time he'd added milk and returned to the table, Alan and Sandra had come in, grunting good-mornings. Sandra went to fill the kettle while Alan slumped in the chair facing Jim.

'Jamie's been invited to a party,' Tessa told them, then explained all about it.

'You're in there, pal, eh?' said Alan, but his voice was flat and his red eyes showed little enthusiasm.

Sandra, on the other hand, was suddenly energised. 'What you going to wear, Jamie?' She took her place beside him, at the head of the table.

'I beg your pardon?'

'Well, you can't go in the shite you usually wear, can you? Not when you're meeting that kind of crowd.'

'What's wrong with what I wear?' He'd a good mind to point to her husband, who was wearing another T-shirt that must once have been an identifiable colour, but now boasted several that were new to mankind.

She harrumphed him. 'Believe me, you're going to need something new.'

'I'm not spending money on clothes for one night.' He was

pretty sure he didn't have money to spend on clothes for one night.

'You could always go to that thrift shop in Inverness,' said Tessa. 'That's the thing now, isn't it?'

'Oh ay,' said Alan. 'Dressing like a tramp is where it's at, man.'

Sandra gave her husband the hard green stare. 'Paul McCartney wears an old demob suit sometimes,' she told Jim. 'You've got the beard coming and your hair's the right length. Though perhaps you should give it a comb, eh?'

'I'm not going to Inverness,' said Jim.

'Maybe you don't have to,' said Tessa. 'I suspect Douglas has some things that will do.'

Jim looked up at the man mountain stood beside her. What was he – six foot five? Not by any means slim, either. Jim wasn't short, but he wasn't more than six foot, and his one sports jacket had a forty-inch chest. 'I don't think that'll work.'

'Luckily for you,' said Sandra, 'I'm a devil with a needle and thread. We've got till ten tomorrow night. It'll work.'

'Be my guest,' said Douglas. 'You're welcome to whatever you can find.'

Sandra's enthusiasm didn't waver for a moment during their game of dress-up in the Campbells' bedroom, but there were several times when she had to sit on that enormous bed while taking in what Jim was wearing. It didn't seem to be because that was the best vantage point, either. Probably, she'd spent all night pursuing that argument with Alan, which they'd decided to keep to themselves, but which kept spilling over into their dealings with the rest of them. Once, just as she was commending one of Douglas's evening shirts – a thing that was all ruffles, with sleeves that came down almost to Jim's knees – she had to stop mid-sentence and leave the room. He could clearly hear her retching in the toilet. Obviously, she had joined Alan in his drinking and they'd got soaked together as they'd rowed.

'Everything okay?' he asked her when she returned. There had been a further hollowing of her usually plump face and her eye makeup was in disarray.

'Hunky fucking dory,' she said. 'Now, try on the velvet jacket.'

Jim found ways to occupy himself for the whole of the time that passed from his leaving Sandra sitting on the bed with her tape measure to his taking the altered outfit out of her hands the next evening.

He spent much of Saturday morning listening to Bert Balfour's account of having spotted something long and black rise above the sur-face of the loch four days earlier, while Jim had been at Loch Meiklie with the film crew. He then drove the old man out in the Land Rover to the spot on the A82 where he claimed he'd seen it, and waited in silence with him until something similar appeared. It happened, as Jim had known it would, just a few minutes after a motorboat had passed them, heading in the direction of the Bona Narrows and the Moray Firth.

'A delayed surge,' Jim explained. 'It makes a shadow on the water. Hard to tell how far away it is, so you can't judge its size.'

'Ah well,' said Bert. 'Worth investigating in any case, I dare say.' Then, without pause, 'Do I still get my dram?'

Jim ate his lunchtime sandwich on top of the van, with the camera pointed down on the loch from the heights past Lewiston, where he'd once seen a bikini-clad swimmer risking the water's near-Arctic chill. He read the latest on Apollo 11, but there was little of substance to report on it now. Those two men, Armstrong and Aldrin, were already being eulogised as pioneers. When they stepped out of the module and trod the surface of the moon – admittedly, in desensitisingly heavy moon boots – they would be a new Cortez and a new Magellan, and though they would be carrying the Stars and Stripes, they would be representing a world.

Back at the farm, he ladled himself a bowl of stew and took it up to his room. He moved the pile of laundered underwear from the chair by the window to the bed, then sat down to read another Sherlock Holmes story. He chose at random, as had become his habit.

To Sherlock Holmes she is always the woman. I have seldom heard him mention her under any other name. In his eyes she eclipses and predominates the whole of her sex. It was not that he felt any emotion akin to love for Irene Adler. All emotions, and that one particularly, were abhorrent to his cold, precise but admirably balanced mind…

He had an inkling that this would not be one of his favourites – that it would prove to be more 'Creeping Man' than 'Speckled Band'. But the inkling was wrong: it was a good story, with Holmes being outwitted by the brilliant Irene Adler, before delivering a satisfying snub to her former lover, the stuck-up European prince who'd hired him. Jim was so engrossed, in fact, that he let his bowl of stew go cold where he'd placed it on the chest of drawers.

He devoted the following morning – the morning of the Sunday when the long-anticipated event would actually occur – to his favourite hobby. With binoculars, notebook and his treasured Leica M3, he headed for the meadow above Urquhart Bay where he was conducting a five-year study. The weather was even better than it had been the previous day, and the sun blazed for the whole of the four hours he spent recording notes on the flora and fauna to be found there. When he was stiff from crouching, he stretched out his spine and scanned the bay with his binoculars. He fixed a trajectory that would have allowed him a close look at Urquhart Castle, had there not been a hefty promontory in the way. April wouldn't be there, of course – not yet. She'd told him she was going to be working late, in the 'golden hour', sharing her twilight with Mr Stephens. Or Bob, as she liked to call him. Colin and Geneviève Page wouldn't be there. Only the director would be, and the crew, and all the other actors involved in the scene…

At the farm again, he found the television duly set up in the living room, and couldn't resist joining Douglas and Tessa for the 6.45 bulletin. It meant exposure to the last couple of minutes of *Songs of Praise*, which was irksome, and afterwards he felt *Dr Finlay's Casebook* working its narcotic effect on him before Douglas got up and switched the set off. But the bulletin itself was a wonder: live pictures from the Command Module, just after the Lunar Module had separated and shortly before Armstrong and Aldrin began their descent to the moon. It almost made Jim wish he'd caught the other bulletins through the week, instead of priggishly sticking to the more informative newspaper reports. It also made him wonder whether tonight's party was really the right venue to watch the main event...

At nine o'clock Jim was standing in the kitchen for the inspection of the household.

'Well, you do look splendid,' said Tessa. 'Very Byronic, I must say.'

'Ay,' said Alan, 'Adam fucking Adamant lives!'

On the whole, he had to admit that Sandra had done a good job. The evening shirt with the ruffles had been snipped and re-sown on the machine so that it fitted almost to a T. The midnight-blue velvet jacket had been expertly tacked, too, so that it sat exactly as it ought to on his shoulders. There was a bulge along his spine where the material had been gathered inside, but it was neither noticeable nor uncomfortable. It was a little warm, however, to be wearing in the middle of the summer.

'They'll let you take your jacket off when you want to,' said Sandra. 'You're not going back to school, for Christ's sake.'

'It's a bit long, too,' Jim said.

'Hems are worn long at the moment. Believe me, I know what I'm doing.'

'And the sleeves?' Those on the jacket were fine, but the shirt cuffs fell low enough to cover his hands.

'Here,' said Sandra, and folded them back over the velvet.

'Oh, that's perfect,' said Tessa. 'Absolutely the right effect. What do you think, Douglas?'

As was almost always the case, it was impossible to interpret that downward-turned smile. 'Cinders,' he said, 'you shall go to the ball.'

Jim insisted that Tessa stop the Land Rover as soon as the headlights revealed the gap in the trees. Dusk had fully descended during the short drive, but the thick sickle of new moon and scattering of stars made it still bright. He got out of the Land Rover and pulled on the velvet jacket again.

'Sure this is it?' she asked.

He looked again at the phone-table notepaper on which he'd written the directions. He could barely see it now, but it didn't matter. 'Unless I've been given false information,' he said, and stuffed the paper in a trouser pocket.

'Okay.' She sounded like a nervous parent dropping her teenager off at his first after-dark party. 'Have fun.'

The sweep outside the house was lit by a private lamp post, an electric light made to look like it ran on gas. There were a lot of cars, which was a good indication that this was indeed the right place. A Land Rover, newer than the Campbells' battered post-war model, and one or two ordinary saloons, but also a big Mercedes and a couple of roadsters, each of which must have cost a packet. The bay windows glowed with the light of table lamps, and the curtains at the open sashes shimmied as if stirred by the music. Growling guitars, of course, but also a woman's voice singing something both soulful and folky – not quite what Jim was used to hearing at the Drum's folk nights, but near enough. He looked at his watch: only 10.25. He felt the first prickles of sweat under his arms, and considered returning to the darkened road to wait there for April's *cortège* to appear…

But he didn't. Instead, he climbed the three steps to the door and pressed the button that protruded from the stone jamb like a navel. The rattle of distant bells was louder for a moment than the music. Then the door, which he now saw was already ajar, was thrown open and a couple of bodies hurtled past him. A girl and a boy, trailing hysterical laughter in their wake, both rake thin and dressed in almost identical bell-bottomed jeans and swirl-patterned shirts. Their hair was of a length, too, sprawling over their shoulders and down their backs. When they'd vanished into the night, Jim was no longer sure that they had been a girl and a boy, and even the quality of their fading laughter gave no real indication either way.

At first sight, the hallway was exactly what he had expected it to be – high-ceilinged, with a crystal chandelier filling the vast space above. But then he noticed the telltale signs of an Eastern influence. Where normally he would have expected to see an umbrella stand, there stood a ferocious ebony idol, which was mostly a gigantic head with a wide mouth full of fangs and glaring orbs that were almost at the level of Jim's own eyes. Along both walls there was a set of prints depicting stylised Indian interiors, and at the centre of each was a pair of human figures arranged in different and sometimes unlikely alignments. Of course, Jim knew what they were before a cautious closer look confirmed it: scenes from the *Karma Sutra*.

From an interior door, out of which issued a haze of smoke as well as the bluesy music, another human figure emerged. She was dressed in a frock made from silk as midnight-coloured as his jacket, but with a silver thread running through it. 'Oh, you must be April's friend,' she said, and swept up to take both his hands in hers. Every one of her fingers was circled in silver and most studded with a stone. 'I'm Victoria,' she said. The dress was cut so low that when she reached up to kiss his cheek, he felt the cold skin of her shoulder against his throat, and feared feeling more. The skirts were very full, however, so that only the turquoise-painted toes were visible below.

'I don't suppose she's here yet?' Jim asked, once she had released him.

The question didn't seem to register. 'I'm April's friend too,' she said, 'so we already have that much in common.' Her voice dripped more old privilege than even Douglas's, which still retained some muted notes of the Highlands. 'You're James, aren't you?'

'Yes,' he said. 'But please, call me Jim.'

Her face was remarkably round, as were her shoulders and the tops of her hoisted breasts. Their pallor made a striking contrast not only with that dress, but with the black hair that fell in torrents from her head to her hips. 'So pleased to meet you,' she said. 'April's not here yet, but that means we can get acquainted, doesn't it?'

Jim felt his gut tighten.

She made a smile that was somehow redolent of both solemnity and decadence. 'It's only proper that we should prepare ourselves for tonight's rite of Artemis. Or should I have said Soma?' She took hold of just one of his hands now. 'Come with me, and I'll help you choose your potion.'

Chapter Eight

She led him to the end of the corridor, jingling a little with the charms on her bracelets and on the anklet that moved with one of her turquoise-tipped feet, and they entered an idealised version of the Campbells' kitchen. The range was a pillar-box red, and the wall behind it white-tiled and tidy. Cabinets and cupboards were a unified powder blue. There was also a refrigerator bigger than any Jim had seen outside of the depictions of American kitchens on TV. By comparison, the table seemed modest, but that was before he took in its surface contents.

'You'll see we're broad minded here, James,' Victoria said, letting go of his hand. 'Take your pick of anything you fancy.'

There were wines with labels in French and Italian, uncorked and already partly consumed. Bottles of Gordon's, Remy Martin, the Macallan and Smirnoff, with a crystal soda syphon. Wine goblets, heavy-bottomed crystal tumblers and highball glasses, clustered in florets. And a white plastic tray, on which was placed a neat row of home-rolled cigarettes with twisted ends. Next to these, a big table lighter made of soapstone.

Jim's stomach turned again and his heart began to pound. News reports of police raids on Mick Jagger and John Lennon came powerfully to mind. He mixed himself a very weak whisky.

'Now, come and meet everyone.'

She took his free hand and led him back down the corridor to the living room. Or was it a lounge? In the low light, misted with fragrant smoke – just incense, he was sure – he could make out about a dozen supremely relaxed revellers. Most were sitting cross-legged or half-prone, propped on elbows, amid wine glasses and ashtrays, on the enormous Persian rug that covered most of the floor. He was pretty sure none of them was Colin or Geneviève Page. A sofa that might have accommodated all of them at a pinch was taken up by only one girl. He recognised her as the runner he'd embarrassed at Urquhart Castle all those weeks ago. A lad who was leaning over the back of the sofa, talking softly in her ear, stood up straight and looked at them as they entered. Everyone was clad like the two who'd nearly knocked him down at the door, in jeans and swirling-patterned shirts. Jim was pretty sure the lad staring at him was wearing makeup, too, and not the kind designed for the benefit of Panavision. The guitar and fiddle sound from the hi-fi seemed to be reaching a frenzied crescendo. Was it meant to sound like courting foxes, he wondered.

'This is April's friend, James,' Victoria announced.

The partygoers waved their cigarettes at him and called out various things above the music.

'Hi, James.'

'Hey, man.'

'*Ciao, bello.*'

Victoria drew him a few more steps into the room then wafted him towards the sofa.

'Come and sit here,' said the girl he'd embarrassed, patting the cushion next to her. Did she remember him? 'I've seen you on a shoot, haven't I?' It seemed that she did. 'At Loch Meiklie, wasn't it?'

'That's right.' If that was all she remembered, all well and good. 'Miss Bloom invited me,' he added, sitting down.

She laughed. '"Miss Bloom" – I like that.'

Over the heads of those on the floor, engaged again in their own conversations, was the dark TV set Jim had come for, positioned high in a modern cabinet that also contained the hi-fi. A brand-new 22-inch colour model – the picture ought to be good, so long as reception wasn't a problem. They'd be watching BBC1, so the colour was surplus to requirements. What really mattered, of course, was how well the original signal survived the long journey to earth.

'So, what is it you do, James?' It was the boy who'd been standing behind the sofa. He was sitting next to Jim now, the other side from the girl. Close enough to make Jim want to shift away – but he wouldn't have been able to do that without imposing himself on the girl.

'He's a fearless monster-hunter,' said Victoria, the only person now standing.

'A Professor Van Helsing?' said someone on the floor, in another impossibly plummy voice. 'That might prove a problem later.'

There was some husky laughter at that.

'The *Loch Ness* Monster,' Victoria explained.

'I'm a marine biologist,' Jim told them, trying to sound like someone who should be taken seriously. The thigh of the boy was resting right along his own now, and he sensed an arm reclined on the back of the sofa behind him. 'We're conducting a scientific study of the loch. The monster, as you call it, is incidental. We tend to speak of "phenomena".'

'Well, would you ever?' said Victoria, shaking her head. 'What will scientists get up to next?'

For some reason, that also made people laugh.

'Well, we're hardly creating the next H-bomb,' said Jim.

He suddenly felt very hot. Without thinking, he fidgeted in his seat, brushing against the girl on his left and the boy on his right. It only seemed to make them close in on him more.

'And have you seen any evidence that there *isn't* a monster?' asked another from the floor.

He was about to explain to him the problem of proofs of absence, when more laughter – a burst of it – sounded from the hallway. Then a dark form shaped like an A cut itself into the bright rectangle of the doorway. Beams from the chandelier caught in the ends of backcombed hair and illumined the edge of a short dress made from some translucent material, so that it glowed like the ring of sunlight around an eclipsing moon.

'Hello, April.'

'Hi, babe.'

'*Ciao, bella.*'

Thank God, thought Jim. He peered at the luminous dial of his watch – 10.35. Could he really have only been here for ten minutes?

The girl got up and April took her place. The boy didn't move.

'So, how you getting along?' April asked him. 'I hope they've been gentle with you.'

'Oh, I'm renowned for my gentleness,' said the boy. 'Gentle Ben, they call me.'

The voice was pure Julian-and-Sandy, even down to the faint Cockneyisms. Jim half-expected to hear some actual Polari.

'This one,' he continued, meaning Jim, 'has been tellin' us all about his monster-huntin'. Sounds dead excitin', if you ask me.'

'I've barely said a word,' Jim muttered to April.

'I believe it,' April muttered back. Then she spoke more loudly, for everyone's benefit. 'Oh, you gotta hear this.' She slapped Jim's knee by way of emphasis, then kept it there. 'But I've got to tell it quickly, before the others get here.'

'Oh no,' said the girl. 'What happened?

'Well—' she was stage-whispering now, '—Mr Wilder went and did it again.'

The laughter seemed very loud, but then Jim realised that it was only because the music had finished. 'Oh, Christ,' said the man in the cheesecloth shirt who was attending to the LPs. 'Who got the sharp end?'

'Well,' April told him, 'it was only Christopher…'

There were gasps, as well as some more laughter.

'He's been having a hard time of it,' she told Jim, as though he should know who she was talking about. 'Not as bad as Bob, and it's only this one scene, but they've been rehearsing it to death, then trying to get it in the can without a hitch. Only a few minutes to do it, too, because it's got to be in golden hour. And poor Christopher has got to remember all these names, and all these strange job titles. And if he doesn't get it right—' she made a Donald Duck quack, cutting a finger across her throat. 'It's got to be "J.W. Ferguson, naval architect" and "W.W. Prescott, co-inventor of the revolving periscope", and not "W.W. Ferguson" or "J.W. Prescott". And there's a lot more stuff like that, all the way down the line, introducing these old guys to the Queen. It's goddamned hard, and he's fluffing all the time. It doesn't help that Mr Diamond's there, mouthing his goddamned script just off camera. And you can see Christopher's beginning to lose his cool, when normally he's the last cucumber in the icebox.

'Anyhow, tonight Christopher turns up and he's focused as all hell. And he goes through the rehearsal like a machine, rattles off his lines perfectly, not a single bum note. He's acting good, too, and Bob's matching him – though it helps, I suppose, that he's not got a lot to say. But then they're waiting for golden hour, and that's when it gets bad. What if it goes wrong again when the camera rolls? You can see Christopher thinking: what if those J's and W's won't get in line? And he's giving off this vibe, like if Mr Wilder shouts "cut" again in the middle of a line, he's going to have a fit. And then, while they're waiting like this, Mr Wilder points up into the sky.

'"Look, Christopher," he says—' she was putting on the director's Austro-American accent, and pointing herself, at the ceiling, '—you see that?" And there's two or three bats flitting about up there, in and out of the castle ruins, like we've seen every night. And he says to Christopher, "That must make you feel at home, *ja?*"'

The gasps were louder, the laughter more forthright.

'He didn't!'

'God Almighty!'

'Bloody hell!'

'And what did the Count say?'

'Well, amazingly, he actually laughed,' said April.

'Didn't sink the fangs in then?' asked somebody else, causing guffaws.

'Uh-uh,' said April. 'And then they started shooting, and it all went like a dream.'

Jim still didn't get it, but it was far too late to ask for an explanation now.

The hi-fi attendant had put something new on the turntable, and at the first, building beats of it, Victoria – who'd drifted out of Jim's consciousness with the arrival of April – exclaimed, 'Oh, it's Davey's record!' There was a murmur of recognition from some of the floor-dwellers, too. 'Oh, you must listen to this properly, everyone. It's absolutely the thing for tonight.'

It turned out to be a story song, and a sad one at that – all about an astronaut who wouldn't be returning from his space mission. Very quickly, the mood turned thoughtful, with the floor-sitters swaying slightly in unison, like corn moved by a night breeze. April was listening intently, her hand still on Jim's knee. The boy made himself even more expansive, which pushed Jim and April closer together. Then the song changed tempo and became strangely euphoric. Then it was sad again, and then it was over. The others were murmuring to one another, still reflective, as the attendant removed the disk – it was only a 45 – and fumbled to replace it with an LP. April whispered in Jim's ear, 'I need a drink. And you need a refill.' His glass was unaccountably empty. 'Come on, let's get them together.'

Leaving the sofa and the boy was like disengaging from a wide strip of Velcro. In the kitchen, April went for the freezer compartment of the enormous fridge. 'Gimme your glass,' she said. 'I'll fill it with ice.'

'Why?'

She looked at him from around the edge of the open door. 'No ice?' She dropped some cubes into the highball glass she'd selected for herself. 'You must be the most British man I know.' At the table, she added a measure of vodka then topped it up with soda. 'So, have you spoken more than five words since you got here? That's as many as I've heard from you, by the way.'

Her tone was as sympathetic as it was chiding, and it eased Jim's mind. 'Well, it's been hard to get a word in edgeways. They did ask me about the work, but then wouldn't let me say anything about it.'

'Big ideas,' she said.

'I beg your pardon?'

'Granted.' She took his empty glass and sloshed too much whisky in it. 'Stick to big ideas and you'll be fine. A party's not a place for details. Well, not coherent ones, anyway. You partaken yet?' She was pointing with her glass at the plastic tray.

'God, no.' He took his drink. 'I don't even smoke normal cigarettes. Have you ever…?'

She smiled, and he realised – even amid his discomfiture – how much he liked her smiles. They had an opulence he didn't see in the smiles he encountered every day. 'I'm from San Francisco,' she said, 'what do you think? Well, we won't jump the gun. Come on, they'll be wondering about us.'

The sofa was off limits on their return. The same boy was still where he'd been sitting, but now another boy, in the familiar shirt and jeans combination, was reclining along the rest of its length, resting his shaggy head in the first one's lap. Jim followed April's lead and sat cross-legged on the rug. The songs on the new LP were less tuneful, more psychedelic Jim supposed, than the 45 had been, and it seemed to ring a change in the party's mood. The conversation among the floor-dwellers had turned serious.

'Nixon, for Chrissakes,' someone was saying, the only American voice other than April's that Jim had heard in the house so far. 'Now, there's a bloodsucker risen from the grave if ever there was one.'

'Well, it could've been Hubert Humphrey,' said another Yank. 'What's the difference, man? And anyway, didn't Nixon say he was gonna stop the draft?'

The first Yank snorted. 'Like shit he will. You'd better stay out of the States if you don't want to be trading shots with the Viet Cong by New Year's – remember I said that.'

Jim couldn't see either of them clearly in the low light, but he guessed they were a couple of years younger than him. Perhaps the age his father had been when he'd gone to war.

'I suppose we'll have an election here next year, too.' It was the girl who'd been on the sofa, now sitting next to them on the floor. 'Another chance for us to watch the English choose our masters.'

'Scotland votes Labour,' said an older voice. 'And we've got a Labour government.'

'Ay,' said the girl, 'but if England chooses Ted Heath, we'll have Ted Heath whether we want him or not.'

'You're a Scottish nationalist, Sophie?' It was Victoria, still standing. Was she capable of sitting? Her round face, and rounded shoulders and bust, seemed incredibly luminous against her dark gown and the surrounding gloom. 'Good for you,' she added, in a way that made Jim bridle.

'Well, I am for my granddad's sake, really,' the girl said, with no sign that she'd taken offence. 'I want to leave, if I'm honest. Leave Scotland, I mean.'

'And go where, child?'

'Well, you know…' She smiled, and it was the British, self-lambasting thing, not like April's at all. 'I want to go to Hollywood.'

One of the Americans scoffed. 'Jesus, doll, that's one shithole you don't wanna get stuck in.'

'Now, Rufus,' said Victoria, 'you're thinking geographically. Sophie isn't.'

The girl looked bewildered. 'I'm not?'

'No, child,' Victoria told her. 'Hollywood isn't a place to you, it's a state of mind. Perhaps a state of being. I feel we're entering James's territory here.'

It took a moment for Jim to realise she meant him. 'Are we?'

'Indeed,' said Victoria. 'Whether you like it or not, you're a dealer in dreams.'

She seemed to expect a response to that, but Jim hadn't one to give.

'When the first hard-handed crofter,' she continued, 'thought he'd seen that beast rising from the dark waters—'

'It was a businessman from Inverness,' Jim told her. 'Or perhaps an English tailor.'

'—what was it he actually saw?'

'Probably not what he thought he saw,' said Jim.

'—I'll tell you, James: he saw the dragon of his granddam's tales, told him as a boy by a midwinter fire.'

Of course, she was talking rubbish. But Jim had to concede that there was at least something in it, if by 'dragon' she meant the folkloric water horse or kelpie.

'Our dreams are real,' she added. 'Dragons did walk the earth and swim in our seas and lakes. Isn't that what our scientists have been telling us for the past hundred years? But here's the crucial point: *we already knew!* Now your task, James, is to find out whether they might still walk the earth, or at least swim in our waters.'

A little firefly of light was hovering near her waist now, and she reached down to take hold of it. Jim supposed it was one of the cigarettes from the tray in the kitchen. Its smell was different from an ordinary cigarette in any case, and it burned with a different light. Reverently, Victoria held it to her lips and drew, making the red spot at its end glow yellow.

'You were talking about Hollywood,' said the girl, reaching up to take the cigarette from her.

'Ah, yes,' said Victoria. 'Our factory of dreams. Now, James—' he felt his shoulders grow taut inside the overwarm jacket, '—April's told me about you. You're a fan of *2001*, are you not?'

'That movie's far out,' said one of the Yanks, entirely lost in darkness now. 'Seen it like five times.'

'I've not seen it once,' said Jim.

'Made only two years ago,' said Victoria, 'and behold, interplanetary travel begins tonight.'

'They're not going to Saturn.'

'And that computer,' she went on, 'that *murderous* computer. As I understand it, our reliance on such machines will only increase in the coming decades. Mr Kubrick is laying down the ground plans for all our futures in that film, and it's a terrifying nightmare and beautiful dream at one and the same time.'

April nudged Jim's arm. He thought she was inviting him to join her in mocking her friend, but then he saw that she was holding out the cigarette to him. Its smoke was still trickling out from between her lips. Without hesitating, he took it and drew in some smoke of his own. It burned the roof of his mouth and he let it out with a splutter.

'Take it easy, man,' said one of the Yanks. 'It's a crime to waste a joint.'

He tried again. Less smoke this time, and he took it into his lungs.

In the 45 minutes that followed – time watered with more whisky and infused with further draws on that joint, and those that came after – discussion ranged over many and disparate topics. A ballet based on *Spartacus*, the banning of the Beatles' new single by the BBC, a movie called *Midnight Cowboy*, which everyone loved, even if they hadn't seen it. Talk of Brian Jones – this when the psychedelic LP was followed with one by the Rolling Stones – ended with Sophie having to be led out by Victoria, to be comforted in the kitchen. And then they were onto the crimes perpetrated by the US National Guard on young American citizens of every colour and creed...

As 11.30 approached, someone even mentioned the Soviet probe that had recently landed on Venus, and went on to claim that Russia was way ahead of the United States in the space race. Jim knew he laughed out loud at that, but it sounded like it came from somewhere else. He also heard Alan say, 'What a load of shite.' Then he remembered that Alan wasn't there, and felt April squeeze his hand.

'What do you know about it, limey?' blurted one of the Yanks.

'Be nice, Rufus,' said Victoria, who was in the room again.

And to give Rufus his due, he was. 'Ah, it's cool, man. We're all fed the same crapola. Who knows what to believe?'

Jim was watching the TV set over the heads of the others. He had no idea when it had been switched on, and the sound couldn't be heard above that of Mick Jagger *et al* – but there was James Burke's great domed head, hovering in the darkened air like some benign, black-and-white Mekon.

What were they waiting to watch again? Oh, yes. 'The moon,' he said and took a sip of red wine.

Something was happening on the sofa and he couldn't quite make sense of what it was. The two lads were still there, he was sure, but they'd been joined by someone else. Could it really be Victoria, recumbent at last? He had an impression of too many legs and arms, and of pale spheres emerging from the deepest blue. He

also detected a slow, deliberate movement, which put him in mind
again of the kitchen table at Yew Tree Farm…

Then he remembered that he wasn't drinking red wine, and
tried to find his whisky. But there were too many glasses, and not
enough light to see them by.

He was outside, walking. Well, nearly walking – others had hold
of him, on either side. He was looking down at the gravel, which
was making an unconscionable noise under their six feet.

'There's gotta be money in it,' said one of the Yanks.

'In what?' asked the other.

'In the Loch Ness Monster.'

'You mean, like, hunting?'

'No, dumbass, I mean in tours. Maybe an amusement park.'

'I dunno,' said the other. 'Tell it to Disney.'

'The moon,' said Jim. He managed to lift his head so he could
see it – well, not quite half of it. Was it the right half?

'Is that fellow all right?' A rich, resonant voice. Was Douglas
here now?

'He's fine, sir,' said one of the Yanks. 'Just needs a little air.'

A tall figure stepped into the light of the old-fashioned lamp
post. An imperious face topped by swept-back, greying hair. The
Prince of Darkness, dressed down in a tan blazer and a yellow roll-
neck sweater. No satin-lined cloak.

The light was too bright and Jim was sitting in a kitchen chair,
drinking water. The bottles were still gathered on the table but
only a couple of the cigarettes remained.

'The moon,' he said.

'It'll wait,' said April, sat beside him. She was resting a hand on
his back. He knew he wasn't wearing Douglas's jacket anymore
and wondered where it might be. 'All they're doing is talking,' she
said. 'The hip professor type and the big guy who speaks too fast.
Drink some more water.'

'I saw Dracula,' he said.

'Yeah, I know you did, kid.'

All lights were off now, and the music, too, so that the only sound and vision came from the television. There was an even greater haze on the moon than there was in the lounge, the fog of 380,000 miles. A bulked figure was almost merged with the ladder he was descending, and below him the white surface glowed like phosphorus against the flickering blackness of the void. James Burke's commentary was a nervous compulsion, dogging everything said and done.

'*Okay. I'm going to step off the LM now.*'

'*Stepping onto the surface.*'

'*That's one small step for man… One giant leap for mankind.*'

'*And the first words of the first man to put foot on the moon: "That's one small step for man, one giant leap for mankind."*'

'Man and mankind,' said Sophie. 'I don't know why the rest of us are even watching.'

Somebody shushed her. It might have been Jim.

'He goofed there, didn't he?' said someone else. 'This movie needs a continuity girl.'

Jim found April in the darkness. He kissed her on the cheek. 'The moon,' he said in her ear.

'I know,' she whispered back, and kissed his lips.

London, 2014 (III)

Her hair is an untreated silver-white, worn short in that pixyish way that looks good on Judi Dench. She's got the crazed skin that all white Californians of her generation have, because they sunbathed too much in their youth. But she isn't terracotta now – instead, her skin is like porcelain, pink and white. She's also trim and well turned out in a navy blazer and a pair of linen trousers the same pale blue as her eyes.

No – that's not true. They're not even close.

Those eyes are nearer the shade Paul Newman should have patented: crisp as new icebergs and more lucid. Why wasn't she dragged from behind the camera and made to aim those WMDs directly at the lens? There isn't a chance she wasn't a supreme beauty in her working days, considering she's one right now.

'It's so good to meet you at last,' she says, kissing Gemma's cheek.

'Really, it's my pleasure, Ms Korzeniowski.' Gemma knows she's grinning, because her face almost hurts. 'Can I get you a coffee?'

They're standing at the table Gemma's been sitting at half the morning, under the awning of the Bankside restaurant attached to the BFI. 'I'd rather walk,' Ms Korzeniowski says. 'A stroll will be better for my jet lag than caffeine.'

Gemma leaves enough money to cover her latte and a tip, and leads the way out of the awning's shade into the shade of Waterloo Bridge. They've an hour to kill before they take their seats in the BFI Studio and record their DVD commentary for the restored version of *The Private Life of Sherlock Holmes*. On another day, Gemma might have spent it at the trestle tables filled with second-hand books that are ranged between the restaurant and the embankment. But today, she leads Ms Korzeniowski past the brutalist blocks of the National Theatre in the direction of the Globe. It's a rule: always show an American something old. Even if it's fake.

'It's good to put a face to the name,' Ms Korzeniowski says.

'It certainly is.' Gemma wonders whether her face and name are a match.

'Do you mind if I call you Gemma? If I call you Dr MacDonald, I'm going to want to tell you all about my sciatica.'

'Of course. Please do.'

'And you'd better call me April. Sometimes I think the Poles do it on purpose with the names, just to annoy Anglo-Saxons.'

'Korzeniowski is your ex-husband's name, I take it?'

Gemma regrets the question instantly. Where has the talk of disappointing in-flight movies and untidy hotel rooms gone? You can't start a conversation with a stranger by dredging up their marital history…

Luckily, her impudence only earns her a shrug.

'I keep it for my daughter's sake,' April says. 'She's still a Korzeniowski. And I never liked my maiden name, anyhow.'

Bloom. Harold Bloom, of course, with his Western Canon, and Leopold Bloom traipsing around Dublin, a Jew amongst Catholics. But also, Judy Blume, the children's writer, and other versions, without the final 'e' and with an umlaut over the 'u'.

'We must've lost the umlaut and added the "o"s sometime in the last century. There was a great-grandmother I never met who lived in New York – Dad used to do a sort of European accent when he remembered the things she said. Mostly, though, the name makes me think of Gene Wilder in *The Producers*, so it sounds kind of desperate.'

They're threading among other pedestrians now, and Gemma sticks close to April. When a cagouled woman wheels a pushchair between them, she feels genuine resentment.

'How about you?' April asks. 'Not related to any terrifying corporate clowns, I take it?'

Gemma laughs. She suspects April is fishing for a story of slavery, and if they'd been talking about the Jeffreys, she might have been able to hint at one – Mum's maiden name didn't come out of Africa, after all. But MacDonald is Dad's name, and comes with a different kind of tale.

'My grandfather was a real Highlander,' Gemma says. 'He

moved to Glasgow from Ross in the 1930s, and understood so little of city ways that he went and married an Irish Catholic.'

'Bad news in those times, huh?'

'And for a long time after. Dad moved down here in 1970, just when the Troubles were starting in Northern Ireland. He met Mum ten years later.'

'And she's a Londoner, right?'

She's definitely fishing now. 'Second generation,' Gemma tells her. 'My grandparents came to Britain in the Fifties. From Jamaica.'

The dome of St Paul's heaves into view across the water. They have to negotiate a crow that's got its beak in an ice-cream cone. It flaps about but won't abandon its spoil. An aproned waiter casts a cold eye over rows of white-shrouded tables, outside a restaurant with no customers.

'Oh, but I'm excited about seeing the full-length movie again,' says April, suddenly jubilant. 'It's been so long. I can barely remember it, you know?'

Gemma hopes she'll remember something. 'Can you remember if you thought it was a good movie?'

She shrugs. 'I was there with my logbook, looking for inconsistencies in eyelines and such. That's not the way to appreciate a movie as a work of art. But you've seen it, right?'

Gemma nods.

'What do you think?'

But she's not ready for that question. She feels that fluttering behind her sternum again, that she's felt recently in another context.

'That bad, huh?'

'Oh, God, no—' she's horrified that April could think such a thing, '—not bad at all. It's just that—' she reaches for something to say, '—it's just that I didn't watch it as a work of art, either. I had my film historian's hat on.' She tries to be brave and say something of substance. 'I suppose I did think that you could understand the producers' jitters. It's definitely a roadshow movie, and for a film released in 1970, that makes it look like it missed its moment by a couple of years.'

Gemma can't tell what April thinks of that, or if she thinks anything of it at all. Those glorious eyes of hers are focused on the pavement just ahead of her. Such non-reaction isn't strange – those who have worked in particular fields of the industry for decades don't necessarily have a handle on the shifts in fashion from era to era, as driven by the appetites of audiences, so that a film scholar's talk of what belongs when can leave them nonplussed.

'But that's only half the story,' Gemma adds, only partly to placate. 'Movie executives like to think they've got their fingers on the pulse, but they're always a step behind – like us critics. *The Private Life of Sherlock Holmes* wasn't a dinosaur, it was the shape of things to come. It's a piece of fanfic if ever there was one...'

April laughs. 'Okay, you've definitely lost me now.'

They're nearing Tate Modern. 'Well, I should probably save it for the commentary. Shall we head back?'

The strange segmentation of the Millennium Bridge is visible now. It makes Gemma think, as it always does, of the fossilised vertebrae of some immense creature that might have lived here when this, too, was one of the dark places of the earth. Today, it also reminds her of the Skarasen from *Doctor Who* – the agent of the Zygons disguised as the Loch Ness Monster and sent to attack Parliament. It's an apposite thought, of course, but she keeps it to herself. April's been exposed to enough of her host's geekiness for the moment.

It's not even eight when Gemma gets back to the flat, but David is already sitting on the sofa wearing only his pyjama bottoms. His laptop is on his knees, fingers rattling over the keyboard like the legs of little tarantella dancers. The lenses of his specs are filled with screen light, hiding his eyes.

'How's it going?' she asks.

He recoils when she tries to kiss him. 'Sorry, babe—' he doesn't sound it, '—I've already started this over twice.'

For a moment, she's captivated by the way his tendons flex and unflex beneath the skin of his lower arms. The rounds of his shoulders remain fixed – she rests a hand on one of them, and it might as well be made of marble.

'You eaten?'

He shakes his head.

In the fridge, she finds half a block of cheddar folded in its wrapper and some close-to-use-by tomatoes. Cheese on toast it is, then. She continues watching David over the breakfast bar while she prepares her meal, willing his attention to waver so that she can tell him about April Korzeniowski. She's toasted her cheese, prepared her salad and is halfway through eating it when he sounds his barbaric yawp.

'All done,' he says, stretching his arms. The laptop teeters on his knees and he has to double up to catch it. 'Thought I'd never get a synopsis out of that fucking stupid plot.'

Gemma, her mouth full, waves her fork in the air by way of celebration.

He gets up and stretches some more. 'So, how was the old lady?'

'Great.' Gemma pauses to swallow a final tomato. 'Not particularly old, either.'

'You get what you wanted from her?'

She's not sure how much she wants to tell him now. He won't get it, after all – the Hollywood she's interested in was dying by the time the movies he loves were getting started. For him, there's before *The Night of the Living Dead* and there's after, and he's only really interested in after.

'Shall I open some wine?' He sidles up to her, kissing the top of her head, where she's parted the hair to make bunches. His lips are hot against her scalp. 'Want to watch something?'

'Yes and no,' she says, finishing the last morsel of toast. 'Yes, to the wine, but I've been looking at a screen long enough today.'

He gasps in mock horror. 'Wash your mouth out, Dr MacDonald. There's no such thing.'

She watches him retrieve a bottle of red from the rack beneath the worktop.

'It was great,' she says, incapable after all of saying nothing. 'She's a real trouper. Everything she told me was interesting – we won't want to lose a thing. Even when she went off on tangents, they were interesting tangents. She's very…' She was about to say American. 'She's an extrovert, you know? A bit of a performer.'

'Sounds like someone you could get tired of quickly.' He's searching through the drawer for a corkscrew.

'Not at all.' Gemma feels defensive. 'She's really lovely.'

He's holding the mouth of the corkscrew over the end of the bottle, and turning the steel fishtail. It's making his trapezoids move. 'Glad to hear it, Gem.' He depresses the steel arms, but the cork barely rises above the bottle's lip. 'Goddamn it.'

'Want me to do it?'

He recoils from the hand she offers him. 'I'm fine.'

He grasps the whole contraption firmly in his right hand, hugs the bottle to his body and pulls again. His biceps bulge and his face turns puce. Gemma feels a tickle of laughter in her throat. Then there's a resonant pop, and David is holding the corkscrew aloft like a sword, with only half the cork attached to it. He looks forlornly at the other half, still stuck in the bottle.

Gemma can't contain the laughter. 'Oh God,' she says, 'we're as useless in the kitchen as each other, aren't we?' She gets up from the stool and places a hand on one of his recently contracted biceps. 'Why don't we go to bed instead?'

Any fears about April Korzeniowski's ability to remember the far-off events of the shoot vanished within the first couple of minutes of the projector rolling. It seemed like every third or fourth frame triggered a golden memory. The first scenes, with Colin Blakely playing Dr Watson's grandson, flown in from Canada to claim his inheritance, sparked stories about that actor's extraordinary gallantry.

'People kept calling him Jesus behind his back,' she said, 'and I thought it was just because he was so nice. It was late in the day before I found out he'd played Jesus in a TV movie that had been shown on the BBC just before we started shooting.'

'*Son of Man*,' Gemma told her. 'Quite controversial at the time. A very bluff, working-class Messiah. Not very C of E.'

When Robert Stephens arrived for the first time, in deerstalker and Inverness cape, April actually let out a sigh. 'Now, Bob was charming in another way.'

Gemma wanted her to pursue that thought, but decided to wait. She picked it up again during another restored sequence: the flashback to Sherlock's undergraduate days, and his seduction by Jenny Hanley's sly prostitute.

'So, the consensus is that it was a very unhappy shoot for Stephens. Is that how you remember it, April?'

'Oh, yes,' she said, with another sigh. But she still didn't run with it and Gemma was forced to say more.

'Billy Wilder supposedly put him through the wringer – multiple takes, lots of different line readings, very precise notes on hitting his marks… That must have been difficult for such a highly regarded stage actor. We're told he resented it. Were there ever clashes between takes?'

'No, nothing like that.' April paused again, and for a moment Gemma despaired. But then she continued. 'I think too much is made of what a taskmaster Mr Wilder was. I mean, it's true – he wanted everything just so. But the actors understood that. It's not as if his reputation didn't precede him, you know? It was bad for Bob, but that was as much to do with what was going on off the set as on.'

'You're talking about the state of his marriage to Maggie Smith?' said Gemma. 'The fact that they had a young child, and she was becoming a big star independently of him…'

'Yeah, all of that.' She paused again, and Gemma waited. 'He was a sweet, sad man,' April added at last. 'Lonely, too – especially when we were up there in the wilds of Scotland. That can be a very – how can I put it? – a very alluring quality. You know what I mean?'

Gemma thought she did. 'So, did you get to know him at all?' she asked. 'Between takes, after a day's shoot…?

April laughed out loud. Her eyes seemed to reflect half the light that came off the screen, straight into Gemma's face. 'You're a naughty woman, Dr MacDonald. What are you implying?'

Gemma shrugged. 'He did have a reputation. He's very open

in his memoirs about the affairs he had while married. Famously, with Lady Antonia Fraser, who was married herself, to Harold Pinter.'

'Well, we were all supposed to be liberated then, weren't we?' said April, with a shrug of her own. On the screen, Jenny Hanley was making her Victorian stays and stockings look very Mary Quant. 'Though I'm not sure how much of that had got into the Scottish Highlands before we were there. No—' she sighed again, '—I don't want to say too much out of school about poor Bob. Maybe I've got some memoirs to write sometime myself…'

Gemma didn't push it. That had been a bit of gold, and she hoped there would be more revelations of the same kind to come.

Other juicy details which did follow included an eyewitness account of the sinking of Wally Veevers' original *HMS Jonah*, out on Loch Ness. She explained how it had been denuded of its buoyant humps because Billy Wilder had decided they didn't look right, and how it had subsequently lost its equilibrium and sunk beneath the waves. April laughed as she spoke, but Gemma suspected there hadn't been much laughter at the time…

'There's more to that story than meets the eye, too,' April added. 'Mr Wilder had invited a Loch Ness Monster expert down to watch the launch, and asked this guy's opinion on how the thing looked. I think it matched up with Mr Wilder's own ideas, so he was able to ditch the humps with added authority.'

'There was a Loch Ness Monster expert there?' This really was news to Gemma.

April laughed again. 'Oh yeah,' she said. 'He thought we were a terrible nuisance, getting in the way of his field research. He was a sweet guy, though.'

Gemma was beginning to believe that April was one of those people who thought everyone was 'a sweet guy'. There were worse ways to be. 'And did it feel like this was some kind of intervention by fate?' she asked, meaning the sinking of the model. 'Did it feel like the shoot was cursed in some way?'

'Not really,' said April. 'Mostly, it was funny.'

Afterwards, with the commentary in the can, April was ready for a black coffee. It was past two now, so Gemma grabbed a sandwich and a glass of red for herself, and they sat at a table in the moodily lit heart of the BFI bar.

'Thank you, Gemma,' said April, sinking into a low armchair. 'I really enjoyed that. I loved all those old episodes. I'm so glad everyone will be able to see them now.'

'Well, you're the one who deserves thanks, April,' said Gemma. 'The commentary is really going to enlighten people.' Then she let herself show a glimpse of misgiving. 'Those restored episodes, though – they are just that, aren't they? Episodes, I mean.'

'Like a TV show, you mean?' April considered that for a moment. 'I don't think Mr Wilder would've liked that at all.'

Gemma shrugged. 'Well, perhaps it's one of the areas where the film was ahead of the curve. TV isn't what it used to be, and at its best, it's a writer's medium. Wilder and Diamond would have thrived in today's cable networks. Look at something like *Mad Men...*'

April laughed. 'That practically is *The Apartment*, isn't it?'

My God, Gemma thought, *it's like we share a brain*. 'According to Matthew Wiener, that's exactly what it is.'

'*Mad Men*,' April echoed, her voice dipping low. 'I really love that show.'

And they spent most of the rest of their time together talking about Jon Hamm.

Lying beside David in bed, with only the TV on, Gemma thinks of the decades of Californian good life that went into the making of April Korzeniowski. Maybe a move to the States isn't such a bad idea. Risky for her career, perhaps, but there would be opportunities, too... She's under just a sheet, while David's swathed in the entire duvet. They're supposed to be watching *The Walking Dead*, but it's only really David who's doing that. He's concentrating as hard as he was when he was working on his synopsis for *Sight & Sound*.

Yeah, Gemma thinks, *and about twice as hard as when he was fucking me.*

That isn't fair, and she regrets giving the thought even an internal voice. She's the one who'd initiated things, after all, and there have been plenty of times when he's made the first move and she hasn't especially felt like it.

Suddenly, she's warmer under the sheet than can be explained by the mildness of the night. She thrashes a little with her legs to make the air move, but that doesn't dissipate the flutter of panic in her chest.

God, she thinks, *there's not much time, there's not much time…*

The episode of *The Walking Dead* will finish soon, and there's a too-real possibility that before David switches off the light he'll want to discuss 'their plans for the future'. That's his routine these days. What if she tells him about Aberdeen now? Well, naturally, he'll ask her when they made her the offer, and if she keeps telling the truth, he'll learn that she's been keeping that bit of information to herself for five whole months…

Aberdeen would take bad news better, she knows. There might be some grumbling, and almost certainly some bridges would be burnt, but the world would keep on turning and no real harm would have been done. She's pretty sure that whatever happens, Anthony will remain his usual gracious self. In all likelihood, he will do everything he can to help, whatever she chooses to do. No, the only person she can really hurt is David.

Oh, and herself, of course.

White credits scroll down the black screen. Then the set pops to standby and David removes his specs. 'Okay,' he says, 'now where were we exactly before the zombies attacked?'

She's the one not feeling it now – but this is so much better than what she feared. How much more time can sex buy her? 'Hmmm,' she says, pulling aside the duvet, 'let's see if I can't find the exact coordinates.'

Chapter Nine

Jim opened his eyes cautiously, mindful of that last time he'd had too much to drink, and saw that he was in a strange room.

There was a stripe of sunlight where the heavy curtains didn't quite meet, brighter than the moon's surface had been on the television. It showed him a high-ceilinged room with walls painted purple and framed pictures on the wall of what were meant to be either big blue pots, or big blue women. He shifted his weight and felt the all-over ache he was expecting. It was most intense in the muscles of his abdomen...

Then he realised he was naked under the sheets.

'Oh, God,' he said aloud.

He was lying on one side of a double bed, the sheets thrown back on the other. Was it possible...? Had they...? He looked around him for confirmation. His borrowed clothes were piled on the floor on his side, though there was no sign of the velvet jacket. On the bedside table, the face of an alarm clock was obscured by a sheet of notepaper.

"*Gone to work. Don't move till you need to. Drink coffee. I'll call.*
April xxx."

He pushed the paper aside. It was nearly eleven o'clock.

He dressed and wandered the corridors of the first floor until he found the stairs. The velvet jacket hung off the bannisters at the bottom. His head ached less than he expected, but it wasn't right. Colours seemed wrong, and he guessed that his brain's chemistry was struggling to recover from the changes he'd made to it. His hearing was off, too – sounds seemed a long way off, then suddenly too near. In the kitchen, the bottles and the plastic tray were gone, and a plate smeared with carbonised fragments was at the head of the table instead. Somebody was filling an Italian-style coffeemaker at the sink. He looked over his shoulder as Jim came in.

'Morning, sleepyhead.' It was the lad from the sofa, using the same voice he'd used last night. 'Make yourself comfortable. I'm under orders to give you everythin' you could possibly desire.'

The short drive in the dark to Victoria's villa turned into a long walk home in brilliant sunshine. Jim carried the velvet jacket and kept to the outside of every bend. The world was absurdly vivid – beech, oak and rowan looked like they were made of jade, with clusters of ruby hanging from the rowan. The zip-zip-zip, chu-chu-chu of pipits' song had a cold-water clarity.

He could remember now. Not everything – not as much as he wanted – but enough to know it hadn't been a dream.

He'd been to bed with April Bloom.

His heart was beating rapidly, and he felt like running. Adrenaline, he knew, and he suspected it might overcome his fatigue and self-poisoning, and take him all the way home at a sprint. It was wonderful, she was wonderful – he had never known someone for whom the adjective wonderful was so completely apt. And she made him feel incredibly, stupidly alive.

But how much did he really know about her?

Until last night, the way she'd treated him might have been thought mocking. Playful, flirtatious – but also mocking. Then he remembered Douglas's remark about her Bohemian experiences in California, and that made him think of her friend Victoria.

How many men had Jim seen her kiss last night? Not pecks on the cheek, either – not even friendly smacks on the lips. Open mouths, the glint of wet tongue on wet tongue... He tried not to think about what she'd got up to when the lights had gone out, but did so anyway. He imagined an immense bed – bigger even than the Campbells' – in a boudoir decked with oriental cushions and silk drapes, with plenty of room to entertain anyone who was keen to join in.

With a mighty effort, he put the thought out of his mind. He was above such unsubstantiated suspicion. What he knew, for sure, was that April had taken him to bed last night – this morning – and that it had been wonderful.

But there was another thing – a sense of collusion.

It wasn't so much that these people were in the LNRG's way – though he still thought conflict was possible, perhaps inevitable, at some point. It was more that his fears about them had been so comprehensively confirmed. If he'd learnt nothing else last night, it was that these were people who didn't see the world the way he did. They disagreed about the basics, about what constituted truth…

At the front door, Jim remembered Sandra, and was suddenly fearful of an interrogation. But it was Tessa who emerged from the kitchen, with Autolycus at her heels. 'They didn't wait for you, I'm afraid,' she said cheerily. 'Wonderful, wasn't it?'

She meant the moon landing. 'Fantastic, Tessa.'

The pine marten ran up to greet him, too, then kept on running. Up his trouser leg and over his shirt, until it reached his shoulder and sniffed his chin. 'Yes, it's me, Autolycus.' He hooked a hand under its belly, but when he tried to lift the creature, the sharp claws pierced the thin fabric of his shirt and then his skin. 'Ow!' He tightened his grip without meaning to, and Autolycus reacted by biting his right thumb. 'Tessa, give me a hand, will you?'

He knew enough to slacken his grip entirely, so that Tessa could deal with the situation with a lightness of touch beyond him. She did so, then bent down and dropped Autolycus on the flagstones. Immediately, it shot out of the still-open front door.

'He's not a pet,' said Tessa sadly. 'We forget that sometimes.'

'I don't,' said Jim. He looked now at the red semicircle of droplets burgeoning over the joint of his thumb, and thanked God it had only managed to engage its front teeth.

'Better wash that,' Tessa said. 'I'll fetch the Germolene. Perhaps you should see about a tetanus booster, too.'

When she'd applied a sticking plaster to his wound, she made him a cup of coffee – not a patch on what the lad at the villa had got out of the coffeemaker – and told Jim about Sandra.

'She's pregnant. She's gone to Glasgow for a couple of days to see her parents. Alan's in a terrible state about it.'

'She's left him?' That was a greater surprise than the pregnancy.

'Oh, no – nothing that bad. But they hadn't planned it, you see, so it came as a bolt out of the blue. I think it's fair to say they've mixed feelings about it.'

Jim sipped at his bad coffee. 'Alan wasn't himself,' he said, 'when we went out on the boat the other day. Philosophical. Didn't suit him at all.'

Tessa looked sorrowful. 'He's a lovely boy, but not terribly mature, I'm afraid. It's not exactly natural the way they've arranged things. Sandra's the one with the common sense and the drive. When they met in Glasgow, she was working as a secretary at the university, you know. She was never a student. Her father owns a hardware store, and I think she'd like to do something similar. She's joked about being her father's only son. But Alan... Well, it's not really work he's interested in, is it?'

Jim felt the way he did when he found himself talking to some evangelically minded member of the Church of Scotland. He feared what she might say next.

'Well, she won't be able to work when there's a baby to look after,' he said, heading her off. 'We need to make sure we secure that funding come October. Then they'll be fine. It's the uncertainty that's worrying them, that's all.'

Tessa's frowns had become almost exactly like Douglas's, confined to the very top of her nose. 'Uncertainty can be a terrible thing,' she conceded. Then she perked up. 'Now, it's a bit late, but would you like some breakfast? Plenty of eggs today...'

Jim was dozing on the screening-room sofa when he heard the phone ring. He wasn't properly awake until he was downstairs with the receiver to his ear.

'Hi,' said April, 'how you feeling?'

The question sounded sincere. He was reassured by her semi-whisper, too. It seemed to indicate a new intimacy. 'Tired,' he said, just as softly. 'You?'

'I could certainly do with some more sleep, but that's only how everyone is today. Now listen—' her voice rose to a more normal pitch, '—you'd better get some real rest, because you've got to be up early tomorrow. *HMS Jonah* is launching, soon as it's light.'

'*HMS Jonah?*'

'Don't pretend you don't know what that is, Benedict Arnold.' She was mocking him again. 'Of course. Temple Pier, right?'

'Uh-huh. I'd better go now. Mr Wilder will be missing me. Sweet dreams, Jim.'

Later, while he was working on the files in the screening room, he thought he saw a correlation between sightings and the movement of currents in stretches of water believed to be of similar depths. He heard the Land Rover pull into the yard at about half-past four and went down to tell Douglas about it.

'How was the party?' He was already half inside the pantry.

Jim made what he thought were the right noises, and they talked for a while about the moon landing. Then he told him about his new theory and Douglas agreed it was worth investigating.

'By the way,' he added, taking a handful of carrots to the sink, 'what would you say to some *ad hoc* lecturing from October? I spoke to Roger Carrick this morning, and he's looking for a generalist in marine biology, and perhaps something more specific on the intertidal zone. I mentioned your name. It'd be good experience, and I'm sure you could do with the money.'

'Well, if we secure funding again that won't be a problem, will it?'

Douglas laughed. 'Your needs really are that simple, aren't they?'

Jim shrugged. 'Thank you,' he said. 'I'll think about it.'

'I say—' Douglas had turned and was frowning at him, '—you've hurt your finger. How did you do that?'

The slamming of the front door brought Jim out of a deep slumber. A slant of light from the peopled moon illuminated his clock, and he saw it was half-past one. Alan must have been locked in with Pete at the Drum, spilling his troubles over a pint or four and a couple of drams. Jim was surprised he hadn't been woken by the Alvis, then remembered it was parked outside Sandra's parents' house in Glasgow. Soon, he heard the heavy thump of a body hitting a bookcase halfway up the stairs. A couple of minutes later, and the toilet was flushing. Then a bedroom door creaked open and shut, and silence fell over the house again.

'So, what do you think?'

April was in her jeans and T-shirt, and her hair was in plaits again. They were standing together on the next quay to Campbell Pier, a little distant from the others.

'It's something all right,' he told her, and meant it, too.

Riding before them, at the landing's edge, was something truly monstrous. A terrible face, set with a pair of angry red orbs, at the end of a long and swanlike neck. Behind it, two humps, like those of a Bactrian camel, rose on its back. How big was it – twenty-foot high, thirty long? Its textured exterior gave a good impression of dinosaur hide, too. It was only its tendency to sway from side to side that gave the impression of a swimming gait that would be more comic than terrifying.

'It's the face I like best,' he said, reaching for the positive.

'Oh yeah,' said April. 'Stuff of nightmares.'

He remembered now what he'd meant to ask earlier, and had forgotten because she'd brushed his hand with hers, and he hadn't known whether he was expected to take hold of it... As they'd watched the crew winch the beast out of the truck into the loch, he'd noticed that it didn't have a keel. He asked about it now.

'A what?'

'A keel,' he said. 'It ought to have one to stop it from tipping over when it turns in the water.'

He looked at the cables attached low on the monster's bows,

drooping into the water and emerging again at the stern of the powerboat moored in front of her.

'Is she completely dependent on that to keep going?' he asked, pointing at the boat.

'Far as I know. She doesn't come with oars, at least.'

The powerboat looked more than capable of its task, but Jim still felt uneasy. 'There should be a keel. Unless she's more buoyant than she looks.'

'Well, I've done my homework there,' she said. 'See those humps? That's her lifejacket. Her whole back is a floatation unit. If she tips too far one way, it'll push her back up again.'

Jim nodded. 'That might work. I suppose it was designed by someone who knows what they're doing.'

'Uh-huh,' says April. 'See the guy taking with Mr Wilder? Not Mr Diamond, the other one.'

Mr Diamond, who was stood to Mr Wilder's right, was the man Jim had seen talking to Colin by Loch Meiklie. He was wearing the same worsted jacket now, done up in the middle. To Mr Wilder's left was a man of about the director's age, but constructed to a boxier plan. His bullet head seemed to emerge straight from his chest, and there was no disturbance in the line from his shoulder to the ground. Red mud flecked his black shoes and the hems of his trousers. Mr Wilder was in his usual sports jacket and flat cap, and was wearing a pair of tan boots. It was he who was doing the talking, left hand on his hip, right hand flapping at every word, scattering cigarette ash.

'That's the special-effects man,' April said. She shot him a look that was part-accusatory and part-amused – mocking again, even. 'If you'd bothered to go see *2001*, you'd know what he can do.'

There were some people there he did know, of course. The camera operator, standing by the big Panavision camera, ready to catch the test footage. Colin, wearing a light blue shirt and an actorly yellow scarf. Geneviève Page next to him, in a long summer dress that snapped about her legs in the breeze.

Jim wanted to reach minimally across and touch April's fingers. He estimated she drew about seventy percent of his attention away from everything else that was going on. He would do it, too – reach for her hand – but he needed to know the consequences…

'Okay—' it was the familiar Austro-American voice, calling through the loudhailer, '—let's see her go.'

The engine of the powerboat made a minor-key roar, then sprang forward. It travelled out some thirty feet before the monster jerked to life and followed. Great surges of white water boiled at both the boat's and the monster's sides, making a wide, double trail.

'So, Mister Monster-Hunter,' called the Austro-American, still amplified, 'there's what you've been looking for all these years. You can retire happy now, no?'

Jim nodded, feeling the strain of the rictus he wished he wasn't making. All eyes were on him, including those of Colin and Geneviève Page. Then everyone looked out at the monster again.

'What do you really think?' April murmured.

Jim dipped his voice and leant towards her. One of her pigtails touched his shoulder. 'Don't think I'd be reaching for a disruption report sheet.'

'It's the humps, isn't it?'

He nodded. They were too proud, too unlike anything that had ever been reported. They took too much away from the strange persuasiveness of that neck and head.

The boat was moving towards Urquhart Castle, where it stood at the tip of its peninsula. Then it made a crisp, white-fronted turn and headed back towards the quay. The monster duly followed. Jim was reassured: there was no undue tipping to the inside. Clearly, the construction was robust and water-worthy.

'What will they do next?' he asked.

April shrugged. 'Make some adjustments, I guess. Mr Wilder won't be happy till it's just right.'

The discussion between the director and his special-effects man had taken on a new urgency. The box-shaped man was doing more of the talking, shaking his low-slung head, looking down at his smeared shoes. A man in a wet suit was swimming out to the monster, while another on the boat was preparing to join him.

Jim considered the model again. 'I can see what they're trying for.'

'What do you mean?'

He explained that, barring the humps, it was a pretty good realisation of the so-called 'surgeon's photograph': a snap that first appeared in the *Daily Mail* in 1934, and had been used to illustrate nearly every story on Loch Ness phenomena since. Of course, the picture bore all the hallmarks of being bogus: over-exposed, blurred through magnification and always presented alongside strongly biased copy. Even an untrained eye ought to have seen that the ripples emanating from the neck were too big to suggest anything larger than a water bird, or a tree stem, or perhaps an otter. Jim thought it just possible that something more sinister was at work. To him, it looked as though someone were holding the front end of a toy brontosaurus above the water...

Mr Wilder turned Jim's way again. 'What do you think of the humps, Mister Monster-Hunter?' he called through the loudhailer. 'Honest answer, please.'

Jim made a proportionally amplified shrug. 'Perhaps a little too pronounced,' he said. Then, to make sure he sounded as little like a critic as possible: 'The neck and head are excellent.'

'Many thanks, Mister Monster-Hunter.' His tone was that of someone whose contention has been corroborated by an expert. 'Okay, gentlemen,' he called, turning the loudhailer towards the water again, 'let's get rid of 'em.'

The two men in wet suits worked either side of the model, removing the large section that carried the humps. Beneath was a hollow, as deep as the monster's body.

'I thought you said that was a floatation unit,' said Jim.

'I did.'

'So, they can't remove it, can they?'

'Tell it to Mr Wilder,' said April. 'I double dare you.'

Even as she spoke, the monster's neck began to swing from side to side again, this time alarmingly. The swimmers shot away, using the humps like a paddling float. But when the monster found some stability, Jim had to admit that the new effect was better.

The neck appeared to emerge directly from the water – she looked more than ever like the monster in that spurious photograph.

The swimmers aided the land crew in hauling the humps out of the water, then one of them got back into the boat. The pilot held up a thumb, and the director called, 'Go.'

The boat moved at a steadier rate, making fewer surges now that the humps were gone and the monster rode lower in the water. Now Jim couldn't be sure that the sight of that graceful neck wouldn't set his heart racing and send him reaching for his logbook.

'Any better?' April said now.

The urge to reach for her was overwhelming. 'Oh, yes,' he said, balling his fingers. 'But I want to see her turn.'

As the boat reached the same limits it had before, Jim could almost hear the pilot's mind working through the dilemma. Even with thirty feet of cable, too quick a turn would make the monster tilt dangerously. It was no surprise, then, when the boat turned shallowly instead, tracing a broad circle that pulled the monster out towards the middle of the loch.

'Taking the long route, huh?' said April.

Jim looked at her hand, relaxed by her side. 'He doesn't have a choice.'

There was a gasp from the quayside.

He had to force his mind away from April to catch a glimpse of the monster's head dipping quickly to port. There was no oscillation – it simply continued to move until it was lost in the water. Instantly, the bow of the powerboat rose high. Jim could see the wetsuited diver frantically working at the stern, loosening the cables. Then the boat levelled with an audible smack.

Another gasp erupted from the spectators. Behind the boat, where moments before there had been a monster, a plume of bubbles broke on the loch's surface.

'Bloody hell,' said Jim.

'Jesus,' said April.

It was hard to gauge how he felt. This was a catastrophe, no doubt: a great failure for those who'd worked so hard to achieve a particular effect. He naturally felt badly for them about that. But then, what was it they were trying to achieve? How could someone in his position not feel a degree of satisfaction in the fact that those who intended to propagate a false notion regarding Loch Ness phenomena had suffered such a tremendous setback...?

'How deep is it out there?' April asked.

'We haven't had a chance to do the sonar testing,' he said. 'We've been waiting for you lot to clear off. Deep enough,' he added, and had to stop himself from smiling. 'You're not getting it back, that's for sure.'

He looked towards Mr Wilder then, and saw something as astonishing as anything else he'd seen that morning. The director was holding the sober-suited model-maker in a bear hug, so that the latter's forehead rested on his shoulder. It looked like he was sobbing, using Mr Wilder's sports jacket to soak up his tears.

April took a firm grasp of Jim's hand, and he felt it like an electric shock.

'You eaten breakfast yet?'

None of his mind was on the model monster now. 'No,' he said, struggling with the one syllable.

'Then I say we go get some,' she said, 'while the getting's good.'

Chapter Ten

Jim got home late after a day's observation, and found Sandra sitting with the rest at the gigantic kitchen table.

He wondered whether the way she looked now might be described as blooming. When she wasn't putting him on his guard, it was possible to see that she was what Douglas called 'a fine figure of a woman'. Not how April was, but in the more old-fashioned, hourglass way. Big hipped with a big bust, which would only grow bigger in the coming months. He could never tell whether her perpetual pout indicated sensuality or irritation with everyone and everything around her. She already carried hints of the jowls she would develop in later life, together with a gentle bladdering under her chin. Neither detracted from her beauty, however – in fact, Jim was certain a stranger would think her an invitingly soft landing place. It took time to discover the wayward springs hidden in the plush upholstery.

After everyone else had gone to bed, Alan told Jim his news.

'Tessa told me already,' Jim said, 'but congratulations, anyway. To you both.'

They were drinking some of the ground coffee Sandra had brought back from an Italian delicatessen in Glasgow. It had been prepared in a French coffeemaker Douglas had found in the back of a cupboard. A little silty, but a big improvement on what they were used to. Still not as good as what the boy at Victoria's had made.

Alan's smile was like something unexpected rising out of a pail of milk. A slice of lemon, maybe. 'It was a bit of a shock, I can tell you.'

'Good job you're not our biologist then, isn't it?'

He almost looked abashed. 'And what about you and the Yank lass? How's that going?'

Jim had known this topic would come up. He sipped his coffee. 'All right, I suppose.'

'All right? Will you listen to the king of the fucking understatement?'

Jim shrugged. 'Better than all right,' he conceded. 'She's an interesting woman.'

'Interesting?'

'Clever, funny—'

'Beautiful,' Alan cut in. He'd finished his coffee and was building a cigarette from scratch, peppering a paper with shredded tobacco. It was part of a new economy, Jim supposed. 'Gorgeous. Fabulous. Sexy as fuck. That's what you're trying to say, isn't it, pal?'

Another shrug. 'Those things, too.'

He rolled the paper. 'Begs the question, though, eh?'

It was a joke, of course, but it was also the truth. Jim didn't have an answer, even now. Why had she chosen him? Why had she picked him out for attention, taken him to bed at the end of the moon party, invited him into her hotel room since...?

'How long's she got left here?'

Another question Jim didn't know how to answer. 'The director won't let anyone go until he's got everything he wants. It's hard to say when that will be.'

'And then where will she go?'

He wasn't going to bloody stop, was he? 'London,' Jim said. 'To the studio where they're shooting the rest of the picture.'

'And what'll you do?'

For a moment, it seemed another of Alan's *non sequiturs*. What did Jim have to do with the continued making of the picture? Then the penny dropped – heavily, somewhere in his lower intestine. 'Don't know,' he said. 'I've not thought about it.'

'Well, it's not so far, pal.' Alan held the very loose cigarette between his lips, spitting out stray flakes. 'You could pay a visit, eh?'

A happy thought occurred to Jim. 'I could drop by the Natural History Museum, too.'

'Natural History Museum?' Alan lit the cigarette – all the paper seemed to go up at once. 'And there was I wondering what she saw in you. You're one cool cat, Jamie Outhwaite.'

Next morning, Jim was woken by a knock at his bedroom door.

'April's here,' Tessa whispered through it. 'She seems upset.'

He threw on some denims he thought were probably clean and found her in the living room. Slumped forward in the sofa, her hands around the mug of coffee Tessa had presumably provided. As far as it was possible, she looked awful. Pale, despite her tan, and hollow cheeked. Snail tracks ran from her eyes, which she'd only partially wiped away.

'It's Bob,' she told him as he sat beside her. 'He's sick. Really sick. They've taken him to hospital.'

Jim's thoughts ran from stroke, through heart attack, to liver failure. The wages of a life lived too richly.

'He's been on pills,' she explained. 'Prescribed ones – maybe others, too. Nobody really knows. He's been in a black mood for weeks. He misses his family, and hates Mr Wilder, and thinks he's doing a terrible job.' She bit her lip. 'Anyway, it seems he got the doses wrong…'

'Oh,' said Jim.

She managed a watery smile. 'Oh, indeed. Anyway, the upshot is, I've got the day off. Not a lot the crew can do when the movie's star isn't around. The last place I want to be is the hotel, so I thought I'd tag along with you and look for Loch Ness disturbances. Is that okay?'

He fought back a smile of his own that would have been the wrong type. Not caring or sympathetic, or even plain understanding. It would have been triumphant. He couldn't help feeling that he'd vanquished a rival, because that's how he'd thought of Mr Stephens ever since that idiotic conversation between Pete and Alan at the Drum. He couldn't help it. Despite the actor's dipsomania and obvious depressive tendencies – or perhaps, because of them – Jim still thought he was by far the better romantic match for April. And yet, here she was, on the day Mr Stephens had apparently overstepped himself, sat on the sofa of Yew Tree Farm, electing to spend her day sitting with Jim on top of a van, sharing his egg sandwiches…

'You might find it a bit boring,' he told her, just to make sure.

'Believe me,' she said, smiling again, 'boring I can deal with.'

It was a good answer. 'Okay,' he said, and then came to a decision. 'We won't go out in the van, though. We'll go walking.' He looked down at her sandals, and at her exposed, painted toes. 'What shoe size do you take?'

It was Tessa who found April a pair of walking boots that were a good approximate fit, at least when worn with a pair of Tessa's socks. The abandoned property of some previous tenant, they were well used but clean. Jim actually liked the contrast they made with April's floral summer dress.

'Moon boots,' she said, making exaggerated slow-motion strides on the flagstones in the kitchen. 'This is one small step for woman, one giant leap for womankind.'

Jim led her up the path to his usual meadow, allowing her to pause from time to time to catch her breath, and to admire the prospect. Across the fields, Urquhart Bay could be seen reaching into the breaks among the promontories. Jim realised now how close they were to that spot where the crew had shot footage of the actors cycling along the track past that old croft. He felt a first pang of guilt over his unkind thoughts regarding Mr Stephens. The man clearly deserved pity rather than malice. And then he thought that pity was ungenerous, too – pity was also mean.

'Look,' said April. Near her, on a big head of thistle, rested a butterfly. 'Not the same kind as last time, huh?'

Jim went down on his haunches beside it. Brassy yellow wings segmented with black ribbing. Cuticles at the end of each segment. Wavy black inkblots nearer the thorax. 'A pearl-bordered fritillary,' he pronounced. 'You do find them elsewhere in Europe, but they're rare in other parts of Britain.'

'What's its real name?'

'What do you mean?'

'Its scientific name.'

He smiled. '*Boloria euphrosyne.*'

'Beautiful,' she said.

'Gorgeous,' he agreed.

He took his camera from his shoulder bag. The moment the shutter snapped, the butterfly flapped away. Then he wound on the film and turned the lens on April.

'Ready for my close-up, Mr DeMille,' she said.

They crossed the meadow and he led them into a plantation of Douglas fir. A kind of twilight overtook them, and their steps were muted by a carpet of needles and moss. Rays of light shot through the canopy, pooling in clearings where yellow broom and bilberries grew in low bunches. Jim tried to pluck some of the latter, thinking to feed April from his hand – but their velvet skins disintegrated at his touch, as he'd known they would, staining his fingers purple.

By a little burn, tumbling among the exposed roots of one of the larger trees, he found a rusty red toadlet. He caught it gently and held it out to April on his palm. It was small enough to fit on her fingertip.

'Got a name for this fellow?'

'The common toad,' he told her. '*Bufo bufo.*'

She laughed. 'Well, that's not beautiful, but it kind of suits him.'

In the open again, in full daylight, they sat on a slope overlooking the bay and ate their egg sandwiches. He wanted to kiss her, but one or other of them always had a full mouth. Kissing would have to wait until after they'd fed.

'You should see the redwoods back home,' she told him. 'We used to go to Muir Park for picnics when I was a kid. You seen *Vertigo?*'

'The Hitchcock picture?'

She looked surprised. 'That's the one.'

'No, I've not seen it.'

She tutted at him. 'Troglodyte.'

She told him of the great cross-sectioned trunk on display at the park's entrance, with famous dates from history – the Battle of Hastings, the Declaration of Independence, etc – marked against the corresponding growth rings. 'Kim Novak points out her dates on it,' she says. 'I mean, the dates of the murder victim whose spirit is meant to possess her. It shows what a blip her life was, overall.'

'Sounds cheery,' said Jim.

April poked his ribs, which he was quite happy for her to do.

'This makes me feel the same way,' she said, gesturing towards the loch, and over the fields, and back towards the plantation. 'All this has been here a hell of a lot longer than we have, hasn't it?'

He shrugged. 'Depends what you mean by "all" and "we".'

She gave him the full arc-light treatment, and he liked that, too. 'Go on then, Mr Scientist, explain.'

'Scotland's a man-managed landscape,' he told her, 'and has been for thousands of years. The primeval forests were got rid of by the first farmers, and we've shaped the land ever since. Killed off bear and lynx early, and wolves in the last 300 years. We've not stopped, either – otters are nearly gone now. Our red squirrels can't compete with your grey ones, so their days are numbered. Gillies are killing off the peregrines and harriers so rich people can shoot grouse and capercaillie. And don't get me started on the sea. Overfishing, whaling, the warming of waters off Dounreay…'

She was laughing, shaking her head at him. 'You're as much a worshipper of Gaia as Victoria, or any of the hippies back home.'

Naturally, Jim bridled at that. 'I'm just a scientist,' he said.

Jim could see a boat headed towards the bit of bank below them that wasn't overgrown with alder. Since they weren't far from where the *Caledonian* was moored, it was reasonable to suppose that this was Alan, coming as close as he could after spotting them through his binoculars. And it was while he was wondering what prank might be in store that Jim felt the familiar visual itch at the bottom of his line of sight…

'What's up?' asked April.

He was reaching in the bag. 'Not sure,' he said. Through his own binoculars, he saw a snaking movement in the water near the bank. A dog? One of those endangered otters he'd just mentioned? An actual snake? No, the movement was wrong for all of them. Only one thing was certain: this was a disturbance and it needed to be recorded.

'Going, are we?'

He was on his feet, pulling his kitbag onto his back again. 'Come on.'

He started down the slope at a lollop that was in danger of becoming a sprint. April, struggling in her heavy boots she wasn't used to, quickly fell behind. He could hear the buzz of the motor-boat now, made louder no doubt by the grand acoustic of the bay. It was impossible to keep an eye on the disturbance, because the uneven ground made him judder too much. And then, seventy feet from the bank, he knew what he'd seen.

It was a pine marten, snaffling bits of bread that were being thrown to it by someone hidden by a gorse bush.

'Good boy, Autolycus,' intoned a patrician voice from behind that prickly screen.

Momentum had taken Jim another forty feet before he'd stopped. Now he walked another ten and there was Douglas sitting on a convenient stone, looking like the statue of some 18th century poet, despite his rolled shirtsleeves and bottle-green corduroys.

'Christ,' said Jim, and the one word cost him the rest of his breath. He planted his hands above his knees and drew in more air.

'Hello, Jamie.' The voice betrayed only the mildest surprise. 'And April, too – how lovely to see you.'

She was at Jim's side now, drawing breath as painfully. 'So, it was only the notorious finger-biter, huh?'

They watched Autolycus move lithely from the water, looking for all the world like a chocolate-brown otter. Then the buzzing got louder and Jim looked towards the approaching boat.

'Well, well, well,' said Douglas. 'If it isn't Stewart.'

He was right. It wasn't the *Cally*, it wasn't Alan who was waving at them now. Instead, Jim recognised the man who'd *ahoyed* them a couple of weeks ago. His blond cap of hair was lifted by the breeze again, and this time sunlight glinted off the brass buttons of his blazer. Douglas got up from his plinth and waved back. And then April waved, too, with both arms.

THE CONTINUITY GIRL

'Who the hell has he got with him?' Jim asked. There was a whole boatful, sat on the benches along the bows.

'Passengers, I expect,' said Douglas.

'Passengers?' There was something momentous about this answer. 'Since when has he been carrying passengers?'

'Oh, since last summer.'

Jim was thunderstruck. 'But why?'

Douglas smiled. 'I expect there was an exchange of money.'

'Actually,' said April, 'he's a pretty good guide.'

Another bolt, straight to the heart this time. 'You've been out on his boat?'

She nodded. 'Not just me, either – Colin, poor Bob, Geneviève, a couple of others... It was during our first week here, when we were trying to find our way around still.'

'But—' he didn't know what to say, so said something he knew was nonsensical, '—we could've taken you.'

He looked out at the boat again and counted thirteen passengers. All were men and women of a certain age, in high-banded trousers or dresses without waists to them. Everyone wore some sort of old-style hat. Christ – so these were Douglas's promised tourists...

'I'm off to do some boating of my own,' Douglas said. 'You're welcome to join me.'

But April declined on behalf of them both. 'One boat tour per summer is enough for me,' she said. She took hold of Jim's hand. 'I think we're ready to head back to the homestead.'

Something more precise was communicated through her palm. He'd never invited her into his room before, and with good reason. It was always a terrible tip. But he wasn't about to turn down what was effectively a direct request.

'Yes,' he said. 'We're all done here.'

There had been two love affairs before this one, and they'd done nothing to prepare him for April.

The first girl, in his second and third years at Manchester, hadn't even let him see her naked, even when they'd shared a bed. The second, in Aberdeen, had sighed heavily at the end of their second date. 'Oh, all right, then,' she'd said, as though he'd been badgering her for sex the whole night, which he hadn't been. Then she'd treated the whole thing like some horrible ritual that needed to be got over, so they could get back to important things, like arguing about the washing-up.

How different this was to all that.

With April, there was no such awkwardness. In fact, oddly, there was very little of anything. The beauty was in the absences. No sense of performance, no struggle for attainment, barely any thought even. Instead, there was a sort of slackening of the self... It was almost as if maleness and femaleness didn't exist. How could that be? Things just unfolded as they needed to, in the right sequence, at their own pace. Things simply *were*.

Afterwards, she asked about Stewart McAllister. 'He seemed a bit of a charmer to me,' she said. 'What have you got against him?'

'Where to begin?' said Jim. 'He's a walking, breathing warning to all scientists.'

'Because he believes in the Loch Ness Monster?'

He shook his head. 'I've no idea what he believes.'

He told her how Douglas had met Stewart in 1964, at a conference in Cambridge on recent discoveries in the Amazon basin. During lunch in some panelled refectory, conversation had turned to the coelacanth – the armoured fish, long thought extinct, which had turned up in the catch of a South African angler in 1938 – and there'd been some speculation about what other 'living fossils' were due a return. Naturally, someone had mentioned the Loch Ness Monster. Stewart had then informed Douglas that he'd grown up on the banks of Loch Morar, and had been fascinated since childhood with the kelpie or waterhorse. Within five minutes, the Loch Ness Research Group had sprung into existence.

'Stewart was still with the group when I started,' Jim told her, 'but tensions were running high by then. He was touting a book to publishers, in which he claimed he'd solved what he called the "mystery of Loch Ness". All the evidence pointed to...' He stopped himself. 'I can't make myself repeat it.'

'Can I make you?'

My God, he thought, *she could make me do anything.*

'He'd come up with a sort of chimera, grafting together all the bits and pieces people have claimed to have seen. A neck from here, a tail from there, a bloody diamond-shaped paddle from somewhere else… It was hard to tell how much Douglas disapproved, because – well, you've met him, haven't you? Then, one morning, I woke up and Stewart was gone. "We thought it best we part ways," Douglas told me. "A disagreement over methodology."'

'Did he publish that book?'

Jim nodded. 'There's always someone willing to publish crap like that,' he said. 'Then, a year ago, he turned up in his own boat. Calls himself the Loch Ness Research Institute, would you believe?'

'Well, I could, because that's what he told us he was.'

She slipped out of bed. Jim had to stop himself from looking away, and then from just staring. She put her hands on her hips and stretched, as though she'd just finished a bout of athletics, which he supposed she had. Then she wandered to the window.

'Still reading Sherlock Holmes, huh?'

She'd spotted the volume on the chest of drawers and now picked it up and opened it. He liked the image she presented now, fused with the sunlight filtered through the yellow curtains, so that she seemed just as golden.

'Just when the mood strikes,' he told her.

'What are they like?' She was leafing through the pages.

'You've not read any?'

'Uh-uh. Just seen the old Basil Rathbone pictures.'

'Well, even I've seen those. The stories are much better. If you want to know my favourite, it's "The Man with the Twisted Lip". The first one I read.'

April brought the book back into bed with her. 'Is Geneviève's character in here?'

'I've not come across her.' Then he remembered. 'There is Irene

Adler, though.' He explained about her, and got April to turn to the right page.

'"The woman", huh?' She pored over the opening paragraph for a while. 'Can't believe there'd be room in Sherlock's life for both an Irene Adler and an Ilse von Hoffmanstal.'

There was a record playing on the hi-fi in the sitting room now, directly below them. A plucked guitar – it must be one of Sandra's folk singers. Then the song proper began and he recognised the nasal drawl. The singer was requesting that the listener pass on his regards to a girl who'd once been a true love of his.

'So, we don't have the house to ourselves anymore,' said April.

'Doesn't sound like it.'

She put the book down on the floor, then lay on the pillow and looked at him directly. There was nothing searing about her eyes now. They didn't project anything, they were deep. He thought again of how idiotic it was that he'd been jealous of that poor actor, who was lying now in another, tightly tucked bed, fighting demons. *I'm the luckiest bastard in the world*, he thought.

'Guess that means we better keep the noise down, huh?' said April.

'Guess we better had,' he said, and leant in for a kiss.

London–Stirlingshire, 2014

Gemma began suspecting David knew something about the Aberdeen job a week or so before they were due to leave for Scotland. Nothing obvious – he just became more reticent, even oddly secretive. She caught him talking on the phone to his mother one night, which was something he never did. He tried to mislead her at first, saying only that he'd 'had to make a call to the States', and only became less ambiguous when questioned. And then, a day or two later, there'd been an awkward conversation.

'Why don't we fly?' he said. 'Your dad can drive the rest of them, if he really wants to. But we should fly, and have a couple of days to ourselves.'

'But we have lots of days to ourselves,' Gemma said. 'I've told you, Dr Kitch, you're getting the full MacDonald family holiday experience. Besides, I need to be with Destiny.'

They had discussed this – how Gemma was going to take her niece in hand, be her guide to a different life.

'Well, that's not going to matter until you're in Scotland, is it?' A furrow was forming above his glasses. 'And as for being alone at home, it's not the same. When you're somewhere else, it gives you perspective.'

Perspective was not a David word.

'And your dad's fine with it,' he added.

That, at least, was funny. 'What could possibly give you that idea?' she said when she'd finished laughing.

'He told me. Last Tuesday, remember? When he called and you were too busy repunctuating that *Screen* article for the 56th time to speak with him.'

Gemma tried to dismiss it with a wave. 'David, he was pulling your leg. Anyway, he's not the fount of all authority.'

They're standing on the pavement outside the flat, and David is smiling in that way that doesn't show in his eyes. Gemma knows she's asking a lot of him: he's about to embark on a near 600-mile journey in a ten-year-old Vauxhall Vectra with someone else's family. She nudges his arm, and when he turns, shows him how smiles are meant to look.

There's one more person to fit in this year's model of old tin can than there used to be. David is filling in for Robbie – as adults, at any rate, they take up about the same amount of room. At first, Gemma imagines that Destiny is the supernumerary, but then she looks at her, and gets another of those out-of-body, time-travelling sensations. If anyone represents her childhood self, it's the skinny ten-year-old with the Afro who is already tucked into the far corner of the back seat, maintaining total control of her sensory experience with a DS, a pair of headphones and her mobile. Twenty years ago, it would have been a Gameboy and a Discman, but the principle is the same.

Gemma thinks of the three CDs she's burnt especially for the journey. She's going to need a strategy to get them played.

'You two getting in,' Dad says, leaning over Mum and speaking through the passenger window, 'or are you going to stand there for ten days?'

Gemma slides in beside Destiny. David follows, huffing and puffing, making a meal out of finding the clasp for his seat belt. She knows she must raise the subject of Aberdeen before he does, because if she doesn't, it will be a disaster. Maybe tonight, when they're alone in their motel room. He wasn't wrong about perspective – when they're in the holiday mood, after a meal and some wine, he'll be able to see things *in toto*, understand that in an age of instant communications, relationships don't have to occupy the same spaces as they used to...

Yes – something like that. It's a line that needs a little development.

Dad pulls away and they join the fairly amiable mid-morning traffic of the Mile End Road. Then Mum turns on the radio and the car is filled with chortles.

'Ah, Gloria,' says Dad, 'not the ginger dunderhead.'

She turns it off again. 'We can listen to whatever you like, Ally,' she says, disgruntled, 'so long as it isn't dreary.'

'Turn it to Five Live,' says Dad.

Gemma joins forces with Mum on that – it's not going to happen. There's too great a risk of the referendum being mentioned. With two months still to go, the media coverage is already hysterical, and shows no sign of letting up.

'What about David?' Dad asks, 'It's only fair to ask the guest if he has a preference.'

'I'm easy,' David lies.

'Destiny?'

But she's busy making her pocket monsters fight other pocket monsters in the 3.8-inch, wibbly-wobbly world she's happy to inhabit for hours on end.

It's time for Gemma to play her first card. 'How about this?' she says, and passes Mum the first of the three discs.

The film programme podcast lasts until they're close to Northampton. It pleases Dad, who's a fan, and offends no one else. Mum is interested enough to ask Gemma whether she's ever met the brash man doing the reviews.

'We're on nodding terms,' she says.

'And does he listen to your show?'

She means Gemma's occasional visits to LBC to talk about the latest blockbuster. 'I wouldn't have thought so, Mum.'

David gives his usual half-admiring, half-mocking analysis of his rival's verdicts. 'He always says *Beneath* is the best of the *Apes* movies,' he says after a glowing review of the latest instalment, 'but that's a crock. *Planet* is a masterpiece and the only original sequel that holds a candle to it is *Escape*.'

When the podcast is over, nobody objects to Mum flicking the radio on again, and so Ken Bruce takes them to Cannock Services. While the adults refuel on bad coffee and sandwiches, Destiny refuses everything but a bag of Haribo, and continues playing her game.

'How's school?' Gemma asks.

It's a terrible question, underlining just how far she is from her own childhood, and not just in years. Destiny shrugs. 'It's the summer holidays, Auntie Gem.' It's a fair reply.

When Dad turns the ignition again, Jeremy Vine bounds out of the radio. There's a real danger the referendum will rear its provocative head. 'Why don't you choose some music, Dad?' Gemma suggests.

And so, the Cannock-to-Kendal stretch is accompanied by various combinations of Crosby, Stills, Nash and Young.

At some point, David starts tapping his fingers on Gemma's denim-clad thigh. It's annoying, of course, but also strangely stimulating. She wonders again how he could possibly have got wind of the Aberdeen job. It seems so unlikely, and she nearly convinces herself she's imagined it. But then, how to account for his odd silences, the phone call to his mum, the suggestion about flying up early…? No – something was up. Nobody at work could have told him, because she hasn't told them yet, either. The best explanation is that he got into her emails, or looked at her text messages. That thought kindles a righteous anger in her, which she's happy to let smoulder. It might come in useful later.

When they draw up outside the stone-clad Travelodge, all the Haribo and screen-watching take their toll on Destiny. Payment comes in the form of a quite astonishingly sustained spray of liquefied sugar and gelatine, which glazes the back of Dad's seat.

'Why didn't you say something before, love?' Mum asks when they're safely on the car park gravel.

'It was all right while we was moving,' Destiny says. 'It was stopping that was the problem.'

After checking in and cleaning up – flecks of vomit had got as far as David's glasses – they get back in the car and head for Grasmere. Passing Lake Windermere, Destiny asks, 'Why aren't there monsters in that if there's one in Loch Ness?'

'There isn't one in Loch Ness,' says David.

'Monsters don't come down this far, hen,' says Dad. 'English water doesn't agree with them.'

'There are monsters here,' says Gemma. 'I mean, people have said they've seen them.'

'Knew it,' says Destiny, deeply satisfied.

She continues to show engagement when they're in Dove Cottage. It isn't centred on Wordsworth, though – she's more interested in the idea that people could have lived in a place even more cramped than Grandma and Granddad's house. She wrinkles her nose when their guide – a retired lady with a local accent – tells them about the twice-used tea leaves being passed to the poor for one more go around the pot. Meanwhile, Dad's tickled by the idea of his countryman, Sir Walter Scott, climbing out of a back window to escape his abstemious English host and find a tavern. 'He's a better writer, too,' he says in a whisper meant to reach the ear of the guide.

David's not a fan, either. 'What exactly did he do,' he asks Gemma in a more genuine whisper, 'apart from write about fucking daffodils?'

It's enough to make her buy him a scholarly edition of *The Prelude* in the gift shop before they leave.

They eat at the same big coaching inn, on a roundabout near the motel, where the family ate the last time they stopped here, seventeen years ago.

Back at the motel, Gemma and David say goodnight and head along a different corridor to the others to reach their room. Panic erupts behind Gemma's breastbone – *It's now, isn't it? I've got to talk to him now.* David's arm is around her waist, and as they near the room, he draws her to him. He will want sex, but she's going to insist on talking first…

They brush their teeth, undress and get under the sheets before she turns to him with any real intent. And then he yawns in her face.

'Sorry, Gem,' he says. 'I'm beat. Nothing like being stuck in a car for half a day and walking around a lake for the other half to wear a guy out.' He switches off his bedside lamp. 'Night, babe.'

He seems to fall asleep in seconds. Gemma feels less tired than she did an hour ago. She gives the latest Ali Smith a go, but can't concentrate on anything above the sound of David's restful breathing. After twenty minutes, she turns off her own light and just lies there.

Next morning, Dad goes off piste, taking them through twisting lanes and up sky-bound gradients. There's a constant to-and-fro with Mum along the lines of 'We won't make it' and 'Ay, we will'. Eventually, Dad's internal satnav brings them back onto the M6, and at some point, they're not in England any more.

'Smell that, Destiny?'

She wrinkles her nose. 'Smells like cow poo.'

'It's Scottish cow poo,' he says, 'and that makes all the difference.'

Radio 2 has been playing softly all morning. There haven't been any complaints, but now Dad gets twitchy. 'Can we have a CD on, Gloria?'

Mum clicks her tongue. 'Old men and guitars again?'

Destiny is having a rest from the DS and looks bored. 'Hey,' Gemma says, 'what movies do you like?'

'Scary ones,' Destiny says. 'Like *Woman in Black*.'

David scoffs.

'Oh, dear,' says Mum. 'Does your mother let you watch things like that?'

'It's only a 12A,' Gemma tells her. 'It's made for ten-year-old girls to scream at. What about Pixar films, Destiny?'

She looks at her aunt askance. 'Like *Madagascar*?'

Gemma resists delivering a lecture on the creative credos of different US animation studios. 'Like *Brave*,' she says, and takes the second CD from her bag. 'I've got the soundtrack here.'

'Disney songs?' It's Dad scoffing now.

'It's the one set in Scotland,' she tells him. 'Julie Fowlis sings on it. Billy Connolly does one of the voices.'

'Is that right?'

And Gemma knows she's got him onside.

He takes them on a diversion, the significance of which Gemma doesn't understand until she sees the sign for Gretna Green.

'This is where English people used to run away to get married,' Dad tells Destiny, 'back when you had to marry whoever your parents chose for you.'

Mum punches his arm. 'You say that like it's a good thing.'

'What d'you think, Davey?' Dad is trying to catch his eye in the rear-view mirror. 'Want to take the opportunity while you're here?'

'We're okay, thanks.' He's smiling again, but has turned to a stone next to Gemma. He even withdraws his hand from her thigh.

Gemma tells Destiny about Gretna's role in *Pride and Prejudice*, and then has to tell her about *Pride and Prejudice*. They don't stop when they pass the blacksmith's shop, and as soon as he can, Dad turns around and heads back to the main road.

They bypass Glasgow, and the remnants of family they might have visited there, and stop instead at a hotel in Milton of Campsie. The big foothills of the Highlands glower all around them now, visible everywhere. After settling in, they take a walk around what's mostly an ordinary estate of boxy houses. Gemma's nervous about the posters peeping out of every other sitting-room window. The blue YES ones predominate, but there are enough red NO ones to set that vein throbbing in Dad's temple. Luckily, the solemn giants surrounding them demand a sort of hushed respectfulness.

Gemma's favourite bit of the walk is when they climb a stile and discover a footpath passing through a tall meadow, back towards the hotel. Scudding clouds throw a piebald pattern across the field, and Gemma has no option but to take out her iPhone and take a snap of her companions trudging knee-deep through grass and wild flowers.

They eat a good meal under a glass ceiling in the hotel's restaurant, and afterwards Dad and David bond a little over tumblers of Glengoyne, and the differing merits of Hollywood and Spaghetti Westerns.

'And what have you liked best so far?' Mum asks Destiny.

Destiny shrugs. 'My Magikarp evolving into a Gyarados,' she says.

Mum is bemused, but Gemma laughs out loud. It's the perfect answer.

Later, in bed, Gemma's phone pings. It's a text from Julia Crosby in Aberdeen. '*Thanks for invitation to screening in Inverness. Looking forward to meeting you again.*'

'Who's disturbing you at this hour?' asks David.

'Just an old text coming through,' says Gemma, which is probably true.

'So,' says David, 'I'm altogether less tired than I was last night.'

Instantly, her heart is pounding again. Nothing to stop her now – the perfect moment. 'I'm glad to hear it,' she says. Her voice sounds wrong in her ears, somehow distant. 'Can we have a chat?'

'A chat?' There's something like a smirk on his face, though it's hard to tell when he isn't wearing his glasses. How can someone be less readable without specs than with them? Under the covers, his hand finds the inside of her thigh. 'I wouldn't say I'm in a chatty mood.'

'Okey-doke.' All the tension leaves her immediately. 'We'll have to think of something else to do instead.'

From the perimeter wall of Stirling Castle, Gemma admires a mighty view.

Below, the city is gathered in loops of the River Forth, while to the north, the hills rise into mountains. They're stuck with what look like giant dandelion clocks, but are actually wind turbines. Not everyone's cup of tea, but to Gemma, they're elegant. Only the Wallace Monument is an embarrassment: a phallic tower, set on a crag in the middle of the city, made from stone that she's tempted to call 'tumescent red'. But even this sore thumb can't detract from the inherent beauty of the place, and Gemma feels an unearned sense of national pride. She wants to shout some *Macbeth* into the buffeting winds: *Then fly false thanes, and mingle with the English epicures!*

She's here with Dad and Destiny. They left Mum and David in the museum, looking respectively at medieval kitchen equipment and the regimental relics of the Argyll and Sutherland Highlanders. David's generous mood of the previous night hasn't lasted, worse luck, and he was testy first thing. He swore at his shoelaces for refusing to tie, and at the toothpaste for spilling on his T-shirt. Then, in the car, he'd been mordantly silent. This was exactly the kind of thing that had made her suspicious in the first place...

'They teach you about Robert Bruce at that school of yours, hen?' Dad asks Destiny.

'Which one's he?'

'The king who watches the spider,' Gemma tells her, 'and learns about not giving up.'

Destiny shrugs again. 'Might've.'

'That's the fairy story, hen,' says Dad, and begins a sermon on the Battle of Bannockburn and its importance to Scotland's status as a nation. The light in his eyes is turning dangerously inward and he's losing a sense of his audience.

'She can find all that out in the visitors' centre,' Gemma says. 'Or we can watch *Braveheart* when we get to the cottage. I'm sure it will be on some channel or other.'

'*Braveheart?*' Dad's disgusted, as she'd known he would be. 'I'll tell you, Destiny, that film's a pile of Aussie baloney.' He's choosing his words carefully, but his good intentions fall away with his next statement. 'The Scottish didnae go around with all that blue shite on their faces and William Wallace was no fucking hero.'

Back in the car, there's a choice of routes. Ever perverse, Dad decides against the more obvious splendours of the west and heads for the interior. Splendour is relative, of course. As they ascend into the Cairngorms, and the landscape becomes a high tundra, like nothing else in the British Isles, Gemma's breath is quietly taken away.

'Any requests?' asks Mum when the *Brave* CD comes to the end of its third run.

Gemma's gained no end of brownie points for bringing it along. 'Is there something else you'd like, Destiny?'

She shakes her head. 'Gonna play my game again.'

'You do that, hen,' says Dad. 'Just let me know if we need to make a puke-stop, all right?'

'Ally!' Mum shakes her head.

Gemma's got one last CD in her bag and now's the time to bring it out. Everything else has been a prologue to this. 'Here you go, Mum.'

'What is it?' asks Dad.

'It's Miklós Rózsa's score for *The Private Life of Sherlock Holmes*.'

'Oh ay?' he says, 'Come on then, Gloria, let's hear it.'

Gemma expects indifference from the rest of them and steels herself for worse. It's always a terrible gamble, exposing loved ones to works of art you love. It's bad enough with students – she's never got used to the failure of most of them to meet the challenge of black-and-white photography, or dialogue in another language, or no dialogue at all. But the prospect of her family rejecting something she cherishes is almost too much to bear.

A brass fanfare gives way to the main theme. 'This is Holmes and Watson,' she explains. 'It's cosy, in a masculine sort of way. It represents their friendship.'

'You giving us a lecture, Gem?' says David.

She does a Destiny and shrugs her shoulders. 'I'll shut up then.'

'No, dear,' says Mum. 'Go on and tell us. It's interesting.'

The music changes tempo, a violin leading a sharp ascending melody now that refuses to resolve. This is Holmes's inner life, the loneliness of a mighty brain. It segues into Ilse von Hoffmanstal's theme, the one Holmes is meant to have composed himself. Ilse is his intellectual equal, trapped in a netherworld of espionage and deceit. She is a pawn played by higher powers – as indeed, unwittingly, is Holmes. Thus, the themes unite them, even as their roles as enemy agents push them apart.

'Spoilers,' says Destiny.

'Don't pretend you're listening,' says David.

'But we've got to watch Auntie Gem's old film, don't we? That's the only reason we're here.'

'You can always sneak in your DS.'

'Nah—' she's stage-whispering behind Gemma's back, '—don't want to make her cry, do we?'

As far as Gemma can remember, this is the first conversation they've had, and they're using it to make fun of her.

'Sounds like something you'd hear at the Proms,' says Mum.

'Well, you might,' Gemma tells her, 'and not just when they're playing film music. Miklós Rózsa based it on his own violin concerto. The director and his co-writer listened to it as they worked on the script. It's where they found the film's mood.'

'I thought it was a funny film,' says Dad.

'Oh, it is.' She's worried he'll tell them that films are just a bit of fun, and aren't meant to be taken seriously. He's said it before, and sounded like he meant it. 'But it's romantic, too, and a little sad. It's about people whose brilliance prevents them from leading fulfilling lives. There's this wonderful ballerina at the beginning, who's at the end of her career and wants a family. She's run her life so carefully that she doesn't understand that you can't arrange for a baby the same way as you can for a tour. Then there's Holmes himself, who has to stimulate his restless mind with cocaine when there's nothing to occupy it. Relationships are too unpredictable, so he shuns them. And then we have Ilse, who's the most tragic of all. She's stuck in a century in which her genius is only valuable because of her sex, which she's required to use to trap enemies of her state…'

'Close your ears, Destiny,' says Dad.

Destiny sniggers.

'Okay,' says Gemma, 'I'll definitely shut up now.'

And so she does, but with a sense that her work is done. David's hand is resting in her own now, and he seems entirely at ease. That conversation they haven't had yet – that they will have, sometime soon – needn't be an ordeal. On the banks of a vast stretch of water, or on top of a mountain, he's bound to see things objectively, isn't he?

For now, everyone in the tin can is listening to the music, and a sense of absorption lasts for the rest of the drive through those heathery uplands, all the way to Loch Ness.

Chapter Eleven

Perhaps this was the last house in Drumnadrochit, though there were a number scattered along the road heading west for which the same claim might have been made. Set high on the inside of a bend, its front door could only be reached by a steep flight of steps. The building was of genuine stone construction, not cladding. Jim guessed that Sherlock and Watson might have pedalled past it when it was new, had they existed. He'd walked past it himself on his way home from Victoria's mansion, the morning after the moon party, and now he remembered its flaking eight-paned sashes looking darkly at him on that bright day.

'What d'you think?' said Alan.

The Alvis was idling on the corner, its engine protesting with little squeaks and splutters. 'I think it's an old abandoned house,' said Jim. 'Let's go before a lorry comes around the bend and flattens us.'

Alan reversed a car's length and turned up the drive to the right of the house. It climbed almost as steeply as the steps, and Jim watched as the first floor at the front of the house became the ground floor behind. Alan parked and got out. By the time Jim had joined him, he was standing in front of a door in what must have been the garden wall, from which good-sized leaves of green paint were peeling to reveal grey planks dotted with black rot.

'Bolted the other side,' said Alan when he'd tried the latch.

'Pity,' said Jim. 'Shall we go then?'

Alan stood back and took in the wall's height. 'Give us a leg-up.'

Jim laughed. 'I'm not helping you break into someone's private property.'

'It's nobody's private property,' said Alan. 'That's the point.'

'The point of what?'

Alan gave him as severe a look as he could make with those milky eyes of his. 'Let's get in and I'll show you the fucking point, pal.'

They found a place where the earth was stacked high enough against the wall to make for an easy climb, then Jim turned his hands into a stirrup. Of course, he'd seen this done weeks ago at Urquhart Castle, and wasn't best pleased to be playing the part of Watson to Alan's Sherlock. He was sure Alan weighed quite a bit more than Mr Stephens, too, though he wasn't a burden for long. Seconds after he clambered over, the flaking door opened from the inside.

There were signs that there had once been a carefully managed garden here, under the feathery tops of the grasses and purple heads of thistle. An apple tree was already so heavy with miniature fruit that the ends of its limbs dipped beneath the undergrowth, like the tips of willow in water. Altogether, there must have been a good half acre here, bounded on three sides by the stone wall and on the fourth by the house itself. More distressed window frames showed on the low first floor, while on the ground a couple of black oblongs squinted at them through iron grills.

'Wait here a while,' said Alan.

He returned from the Alvis with a bundle under his arm: a hacksaw, a hammer, a chisel and an electric torch. 'You're not planning to do what I think you're planning to do,' said Jim. 'I'm telling you, I'll walk home.'

'Ah, don't be a big baby.' Alan knelt in front of one of the cellar windows. 'What are you afraid of?'

'Well, the police, for one thing.'

Alan rolled his eyes. 'Do me a favour. The police?' He stressed the first syllable. 'How would they know we're even here?'

'That idiotic car of yours is quite a big clue.'

Alan blew out his cheeks. 'And why would they give a shite? I told you, nobody owns the place. Now, wait another minute and I'll get us inside.'

It took more than a minute, but Jim soon found himself engrossed in what Alan was doing. There was a deftness to the way he sawed through all but one of the rusty bars that seemed worthy almost of admiration. Then the hammer and chisel were applied, loosening the last bar to make it into a hinge on which to turn the grill inward. Alan switched on the torch and peered inside.

'There's some kind of chest down there,' he told Jim. 'It's like they knew we were coming. Careful of the broken glass, though, eh?'

The chest turned out to be an old hardwood box, not a tea chest, so it easily supported their weight. From the floor, the windows showed bright as the moon on Victoria's TV set, making the rest of the cellar a black void. Then Alan's torch picked out the room's limits: the whitewashed walls, the stone flags, the steps set against the farther wall, leading to a door near the ceiling...

'Probably locked,' said Jim.

'Probably not,' said Alan.

He was right, and they passed into a room lit well by one of the windows that looked out onto the overgrown garden. Alan switched the torch off. 'Needs some work, eh?'

There was a big, old-fashioned tub sink, cracked and covered in a soot-like dust. No taps – Jim supposed that somewhere among that tangle of flora outside they would find an iron pump. All the cupboards were missing their doors. What had once been the pantry gaped at them, its empty shelves and ventilation grill grained black with the same dust that covered the sink. Alan led the way through another unlocked door to the front of the house. This was an upper room, of course, and Jim looked down from one of the eight-paned windows onto the bend in the road where they'd been just minutes before. Above the level of the roadside trees, he saw the pastures and purple heath extending as far as the ridge of woodland bordering the loch. There was a worrying degree of give in the floorboards under his feet. Something made a scuttling noise nearby, and he couldn't decide whether it was behind the skirting or above his head.

'Well, what do you think?' asked Alan.

'Fabulous,' said Jim, 'for a student of fungi.' Suddenly, he knew why they were here. 'You're thinking of buying, aren't you?'

Alan was examining part of the wall, his nose nearly touching it, as though it held some feature of special interest. 'Ay,' he said, almost blithely.

'What with?' Then Jim remembered his manners. 'If you don't mind me asking.'

'Not at all, pal.' He was looking even more minutely at a dark spot on the otherwise tea-coloured plaster. 'Sandra's old man's going to make us a loan. She talked to him about it when she was over there. It'll not be enough, but it's a start.'

Jim steeled himself to ask another impertinent question. 'So where will you get the rest?'

'Well—' Alan turned to face him, beaming like a gameshow host, holding out his hand, '—thank you for agreeing to see me today, Mr Outhwaite. May I say what a lovely shirt you're wearing there? Only the one button missing, I see. Now, I'd like to tell you about a once-in-a-lifetime opportunity...'

'Wait a minute—' Jim didn't take Alan's hand, '—are you asking *me* for money?'

The smile morphed into something so serious, it looked comic. 'You've got to use your imagination, Jamie. I'm not thinking about this as a place to live in. I'm thinking about a shop.'

Jim had prepared himself to hear this dump proposed as a place where Alan might try to live with his wife and bring up a baby, which was bad enough as ideas go. But this was worse.

'I thought you hated businessmen,' he said.

'Oh, I do,' said Alan. 'The big fucking bosses who ruin the lives of decent working people. Those bastards at the shipyards who laid off my old man. But this'll be us, Jamie.' He nodded at the door to the landing. 'Let's look at the rest of it, eh?'

It took time and effort to find which steps on the staircase would support their descent to the ground floor. There were two rooms down there, each lit by a sash window. Someone had started to knock through the wall between them, but had abandoned the attempt after a few swings of the sledgehammer. The small hole was covered by a spider's web.

'Can you not see it, Jamie?' said Alan.

He couldn't. 'What would you sell?'

'Everything.'

'Everything?'

'To do with what we do,' said Alan. 'Postcards and posters. Wee rubber plesiosaurs and ichthyosaurs for the wains. Books. They'd be by us, so they wouldn't be the kind of shite Stewart writes. It'll be you and me, so it'll be good.'

'But—' Jim wanted to yell it, '—we can't, Alan. There's no chance the university would permit it. We're publicly funded. We couldn't start anything commercial.'

Alan made a sound that was stranger than any Jim had heard him make before, even at his drunkest. A yowl, which rose from the back of his throat and reverberated around the little room. 'Jesus Christ,' he spat out when it was done, 'will you listen to yourself, for fuck's sake?'

It was a shock after all the charm. 'I don't know what you mean.'

Alan said nothing for a moment, and Jim felt the effort he was putting into controlling himself. 'There's not going to be any funding,' he said, quietly now. He ran a hand through his flop of blond hair, as though he could soothe his brains that way. 'It's over, pal. Kaput.'

'You know that's the case, do you?' It occurred to Jim that he might.

'It's always the same. Every fucking August.'

'So, you don't.'

Alan's body sagged and the light in his eye dimmed. There was no vibration in the air now. 'It stands to reason,' he said. 'We've got to look to the future.'

'Is that you talking,' said Jim, 'or Sandra?'

Alan was looking out the window at the road. He didn't answer Jim's question. 'It's okay for you,' he said. 'Douglas has seen you all right.'

Jim smiled. 'That bit of *ad hoc*? Hardly the future. And there's nothing to stop you finding some of that for yourself. There must be someone you can talk to at Glasgow.'

'You'd think so, wouldn't you?' He leant forward now, so that his forehead rested against a pane of glass. 'But it seems my face doesn't fit. And Douglas never thought of looking out for something for me, did he?'

'Did you ask him?'

Now Alan smiled, and it was morose. 'Oh ay, I asked all right. And when it was obvious there was nothing doing, I asked him about money. I'll be honest with you, pal, I made him the same offer I've just made you. "Wish I could help, old boy," he said, "but the farmhouse is mortgaged to the hilt, and I've no savings." That's when I thought about your new job. You'd have no problem getting a loan from the bank, would you?' Something of his recent enthusiasm resurfaced. 'You won't need much, and it'll be an investment.' The sunlight, filtered by grime, showed up the yellowish patina of his skin. 'We'll be partners. The three musketeers. Well, nearly...'

Jim spoke gently, but he hoped he sounded firm, too. 'I've told you, all I've been offered is some *ad hoc*. I doubt I'd succeed in getting a loan on the strength of that.' He didn't know, of course, but the idea that he might succeed terrified him. 'Sorry, Alan, but I'm afraid you're barking up the wrong tree.'

Alan turned away from the window and took in the fading room. 'So that's that.' It was a statement, not a question.

'Sorry,' Jim said again. Then, with another smile, 'Let's wait and see what the university decides, eh?'

'Ay,' said Alan, but the disappointment broke the single syllable before it could leave his throat. 'We'll do that, pal.'

Jim sat beside April at the kitchen table. She was stirring her coffee, though she hadn't put any sugar in it.

'He's better than he was,' she said, 'but still looks awful. Mr Wilder's close to deciding we're done here. He's got location scouts looking for places near London where we can pick up shots. I don't think he's happy about that, but he'd rather his leading man was fit and healthy. He's not a monster.'

'So, you're nearly finished?' A clammy heat crept across Jim's forehead.

'Well, up here at least.' She smiled. 'It's a funny kind of a vacation that depends on someone you like nearly killing themselves.' She put the spoon down on the tabletop and reached for his hand. Her hold looked light, but when he tried to move his fingers, he found them tightly gripped.

'I haven't been to London for years,' he told her. 'Not since I was doing my masters. I went with one of the lecturers to hear someone speak at the Royal Society. Took a while to get used to nobody saying "How do?".'

'You should go to New York one day,' she said. 'Experience some real discourtesy.'

'I'd like to.' Jim was responding to the first statement before he'd taken in the second. 'And to San Francisco, of course.'

She let go of his hand and picked up her mug. 'Oh, you should. You should see as much of the world as you can.' Then, 'Hey, you know where I'd really like to go?'

'Paris?' His mind was instantly in the bureau in Kendal where his passport lay. 'Rome?'

She shook her head. 'Been to Paris. Would love to go to Rome, but it's not what I was thinking. No, I'd like to go to India.'

He hadn't expected that. Now his mind was in a region of oppressive heat, extreme poverty and food far too spicy for an ordinary English gut to cope with... It was hard to think of somewhere he was less inclined to visit.

'Well,' he said when he'd given it some thought, 'I suppose I wouldn't mind seeing a tiger in the wild.'

'Before Bungalow Bill shoots them all, huh?'

'Or a gharial.' He was warming to the idea. 'That really would be something to see.'

She shook her head, and even as he described the rare, narrow-snouted crocodile to her, he could sense that she was withdrawing from him.

'I'm more interested in the people,' she said. 'Wouldn't you like to meet folk who see the world in a different way to you? Who live their lives by different values? There's so much we can learn by looking outside our own little TV-commercial lives, don't you think? I'm not talking about the rich Indians either, the ones who live like it's still the Raj out there. I'm talking about the ones who live the way they've always lived, down through the centuries.'

Jim wondered how well April would really cope without her morning coffee, her hot and cold running water, her flushing toilet. She had enough problems with Scotland's restricted trading hours and limited cuisine. But something else was niggling at him, too. He was remembering that hotchpotch of requisitioned articles in Victoria's mansion: the ebony idol, the burning incense, those mucky prints on the walls in the hallway… Since the night of the party, he'd learnt all about Victoria's trips to Goa, too, and of the spiritual life she'd found there that sounded much more to him like a carnal life. It really did seem to consist of little more than an attempt to sleep with as many men, in as many locations, for as sustained a period as was humanly possible.

'Of course,' April was saying, 'back home I've friends who've devoted their lives to Krishna. They seem happy – and not just happy, either. But I'd like to hear the message from company HQ, you know, rather than a branch office…?'

'You should talk to Douglas,' said Jim, suddenly inspired. 'He's been to India. A while ago, mind. Alan says he was working for Lord Mountbatten.'

'And what does Douglas say?'

'That he was looking for the Yeti.'

April's eyes grew bigger, and it was another sight worth seeing. 'Was he?'

Jim laughed. This was better – this was firmer ground. 'Well, yes and no. He was compiling a record of stories the locals tell about the hairy mountain men they believe they share the Himalayas with. That's what he's interested in: what people believe and why they believe it.'

Then he told her about the other creatures Douglas had gone in search of over the years. The Loch Ness Monster's cousin in Lago Maggiore on the Italian-Swiss border, who'd first appeared a year after Mr and Mrs Spicer's drive had been interrupted by an amphibian jaywalker. The ridiculous bat creature apparently terrorising the people of rural New Jersey. The Sasquatch, or Bigfoot, in British Columbia. And finally, back in Britain, those big cats blamed for killing cattle in any number of English counties over the past several decades.

'Well, that's not such a stretch, surely,' said April. 'People keep lions and such as pets in California. They've been known to escape. That's got to have happened here, too.'

'Perhaps,' said Jim, 'but Douglas's theory is that it's essentially a modern version of the old legend of the demon dog.'

'Like the Hound of the Baskervilles?'

Jim nodded. She was holding his hand again and her grip was as firm as it had been before. 'Yes, exactly like the Hound of the Baskervilles.'

Roger Carrick's office seemed an emanation of the man himself, like a shell is to a crab. It was perhaps fifteen feet by eighteen, but its high ceiling made Jim feel as though he were sitting in a perfect cube. Two tall windows looked out over the grey peaks of Aberdeen's skyline.

'Sorry to have kept you, James.' Carrick's accent was that refined Edinburgh thing that turned every sentence into a question. He was a small-framed man of 45, dressed in a charcoal suit and a black woven tie. His eyes and hair were also grey, and his fine features might have been hewn into existence with a hammer and chisel. Even his handshake was like stone. 'Did Mrs Crosby offer you tea?'

'She did, thank you,' said Jim, sitting again in his black-cushioned chair.

'Good, good.' Carrick crossed the room and sat behind a desk made from tubular metal and a slab of highly polished granite. It must have caused extraordinary difficulties for the porters who'd hauled it up the narrow staircase when Carrick was awarded this enviable office. 'So, how are things on the bonny banks of Loch Ness?'

'Well, I think we're doing some useful work,' said Jim. 'I was a little concerned when a Hollywood film crew arrived—'

'Oh, I heard about that. Billy Wilder, is it not? A fine filmmaker. Have you seen *Sunset Boulevard*?'

Jim shook his head. 'I've seen *Some Like It Hot*,' he said, to save Carrick the trouble of going through the whole catalogue.

'Ah, yes – the divine Marilyn! What a sad loss, eh?'

Jim tried to agree, but Carrick had already moved on.

'Now, I've some good news for you, my boy.' He paused to smile, then stopped smiling and spoke. This was what he did – spoke or smiled, never both. 'You know Daniel Macpherson?'

'The whale man,' said Jim.

'Ay, the whale man.' Smiled, stopped smiling, spoke. 'Well, he's succumbed to the brain drain, I'm sorry to say. Been offered a post at the Marine Institute in Newfoundland, with funding for a research project on the migration of baleens. I'm sad to see him go, of course, but it's a dream come true for the lad. However, it means I've more than a bit of *ad hoc* to offer you.'

Jim had to let that sink in. 'You're offering me Macpherson's job?'

Carrick laughed, stopped laughing, spoke. 'Not quite. It's more a question of moving people around, like pieces on a chessboard. Tom Percival will take on Macpherson's role, but that still leaves me shy a lecturer. That's where you come in, if it suits you.'

That made more sense, but it was still quite an offer. 'And this would start in October?'

'Ay.' Carrick paused. 'But there's something else, too, for which you would indeed be replacing Macpherson almost directly. He was about to start work on a behavioural study of killer whales in the Hebrides. I know you're no cetologist, but it's important work, and if you like, we could use it as the basis for a PhD. Fund it, too, which is perhaps more to the point. There's a bursary we could apply for, something bequeathed just recently. With that and the teaching, you'd be well set up. What do you say?'

Jim had nothing to say – not for the moment, at least. It was true he was no cetologist, and certainly no expert on killer whales. Macpherson, who had all the right credentials, hadn't been keen on them himself. 'There's no record of one attacking a human,' he'd told Jim, 'but I don't want to be the first statistic. Christ, they could eat you in two bites.'

Eventually, Jim said, 'It's a lot to take in, sir.'

'Well, sleep on it, if you must. But don't delay too long, eh?' His tone was growing brisker. 'If we can't rely on you, we'll need to look elsewhere quickly. But you know—' he paused, smiled, stopped smiling, spoke, '—it really shouldn't be a hard choice.'

Jim nodded, but knew his misgivings were showing in his face.

'What could possibly be worrying you, James?'

Jim knew the answer, but not how to give it. He felt as though he was being asked to commit an act of deep betrayal, and the feeling threatened to swallow him up as comprehensively as one of those killer whales might do, one day soon. 'I'm thinking of my colleagues,' he managed at last. 'I mean the Loch Ness Research Group. I do believe we're doing important work, and I'm reluctant to leave Douglas and Alan Stirling in the lurch. Alan's wife's expecting – had you heard?'

Carrick remained impassive. 'I hadn't, no.'

'Well, he's naturally anxious about the group's future. I'd hate to think that my withdrawal made things difficult. And if I'm honest—' he swallowed before he said it, '—I would miss the work. It's good, as I said, and I'd hoped to be there when we mapped the floor of the loch.'

Carrick's eyes dipped to the desk, and he seemed for a while to be picking out all the white grains in the otherwise black surface. 'You understand,' he said, 'that nothing lasts forever, don't you? You ought to be looking elsewhere, and so should Mr Stirling. Douglas certainly has been. To be frank with you—' he paused, pursed his lips, continued, '—I wouldn't rely on the group securing any more money beyond the end of next month.'

'Oh.' That was certainly unambiguous. 'So that's it?'

'I rather think so, James. But it was good while it lasted, eh? Fun and so on.'

What did he mean by that? Again, Jim's feelings must have shown in his face.

'Oh, come now,' said Carrick, 'you know your Bible, I'm sure.'

Then he adopted the tone he must have heard every Sunday as a boy, sitting with his family in the local kirk. '"When I was a child I spake as a child, I understood as a child, I thought as a child. But when I am become a man, I put away childish things."'

'Right,' said Jim. 'I see.'

'Have a think about what you're being offered.' He rose from the desk and crossed the rug to the door again. 'But don't leave it beyond a week, eh?' He opened the door. 'Then, when you're ready, you can come and sup with the adults at the big table.'

Chapter Twelve

Tessa made the announcement while they were eating breakfast.

'Autolycus has been gone nearly three weeks now. I think we've seen the last of him.'

Jim was surprised by his own response to this news. There was something strangely significant about the pine marten's disappearing just now. 'It isn't the first time,' he said. 'Are you sure it's permanent?'

'He's never been gone so long,' said Douglas. 'I'd hoped he wouldn't return when he left us last spring – that he'd found himself a mate and was busy making more *autolykoi*. But he was back after five days.'

'Perhaps he's in a poacher's snare,' said Sandra. 'Or perhaps a gillie's shot him.'

Tessa actually flinched. Her eyes, already enlarged by the thick lenses of her spectacles, seemed magnified further by incipient tears. Here was more proof that pregnancy wasn't causing Sandra to mellow.

Douglas threw a long arm around his wife's shoulders. 'There's no reason to think that, darling.'

Sandra soon made it clear that she wasn't picking on Tessa in particular. She spent the next hour making sure everyone was fully aware of her presence. She clacked the heels of her clogs against the flagstones, made crockery ring and cutlery clatter, turned up the radio so that the inane babble reached into every room of that fairly substantial house... Tony Blackburn's quasi-American accent was the last thing Jim wanted to hear now he was being denied the real thing. April was on an early call, out at some country house near Culloden, and had thought it best they didn't spend the night together.

'I'm going down to the van,' he announced at nine, putting aside the newspaper he'd been failing to read. 'Anyone else planning on taking the Land Rover?'

'Me,' Sandra said, and it seemed inevitable that she would. 'But I'll give you a lift.'

He slumped back in the chair and watched her putting things away, slamming cupboard doors to add extra percussion to Elvis Presley's song about a lad falling into bad company in the ghetto. The flamenco flounces of her yellow dress flared about her knees as she turned. She had piled up her hair again, and it seemed to add another foot to her height.

'Okay,' she said, wiping her hands on a tea towel. 'I'm ready. Are you?'

The flesh between Sandra's thumbs and forefingers turned white with the grip that she maintained on the steering wheel as she drove. She didn't say a word from leaving the kitchen to coming to a concussive stop beside the van at the quayside. An early mist lay over the water, turning the far shore into a ghost of itself.

'Thanks,' said Jim, opening the door.

'That it, then?' She turned off the engine.

His left leg was already swinging free. 'Sorry?'

'I was waiting for an explanation.'

'For what?' He let the leg dangle.

Was it pity in those kohl-rimmed eyes? 'You really have no idea what Alan's offering you, do you? For some reason, he's decided he'd much, much rather work with you than anyone else in the world. Now, me? I'm not so sure that's a good idea.' Pity had slid smoothly into contempt, and it suited her better. 'But Alan thinks you're the only one around here who takes him seriously.'

'That isn't fair,' said Jim.

She arched an eyebrow. 'You sure about that? Because I think he's got a point. Where did he go to school, d'you think? Eton, Fettes?'

She meant Douglas, of course, 'Stowe,' said Jim.

'That's in England, I'm guessing.'

Jim nodded.

'Well, there you go. No wonder he looks at the likes of Alan and me the way a hillwalker looks at the shite on his boots.'

'Now that really isn't fair—'

'Don't you tell me what's fair or not.' She said it as though it were Jim who'd been bandying insults. 'He's always treated Alan like a child.'

And so have you, Jim thought, *and so have I*. How could it be otherwise?

'Even if it were fair,' he said, 'what can I do about it?' Then he said something that would have come easier before his trip to Aberdeen. 'I told Alan what my position was—' a lot rode, he knew, on his choice of participles, '—that I didn't have any money.'

Sandra threw back her head and gasped. 'Jesus, Jamie, can you really not see the wood for the fucking trees? This isn't about money. It's about you and him, Jamie Outhwaite and Alan Stirling, working together. Money can be found. Really, it can – Alan had the gumption to ask me, and then I asked my old dad. It was as simple as that.'

And then Jim knew exactly where this was headed. The knowledge caused a flame to flicker, just below his solar plexus. 'You want me to ask April?'

Sandra looked him straight in the eye. 'Well, she cannae be short of a dollar, can she? Just look at her. Just listen to the way she speaks. Drips money, that one.'

He looked out past the *Cally* towards the southern shore, into the white haze. He knew April's father was some sort of businessman, but had no idea what he made, or how successful he was at doing it. Was April rich? He couldn't tell – couldn't judge by the quality of her clothes, or by her accent, because he didn't know what rich American women were meant to wear, or how they were meant to sound. 'Jesus, Sandra,' he said, 'I'm not asking her for money.'

'I'm not suggesting you do.' Her voice was calm now. This was a part that she'd clearly thought through. 'I'm suggesting you make her an offer. Tell her it's an investment, a way of maintaining a wee stake in this country she's had the privilege to be work-ing in for the past few months.'

Thought through, but still ludicrous. Was this the preg-nancy? Was the source of this lunacy the same as those cruel words that had been shot at Tessa over the breakfast table? 'I'm not going to do it,' he said. 'What would she think of me?'

'So she doesnae trust you?' Anger was seeping back into her voice. 'Is that what you're telling me? And here was me thinking you were more than just a holiday fling to her.'

The flame she'd lit inside him flared. He wanted to be indig-nant – the way she was behaving, she deserved indignation. But he couldn't give it her, because there was nothing he could say that didn't depend on a decision he hadn't yet made. *Sod you, Roger Carrick*, he thought. And *Sod you, Alan*. Even, *Sod you, Douglas*. They were all making demands of him that he couldn't fulfil...

'I know you, Jamie Outhwaite,' she said. 'What's she planning to do when they're finished here?'

He told her about the studio shoot near London.

'And after that?'

'I don't know.'

Her grip on the steering wheel was turning the flesh between thumb and forefinger white again. 'But you should,' she said. 'Really, you should. What do you think happened between her old man and her mother, down there in fucking Norfolk at the end of World War Two? Do you think he was happy not knowing what was going to happen next, or do you think he did something the fuck about it?'

He still couldn't answer her.

'You need to throw her a line, pal,' she said. Then she started the engine. 'Now, hop out. I've things to do.'

He dropped to the ground, and had hardly closed the door before the Land Rover's wheels span and it leapt away from him.

Most of the mist had cleared by noon, by which time Jim's mind had spread over the loch's surface the way it did when he was super-sensitive to any disruption. But today, not a single ripple appeared out of place. There was little to distract him beyond some new-feathered mallards, among which he caused a scuffle by throwing them most of his lunchtime sandwich. By four o'clock, he was happy to call it a day.

He drove the van to the Drumnadrochit Hotel. April had indicated that Mr Wilder was committed to going easy on his leading man for a while, and that they were likely to be done by early afternoon. As Jim parked on the front sweep of the hotel, next to one of the crew's Land Rovers, he felt that flame Sandra had lit burn again in his belly. *Sod her, too*, he thought. He was damned if he was going to talk to April about money.

She came down in her workaday jeans and white T-shirt, but with her hair already unravelled. The curls cascaded over her shoulders and chest. She reached up and kissed him lightly on the lips.

'I tried to call you,' she said. 'Do you mind if we take a rain check?'

He tried to keep the disappointment from his voice. Her eyelids drooped and she wasn't smiling. 'Tough day?'

'I'll say.' She did smile now, but it was that watery thing Jim had seen on the morning Mr Stephens had been taken to hospital. 'I just want to eat some aspirin and hit the hay.'

'You do that,' he said. 'We'll do something tomorrow.'

She frowned. 'Look, since you're here, why don't you buy me a Coke? That won't do any harm, will it?'

The bar wasn't open, so they left the hotel and crossed the bridge to the Post Office. The postmistress – the always-severe Muriel Mackey – was just shutting up, and tutted as she handed over the bottles. They drank sitting on the bench on the green, and Jim became aware again of a warmth in his gut that had nothing to do with the fizzing soda.

'So,' said April, 'what's up?'

Without intending to do so, he told her everything about the intrigue engulfing the Loch Ness Research Group. Except for the last details – he didn't tell her what Sandra had said to him in the Land Rover.

'You mean, all this could be over?'

He thought at first that she meant the moment they were in, with the afternoon air raising goose pimples on her bare arms, and rooks calling from the tops of the beeches beyond the crescent of pebble-dashed cottages. 'Depends what you mean by all,' he said when he knew better.

'The monster-hunting, the farmhouse, you and Alan, and Douglas and the girls...'

He let warm Coke foam on his tongue and in his throat. 'Nothing lasts forever.'

'Will you take the teaching job?'

He shrugged. 'Don't know.'

April tipped the last drops of Coke into her mouth. 'Okay,' she said, dropping the bottle in the bin beside the bench. 'I'm done. You sure you don't mind me postponing our date?'

'Really, it's fine.' But then, when she got up, he took hold of her arm. 'You do know I don't have to do any of this, don't you?'

She sat down again. 'Any of what?'

He was trembling – why was he trembling? – and that fire inside him was blazing now. 'I don't have go to Aberdeen, or somehow scrape some money together to go in with Alan. I don't even have to stay in Scotland. I'm not Scottish. I can go anywhere I like.'

'Jim, can we talk about this some other time?' For the first time since they'd met in the lobby, he saw pain in her face as well as weariness. 'I'm really not fit to think about anything except getting rid of this headache.'

'Of course,' he said. It was a lot to take in, he knew. They could pick this up tomorrow, and something would be decided then. And it would be *good*...

But as they walked back to the hotel, she talked anyway.

'Listen, Jim, there's something you've got to understand about this life I lead.'

Because they were walking side by side, holding hands, he couldn't see her eyes. 'Go on.'

'There's nothing stable about it,' she told him. 'This is one hell of a long shoot, but on the whole they take up about two months, and then I'm on to the next thing. I'm a vagabond, Jim. I make friends along the way, but I often don't see them again. Now, listen—' she stopped a few yards short of the hotel door and stepped in front of him, looking up into his eyes, '—what we've got is good, and it can stay good, even when it's over. You understand what I'm saying?'

No, he didn't understand a word of it. 'I think so,' he said.

She reached up and kissed him, then rocked back on her heels and gave him a questioning look. 'That wasn't right, was it?' She kissed him again, and this time he responded. They kissed for a long time.

'Okay,' she said, dropping back again. 'Now I've got an appointment with a couple of aspirin and my pillow.' But she had another thought before she moved. 'I ought to be finished early again tomorrow. Why don't you pick me up at five and we can drive someplace? Maybe eat something terrible in a pub. What do you say?'

'Sounds perfect.'

He watched her disappear into the hotel. Then he poured the last of his Coke out on the verge and chucked the bottle on the passenger seat of the van. He was reversing when he noticed the second Land Rover, parked on the sweep behind him. Even with it inverted, he recognised the plate. Was Sandra in the hotel? Part of him wanted to go in and find out. But the other part – and by far the more persuasive – wanted to get as far away from the hotel as it was possible to get.

No fire now, just numbness.

On the walk from Campbell Pier to the farmhouse, he tried to focus on things outside himself. A tussle between two hooded crows over the remains of a wood pigeon, a brown hare running full pelt across a meadow, a mistle thrush singing from the top branches of an elm. At one point, he emerged from a portion of road that the hedgerows had almost turned into a tunnel and was surprised by a skirmish of swallows, swooping low for the midges that were beginning to gather now like the mist in the morning.

But try as he might, his mind kept returning to the bar of the Drum. He kept sifting the overwhelmingly masculine crowd that was always there, picking out likely candidates. There was that big Australian lug, for a start – the electrician who was always laughing at him, and only half concealing it. He had a skilled-workman manliness about him that Jim couldn't hope to compete against, and the same thing could be said for about half the rest of the crew, too.

And then, of course, there was Mr Stephens.

An artist, not an artisan, on the cusp of becoming a new movie star. How stupid of Jim to fail to see that his weaknesses were actually strengths. His self-inflicted ordeal only made him a sort of Lord Byron, or Brian Jones of the Rolling Stones… What worthier subject could there be for April's sympathy? What more deserving recipient of the kind of comfort that was the cure-all of the age, if you believed what you read in the newspapers – which everyone did?

But it was worse than that, if you believed the newspapers. Particular people weren't the point, were they? Jim couldn't help but conjure up images from the moon party of slow-writhing limbs, and of open mouths and rounded, white flesh. It was April's friend, Victoria, who provided the model, wasn't it? Sex with anyone, at any time, in any place…

Neither the Land Rover nor the Alvis were parked in their places outside the farmhouse. But as Jim passed the kitchen door, intent on making it upstairs and into his room, he heard Douglas call to him from the kitchen. Jim looked in at the door, but didn't enter.

'I've just been on the phone with Roger Carrick.' Douglas was sitting at the head of the table, sliced onion and marrow already heaped on the chopping board before him. 'He's wondering why you haven't called.'

Jim was instantly filled with rage. 'He gave me a week,' he spluttered. 'I've still got a day.'

There was a neat snick as the knife cut through the potato on the board. 'What did you need a week for?'

'I think you know.'

Douglas seemed to be preparing enough food for an army. But then, there was no Autolycus to steal any of it now. 'It's quite an offer he's made you.'

Jim shrugged. 'There are other things I need to think about. And other people.'

'You mean April?'

More fury flared in him. 'No, I don't mean April. I mean Alan – what's going to happen to him? With a baby on the way, too.'

Douglas frowned minimally. His aura of calm threatened to make the whole exchange a reasonable one, throwing sand onto Jim's fire. 'What's your worry about Alan?'

Jim moved to the other end of the table and sat down. 'That you didn't find him a job when you found me one.'

The downturned smile made an appearance now. 'Well, I didn't go looking for a job for anyone. One presented itself, and it happened to be in marine biology.'

'So, you didn't ring Roger Carrick and ask if there was anything going?'

'No.' He decimated a potato, and moved on to another. 'But after Roger contacted me, I did give George Loomis a call. He told me there was nothing equivalent in geology.'

'Nothing equivalent,' Jim said. 'Then there was something.'

Douglas got up and carried the loaded chopping board to the range. 'You have to understand,' he said, placing the board between the hotplates and bending down to rummage in a floor cabinet, making the pots and pans clang, 'that Alan's a lot to take on. We love him, of course, and in some ways, he's flourished here. But he has his—' he paused in his rummaging to fish for a word instead, '—he has his eccentricities, doesn't he? You must see that.'

'So, it's Loomis who's the snob.'

That wouldn't be a surprise. Loomis was even worse than Carrick: a would-be Highland laird, who wore three-piece tweed suits and smoked a briar pipe. He'd been known to wear a cape in the winter.

'That's unfair.' Douglas unbent himself, bringing a heavy-bottomed casserole dish up with him. 'He's old fashioned and likes to run a tight ship. Some professors prefer their departments to have a balance of insubordinate types and those who'll toe the line, but Loomis isn't one of them.'

'You mean he wants drones?'

Douglas sighed. It was the nearest Jim had ever heard to an expression of impatience from him. 'No, that's not what I mean.' He pared off a yellow hunk from the butter dish and dropped it into the casserole. 'I mean he wants men who can master themselves. Thinkers, but judicious ones. People with a little self-discipline. I think that's fair enough, don't you?'

Jim supposed it was. 'And what are you going to do?'

'What do you mean?' He was adding the onions to the spitting pot.

'When the group's finished. When we're all done here.'

Douglas placed his hands on the back of the chair he'd been sitting in. 'I'm going to put this place in mothballs for a while. Tessa and I will go travelling. Funnily enough, I've been invited to California.'

Jim didn't know why that was funny. 'Why there?'

'Oh, I've been invited by some people interested in cryptozoology.'

It was a horrible word – one that had hardly been spoken within these walls in all the years Jim had lived here.

'I've told you about my days in Canada, recording stories of Sasquatch sightings. Well, now it seems the old chap has removed himself to the West Coast of the United States.'

'And meanwhile,' said Jim, 'Alan will be on the dole, or forced to do something that makes a nonsense of his education.'

Douglas's eyebrows converged a very little more. 'Whatever makes you say that? Hasn't he told you his plans?'

'Of course,' said Jim, and he almost hated Douglas now. How could he be so obtuse? 'I know he went to you first. I've told him I can't help either.'

Douglas was at the range again, adding the other vegetables to the pot. 'Well, I did have to decline, but it didn't sound like a bad plan to me. And it might be a way of keeping the research going.'

Jim couldn't believe what he was hearing. 'But they can't afford to do it,' he said. 'Not without another investor.'

'Oh—' Douglas was pouring water from the kettle, making a great cloud of steam rise over the range, '—they haven't told you?'

'Told me what?'

'Pete Leith's going in with them. A sleeping partner, I understand, since he already has a lot on his plate. He has no grounding in science either, of course, but he does have some business sense. I think it ought to work out rather well, don't you?'

It was strange, but Jim's awkward encounter with Douglas in the kitchen made him feel more detached from his other problems. Lying on his bed, he was able to concede that there were other ways of looking at things.

First, he would accept Carrick's job. If circumstances changed, he could hand in his notice and be a free man again in a matter of weeks. Some bridges might be burnt, but nothing that couldn't be repaired in time.

Next, he'd go on his date with April and explain things properly to her. The storm of jealously had passed, and he could see more clearly now. April was not Victoria. He hadn't once seen her making eyes at anyone else, other than perhaps at Douglas that time in the Drum, which really didn't count. She was too intelligent, too much her own woman, to play stupid games of that sort. She'd picked Jim, hadn't she? It hadn't been the other way around. Whatever he represented – which wasn't what those workmen represented, or even Mr Stephens – was the thing she had decided she wanted. And tomorrow night, he'd tell her the truth about how he felt. Despite the short time they'd had together, he knew that he loved her. Wasn't just *in* love with her – he loved her, plain and simple. So much so, that, just as her mother had done with her father, he was willing to go wherever she went. Uproot himself, if he could be said to have any roots, and plant himself on the other side of the world if necessary. And if she were determined to be an itinerant, he would roll wherever she did, too…

And now he wasn't detached any more. He was excited about what lay in the future.

A brisk voice on the other end of the phone line ran through the number Jim had just dialled. He hadn't expected to be talking to the man of the house straight away.

'Hello, Professor Carrick,' he said. 'It's James Outhwaite.'

'Ah.' A world of mockery was condensed into that one exclamative. 'Douglas caught you, did he? You're elusive, my lad. So, have you an answer for me?'

Jim did, and gave it.

'Splendid. Now, we could blather over details on the telephone, but I'm expecting the dinner gong to sound at any moment. Tell you what, why don't you join us here tomorrow night? Mrs Carrick's a tremendous cook, and the boys are still home for the long vacation. They'll quiz you about the monster – you'll enjoy that. Then we can retire for whisky and cigars and talk like men. Bring a sponge bag – you'll not want to drive back all the way to the wilds at that hour. Now, what do you say?'

It sounded horrendous, and Jim was glad of his perfect excuse. But then, when he tried to make it, the words wouldn't come.

'I cannot hear you, James,' said Carrick. 'Are you still there?'

'I am, Professor,' he said, and then a lie came easily enough. 'I'm just looking in my diary.'

'You have a busy social calendar, Mr Outhwaite?'

'No.' He said it without thinking. 'I mean, sometimes I… have engagements.'

He was feeling now the full weight of the inevitable rejection that lay ahead of him. In truth, April hadn't left any room for doubt. In fact, she'd been at pains to make herself as clearly understood as possible. She'd fixed on an end point to their love affair, and that meant it was already over. Nothing he said on their date would change that. At best, he risked embarrassment; at worst, humiliation. Whatever Roger Carrick had to offer was better than that…

'Yes,' Jim said. 'I'm free tomorrow night. I'd be very happy to join you for dinner.'

'All right then.' More briskly than ever. 'Now, write down this address.'

He grabbed a biro from the jam jar on the table and did as his new boss told him. His hand didn't stop shaking the entire time.

Inverness-shire, 2014 (I)

We've come across this situation before, Gemma thinks. *There's a lake, and there's a castle, and there's a swan that isn't really a swan...*

She's trying to see it through Billy Wilder's eyes. Where exactly would he have been standing while dishing out those infuriatingly precise instructions to cast and crew? Had she thought to bring her laptop, she might have frozen the DVD on an appropriate image, and tried to match it to frameless reality.

Urquhart Castle seems even less substantial than in the film. Its weathered walls support nothing, and there's no way of knowing, without being told, how each roofless room had differed in its function from another. Its lack of substance means that the loch dominates, a grey and level slab stretching away into mist in three directions.

'Well, this brings back a whole heap of memories.'

April is also looking out on the waters, shielding her eyes. It's as overcast as when they walked together by the Thames, but the wind is more blustery. It's stinging Gemma's eyes, too. Their fellow tourists are wrapped in bright cagoules, or some more serious style of waterproof. One woman leans on a couple of those telescoping walking sticks that turn hikers into quadrupeds, looking as though a sudden gust will topple her over. The breeze continually lifts and parts April's hair, showing lines of pink scalp beneath the snowy whiteness. It sounds in the gaps of the surrounding monuments, too, like breath blown over bottle tops.

'Is this the wall Robert Stephens looks over in the movie?' Gemma asks.

April considers it for a moment. 'Could be,' she says. 'There was some trouble shooting that scene, I recall. On the first day, a couple of locals got curious and came to have a look. One was in a boat, and another—' she's pointing inland, towards the wooded slopes, '—was up there a-ways.'

She reaches out and touches the wall's belichened surface with the tips of her fingers. Gemma is reminded of the time she went to see the Rollright Stones in Oxfordshire, with a university friend going through a neo-pagan phase. The friend had touched those stones in much the same reverent way April touches these ones now.

April laughs. 'You know about Mr Wilder's joke about the bats and Christopher Lee?'

'Yes,' says Gemma. 'It's in Lee's memoirs.'

There's a similar story about Stanley Holloway, and she wonders if April knows that one, too. While standing in the graveyard of some English church masquerading as Scottish, the director had subjected the old trooper – playing a gravedigger, in a nod to his role in Olivier's *Hamlet*, but famous at the time for his performance in *My Fair Lady* – to a rendition of 'I'm getting *buried* in the morning'.

'It was much more deserted back then,' April says. 'No tourists at all, no visitors' centre, no little movies about Saint Columba and whatnot. Honestly, the only people I met were locals.'

'Historic Scotland and the Tourist Board have worked tirelessly to change all that.'

April nods. 'Good for them, I guess.'

She turns towards the interior and her eyes relax. She's echoed their colour again, in a muted way, with the blue petals printed on her thin cotton blouse and the milky stones in her silver necklace. Moonstones, Gemma thinks.

'I liked how it was,' April tells her. 'I've mostly lived in cities – San Francisco, and London, and Los Angeles. I went to parks when I was a kid, and in England I visited my mum's folks in East Anglia.' She really does say 'mum' instead of 'mom', the English way. 'That's a pretty desolate part of the world, you know? Awfully flat. I used to swim in the North Sea...' She remembers something then that makes her laugh. 'Oh, would you believe I tried to swim in the loch?'

'Loch Ness?' Gemma's blood rebels at the idea.

'Yep. The North Sea was no picnic, but I'd done it, so I had a false sense of what I was able to endure. I didn't last more than a couple of minutes out *there*.'

She's gesturing at the water, laughing again. But there's something qualified about the laughter, and when she's finished, Gemma thinks she detects something rueful in the corners of her smile. 'I got to commune a little with the place when I was here,' she says. 'Perhaps I should find a forest to stand in for a while before I leave again.'

Gemma nods. She can't shift the mental image of April swimming in the loch. *There's a swan*, she thinks, *that isn't really a swan…*

There's no avoiding the visitors' centre. It's set beneath the car park like a nuclear bunker, or a Bond-villain lair, and like everywhere else that's unavoidable in Scotland, is a shrine to all things sellably Scottish. Tins of shortbread and fudge, bottles of beer and whisky, calendars and jigsaw puzzles. About half of everything available carries an image on its label of a certain serpentine water beast.

Once through this resistible grotto, it's a twenty-minute walk to April's rented cottage. The wooded slope is to their left, rising almost to the level of clouds, while the drop to their right gives them a comprehensive view of Urquhart Bay. A couple of motorboats cut white lines across the loch's dark surface. They chat about nothing – the toils of travelling north by car compared with those of travelling by plane – and when approaching April's cottage, Gemma suggests grabbing a coffee at a nearby pub.

'I can give you better myself,' says April. 'That's one thing I've made sure of this time.'

The cottage is tiny but well furnished, in much the same creature-comforts style as the lodge where the MacDonalds and Dr Kitch are staying. Gemma perches on the edge of a floral sofa while April is busy in the kitchenette.

'I didn't hear anything about Colin and Bob in the States,' she tells Gemma, spooning grounds into a cafetière. 'They had no kind of profile there, which is a tragedy, considering how talented they were. But I saw Bob one more time. I was visiting friends in London and we went to see the Royal Shakespeare Company perform *Henry IV Part One*. I was taken backstage afterwards, and Bob did a good job of pretending to remember who I was.'

'I'm sure he did remember.'

It's the perfect cue for Gemma to press April for corroboration on that story she has already fully imagined. The one about the love affair between the lonely lothario of the National Theatre and Billy Wilder's stunning Californian continuity girl, set against a backdrop of purple mountains and running deer...

But April has already moved on. 'Anyhow,' she says, filling the kettle, 'I honestly didn't know about Colin till I asked about him then. Leukaemia, right?'

Gemma nods.

'You know, Gene Hackman always reminded me of him. Gene's taller, but they're similar types of actor, I think, and similarly lovely men.'

She's leaning against the oven, fingers tucked in her jeans pockets, pensive again.

'I didn't hear about Bob till he'd been gone a couple of years. Well, it wasn't a surprise – he looked terrible that time I saw him in his dressing room. I mean, onstage he'd been playing Falstaff, so that was to be expected. But even with the belly off, and without the white wig, he looked bad. Hardly the same person, in fact.'

'He did have a late career surge,' Gemma says. 'Falstaff, and then King Lear. The critics loved him. He had a liver transplant after that, but it wasn't enough to save him.'

April makes a downturned smile. 'I just wish he'd looked happier that last time.'

She seems pretty melancholy herself. In London, she'd shown no sign that she was capable of anything other than extreme ebullience. She'd seemed wedded to the moment, too, despite the reminiscences.

'Not everyone's gone,' Gemma tells her, trying to change the tone. 'I'm hopeful of interviewing Christopher Lee at the BFI in

October. He's frail, by all accounts, but still working at 92. Tim Burton won't make a film without him.'

'Good ol' Christopher,' says April, and the smile blazes again. 'What a gentleman.'

'I understand Geneviève Page is hale and hearty, too,' Gemma adds.

'Oh, I bet she's a beautiful old lady. My God, she was a doll.'

'And we found no end of crew when we went looking. All retired now, but mostly fit. I'm sure if you stick around for the London premiere, you'll see some faces you recognise...'

April insists on driving Gemma back to the lodge in her little hire car. By now, the cloud has lifted and the sun turns the roadside trees and the tops of the hills into an extraordinary, vibrant green. 'I'm pretty sure we're close to where my friend Victoria had a house,' April tells her as they approach the final turning. 'Where we watched the moon landing.'

'The moon landing?' Gemma says, 'Of course, that was then. What a fucking idiot.' She collects herself. 'Sorry, April – I mean me, not you. I'm so obsessed with that film of yours, I forget other things were happening in 1969, too. Like Vietnam, and the Troubles, and the clocks not changing...'

'The clocks not changing?'

Gemma explains that between 1968 and 1971, there was no GMT. British Summer Time was retained throughout the year, renamed British Standard Time. 'Still BST, you see.'

'Well, that totally passed me by,' says April. 'Or maybe I knew it and forgot.'

There's a warmth to their goodbye hugs that Gemma's glad about. Their friendship seems more than professional now.

The Vectra isn't parked outside the lodge, which means Mum and Dad succeeded in getting Destiny up and out to see the Cairngorms' reindeer herd. She finds David lying on the sofa, momentarily irradiated by orange light emitted by the TV. She pushes his feet aside and joins him.

'How long have they been gone?'

'Couple of hours.' His eyes stay on the screen.

Bruce Willis is crouching behind a truck, watching the wreckage settle from the explosion he's just caused. Sweat beads on his razor-cut scalp and trickles into his wrinkles.

'What's this?' she asks, '*Die Hard 48?*'

'Something like that.'

Gemma feels fidgety, despite having just sat down. She's always restless in David's company now, and knows full well the reason why. He hasn't said anything to her, and his moods haven't grown less erratic. She hasn't said anything either, but since he's so changeable, she no longer feels she can judge when's a good time.

'So,' she says, 'what're we going to do?'

He glances at her, and for a moment she fears she's been misinterpreted, and that he thinks she's about to tell him all. But then he reaches to the side table and tosses her a leaflet from the wad the landlord has left there. On the front is a picture of a motorboat skimming sun-stippled water. Above it, a yellow banner entreats the reader to '*DISCOVER LOCH NESS with DISCOVERY TOURS*'. Overleaf are the predictable shots of all-white families in pristine shirtsleeves and T-shirts, pointing off camera and laughing under suspiciously Mediterranean-looking skies. '*See the wonders of the Great Glen from a unique perspective,*' Gemma reads. '*Our experienced guides will help you explore this beautiful and historic inland Loch from the best vantage possible.*'

'This really what you want to do?' Gemma asks him.

He shrugs. 'Well, we're here, aren't we?'

Bruce is leaping into the open now, a bazooka on his shoulder. He's facing down a diving helicopter, like a gunfighter confronting the black-hatted baddie in an old Western.

Gemma shakes her head. 'Okay, Dr Kitch, let's go cruising.'

They wait by the Tourist Information Centre in Drumnadrochit for the minibus that will take them to the boat. The centre is a single-storey structure that's mostly shingle roof, standing near the entrance to a large municipal car park. Over the road, there's another gift shop baited with stuffed Nessies and tins of shortbread with shaggy cattle and thistles on the lid. Some distance away, a group of Euro-retirees in dayglow casual wear are standing by the door of a big coach with smoked windows, speaking rapidly in what Gemma takes to be German. The invisible coach driver is apparently in no hurry to admit them.

'Let's see the tickets again,' she says.

David shows her the screen of his Android. The plain e-ticket says 14.30, and it's 28 past now.

'Do you think they've forgotten us?'

David laughs.

Precisely a minute later, a white minibus turns off the road and parks some twenty yards away from them. The driver is a barely moving splash of grey behind the windshield's glaze. He turns off the engine, but doesn't get out. Gemma can see a white hand gripping the two o'clock position on the steering wheel. 'That's got to be us, hasn't it?'

'I guess.'

But neither of them attempts to find out. It's something that continues to confuse Gemma about David: the way his Yankee brusqueness hides a soul as retiring and undemonstrative as any Brit's.

'I'll ask,' she says, and wanders over.

Seen more closely, through the passenger window, the driver becomes a little more defined. There is a peaked cap that's a bit Captain Birdseye, a bit Bob Dylan, a scrub of white beard, two pin-pricks of light where the eyes should be. Then the driver's door creaks open and the apparition vanishes. A moment later, it appears in full, from around the front of the minibus.

'Are you Discovery Tours?' Gemma asks.

He nods. 'Let's give it a minute,' he says, 'and I'll decide if it's worth our while.'

He isn't Scottish – is it a Yorkshire accent she can detect?

'I usually charge extra for a private tour,' he adds, and Gemma's not sure if it's a joke.

His cap's nautical air is echoed in the rest of his outfit. He's wearing white canvas trousers and a striped jersey, with a knotted red bandana at his throat. An expensive-looking yellow waterproof hangs a little too loosely from his shoulders.

David ambles over now, hands deep in the pockets of his somewhat cheaper waterproof. 'We set to go?'

'He's waiting to see if anyone else turns up,' says Gemma. Then to the guide, 'That's right, isn't it?'

'Ay,' he says. 'I'm used to a few more passengers.'

Something changes in David's face. His eyes widen behind the lenses, and Gemma's not sure if it's a display of surprise or relief. He's going weird again. 'Oh, is that really a problem?'

The guide's grey whiskers knit over his lips. Then he tugs the handle at the side of the minibus and the big door slides open. 'Mind the crush,' he tells them.

Gemma and David strap themselves in near the front while their guide starts the engine. He turns left out of the car park, going the way he came. At the top of the road, over the bridge, he takes the right and heads for Inverness. To their left is what looks like a Victorian hotel, with an unsympathetic Seventies annex stuck to one side of it. A painted sign reads: *Loch Ness Experience & Museum, Headquarters of the Loch Ness Research Group*. This is where the festival has been screening documentaries about Loch Ness Monster sightings, made by locals. She feels a pang of guilt that she hasn't seen anything yet.

They don't go far before the driver takes another right, sending the minibus through a screen of leaves and onto a narrow, descending lane. Both the sides and the roof are thrashed by branches, so that it seems like they're delving into a jungle interior, rather than approaching a temperate lake. When the gradient settles, they emerge onto a modest landing, with a little concrete lock-up at one end and an old motorboat moored to the embankment at the other. Black Roman letters on the vessel's white side proclaim its name: *CALEDONIAN*.

Their taciturn guide becomes suddenly garrulous as they step out of the van. 'One foot in front of the other's the usual way, young man,' he says as they climb aboard the boat. 'No, don't hold onto anyone else, especially not the young lady. Not unless you both want to swim in the loch, which I don't recommend. Colder than a polar bear's beard in there…'

Of course, it's patter, the sort of thing he will have said scores of times before, perhaps hundreds. But it's amusing enough, and Gemma begins to believe this might be fun. She sits beside David on the cushioned bench that's fixed to the middle of the deck, and nudges him with her elbow. 'How about that?' she says as their guide casts off, 'We really are getting the private tour.'

David gives her a tight smile. She almost reminds him that this was his idea.

'I'll take us out to the middle,' the guide declaims over the rattle of the boat's diesel engine. He's got his back to them now, sitting in a black upholstered chair that swivels on a hydraulic steel leg and looks vaguely ergonomic. 'Then I'll shut down the engine and deliver today's lecture. Pay attention, there'll be a test. Detention and demerits if you don't get ten out of ten.'

The boat breaks away from the quayside and, when they have picked up speed, the engine's rattle turns to a high-pitched hum. The ride is smooth, the boat cutting elegant curves of white spume on either side. Gemma feels a cold tingle of spray on her arms, then David grips her hand tight. More uncharacteristic behaviour – is it possible he's nervous of water?

The boat begins to rattle again as it slows, and then their guide resumes his act.

'Loch Ness is the largest lake by volume in the British Isles,' he tells them. 'It owes its existence to the tectonic fault line along which it lies, and to glacial erosion. It is the second deepest loch after Loch Morar, its deepest point falling to 226 metres.' Here he points to a little monitor stuck to the cabin ceiling near the windscreen, with a curved white line on its screen and a current figure of 150. 'Loch Ness contains more fresh water than all the lakes in England and Wales combined. It stretches through the Great Glen from Loch Oich, via the River Oich and the Caledonian Canal, to Loch Dochfour, via the Bona Narrows…'

Gemma tries to take in her surroundings without the context

she's being offered. From this low perspective, she's reminded of when she would lie on the living-room floor at Bow as a kid, looking up at armchairs and sofas that were suddenly tower blocks. Here, it's like she's at the bottom of a trench, scooped out of the land by some Titan who has one foot in Norway and the other in – where? Northern Ireland, perhaps. The banks of the loch are nearly equidistant now, and similarly hazy. Looking towards Fort William, the valley of middle- and far-distant mountains arranges itself into a kind of View-Master stereograph. It's clear that the weather's worse over there, the farther peaks blunted by low cloud and diagonal brushstrokes signifying real rain. Gemma begins to wish she'd brought her waterproof, too…

The guide shuts off the engine and the silence breaks into her thoughts.

'We've a good view of the most important locations here,' he tells them. 'We've come from Urquhart Bay, and that over there—' he's leaning out of the cabin, pointing towards a stony break in the bankside trees, '—is Urquhart Castle.' Of course, Gemma can see that now. 'Across the loch is Foyer, and up that way—' he's pointing again, the opposite way to Fort Augustus, '—is Lochend. This triangle is the area where, more than anywhere else, there have been recorded sightings of the monster…'

'The monster?' David blurts it out. He doesn't sound surprised so much as disgusted. 'The *Loch Ness* Monster?'

Gemma squeezes his hand. *Be nice*, she tries to tell him.

The guide's face remains implacable. 'That's what I'll be talking about for the next forty minutes, young man. If you were expecting the Pyramids of Giza, I'm afraid you picked the wrong continent.'

Gemma squeezes again. 'Sounds interesting, doesn't it?' she says.

'If it helps,' the guide adds, 'I'll tell you for free that no such thing exists.' He cracks a smile that only shows on his lips. 'I'm in a better position than most to pronounce on the matter, too. Took my doctorate in marine biology, studying populations of orca – not monsters, you may say, but that depends on whether you're a seal – and then worked for over thirty years as a research fellow and lecturer in biology at the University of Aberdeen. On top of that, I've made a special study of Loch Ness phenomena for over forty years, on and off, and have published on the subject.'

He reaches to the base of his chair and picks up a hardback book, which he tosses onto the bench. Then he tosses a black plastic ring binder after it. David picks up the book. It has a sober brown dust jacket and an emblem on the spine that Gemma thinks belongs to a small academic imprint. She picks up the binder. On the white card fixed to the front cover, the title is printed in Arial: 'DIS-COVERY EXPLORATIONS – A HISTORY IN PICTURES.' It's filled with printouts of digitised copies of old photos, stuffed in plastic wallets. There are some sheets stuck with real, chemically developed photos, too. Mostly, they're better than amateur, taken with a proper lens, with a few Polaroids scattered among them. Broken-cornered black-and-white shots give way after a few pages to bright colour. Few have faded, so it's clear they've not been exposed to much light. The loch features in almost every one of them, if not centrally, then as a looming photobomber, peeping over the shoulders of the men and women smiling for the photographer. There's an old model of van that appears from time to time, with a movie camera attached to its roof. An ancient Land Rover makes a couple of appearances, too, and a white car of a type Gemma doesn't recognise. Each entry is labelled with a date and place name in a neat hand. 'Dores, 12-09-1967', 'Nr Abriachan, 4-11-1968', 'Above Lenie, 14-05-1969'...

'You'll recognise me there if you squint,' the guide tells her.

There's a tall man with shaggy salt-and-pepper hair, a blond lad in a T-shirt that doesn't quite reach the waistband of his jeans and a skinny boy with a dark beard, in a denim shirt with the sleeves rolled up... In one of the pictures, this last one is standing on the roof of the van – it's a colour shot, so she sees the van is green – operating the camera.

'That's you making movies?' she says.

He nods. 'A young god, eh?'

In the next picture, a couple of women are standing by a camp stove. A twentysomething hippy in a long purple dress, with toppling heaps of red hair, and an older woman whose face is hidden by her tortoiseshell frames, a dark bob and the mug she's holding to her lips.

'So how do you know there isn't a Loch Ness Monster?' Gemma asks.

'Your young man can tell you when he's finished that book,' he says. 'If he's not done by the end of the tour, he can pick it up in any good bookshop. Well, any that sells remainders.'

David doesn't raise his eyes from the page he's on. He had opened the book at the beginning, so now it really seems as though he intends reading it from cover to cover.

'In the end, it's an easy calculation,' the guide says. 'There simply isn't enough of anything alive in there to support a creature of the size people report having seen. There's only about twenty tonnes of fish, which is only enough to feed about two tonnes of something bigger. I'll show you the video I've made about it in a minute.' He taps the bigger monitor that's fixed to the cabin ceiling, a little way from the depth gauge. 'Moving pictures of the infant me this time, I'm afraid.'

There's a swan that isn't really a swan, Gemma thinks. 'Or in this case,' she says, 'a monster that isn't really a monster.'

'I beg your pardon, miss?'

She shuts the folder and puts it down on the bench. 'Do you mind if I ask you a couple of questions?'

Chapter Thirteen

'Do you mind if I ask you a couple of questions?'

Jim was taken aback by her manner of speaking, more than by what she said. 'Well, I haven't stopped you so far, have I, miss?' It was time they headed for Urquhart Castle, so he started up the engine again. 'Usually, I ask if there are any questions at the end,' he added, 'and the kids ask me how many times I've seen Nessie, even though I've told them ten times that she doesn't exist. The little imps, eh? But be my guest, fire away.'

She didn't speak at once, and after he'd got the *Cally* going again, he looked back and saw a half-smile on her face. Clearly, there was a different conversation going on in her head, and she needed to finish it before she could start another. Her Yank boyfriend, or husband – they weren't wearing wedding rings, so he presumed it was the former – seemed entirely engrossed in that old book. He couldn't be as bad as he seemed, then.

'Would you have been here,' the woman asked at last, 'in the summer of 1969?'

Jim shrugged. 'Well, I've been here since 1967, so yes, I would have been. There will be photos in there, I'm sure, from '69.' Then he remembered when that was, and added, 'I took a bit of a break soon after that, but still, there'll be something.'

The secret smile returned. 'And were you aware of a film crew operating on the loch at that time?'

'A film crew?'

She nodded. 'They would have been here for a couple of months.'

Nobody had asked him about the film crew in all the years he'd been taking people out in the boat. Then he knew exactly why she was here. 'You're something to do with the film festival, are you?'

'Well deduced,' she said, a little pertly. 'We're showing a restored version of the movie they were making back then, tomorrow night in Inverness. I'm introducing it and then interviewing a member of the crew.'

For a moment, he thought that perhaps she, too, had been here all those years ago. He even tried to place her among the faces that had crowded the bar every night at the old Drumnadrochit Hotel. But he was being an idiot, of course. Not only was she far too young – what was she, thirty, tops?—but none of the faces in those days had been anything other than very white indeed. He was making the same mistake he'd begun to make with his students towards the end of his lecturing career: losing a sense of their place in time, of what they might be expected to know, and of where they might reasonably be expected to have come from.

'Yes,' he told her, 'I remember the film crew. I was concerned they'd be a nuisance, if I'm honest. Thought they'd cause a disturbance on the loch that would interfere with the work we were trying to do.' Then he remembered something that made him laugh. 'I did get to see their Loch Ness Monster sink, though. That was fun.'

The woman's jaw dropped. 'Wally Veevers' original?'

It was the first time he'd heard that name since he'd seen the man weeping against Mr Wilder's shoulder at the quayside, all those years ago. 'Ay, that's the one.'

'But that's incredible.' Did that mean she thought he was lying? 'How were you allowed to get close?'

He told her he'd been invited there by one of the crew, and then, as accurately as memory allowed, told her about the questions he'd been asked by the director after the model's first run on the water. 'He was a big name at the time,' he added. 'Had made films with Marilyn Monroe.'

'He was and he did.' He'd forgotten that the woman was meant to be some kind of expert. 'I'm a bit of a fan, actually.'

'A bit?' The Yank boyfriend's eyes hadn't left the book.

She struck his ribs with her elbow. 'I was still at school when he died,' she said, 'so never got a chance to interview him. You've made me very jealous.'

Jim shrugged. 'Well, all he did was yell at me – hardly an in-depth conversation. I offered to give him some advice about the monster, but he wasn't interested. I was really only there so he could show off, I think.' The memories were coming thick and fast, and now they made him laugh again. 'Then the bloody thing sank.'

They were approaching the broken walls of the castle, and for the first time in years Jim thought about the time he had crouched above it, watching the *Cally* take this exact route, while Mr Wilder tried to put the actors through their paces for a scene...

He snapped himself back to the present and at the correct moment switched on the monitor above his head. 'All right, time for a movie of my own. It doesn't star Marilyn Monroe, I'm afraid, but it's still a damned sight better than anything you'll see on this subject anywhere else while you're here.'

But he wasn't convinced they would pay it any attention. Nobody did these days: they stared at the screen, because everyone is trained to do that from the cradle, but they didn't take anything in. 'The problem,' Bill Ogilvy had told him once over a pint in St Machar's Bar, 'is that you don't give them what they want. You only disabuse them, and nobody likes that. They want to believe in Santa, and the Tooth Fairy, and the Easter Bunny...'

Jim's own voice began speaking above his head, high-pitched and slightly too fast. He was talking about the first recorded sightings, from the 1930s. On the screen he couldn't see, there'd be accompanying images of the 'surgeon's photograph' and those supposed monster tracks that Marmaduke Wetherell claimed he'd discovered. Soon, this other self would talk about the interest that actual scientists began to show in the 1950s, and the discussions that followed about whether some prehistoric creature – a plesiosaur, perhaps – might have somehow survived into the present era. This section would be illustrated in part with moving images of the first scientists to come here looking for evidence: Douglas Campbell, Stewart McAllister, Alan Stirling, Jim Outhwaite... Then there would be the underwater shots of silt-covered beer cans and plimsolls – those plimsolls really were a mystery that needed solving – and visualisations of the sonar scans conducted over the past four decades.

His passengers didn't upset his gloomy predictions. While his disembodied voice was dispensing all this wisdom, the Yank never looked up from the book. At least the woman's eyes were trained on the monitor – but there was a glaze to them that suggested they were really fixed on another screen altogether, watching a different film. Jim reached up and pressed pause.

'Now, young lady, can you tell me what you see there?'

As if waking from her dream, she squinted. 'A trainer?'

'Ay,' said Jim. 'Well done. But it's not so easy to make out, is it?' She shook her head.

'That's because, even with a portable light source, it's difficult to penetrate the suspension of particles down there. You see the particles, don't you?'

She nodded.

'That's peat. It stops sunlight from getting very deep into the loch. Without sunlight, you can't have photosynthesis. Without photosynthesis, you can't have organisms that feed on others that rely on photosynthesis. So, your food chain's broken at the start. If you're looking for a large predator of some kind – a piscivore, which most people imagine – then you're looking for one that's happy to go very hungry indeed.'

'So, there isn't any Loch Ness Monster,' said the Yank, snapping the book shut. 'Well, you've convinced me.'

'That's fascinating.' The woman was overcompensating just a little. 'But what's more interesting to me is that people actually believe they've seen it. I mean, other than the guy with the hippo foot and the one who took the famous photo, we're not talking about charlatans, are we?'

This one, Jim thought, *has a brain*. 'Which leads to the next bit of the film, young lady. I'll start it up, then get us going to the other side of the loch.'

This was the real nitty-gritty stuff: the geometric formula Jim applied to photographic monsters to help him identify apparently dinosaurian necks as the washed-out branches of dead fir trees;

the demonstration of how wakes from motorboats might appear as roiling serpents long after the boat itself has passed from view; the way that ducks or cormorants might trick the eye into thinking they were something much larger and faster, especially on a hot day... Then there were the theories about red deer crossing from one bank to the other, of Labradors seen from afar, of introduced or otherwise displaced species swimming upstream from the North Sea: sturgeon, dolphins, whales, seals...

'And you do all this alone?' the woman asked when he was done. 'Not with the... What was it called?'

'The Loch Ness Research Group.' They were following the southern bank now, close to where he'd started his monster-hunting career. 'Ay, since we disbanded the group, I've worked alone. There have been rivals, but no other colleagues.'

She smiled. 'You remind me of the man in the film.'

He rolled his eyes. She was referring, as he knew too well, to one of the two fictional captains with which he was always being compared. Any moment now, the boyfriend would chip in with 'From hell's heart I stab at thee', or start wittering on about the *USS Indianapolis*. 'Go on, then,' he said, 'tell me who I am.'

'Well,' said the woman. 'Sherlock Holmes, of course.'

At the quayside, before disembarking, he ran through his usual end-of-cruise spiel. 'I calculate that about ninety percent of what you're told or what you read about the Loch Ness Monster is pure bunkum. Don't trust it. If you're really interested in knowing more, I recommend this website.'

He handed each of them a business card with his name, credentials and web address printed on it in yellow serif, over an ochre-hued shot of the loch at twilight. The Yank stuffed his in the pocket of his waterproof without a second glance, but the woman perused hers carefully.

'Well, thank you for the tour, Captain—' she read the name off the card, '—Captain Outhwaite. It's been fascinating.' Then she said what he guessed she'd been wanting to say for a while. 'Why don't you come and see the film tomorrow?' She reached into an outer pocket of her rucksack and brought out a plain white card of her own. 'My number's on that. Let me know and I'll make sure there's a couple of tickets waiting for you. I think you earned them back when you watched *HMS Jonah* sink.'

'I'll think about it, miss.' He tucked the card in a trouser pocket, reminding himself that his interest in film was virtually nil. But when he'd got them onto *terra firma*, curiosity overwhelmed him. 'Who will you be talking to?'

'Her name's April Korzeniowski,' the woman said. 'She was the movie's script supervisor. At the time, they would've called her the continuity girl.'

He's sitting in his easy chair in his front room in Inverness. One hand cradles a tumbler of neat Tomatin, the other glides over the touchpad of the laptop that's on his knees. His eyes are stinging, and he knows he ought to give them a rest and turn on the lights. Propped against the screen is the woman's card, on which her credentials are printed, along with her contact details.

'*Gemma MacDonald, MA (Cantab), PhD (Sheffield)*
Lecturer in Film'

His researches have told him that she's the author of several scholarly papers on post-studio-system Hollywood. In 2009, she contributed a chapter to a book called *The Rise and Fall of Noir* that dealt with a Billy Wilder film called *Fedora* and, in 2011, she published a monograph on *The Private Life of Sherlock Holmes* for the BFI. No wonder she was chosen to introduce the screening tomorrow night. He looks that up, too: 'The Loch Ness Film Festival is proud to host the UK premiere of this newly-restored print of Billy Wilder's "lost" masterpiece. Includes pre-show Q&A with the film's continuity supervisor April Korzeniowski, who is returning to Scotland for the first time since the film was shot here in 1969...'

'What a name.' He's talking out loud, because that's what he does when he's alone in the house, which is every night of the week.

It's years now since he first tapped the words 'April Bloom' into a search engine and sorted the wheat from the chaff until he discovered that the surname had changed. That had been something he'd expected, of course. Now he places his whisky on the arm of his chair and types the new name into the search bar. An Apollo and an Abel Korzeniowski come up first, both clearly more famous than April, and then she appears, placed number three. 'You've visited this page many times,' Google tells him. 'Last visit: 29/03/14.'

Well, that's nearly four months ago. Not bad going, really.

He selects the page and scrolls down so that he can read her credits from the bottom up. *Where the Spies Are* (continuity – as April Bloom), 1965. *Lost Command* (continuity – as April Bloom), 1966. *2001: A Space Odyssey* (continuity – uncredited), 1968. *Battle of Britain* (continuity – as April Bloom), 1969. *The Private Life of Sherlock Holmes* (continuity – as April Bloom), 1970. He can't remember her talking about any of these films other than *2001*, and that was only because she'd seen him reading the book. He continues scrolling up. *The Games, Fiddler on the Roof* and *Diamonds Are Forever* are all still script-supervised by someone credited 'as April Bloom'. They're still made in Britain, too – Jim knows this because he checked on one of his previous prolonged searches. How had she maintained that tan while working so consistently under a British sun? But this is the point where things change. Her first movie in America is *The Way We Were* in 1973. Both that and 1974's *For Pete's Sake* are credited to 'April Bloom', but for 1975's *Once Is Not Enough*, she's emphatically surnamed Korzeniowski. There's a longish gap between 1976's *A Star is Born* and *Endless Love* in 1981, but from then on, she works pretty solidly until 2003, when presumably she retired. Sometimes, he's heard of the films she's worked on. Once or twice, he's seen them.

He folds the laptop, leaving Dr MacDonald's card in there, and knocks back the last of his whisky. Too quickly: his throat closes after it and water springs to his eyes. It's almost completely dark, but he doesn't switch on a light until he's in the kitchen. The tube blinks to life like a newborn. He'd meant to stop off at the supermarket on the way home, but his renewed preoccupation carried him all the way to his front door. It's too late to go out now. There's half a packet of cheddar in the fridge and the end-slices to a loaf on the table. That'll have to do. He stands for a long time with the fridge door open, so that the skin on his bare arms and forehead puckers with the cold. He also senses a quickening in his chest.

'Christ,' he says, talking out loud again. 'Why now?'

He wakes before the alarm, as he always does in the summer. He would happily lounge about in his dressing gown for an hour or so, but there's no milk or coffee, so he gets dressed and walks to Sunil's. It's bright, but with a chill in the air, the sort of morning that makes him yearn to be up on the heath, recording things in a notebook. He promised himself he would do that again now he's retired, but the loch just won't let him go.

'You all right there, Jimmy?' Sunil asks, tapping prices into the till. He must be sixty now, but with his film-star looks, and entirely – suspiciously – black hair, he could pass for 45. Only his buff overall ages him, recalling the shopkeepers of Jim's childhood. Sunil came to Inverness from Glasgow 25 years ago, so he's as much an outsider as Jim. 'How's business?'

It's an invitation to moan and Jim's happy to accept it. 'Just two yesterday, would you believe. A lass from London and a cocky Yank who didn't really want to be there. You?'

'Mustn't grumble. The supermarket made me another offer last week. Never know, I might take them up on it. Have myself an early retirement.'

'But what would you do with yourself all day?'

Sunil laughs. 'You've got a point there, Jimmy. We're in the same boat, aren't we? Our hobby is our profession. Not a bad way to live though, you ken?'

By the time Jim has eaten his muesli and drunk two cups of strong, percolated coffee – the latter cancelling out all the good the former has done – he knows there's no avoiding today's overwhelming question. The film is showing tonight, and he has no idea what will happen tomorrow.

He moves from the kitchen to the living room and picks up the laptop from the floor by the easy chair. He unfolds it and the card flitters out. For more than a minute he stares at where it lies on the carpet by his feet. Nothing is certain. What if Dr MacDonald, quite properly, refuses to act as go-between? He's pretty sure that he would keep out of it, if he were the one being put in that position. And even if she does show willing, what good can it possibly do? Right now, dozens of versions of that imaginary conversation he's had with April many, many times over the past 45 years, are competing for ascendency in his subconscious. He's not sure he could ever fix on any one of them.

Then, suddenly, he is resolved.

Who am I kidding? he thinks, and bends stiffly to retrieve the card. It's not as though he has anything to lose.

Inverness–shire, 2014 (II)

'Hi, April?'

'Morning, Gemma.' She sounds a little distant, like she's switched to speakerphone. 'What's up?'

Gemma leans her elbows on the picnic table and fulfils her promise to the monster-hunter in little more than a murmur. It's like being in Year 9 again, when Suzi Skinner got her to pass a note to Brandon Jackson in the middle of a Wednesday-morning maths lesson. Gemma had darted a hand across the aisle, dropping the folded graph paper on the pustulated wonder's desk so stealthily that he hadn't noticed it. He carried on working on his quadratic equations until Suzi *psst!*ed him. She got into trouble for that, and when the whole story came out, so had Gemma…

When this equivalent task is done, there's a long silence at the other end of the line. Gemma hears a car struggling with the incline of the road beyond the trees. 'Sorry,' she says, 'I know it's inappropriate. I didn't give him your number – well, he didn't ask for it, to be fair. Is he a total creep?'

April laughs. 'No, he's not. But I'm mightily surprised to hear he's still around. He isn't a local.'

'Perhaps he has family here now.'

'That's possible. You say he's still looking for the Loch Ness Monster?'

'Well, he made it clear to us that he didn't believe it existed. Oh, and he told us he'd seen *HMS Jonah* sink.'

There's more laughter at that. It's light, and maybe a little melancholy. 'Yeah, I was the one who took him along to that. He came to watch us shoot for a day, too. Access all areas.'

It takes a moment for Gemma to realise that the *double entendre* is intentional. 'So, there *was* something between you?'

'I thought so.'

If not melancholy, there's at least something wistful in her voice.

'A holiday romance?' Gemma suggests, and thinks, *Was this instead of or as well as Robert Stephens...?*

'You could say that,' says April. 'Except that it was a damn long holiday, and I was working, so it wasn't a holiday at all.' There's a pause, then a clear intake of breath. 'Okay, I guess you'd better give me his number.'

They finish the phone call with some words about the screening. The sound check is at seven o'clock, and April will be introduced to the audience at 7.30. The movie is set to begin at eight. 'It'll be a long night,' Gemma tells her, 'especially with the interval.'

'They'd better be serving wine.'

'Wouldn't have persuaded Dad to come along otherwise.'

A moment after Gemma's rung off, the phone buzzes again. It's a text from Julie Crosby: *'Thanks again for ticket. Hope to catch you before show. Looking forward to it.'* She fires off a text as quickly as her clumsy thumb allows, then gets up from the table and heads inside.

The telly's turned up louder than necessary, considering only one person's watching it. Destiny, sitting cross-legged in her pyjamas, is guzzling Coco Pops and immersing herself in a world of hyperactive, anthropomorphised sea life. In the couple of seconds of dialogue Gemma catches, there's enough postmodern jokes to keep a culture studies department busy for a term.

Mum's in the kitchen area, fixing Dad a Scottish grill. There's a Styrofoam tray next to the hob, displaying the full range of Highland delicacies: squares of Lorne sausage, rounds of black pudding and haggis. There's an open box of eggs, too, and a tin of baked beans with the lid removed.

David is crammed into a corner of the sofa, legs crossed at the low hems of his khaki shorts. He's wearing that mould-green T-shirt with the distressed print of Godzilla on it and some Japanese script, which she bought him for his birthday. He's making a show of reading a Jo Nesbo paperback, but his glazed eyes – double glazed, one might say – don't fool her. He hasn't said much this morning, or indeed since yesterday's boat trip. His odd mood continued into the evening. He said almost nothing when they went to the restaurant in the village, and left much of his venison steak untouched. What conversation there was had very naturally focused on Destiny's trip with Grampa and Nanna to see the Cairngorm reindeer herd, which gave him a pass at least. But Gemma knew he was sinking further into the gloom that had begun nearly two weeks ago now. Surely, the crisis was near…

But later, when they were alone in bed, she still couldn't bring herself to say what needed to be said. How would he respond in this mood? She was beginning to believe there would never be a perfect time for it. When he was happy, almost ecstatic – as he'd been at the hotel in Milton of Campsie – she felt it would be an act of cruelty to bring him down again. And now, when he is in the doldrums, it seems like she would be pouring salt on an acid burn…

She decides to nuzzle next to him on the sofa. He glances at her, and she tries to communicate something a little complex through her eyes: *You know what I'd like to do, don't you? But everyone's awake now, and the walls of the lodge aren't as thick as they need to be, and anyway, you weren't up for it last night when everyone was asleep, were you?*

Dad comes in from the bedroom, towelling his hair. His shorts are the same basic design as David's – do men wear anything else in the summer these days? – but he's got a checked, short-sleeved shirt on instead of the geeky tee. His legs, very skinny despite the bulk they're carrying, are obscenely hairless. 'I love the smell of fry-ups in the morning,' he declares. 'Hope that's lard in the pan, hen?'

'You ought to be eating porridge,' says Mum.

'With salt in it,' says Gemma. 'The way they eat it in *Kidnapped*.'

'You'll not catch me eating that shite.'

Mum clicks her tongue and nods at Destiny.

'Apologies, hen.' He's speaking to the back of his granddaughter's head, since her eyes are still glued to the TV. 'From now on, I'll only use language you've heard in the playground.' He tosses the towel over the back of a breakfast-bar stool. 'Anyway, David's got to try a real breakfast while he's here. Isn't that right, son?'

David nods. 'Got some maple syrup to go with that?'

Dad grimaces. 'Christ, I don't know how you Yanks do it. Drown those crispy wee bits of bacon in that sugary—' he slides his eyes Mum's way, '—sugar.'

'You'll be needing some exercise later,' Mum tells David, transferring the protein products to the pan with a spatula. 'Why don't you and Gemma go out and explore the local area?'

'Sounds good to me.' He does a reasonable job of simulating enthusiasm. 'If Gem's up for it.'

'Of course,' Gemma says. 'We can do that.'

'Now you listen to me,' Dad says, doing his bad Sean Connery, 'after that little lot, you won't want to do anything but sit with your feet up reading the newspaper and watching the telly. That's the Highlands way.'

Suddenly, Destiny's bouncing on the sofa, next to her aunt. 'But I thought you was gonna take me with you today.'

She's right – Gemma promised. It was the whole reason she'd insisted Destiny come here, after all.

'Oh ay,' says Dad. 'She kept asking why you weren't with us yesterday.'

'I had to meet someone, sweetheart.'

'But I could've gone with you.'

'Didn't you want to see the reindeer?'

'Yeah.' She said it as though it had been possible to do both at the same time. 'But I can go out with you and David today, can't I?'

David stiffens beside her, like he did in the car when Dad was teasing him about Gretna Green. He's clearly already had enough of the clan MacDonald. She doesn't blame him – but he's going to have to get over it, seeing as they've still got five days to get through...

'We'll see,' Gemma says.

'Grampa and I can take you out again, sweetheart,' says Mum, stepping back from the animal fat as it begins to spit. 'You wanted to see the ospreys, didn't you? We can take you there.' Then, to Gemma, 'She's a budding naturalist, that one.'

'Can't Auntie Gem take me?' says Destiny.

'Why don't you ask her, hen?' says Dad, 'Maybe that fits in with her plans, too.'

Mum gives Dad a hard look, as though she's trying to convey something complex, too, though not at all the same thing Gemma had been trying to convey to David. If Gemma didn't know better, she'd swear Mum was trying to give her some space with her boyfriend…

'You promised, Auntie Gem,' says Destiny.

'Well,' says Gemma, 'I'm saying it's up to David.'

She knows she isn't really giving him a choice, and that this isn't the way to improve his mood. But what alternative does she have? 'Sure,' he says, exactly as though it's the only thing he can possibly say. 'We'll go see some birds.'

'Well, that's settled.' Mum cracks an egg over the pan. 'Make sure you bring us back some lovely photos.'

It's a bit of a drive, and Gemma's the one doing it. She reminds them that tonight's her big night, and she needs to be back in time to get ready for her appearance before a paying public. Loch Ness glimmers at her right shoulder for the first stretch, under a sky as nearly cloudless as any they've seen since crossing the border. David is mute beside her, while in the back, Destiny is plugged into her DS.

When they're through Inverness, headed towards the Cairngorms on the A9, they pass a sign to a distillery that does tours. Gemma nudges David. 'Look,' she says. 'We could go there on our way back, if you like. You and Dad can load up, and I'll take the wheel till he's sober again.'

David nods, but is otherwise unresponsive.

After a while, they turn from the main road onto tiny tarmac trails, going deep into a forest of conifers. The canopy almost closes over them, leaving just a green-edged river of sky directly above. Then they enter an occluded car park, where sun-mottled portions of another loch – more modest than the one Gemma feels is her own now – shows through gaps in the tree trunks.

Inside the RSPB centre, David enters into the birdwatching spirit with surprising gusto. He takes off his glasses and sights along all the telescopes that are lined up before the panoramic window looking out on Loch Garten. As well as this viewing gallery, there's a display on the nesting ospreys, and an adjacent window offering a view of the forest. When Destiny's had enough of looking at the apparently lifeless stacks of twigs that are meant to contain baby ospreys, she gravitates to this other window. Gemma joins her. There are bird tables set up just the other side, and feeders attached to trees; all are well attended by tiny visitors. Destiny starts marking off what she can see against the laminated chart pinned to the wall.

'That's a great tit,' she says, 'that's a bullfinch, that's a greenfinch, that's a lady blackbird…'

'You know you can see all of those in London, don't you?'

'Yeah.' Then Destiny spots something new. 'What's that?'

Gemma squints in the direction her niece is pointing, over the top of the biggest bird table and deeper into the forest.

'Right there,' says Destiny. 'See? It's moving.'

Gemma catches a quick, flowing movement on the grey surface of a fir tree. 'Is it a squirrel?'

Destiny shrugs. 'Too big, ain't it?'

'A wee bit, young lady, yes.'

It's a woman with white hair who has spoken, standing beside them now. At first, Gemma thinks she's the grandmother of the ginger preschoolers who have got in front of Destiny, trying to see what the fuss is about.

'It's a pine marten,' the woman tells them, and Gemma spots the RSPB lanyard hanging around her neck. 'Not so long ago, we thought we'd seen the last of them, but they've made a comeback. They're opportunistic wee devils, mind – love nothing better than to take a clutch of eggs, or even a fully grown bird.'

'It looks like a giant weasel,' says Destiny.

'That's very perceptive, my dear. Part of the same family, with stoats and otters. You know, we've been honoured by its appearance. They're really nocturnal animals, and shy of people. This one's risking a lot for a go at those fat balls.'

'Hey, Destiny—' David's calling from the biggest of the telescopes, '—come and have a look at this.'

The pine marten undulates away behind the trunk.

Gemma takes her turn at the telescope, after her niece. Both the big black-and-white birds of prey are standing in the nest, the mamma and the papa, looking as though they're wearing baggy white shorts, like David's and Dad's. They're dropping fish into the raised maws of their young.

'You can see them up on the screen, too,' says the official, who seems to have taken a shine to Destiny. 'We've set up a camera just outwith the nest.'

On the monitor, the birds appear in larger, grainier form. Sometimes they get too close, and the screen is filled with an enormous eye.

'That's sick,' says Destiny.

The official looks taken aback. 'I assure you, young lady, they're all perfectly healthy.'

On the way back to the car park, Destiny races ahead, weaving through the trees to the loch.

Gemma gives David's arm a nudge. 'Glad you came now?'

He smiles, and it's the most natural response she's got from him in days. 'That was surprisingly okay,' he says. 'You know, I never took advantage of the great outdoors back home. Lake Michigan makes these Scottish lochs look like puddles. It's got actual beaches, with sand. But I was a stay-at-home kind of kid, you know?'

'I know,' she says. How could she not?

'We really need to check out the wide-open spaces when we get over there.'

Over there – it's the first time he's spoken about *over there* since he started acting strangely. Through the tree trunks, Gemma can see Destiny climbing onto one of the substantial red boulders that squats at the water's edge. She wants to run over and join her up there, as though that would would save her from any requirement to think about *over there*. But she knows that this is the dramatic moment of fate, as Holmes would no doubt have it. The reason she hasn't spoken about Aberdeen is that he hasn't been speaking about Chicago, and it's been too easy to ignore the fact that he's leaving Britain altogether in a few weeks time, and expects her to follow him...

'David, we've really got to talk.' She keeps her eyes on Destiny, who's standing like a sentinel on her chosen rock.

'Wait a minute, Gem.'

He stops walking and takes hold of her arm. But he misjudges it, and his fingers dig painfully into the tendon above her elbow. She pulls away sharply, though she knows he didn't mean to hurt her. She turns to look at him, but he's below her eyeline, down on one knee.

'Oh, God, David, no—'

He's tearing at a flap on his shorts. 'I've been waiting for an opportunity since yesterday. If that old geezer on the boat hadn't been such a windbag—'

'Please, David—'

'And I was supposed to take you out someplace quiet this morning, just the two of us.' He's struggling with the lid of the little cushioned box he's taken from his pocket. His fingers are atrophied, have turned to wood.

'David, don't—'

'Gemma—' he's prising at it with his nails.

'David, no—'

'Would you do me the honour—?' He's got it open and looks triumphant. He's holding the box up to her.

'No—'

'—the honour of becoming—?'

'Auntie Gem!' Destiny's voice is muffled by the trees and fallen needles, as well as the distance from the loch. But it's all Gemma is prepared to hear. 'Come and have a look at the funny orange water.'

They haven't driven far before Destiny starts complaining about hunger pangs. Though it's lunchtime, Gemma's not sure she'll be able to eat anything herself. She's pretty sure David won't.

'There were signs to the Heather Centre back there,' he says. 'That was in one of those leaflets, too. I'm guessing they do food. That sound okay, Destiny?'

My God, Gemma thinks, *he really is a decent human being.*

Even with the satnav, it takes a couple of goes to get the turnings right. Her heartbeat is crazy, her palms feel tacky on the steering wheel. She's in full flight mode, but since she's the one in charge of the space out of which she wishes to fly, there's nothing she can do about it. *Christ*, she thinks, *human nature can be a real bitch.*

In the Heather Centre's canteen, Destiny tucks into a big plate of cottage pie and chips, while David follows Gemma's lead and has a go at some Scotch broth. Neither manages more than a few spoonfuls. Then Destiny insists they look around the exhibition.

It seems a disastrous turn of events – but it's while they're passing through the screened corridors, looking at displays on the natural history and many domestic and industrial uses of *Calluna vulgaris*, that Gemma decides she's aunt to a truly remarkable niece. If anything deserves to be the straw of tedium that breaks a ten-year-old's attention-deficient back, it's a museum dedicated to a single shrub. Instead, Destiny shows every sign of active interest in the role that little twigs and tiny petals have played in the history of a hardy people with few life choices.

At one point, when Gemma lets Destiny get away from her, David comes very close. 'I take it that's a *no*.'

She can't bring herself to look at him. 'Let's talk about it later. Not in front of Destiny.'

His whole posture changes, losing its dangerous energy. She knows he's not going to pick a fight in front of a child. He isn't a monster.

They catch up with Destiny and Gemma asks her if she's set to go.

'Of course, Auntie Gem,' she replies. 'It's your big night, ain't it?'

Somehow, Gemma doesn't drive them off the road on their way back to the lodge. Destiny jumps from the car as soon as it's parked and runs off to find Grandma and Grandpa. Gemma follows, but doesn't get far before David calls her name.

'Tell me now,' he says. He's standing by the car, his posture registering defeat and offering an argument at the same time. 'Tell me before we go in.'

She indicates the picnic table and, when they're sitting either side of it, tells him everything.

He takes off his glasses while she speaks and rubs his eyes. 'Aberdeen?' he says when she's finished.

She might as well have said the University of Timbuctoo.

He puts his glasses back on. 'And you've sat on this since *December...?*'

'That was when they made the offer,' Gemma says. 'And I haven't accepted.'

'But you will.'

She doesn't respond.

He takes the jewellery case out and sets it open on the table. For a moment, Gemma thinks he's gone mad – hasn't listened to anything, or hasn't understood. 'Granny Anderson's ring,' he says, and his tone tells her that he understands very well. 'Mine to give to whomever. Grandpa Anderson gave it her in 1956, and he'd got it from his own grandmother. It came to America from Sweden in the 1890s.'

At first sight, it could be costume jewellery. A big purplish stone surrounded by rose-cut white stones, on a thin band of yellow metal. But Gemma can see now that it's an amethyst set among diamonds, on a ring of high-carat gold. 'That's what you were talking to your mother about, isn't it?'

David snaps the case shut and puts it back in his pocket. 'My God, I was nervous. Nervous to talk with her about it – she's never met you. And then nervous about finding the right moment to talk with you. But there was never a right moment, was there?'

'Tell me about it,' Gemma says, and attempts some air-clearing laughter. 'I couldn't work out when it was best to tell you about Aberdeen, either. When you were in a good mood, when you were being pensive...'

David throws up his arms and gets to his feet. 'Fuck's sake, Gemma – are you claiming an equivalence?'

'No,' she says, though she isn't sure. She has certainly said the wrong thing.

'It was a shitty thing you did, Gemma – or failed to do. It wasn't anything like trying to propose to someone you're in love with.'

'You're right.' She's worried their raised voices will reach the lodge. 'You didn't deserve it. But look at you—' and she does look at him, as handsome as ever, hair ruffled where he has just run a hand through it, downturned lips almost a child's mime of grief, nearly irresistible, nearly forcing her to get up and embrace him, give him whatever comfort he requires, '—you're never going to be lonely. You're going to find someone who wants exactly what you want.'

'What I want?' He throws up his hands again, as if imploring the gods to help him in this impossible task. Then he rests them on his hips and looks down at her. 'Do you remember, by any chance, my theory about the three types of lecturer?'

She shakes her head. 'Vaguely, perhaps.'

'Well, that's par for the course. Let me remind you while I've got your attention. The first type is those who are always down with the kids, because they're practically kids themselves – and I'm not talking about how old they are. Then there are the ones who treat the students like they're idiots and laugh about them in the senior common room. I've worried about being both those types in the past. But you're different. You treat everyone in the world, including your mom and dad, and your brother, like you're their personal Jesus. You don't know what the fuck you want to do with your own life, but you can't stop yourself telling everyone else what they should be doing.'

'That's not true,' she says. But she's thinking, *God, he's right – I am like that, aren't I?*

'I'm glad about two things, though,' he adds.

'What are they?' While his voice has become calm, pitched almost normally, she can hear a coldness in her own. She hadn't wanted to put up the barriers, but they're there. This is hurting like hell.

'Now that I know this about you,' he says, 'I can't be too upset that you won't marry me.'

'Good for you.' Her voice is practically a murmur. 'What's the other thing?'

'Well—' he manages a kind of smile, '—I don't have to watch that fucking movie again, do I?'

Chapter Fourteen

'May I speak with Benedict Arnold?'

Jim takes his phone into the front passage, as if there's more privacy there than in the kitchen. Of course, no one else is in the house.

'Hello, April. I'm glad you called. I wasn't sure your friend would give you my number. I think she thought…'

But he doesn't know what he thinks she thought.

'She thought you were a Loch Ness Monster-hunter. She had no idea you were an expert in leaving a girl in the lurch, too.'

Is she really angry after all these years? 'Look, can we talk properly?'

'Isn't this talking properly? I know you can't see me, but I'm opening and closing my mouth at the right times, honest.'

'I mean, I'd like to meet with you, wherever you think best.'

'The way you were meant to meet with me last time, where I thought best?'

He knows she's pulling his leg, but it's fierce. Almost an amputation. 'Yes, another go at doing that.'

'Okay, Benedict, we'll give it a try. Do you know where the Dores Inn is?'

On the drive there, Jim tries to prepare himself for the shock of the new April. He knows he's got off lightly in the intervening years, enjoying a pretty much unbroken run of good health. There's been the odd bout of flu, and one nasty case of norovirus – but since his appendix was whipped out one spring morning in 1959, he's never again been under the knife. Probably, it's a case of good genes: at 94, his mother is living a comfortably diminished life in a Kendal nursing home. But he has also kept active, and outdoors active at that.

Nevertheless, the passage of time has done its usual job of work on him.

First, there's the wide disc of bare scalp, which he wears like a skullcap now. What remains of his hair is badger-streaked, like his beard. True, his eyebrows are still dark, but they are also over-luxuriant, like the hairs he periodically has to remove from his nostrils and ears. His belly began to bulb when he was in his mid-forties, and the muscle of his arms and thighs turned skimpy over the following decade. He has recently considered giving his belt a helping hand with a pair of braces, but he's not quite ready to make that leap.

He knows April won't have escaped time's cruelties, either. Her smooth skin will be desiccated and age-blotched, and it's reasonable to suppose that she will have succumbed at some point to one of the many diseases associated with age in women. Osteoporosis or rheumatoid arthritis, or any one of the usual cancers. Given her earlier life habits, cancer of the skin or of the lungs seems almost likely. Though a committed sceptic by profession, Jim knows that in life he's a plain pessimist. And so, it's with a sense of impending disappointment that he turns into the car park of the Dores Inn.

She's standing next to a Vauxhall Corsa in a frock that shames his own choice of khaki jacket and chinos, blazing like a gas flame against the bronze-shingled crescent of Dores Beach. My God – how has she done it? It isn't as though she hasn't aged. It's not a 23-year-old who's watching him climb out of his Land Rover. But clearly, she's found a way to roll with time's punches.

'You've had a haircut,' he says.

She laughs. 'So have you. They took a lot off the top, didn't they?'

They're standing two metres apart. He's wondering whether he should offer her his hand.

'I'm not going to kiss you, if that's what you're thinking,' she says. 'Not yet. I want to hear your explanation first.'

Is she still pulling his leg? There's a note in her voice to support that theory, maybe even a turn of the lips, too. But he's not taking chances. 'Of course, April,' he says. 'I owe you that.'

'And when you're done,' she says, 'I'm going to tell you my side of the story.'

She was woken not by the alarm, but by the band of light that had stretched from the gap in the drapes to her pillow, like a luminous snake. She felt rested despite the early hour, and optimistic – her old self again.

Then she remembered the conversation she'd had with Jim last night, on the green and outside the entrance…

All day at work, shooting at the house in Culloden that was standing in for the movie's Caledonian Hotel, the memory flitted in her head like a bird in a cage. She'd hurt his feelings. That much was clear from the way he'd kissed her, and in his uncommon willingness to say goodbye. His lips had stood out from his beard in that way she liked, but now it had looked like peevishness. He had seemed a little boy lost.

Of course, she wasn't going to take back what she'd said. It was what she believed, how she felt, the truth. But she'd chosen her words clumsily, hadn't considered how they would sound in his ears. She valued the time they had spent together, and didn't see why their last days shouldn't be golden ones. Why shouldn't the end of a love affair be celebrated the same way that any great enterprise was celebrated? When this goddamn shoot was over, there would be a hell of a party. Why did she and Jim deserve less?

She longed for the final 'cut' to be called, so she could get back to the Drumnadrochit by five, and find Jim waiting for her in the lobby. But when she did get back, Pete Leith was there instead, encouraging the returning crew into the bar, like a grizzly hooking salmon from the rapids. 'Afternoon, Miss Bloom.' Was he really oblivious to how blatantly his eyes undressed her? 'I trust you've had a bonny day?'

'It was fine, Pete.' She carried on towards the stairs, but turned back before she reached them. 'Say, do you know a really good pub that does food?'

He dropped the leer and gave his scalp a rub, tousling the scant hairs there. 'Well, I'm not in the habit of recommending my rivals, Miss Bloom, but you could try the Dores Inn. Not a bad spot, and far enough away so I cannae take offence.'

She gave him a smile he would remember and went on her way.

The general demand for hot water was putting a strain on the boiler, and she washed in tepid water in the second-floor bathroom. When the shoot moved to London, and she was living with Victoria, she would have access to all the hot water she could possibly want. She would even have the use of a shower, by God…

She slipped into the dress she wore when she first visited the farmhouse. Then she struggled with her boots for ten minutes, like a female Tarzan wrestling a couple of pythons. They looked fabulous, but she would be happy when fashion dictated that some more practical kind of footwear looked better.

By five, she was in the bar, drinking a soda and shooting the breeze with Owen. He was an Australian grip, about three-parts lean muscle to two-parts beer gut. He was always talking to her about surfing, as though that was something people did in San Francisco. His tan had long disappeared, but his face had creases in it like the morocco hinges on a Webster's dictionary.

'You waiting for someone, darling?'

She had just looked at her watch for the fourth time. 'Uh-huh.' It was twenty after now.

'He's never left you in the lurch, has he?'

'You know the Brits, Owen. Never in a hurry for anything.'

But she wasn't convinced that was true, and called Pete over from the other end of the bar.

'You haven't heard from Jim, have you?'

Pete shook his head. 'Not today, Miss Bloom.'

She finished her soda and left the hotel. In the phone booth on the green, she rang the farmhouse and waited with a sixpence poised for ten repetitions of the dialling tone.

'No joy?' asked Pete when she returned to the bar.

She shook her head.

'Well, I wouldn't assume that means no one's home. It's a big house, and you cannae hear anything if you're in the yard. Try again later, lassie.'

She could never hear anyone call her that without thinking she was being compared to a dog. 'Maybe I should go over,' she said.

'I'll give you a lift, if you like.' There was something horribly hopeful in his tone. 'Kevin can take charge for a wee while. He would benefit from the experience.'

Kevin was the eighteen-year-old beanpole whom Pete had taken on when the double duty of running the hotel and gassing with guests had proven too much for him. The boy looked up from where he'd been drying the same glass since before April had left to make her phone call. 'Ay, I could do that, Mr Leith.'

'Thanks,' said April, 'but if it's all the same, I'll walk. It's a nice evening.'

It certainly was that, and it followed on from a day as clear as any she'd experienced in Scotland. If it hadn't been for the early start, and Mr Wilder's resolution not to tax poor Bob's stamina, they would surely have been shooting for a lot longer. She followed the route as Pete had instructed her, keeping to the right-hand hedgerow along the narrow roads that led to Yew Tree Farm. The air was full of birdsong, and she tried by an effort of will to commit the sound to memory, so that she could recall it again when she was back in the city, and there was nothing to hear but cars.

She felt almost like her own ghost as she walked through the gate and down the path to the door, and pressed the doorbell. Ghost rain seemed to be falling all around her in the evening sunshine. But this time, the door wasn't answered by Sandra, nor even by Douglas, with whom she might have had a serious conversation. Instead, it was Douglas's wife, Tessa, who appeared.

'Oh, hello, April.' She looked as though she'd had a fright, as though April were actually a ghost. She was dressed for comfort in bottle-green corduroys and a soft blouse that was the colour of baby puke. 'Please, come in.'

'I don't mean to be any trouble,' said April, following her to the kitchen. 'I was supposed to meet Jim at the hotel, but he didn't show up. I tried calling.'

Tessa pulled a chair out from the table. 'He's not here, I'm afraid. You sure you were meant to see him tonight?'

April nodded. 'Yeah, I'm sure.'

Tessa looked stricken again. How old was she? It was almost

impossible to tell. She could be anything between 35 and 50, a bit like the dame in the Dylan song. 'I'm so sorry,' she said.

For the first time she could remember, April was irritated by the British habit of apologising for things that weren't their fault. 'So, where's he gone?' she asked, sitting down now. 'Or do I not want to know?'

Tessa was filling the kettle, another British habit that was suddenly annoying. 'Nothing like that,' she said. 'We're talking about Jamie here.'

But April thought, *Why the hell not?* Hadn't she told him they were both free as air?

'No,' Tessa continued, putting the kettle on a hotplate, 'he's dining with the Professor of Biology in Aberdeen. He's a bit of a berk, if you ask me – the professor, I mean – but he's offered Jamie a job at the university, you see.'

'I do see,' said April. 'He told me all about that.'

'And you're certain he said he'd meet you tonight?'

April nodded again. 'Have to say, this is a first. Never stood anyone up before, never been stood up before.'

Tessa looked as though she might burst into tears. 'It really was remiss of him not to tell you. I'm so sorry.'

April felt a lightness bloom inside her chest. She had to wait a while before she could speak. 'No, it was my fault. I said some things, and didn't say them well. I don't think he knew what to do.'

She gave a summary of that last conversation, and watched as Tessa drew back from her.

'Well, anyone could see he'd fallen for you,' she said. 'It was much more than a schoolboy crush. I think he would have followed you wherever you wanted him to go. I was half prepared for him to leave us when you left.'

April opened her mouth, but no words emerged.

'You really didn't know?' said Tessa.

April shrugged. 'I imagined he would find a local girl when the time came,' she said. 'I thought he planned on sticking around here forever.'

Even as she said it, she remembered Jim's words about not belonging in Scotland, or some such. She hadn't been able to pay attention through her headache. Tessa laughed now, but it was sad laughter, and a little scornful. 'Well, forever's not a thing any of us can rely on.'

She explained, pretty much as Jim had already explained, how there was every likelihood that the Loch Ness Research Group would come to an end in September.

'Alan and Sandra are going in with Peter Leith,' she added. 'They're forming some sort of business to do with the monster. Don't ask me how that's meant to work. And Douglas and I will probably put this place in mothballs and go travelling. So, Jamie had to make a decision about his own future.'

'I see that now,' said April.

Tessa took hold of her hand with one of her own that was warm and a little moist. 'Would you like a nice cup of tea, dear?'

'No, I wouldn't,' said April, emphatically. 'What I would like is a cigarette.'

'I wish I'd known,' says Jim. 'As I said, I was just plain jealous. My head was full of free love, the permissive society, the wisdom of the East... All that stuff I'd missed out on. Grew up eighty-odd miles north of the Mersey, which was no good, you see? To me, it might as well have been 1959 as 1969.'

She's not listening. Telling her story has dragged her into the past. She's leaning on the pub table, her elbows planted either side of her drink, peering into it. That extraordinary dress shimmers in the light from the window that looks out on the loch. Jim's sure that the colour's the same as the dress that Jephro Rucastle makes Violet Hunter wear in 'The Copper Beeches'—*i.e.*, electric blue. Even he can tell that real money has been spent on it. It's nothing like the hippy frocks she must have relinquished soon after the time he'd known her, but it suits her just as well. As does the short white hairdo, which is somehow witty. Is it possible she's wearing contact lenses? He thinks it is, but when she had been looking at him, her eyes had still been the frisson-powered lamps that had burned their image onto his retina in the Drum, that first time he'd seen them.

'We went outside,' she tells him. 'I got to watch Tessa feed the pig and chickens while I smoked three cigarettes. You never took me out there, did you?'

'Never had anything to do with that side of things,' Jim says. 'Except eating the eggs and bacon.'

She's training those eyes on the brown heart of her rum-and-coke, as though she's conjuring up pictures there, like a clair-voyant. Then she turns their light on him. He has to clutch the wooden arms of his chair. 'I preferred the butterflies and the toads,' she says.

He nods, and thinks, *I know*.

'Well, I misspoke, you turned into the Jolly Green Giant, and that was that. But here we are, anyhow – the Dores Inn. Guess it hasn't changed a lot since we didn't make it here back then, huh?'

Jim shrugs. 'Don't know about that. Pubs have aged about a hundred years in the last couple of decades. Blame Margaret Thatcher and her Victorian values. Nostalgia's been one of the only growth industries since then.'

He thinks he's been in here before, but can't remember the when or the why. For the past forty years, he's mostly made do with just two pubs: St Machar's Bar in Aberdeen, the nearest watering hole to his place of work, and the Thistle Inn, his local since moving to Inverness nine years ago.

'Well, I like it,' says April. 'Just what an old Californian like me wants in a British pub.'

He remembers something else about her. 'Did you never go to a pub in Suffolk?'

She looks impressed by this feat of memory. 'No. My folks weren't the type who went into pubs.'

'Still got a British passport?'

'Uh-huh.' Then she asks, 'Was dinner with the dean all you'd hoped for?'

Another memory surfaces now, and it's a fusty one. Tough meat and overcooked vegetables, the ticking of a grandfather clock in between lags in the lacklustre conversation, a dark-panelled room as consciously antiquated as this one, but much less welcoming.

'It was bloody awful,' he says. 'God, I'm sorry, April.'

But that makes her shake her head. 'Far too late for that, bud.'

He thinks she means she can't forgive him, but then knows it's not what she means at all. 'Well, obviously, it's pointless being sorry now, but I wish I hadn't acted like a complete pillock.'

'Do you regret your job in Aberdeen?'

'No,' he says, truthfully. 'There were times I wasn't so sure but, looking back, I can see it wasn't such a bad way to earn a living.'

'Then what you did way back when didn't turn out so bad, did it?'

She's being kind, but he lets her. 'How about Hollywood? Was that a good life?'

She dips her eyes. 'Can't complain. But I was one of the lucky ones. The directors I worked for liked having the same faces around. For a while there, I was on all the right Rolodexes.'

Their conversation suffers its own lag now, and the pub noises close in on them. Clinking glasses, cutlery scraping against plates, and the unimpeded talk of people who couldn't possibly have as much to say as a couple who haven't met since 1969.

'You never married,' April says, a statement not a question.

'No.' He fears she'll require an explanation, so keeps talking. 'You did, though, and only once. That's not very Hollywood, is it?'

That makes her laugh, and he thinks he's got out of jail. 'You should hear some of my best friends' stories.' She shrugs. 'But my ex is a good man. Still love him dearly.'

'So why the divorce?'

Another shrug. 'We'd gone as far as we could. The kid had grown up, left home, been through college… She was even earning a living, more or less. And she knew that both of us would be there for her if she needed us, which she didn't. It was simply time to move on.'

A pulse sounds and April reaches into the clutch bag. 'Excuse me a minute.' She peers at her phone, then makes little percussive taps at the screen with a long-nailed finger. When the phone is back in her bag, there's a further, single pulse, which she ignores. 'So, what about you? There's got to have been a somebody. More than a somebody, I'm sure.'

There has been, of course, and he decides to tell her about the three long-termers. Caroline, a colleague, with whom he'd shared a house for most of the Seventies and a part of the Eighties. Juliette, who'd been someone else's PhD student, which had caused a minor scandal because the someone else hadn't liked it. And Francine, the widow, to whom he'd been introduced by a friend, just before the turn of the millennium. He might have shared his retirement with her, had she not heard the siren call of a daughter's new child and been lured away to New Zealand instead. He doesn't tell her about the really passionate one: the American whose name he can't quite remember – was it Janet, Janice? – who, on an absolutely superficial level, had reminded him of the only other American he'd fallen for. He'd met her at a conference at Stanford University, in the home city of that other American, and their flash-fire romance had lasted all of six days.

'I'm amazed,' April says. 'I absolutely had you down as the marrying type. I thought you would have founded a whole dynasty of monster-hunters by now. Why didn't it happen?'

He sips at the fizzy water he's allowed to go warm. 'You know I still do the monster-hunting, as you call it, don't you?'

She nods. 'My friend Gemma told me all about her tour of the loch.'

'Well, there's a reason I can't stop, even though I've been convinced there's nothing there since probably the time I knew you.'

'So, what is it?'

He takes some air in first. 'Because of the problem of proving that something is absent. You see, it's much easier to point to a photograph of something long and snake-like, sticking out of the water, and say, "Look, there's the Loch Ness Monster", than to point at the water surrounding it and tell people what *isn't* there: sufficient nutrients and sunlight to sustain phytoplankton in the quantity needed to produce a decent number of copepods and cladocerans, which might then feed a big enough population of charr to support a single large predator, let alone a pod of them over many generations, which is what it would have to be. You can't hold up a photo and say, "Look at what isn't there," and expect people to listen.'

'What are you telling me?' She narrows those eyes, which only makes their light more piercing.

'I'm saying that unlike most people, I understand the problem of proof of absence. Those women I shared my life with – Caroline, Juliette, Francine, the others – they were all wonderful in their way, and I really did care for them. Perhaps I even loved one or two. But in the end, their presence only showed up what wasn't there. Or who wasn't there. Do you see what I'm saying?'

Her eyes dip again to her rum and coke. 'We never did kiss hello, did we?' she says.

He shakes his head. 'No, we didn't.'

'Well—' she gets up, abandoning the drink, '—it's time we put that right. Know any place where we can do it?'

Inverness-shire, 2014 (III)

A minute after the failed call, Gemma's iPhone pings.

'*Hi*,' she reads, '*sorry I missed you. Hope all well. Busy atm but will call when I can. xx.*'

She lets the phone slide from her fingers onto the slats of the picnic table. She's all dressed up with somewhere to go, but isn't sure she can face it now. Above the trees that screen the road, the brow of the nearest hill rises like the humped back of something living – her very own white whale, except that it's green. She dips forward, lets her forehead rest on the table, gazes at the pointed toe of one of her ruby shoes… David is in their room. Dad is slumped on the sofa watching Formula One highlights, with Mum beside him, trying to lose herself in Khaled Hosseini's latest. Destiny is folded up on the floor in front of them, subsumed again into a culture of fighting slave monsters.

'You got ready too early, girl.'

Mum's framed by the lodge door, the Hosseini clasped to her chest. She's still in her daytime skirt and blouse, but she's done something to her hair that's a bit Downton Abbey. It's an indication of what's to come.

'Couldn't think of anything else to do,' Gemma tells her. 'Bit nervous, I suppose.'

'But you give lectures all the time.' Mum sits the other side of the picnic table, where David had sat, and lays down the book. The gleam in her eye means, *I know you, girl.*

'A paying public is a bit different. I've got to actually be interesting.'

Mum laughs, the look still in her eye. 'You're never anything else.'

'How's Dad?' The question is only partly tactical. 'He doesn't seem as full of beans as he was.'

Mum's eyes and mouth widen. 'Oh, it was terrible, love.' It's a half-whisper, and she looks around at the door of the lodge, as though somebody might be listening. 'We stopped off at a pub after our walk, and got talking there to a couple who were about your dad's age. The chap had grown up not far from your dad in Glasgow, so they had something to natter about. Then somebody, I'm not sure who, mentioned that blasted referendum.'

Gemma rolls her eyes. 'And he turned out to be a NO campaigner?'

'Worse.' She's rasping now. 'I think we bumped into the last two Tory voters in Scotland.'

Gemma laughs unconstrainedly. Too much, perhaps – it's a release, though, and it feels good. Mum describes how each party trotted out their own side's usual accusations, until the barman or landlord told them to pipe down or get out. Dad said he would happily continue the discussion in the car park, and that was when Mum and the other woman intervened. They weren't teenagers in Govan anymore, they pointed out. The row fizzled into mere grumbles, and something like a sense of shame took hold... By the end of the story, Gemma is dabbing her eyes with the back of her hand, and Mum offers her a tissue from a packet in her handbag.

'So,' she says, 'tell me what's going on with you and David.'

It's a killer move. Gemma's tears of laughter are in danger of turning into something else. She brings them to an end by blowing her nose. 'He's got a migraine,' she says. 'I don't think he's going to be able to come tonight.'

She knows she's about as convincing as Lennie in *Of Mice and Men*, repeating the guff about Curley getting his hand caught in a machine.

Mum takes hold of the hand not holding the tissue. 'I think you should tell me, love.'

And suddenly, Gemma knows this isn't Mum's intuition at work.

'Jesus Christ,' she says, knowing full well it's the kind of swearing Mum likes least. She pulls her hand away, too, stashing it under the table. 'The twat asked you and Dad for permission, didn't he?'

'Don't be angry, love. It's difficult to know what to do these days – we're still between times.'

'What times?' Gemma can't believe she's hearing this. 'The fall of feudalism and the rise of the British Empire?'

'He didn't want us against him, that's all.' She's frowning, but she isn't rising to her daughter's bait. She's staying calm. 'You know we haven't been as friendly to him as we might have been. So, he took the initiative and tried to make peace with the family he wanted to join.' She smiles softly. 'He didn't ask your father for consent, if that's what you're thinking. And your dad didn't offer him a dowry. I told him it was a mistake not to talk to you first, and he saw the truth of that straight away.'

An odd shift inside Gemma's chest makes her feel both better and worse. 'Oh, God,' she says, and she lifts the tissue to her face again. 'I've been horrible to him.'

'You can't say that, love.'

Gemma shakes her head vigorously. 'Oh, I can. I don't mean turning him down. I mean what I should've told him months ago.'

Then the whole story unspools in a ten-minute montage that deserves a different soundtrack than the birdsong and the sound of oak leaves caught in the wind. She feels the load lifting, the muscle in her shoulders unbunching, her pelvic floor letting her breathe again. It feels more like a life-change than anything she has experienced for a while – the end of the age of indecision. She wonders how long that will last…

'You're going to take the job?' Mum asks, her hand in her daughter's again.

'Yes,' says Gemma. 'I'm sorry.'

'Oh, love – what for?' The smile she gives her now is multi-layered. There's pride in it, and sorrow, a new contentment, and piles of an otherwise inexpressible level of unconditional love. 'You wouldn't be doing it unless it was a wonderful opportunity, I'm sure.'

It's another tremendous relief. 'It really is, Mum,' Gemma says, having to talk through laughter. 'It means I'm leapfrogging – I'll have more responsibility than I thought I'd ever get, to be honest. It's only—' she squeezes Mum's hand, '—it's only, I'll be so far away from you and Dad, and Robbie and Destiny…'

'You can't worry about that, love,' Mum says. 'Besides, Scotland's not the moon. We're here now, aren't we?'

But Gemma isn't finished. 'I know I'm giving up another opportunity, too. David's a good man.'

'He is,' says Mum, 'and because you would give him up, you must.'

It's a sinewy phrase, and Gemma has to untangle it.

'I wasn't a bad student myself,' Mum tells her while she's thinking. 'Top stream, and always near the top of the class. I hope that doesn't sound like I'm boasting.'

Gemma smiles.

'Well, I had this wonderful English teacher called Miss Riley, who was the old spinster type. A little manly, you know. There was some silly gossip among the silly boys… No one would bat an eyelid now. Anyway, she was very keen for me to take my A levels at the college and perhaps train as a teacher, or go into something like the law. She told your grandpa and grandma as much at parents' evening, and they said, "Sure thing, Miss Riley," and, "We very proud of our daughter, Miss Riley," and "Thank you for all you doing for Gloria, Miss Riley."

'But when we got home, they changed their tune. "What the point of you doing A levels?" they told me, "All you going do is get married and have babies. You no need A levels for that, child."'

Gemma is as angry now as when Mum first told her this story, before she went to college herself, when she was sixteen.

'Still,' Mum continues, 'I have to count myself lucky. Your Dad wasn't a knight in shining armour, he didn't save me from anything, but he did let me be. We got the measure of each other straight away. I know we argue a bit—'

Gemma snorts.

'—but arguing is a luxury, dear. At least, it is the way we do it. Your Dad never underestimated me, and never undermined me. He's never said the kind of things my ma and pa said to me. We raised you and Robbie together, and when I got the job at the council, he didn't say a word against it. Didn't say anything else either – he just accepted it as a fact of life.'

Gemma's never appreciated that before: how tacit acceptance can be as affirming as vocal encouragement. There's a buoyancy inside her chest now, and she feels like it might lift her from the bench. Mum's still got hold of her hand, but she'll need more anchoring than that.

'Now, you've got a job to do,' Mum says, throwing her a line, 'and I need to get ready so I can watch you do it. Go sort your eyes out, dear. You don't want to face a crowd looking like the *Phantom of the Opera*, do you?'

David emerges from the bedroom into the living room with his rucksack slung over one shoulder, and Gemma tells the others to wait for them outside.

'What are you doing?' she asks.

His glasses are tilted downwards, and his eyes seem fixed on a middle distance lying somewhere just short of the earth's core. 'Catching a flight.'

It takes a moment for Gemma to understand what he means. A flight from Inverness to London, he means, not London to Chicago.

'I can't do that road journey again, can I?'

She shakes her head. 'I don't suppose you can.'

He looks up now and attempts a smile. Some of it even reaches his eyes. 'I know there's no point fighting this,' he says. 'You couldn't tell me because you didn't want to hurt me. And I don't want to hurt you either. I'm sorry if I was—' he thinks about the word to use, '—intemperate.'

My God, she thinks, *he's as brilliant as he's ridiculous.*

The drive to Inverness is normal enough for Gemma to go over her intro with Dad in the front, while Destiny explains the rules of a new DS game to Mum and David in the back. When they reach the outskirts of the city, David leans into the driver's seat and says, 'Do you think you could drop me at a bus station, sir?'

'Ah, that's not necessary, laddie,' Dad says. 'I'll drop this lot off and take you to the airport.'

But David refuses to risk responsibility for anyone missing Gemma's show, and the last they see of him is his rucksacked form waving a final goodbye from in front of the bus station's doors.

Two chairs are set up on the apron below the screen. It's not a big auditorium, because they're in Inverness, not London, and it might even be described as intimate. Gemma sits in one of the chairs now, and is desperately aware that the other one is empty. She checks her iPhone again, but there's been nothing since 'OK. I'm ready. Be there soon'.

That was sent just fifteen minutes ago.

'Hi, Gemma.' It's the man in the red-and-green tartan suit who introduced himself when she arrived, and whose name she's already forgotten. He's in charge of the event, and they've probably exchanged emails. 'We're going to start in five minutes.'

'Ms Korzeniowski isn't here yet,' says Gemma. 'She's on her way.'

He's got a goatee and tufted eyebrows, which give him a Mephistophelean look. 'That's fine,' he says, as though it's an appropriate response. 'We'll show her up when she gets here.'

Then he leaves, and all Gemma can do is sit and wait, aware again of the pre-show drone of the audience, and fearful that she'll catch a stranger's eye. A disturbance in the visual pattern turns out to be Destiny and Mum waving. She waves back, and even that makes her feel self-conscious. Dad's sitting the other side of Destiny from Mum, looking up at the screen, already expectant.

'Hello, Gemma.'

It's a woman in her sixties, dressed in a fitted suit of violet tweed that's a bit Jackie O, looking up at her from in front of the apron. Gold at her wrists and neck sets off freckles and a helmet of strawberry-blonde hair. She's holding up a tiny hand.

'I'm Julia,' she says, then adds needlessly, 'from Aberdeen.'

A pulse sounds inside Gemma's handbag, tucked between her hip and the arm of her chair. She takes the hand that's been offered, and feels she must be careful not to break the bones in it. 'I'm so glad you could make it.'

'Well, I'm intrigued. I've never seen the film before, in any version.'

'Good,' says Gemma. 'That'll make you a test case.'

She laughs at that, and grows a little warmer. 'Can we still meet tomorrow? I'm staying with friends in town. We can have lunch, if you like.'

'Why not?' says Gemma, 'Oh, and yes.'

Julia looks at her quizzically.

'I mean—' she tries again, '—I'd like to take the job, if you're still offering.'

More laughter, and it's even warmer. 'We are. Let's talk about it properly tomorrow. Give me a call.'

While the professor makes her way to her seat, Gemma gets out her phone. '*Nearly there,*' she reads. '*Sorry we're running late. April xx.*' We're…?

The devilish man in tartan is standing next to her again. 'All set?'

'She's nearly here,' Gemma pleads.

'Good,' he says.

The lights come down low enough to prompt the audience to settle. For a blessed two minutes, the infernal official talks about the festival. Gemma spends them taking multiple sips of water. Then she hears her name, and knows she's being introduced. There's a round of applause, and then she's on.

'Thank you, Andrew,' she says, conjuring the right name. 'In a few minutes, you will see a battered dispatch box being laid on a table in the vault of Cox & Co, Charing Cross, for the benefit of the Canadian veterinary surgeon to whom it has been bequeathed. His grandfather's name is inscribed on the side of the box in gold curlicues. It is that of John H. Watson, MD, famous biographer of the world's most famous detective.

'There follows an inspection of the box's contents, in a sequence which has, since 1970, accompanied the opening titles of Billy Wilder's *The Private Life of Sherlock Holmes*. While Miklós Rózsa's wonderful music plays, we are shown in turn a posed sepia-washed portrait of the famous pair, a deerstalker hat, a meerschaum pipe, a magnifying glass, a pair of handcuffs, a pistol and Dr Watson's stethoscope. None of these are surprising, of course – all pertain to life at 221B Baker Street as we know it from reading Conan Doyle's stories, or at least from watching the films and TV shows based on them.

'Then things change. A manuscript sheet of music emerges with Holmes's signature on it, followed by a crumpled seven of diamonds and a pocket watch, the casing of which is opened up to reveal the image of a woman peeping at us with soulful eyes. These are elements of a new mystery, and one the audience might reasonably expect to see solved by the end of the movie. And yet, for 44 years, no cinema-goer has been able to make them entirely add up.'

This is when Gemma had wanted to introduce April. She can see Andrew in the wings, but he's not even looking at her. She's going to have to wing it.

'Shortly, I'll be speaking to April Korzeniowski, who was Wilder's continuity supervisor on *The Private Life of Sherlock Holmes*. She will be able to give us a unique insight into the hopes the director had for a project that was, by all accounts, a labour of love.'

Talking about her hasn't made her appear. Gemma decides to step out onto the ledge.

'But before we meet Ms Korzeniowski, I'd like to say something about what the film, and the rediscovery of this first director's cut, means to me. For a few of us,' Gemma finds herself saying, '*The Private Life of Sherlock Holmes* is the best Sherlock Holmes film ever made. But I'm tempted to go even further. In my assessment, Wilder's film is the greatest work to deal in the mythos of Baker Street in any form, and I include the original stories.'

There's no sign that Gemma's controversial pronouncement has disturbed the audience in any way. There are places, she knows, where it would have started a riot.

'There's a film-making maxim that Billy Wilder was fond of quoting, which he got from his mentor, Ernst Lubitsch. While bad directors tell you "two plus two equals four", a good one only tells you "two plus two". It's a consequence of his sticking to this that means you won't find easy morals at the end of a Wilder picture, even when made under the baleful eyes of the Hays Code enforcer Joseph Breen.

'Now, I think you can see this Lubitschian approach in *The Private Life of Sherlock Holmes*. We tend to think of iconic characters like Holmes as bold monoliths that can withstand whatever is thrown at them. Get them fighting Nazis, parody them, drop them into some other icon's story, and they'll survive every time. But Wilder understood that the opposite is the case. Icons are delicate – to retain their essential nature, their mystery mustn't be fully explained. Wilder's understated, two-plus-two approach is what allows Robert Stephens's Holmes to remain opaque, even while a Freudian light is being shone on his troubled psyche...'

At last, there's something going on at the back of the auditorium. It's too dark to make out what, though. Then there's movement along the further side aisle, and a flash of white hair. She's here!

'And now, I'm delighted to introduce our special guest. Please welcome April Korzeniowski.'

The audience applauds as April climbs to the stage, directed by the man in tartan. But Gemma is thinking, *I haven't finished what I was saying*. She'd been on a roll, moving towards something she's never told anyone. But perhaps that's a blessing... Could she really have confessed that she'd always found knowledge of the missing scenes a burden? That they had hung as an annoying caveat over a film she'd previously considered perfect? It certainly wouldn't have been wise to tell this audience for the restored version that, in her opinion – an opinion being formed even now – it is a diminished thing, stripped of much of what made the abridged version so tenderly ambiguous.

April takes her seat, and her dress turns to sheet lightning under the lights. 'Sorry I'm late,' she whispers.

'No problem,' says Gemma. 'I warmed them up for you.'

April's hair is darker than it ought to be, grey rather than white.

Some strands are clumped together. But Gemma knows it hasn't been raining. Someone was with her in the side aisle, someone who is seated now and invisible among the crowd. There's no mystery here, though – it's the captain of the *Caledonian*.

Damn, girl, Gemma thinks, *there's no stopping you, is there?*

The crowd settles again. 'So, April,' Gemma says, 'can you say something about what life was like for a continuity girl in the summer of 1969?'

Chapter Fifteen

It was April who brought up the subject of the Stirlings, as they lay covered by a sheet in the attic bedroom of her rented cottage. Too much sun came in through the pale curtains, so they'd been awake since dawn.

'So,' she said, 'who are the other survivors?'

He told her how Pete Leith had gone relatively early, in the purple miasma of the 1970s, in amongst OPEC, the drought and the three-day week. She was sorry to hear that. Despite everything, she'd liked the old goat. Then he told her about Tessa, whom he'd seen in her new home in Edinburgh just a couple of months ago. 'On her own,' he said, 'but her daughter and grandkids live just around the corner, so it suits her.'

'How old is she now?' April asked. 'I could never tell.'

Jim shrugged. 'About eighty.'

'Was Douglas with her until the end?'

Jim nodded. 'He had a good innings. Ninety-one when he popped off.' He smiled. 'You know, I'm not sure Alan was completely wrong about him…'

'Oh, Alan,' April smiled and turned his way again, 'and Sandra. What a couple! I always imagined that was a fun relationship. A lot of fighting, a lot of make-up sex. How're they doing?'

Another shrug. 'That's the last time I saw them. At Douglas's memorial service, I mean. In Aberdeen, January before last. I didn't really talk to them then, either.' Then he remembered. 'Well, I did talk to Alan, briefly, but it was only about Douglas. I think Sandra was deliberately avoiding me.'

April threw off the sheet and got out of bed. He felt a momentary jolt, but it subsided quickly. 'That's a crying shame,' she said. She picked up her dressing gown from where she'd dropped it on the floor and wrapped herself in it. 'You can't do that to friends.' She sat in the bedside chair and glowered at him. 'You can't possibly hold anything against them. That would be obscene.'

aid, truthfully. 'But I was angry for a long time. I
e a habit.'

head, but at least she was smiling. He knew the
........ance of that smile – of the teeth, at any rate – must have
cost some dollars, but God, the job had been a good one. 'I was
pissed, too,' she said. 'Notice how well I've gotten over it?'

'You've a fucking nerve, Jamie Outhwaite.'

He wants to take a step back, but there's not enough space
between the doorstep he's standing on and the precipitous flight
of stairs behind. The woman filling the doorway is clearly the one
Sandra Stirling was always going to be. No longer voluptuous in
the way he'd always secretly admired, she now looks like she could
take out an enemy with one well-judged cuff on the chin. Her hair
isn't up, but it's still long: two white torrents foaming over her big
bosom. Her eyes aren't kohl-rimmed now, but they still smoulder.
Her summer frock – it's got daisies on it – ought to fall below her
knees, but it's hitched higher by that bosom and her wide hips.

Suddenly, he's enfolded in a pair of soft arms and the white hair
smothers his face.

'Too fucking long,' she says, and plants a hot kiss on his cheek.
'Would you look at you?' She's holding him at arm's length now,
by the shoulders. 'Barely a change. Apart from the hair, eh?'

He puts his sailor's cap back on. 'You look fantastically yourself,
Sandra.'

'Ay, a bag of shite. Haven't had a chance to put my face on.'
Then she frowns. 'For fuck's sake, come in.'

He follows her into a room he last stood in 45 years ago, when
the house was near derelict and he and Alan were trespassers. But it
isn't the memory of that day that causes him a kind of time-travel
sickness. It's the line of boots by the wall, the floral covers on the
three-piece suite, the fraying rugs on the stone floor, the pile of
unopened envelopes on the mahogany occasional table with the
barley-twist legs... There's an overstuffed bookcase, too, and more
books in little piles on nearly every step leading to the first floor.

In spirit, if not physical dimensions, he's back in the headquarters of the LNRG.

'Shove that rubbish on the floor,' Sandra says, pointing at the sofa.

Jim sits next to a multicoloured plastic water cannon that's leaking from the muzzle onto the upholstery.

'You'll have some tea,' she announces at the door to the kitchen. The radio is playing in there, a soft Glaswegian brogue murmuring comfort to millions. 'Alan will be down in a jiffy.'

'I'll sit tight,' says Jim.

But it's hard to, because he feels like he's waiting to have a filling. A lot of noise comes out of the kitchen, and he remembers again how Sandra had made her presence constantly felt in the Campbells' farmhouse. Water roars into the kettle and the washbasin, metal clangs against metal, ceramics clack and clatter and splash. She turns up the radio so she can hear it above the racket that she herself is making.

'Jamie,' says a voice from above, 'you're a sight for sore eyes.'

Alan has lost some weight, even since Douglas's memorial service. Jim gets up and takes his hand before he reaches the bottom of the stairs. He's clutching the bannister, making it creak, and taking each step with a good deal of care. When he's on firm ground, he keeps hold of Jim's hand and draws him in for another hug. It hasn't the strength of Sandra's, but it's as keenly meant. 'Couple of fucking bastards we are, eh?' he says, 'What's been keeping us?'

'Sheer stupidity, I suppose,' says Jim.

Alan eases himself into an armchair. 'Diabetes,' he says, without being asked. 'You came just as I was shooting up.'

Jim sits by the leaking gun again. 'Sorry to hear that.'

Alan shrugs. 'Could be a lot worse. And it's not so bad to deal with these days. I'm trying to keep fit, too, you know? Knocked the drink on the head. Not a drop in three years.'

Though he'd clearly been overweight 18 months ago, there's a quality to Alan's new leanness that isn't altogether encouraging. His jowls sag, his eyes are sunken and there's a loose ridge that hangs under his chin. There's something urological in his pallor too. But he's got as much white hair flopping over his forehead as he had blond – that, at least, is something to be jealous of. 'And here was I,' says Jim, 'about to suggest we go to the pub.'

'Jesus,' says Sandra, coming in from the kitchen with the tea things on a tray, 'those days are long gone. Do you mind moving that shite out the way, Jamie?'

Jim clears a space on the coffee table, making a heap of the kids' picture books and a couple of copies of *Heat* magazine.

'So,' she says, taking the other armchair, 'what's got you out of your bunker, eh? I'm guessing you didn't just wake up and think "Oh, isn't this a fine morning for visiting friends I've not thought about for fifty fucking years".'

Something in those still-fierce eyes lets him know she's only joshing. 'Do you remember April Bloom?'

'Miss fucking California 1969? Who could forget her, pal? This bastard couldn't, believe me—' poking her husband with a finger, with enough force to tilt him against the further arm of his chair, '—practically had to roll his tongue back into his mouth every time she entered the room.'

Alan doesn't attempt to refute it. 'What about her, Jamie?'

He tells them nearly everything: from his meeting the film lecturer on the loch, to his date with April at the Dores Inn, to attending the film premiere together. He lays it on lightly – doesn't let on that this is the first day they've spent apart since meeting again, five days ago. When he's finished, Sandra gets up and begins to gather their empty mugs. 'Well, I'm happy for you. A nice wee trip down memory lane.'

Jim wonders what he's said wrong.

'You're all right, Jamie,' she tells him, 'it's just that I'm running late. I'm meeting Mary in town.'

'Oh, right,' says Jim. 'And how is Mary?'

'Forty-fucking-four, that's how she is. Her son's the spit of this bastard—' she means Alan, '—and is studying geology at Glasgow. Chip off the ol' block, poor laddie.'

Then Jim is told about the rest of the Stirling clan. Doug is 36, and it's his kids whose colouring books and toys clutter up the house. Their youngest is 27, and another research scientist in Glasgow, working with his own nephew.

'What did we call that one, hen?' Alan asks his wife.

She pauses with the tea tray on her knees. 'Well it wasnae fucking Autolycus, was it?'

Jim has heard already, through the grapevine, but still has to brace himself to hear it again now.

'Jamie's the genius of the family,' says Alan. 'If there's an answer to how we're going to save the planet, he's the one who'll find it.'

Jim bought the *Caledonian* off Douglas in 1971 for a knock-down price. It had been strange going out in her at first, because it had seemed as though she belonged to Alan. He couldn't quite imagine one of them without the other.

Alan stands on the deck with his eyes closed as they pull away from the quay. 'Better than a pub, eh?' He opens his eyes. 'She sounds different, mind. You've had to do some work on her over the years, I suppose.'

'She's an old vessel,' says Jim. 'Luckily, you can replace her component parts.'

Alan nods. 'I could do with replacing a couple of component parts myself.'

Out of habit, Jim guides the *Cally* to where there's a clear view of both banks. Compact clouds skim the skies like tossed paper, and there are white heads on the waves of the loch.

'Which way you voting?' Alan asks.

It takes a moment for Jim to realise what he's talking about. 'Oh, I'm not going to.'

'Why the fuck not?'

Jim shrugs. 'I'm English,' he says. 'It wouldn't be right.'

Alan shakes his head. 'How long you lived here, pal?'

Jim has to think about it. 'Started my master's in Aberdeen in October, '66. So, nearly 48 years.'

'Then you're at least as Scottish as my kids are.'

Jim takes that as a joke, but he knows it isn't. If he isn't Scottish, what is he? His visits to Cumbria stopped feeling like visits home years ago, and nowadays they don't even take him to the house in which he grew up.

'What way will you vote, then?' he asks.

Alan answers without hesitation. 'Our business relies on a steady trickle of foreigners. I'm sticking with the Sassenachs and the EU, thanks very much.'

For a while they listen to the engine and to the old loch sounds that haven't changed in all the time they've known each other. Then Alan starts laughing again.

'What?' Jim asks.

'Fucking Nessie.' He laughs some more – almost belly laughs. 'How good has she been to us, eh? I raised a family on her. And you? She's *been* your fucking family.'

Jim flinches. 'What's that supposed to mean?'

'Well, who else is there?'

So, this is where it's all been leading. Forgive-and-forget when they're on *terra firma*, but once in the middle of the loch, time for recriminations.

But Alan reads his thoughts the way Sandra read them earlier. 'For fuck's sake, Jamie, I only mean you've been loyal to her. I sold her down the Swanee – course I did. You know about the Cuddly Nessie Room at the Experience?'

Jim does know. A room filled with every conceivable design of Loch Ness Monster that can be rendered in napped cloth and stuff-ing. He's aware that he's pulling a face just thinking about it.

Alan laughs some more. 'Oh, I love that room,' he says. 'One of Pete's last good ideas, along with persuading us to set up shop at the Drum so we'd be nearer where people actually are. It's a fucking lightning rod, Jamie. We can have any number of rooms dedicated to real analysis of data, or real history, or records of folk-lore, because people know they're going to end up in the Cuddly Nessie Room and get their photo taken against the green screen with Big Nessie.'

'But do they remember anything of value?'

Alan shrugs. 'The ones that'll remember anything do. You and me, we would've remembered, wouldn't we?'

Jim shrugs. 'Probably.'

'And look at the work we've been able to do. Okay, Douglas got Vickers-Armstrong to come in and do that sonar mapping, just before you jumped ship – calling in some favours from the old boys on the board. A few fellow intelligence men there, I don't doubt...'

'Bloody hell, Alan.' Now Jim's laughing. 'You're never giving that one a rest, are you?'

'But as soon as Douglas was out of the picture, it was a sound business plan and a bit of ready moolah that made the difference. If you've got a little already, people are much more willing to give you a little more. Look at what we've done – that sediment logging, for instance. Who'd have dreamt it? Ten millennia locked up in a tube of mud...'

'I read your article on that,' Jim tells him. 'Fantastic stuff.'

'Thanks, pal,' says Alan, beaming. 'That means a lot. Anyway,' he continues, getting back to the point he has been trying to make, 'I know you're not the type to go for a Cuddly Nessie Room. You're not a means-to-an-end sort of guy. You're more the Sherlock fucking Holmes of Nessie hunters, you know what I'm saying?'

That comparison again – he tries not to let his surprise at the coincidence show in his face.

'It's all got to be based on reason with you,' Alan is saying, 'and be *seen* to be based on reason. I love that. You know what I've mostly heard about you over the past few years?'

Jim stiffens again. 'No, but I suppose you're going to tell me.'

'Customers who've been in the *Cally* before they come to us say that you've told them not to believe anything anyone else says about the Loch Ness Monster. Everyone else has an agenda, a motive for believing in the monster that's got nothing to do with science. But here's the thing I've realised about you, pal...'

'Go on,' Jim says, 'enlighten me.'

Alan jabs his arm with a finger. 'You're the only person I know who really *does* believe in her.'

Jim laughs again. He makes sure it's as loud as Alan's laughter was, and that it doesn't sound too forced.

'I'm not joking,' says Alan, and it's true that he isn't smiling. 'Everyone else – that tosser Stewart McAllister, may he rest in peace, and all the other showmen, spivs and conspiracy theorists who've come here down the years – they just decide she exists and pick and choose their evidence to suit. But you want real evidence, something rock solid. You're desperate for tried-and-tested, peer-assessed, in-fucking-controvertible proof that the Loch Ness Monster exists. And you're not going to stop until you get it, are you?'

Jim shuts off the engine, so that the only sounds are the slap of waves on the hull and the cries of gulls above them. 'If I'm Sherlock Holmes, who does that make you?'

'Not that thick bastard Watson, if that's what you're thinking.' He considers a moment. 'I'm the fat fucker who runs the whole outfit. Sherlock's more intelligent brother.'

Jim laughs for real. 'Mycroft,' he says. 'Well, you might be right.' Then he remembers something, and reaches up to switch on the monitor. 'I've something to show you.'

'Not porn, is it? Because it's all over the internet these days, pal. No need to buy it under the table down the pub any more.'

Jim slides a DVD out of its slipcase and slots it in the monitor's side. The screen turns from uniform blue to various shades of grey. 'That's the night camera,' he says. 'Those are the planks just there.' He points past Alan's shoes to the foot of the central bench. 'And that—' pointing to the screen now, '—is a Tupperware box with some of my lunch left in it.' He presses fast-forward and, for a while, nothing disturbs the screen save the white blips of passing moths. Then something bigger appears and Jim presses play.

'Well, well, well,' says Alan. 'Cheeky wee bastard.'

It's young and sleek, and its eyes show on the screen like two little supernovae. It turns its triangular head in every direction, then thrusts it into the box and lifts out a white triangle in its jaws. It seems to stare directly at the camera, then slips away.

'Douglas always hoped Autolycus would found a whole colony of little thieves,' Jim says. 'I think we've just seen a descendant. But, you know,' he adds, 'I don't have any proof.'

Jim tells April everything about his meeting with the Stirlings. It's like a confession – or rather, a report on what you do after a confession, when you try to put everything right.

'You did good, Dr Outhwaite,' she says. 'Feel better now?'

He nods.

They're taking a rest from climbing the slope of the meadow. The heather isn't at its best, but there are white flowers on the bearberries, and they have already identified three species of butterfly. Jim has been required to pronounce their scientific names, and one turned out to be an old friend – *Aricia artaxerxes.*

'I'd like to see them again, too,' she says, meaning Alan and Sandra. 'Or maybe they can come out and see us in San Marino.'

It's a new game she's playing, that's not really a game: talking as though it's all done and dusted, and that he will be following her to California as soon as he's made the necessary arrangements. He's not sure he finds it much fun. He feels a tremendous yearning, a horrible sense of impending loss, whenever she reminds him that she's got a flight to catch, and there's no doubt that thinking of a future for them eases that feeling. But then, when he thinks of losing all this…

'You were an environmentalist,' April says, looking out across the deep greens of pasture and woodland, the bright incursions of loch, the gorse-yellow on the hills. 'I remembered that every time I heard more about the hole in the ozone layer, or global warming, or people arguing about wolves in Yellowstone.'

'I still am one, I hope,' he says. He's catching his breath, and watches as she catches hers, too, hands on hips. 'An environmentalist, I mean. We've made some progress since those days, with pesticides and so on. Some populations are beginning to boom again. Some raptors are making a resurgence – bet I could show you a golden eagle if we went into the Cairngorms. And pine martens are back, too. You remember Autolycus?'

'The finger-biter?' Her voice is a little husky. 'Yeah, I remember.'

'Global warming's another matter,' he adds. 'We'll die with that only getting worse. Hang on, I've something I meant to show you.'

He takes a photograph out of a pocket in his rucksack. One corner is curled, but the colours are still vivid. A young woman standing in a meadow identical to this one, her hair in two thick braids, wearing a smock dress with little flowers on it. She's smiling, the end of a word dropping eternally from her lips...

'It was a couple of years before I developed that,' he tells her. 'I'd forgotten it in my move to Aberdeen.'

He doesn't go into details – doesn't tell her about the blue funk he fell into as the image materialised in the developing fluid. How it led him to write the first of the seven letters he never sent her.

'I've got one to show you, too.' She dips in her shoulder bag and brings out her wallet. 'That's Maisie.' It's a print the size of a credit card. 'She's a little older in this than I am in yours. But there's a resemblance, I think.'

The woman is standing in front of a brick wall, with a lamp post to her left and the rear wheel of a motorcycle bisected by the frame on her right. She is wearing a leather jacket, jeans and heavy cycling boots. Wing-framed sunglasses are pushed up into her pompadour. She's a rocker, not a hippy, but Jim sees what April means – there's something in the eyes. Her lips, too, are biting off the end of a word. 'She's a film director?'

'Uh-huh.' April is staring hard at the photo. 'Documentaries. She likes real people.'

'And does she have children?'

It's an obvious question, the sort everyone asks.

'No,' April says. She's having trouble returning the photo to the pocket in her wallet. 'Not yet. People wait these days, don't they? You were starting a trend and you didn't even know it.'

Jim persuades her to hand in the keys to her cottage a day early, and spend her final night with him in Inverness. He wakes too early, and is tempted to wake her, too. He wants to steal another couple of hours in her company. But the day ahead of her is long, and she needs as much sleep as she can get. He contents himself with lying beside her for a while, marvelling at these last few days. Then he gets up to prepare their final breakfast in bed.

When he returns with a tray – mugs of coffee, toast, jam, orange juice – April is awake and sitting up. She's drawn the curtains, and is staring at the oblong of faultless blue. Jim feels like he's caught her in a thought, and she smiles and flashes those eyes at him. For the first time, he recognises that look as a cover for something. 'It's a beautiful morning,' she says. 'It's only been beautiful mornings the whole time I've been here. We should have waited to shoot the movie till now.'

While they're eating, Jim asks a question he's wanted to ask all week. 'What exactly did Douglas say to you, that first night at the Drumnadrochit?'

She gives him the arc-light treatment again. 'Not sure I can manage "exactly" – I'm not a Dictaphone.' Then her gaze turns sceptical. 'What do you know? You tell me, and I'll confirm or deny, as far as I can.'

It takes Jim no effort of memory. 'I know that Douglas had been contacted by Mr Wilder, or a representative of some kind, and asked about the use of Campbell Pier. Douglas was a great defender of the film being made here, right from the start, when I wasn't so keen. And then, his behaviour that night at the Drum wasn't normal. I mean, he never had a problem talking to strangers, but he made an absolute beeline for you – I'd never seen him do that before. I interrupted the two of you because I had an inkling something wasn't right. Well, also, I suppose, I was jealous of him talking to the most beautiful woman in the room. But afterwards, I couldn't help thinking that he was always the sort of man who could make things happen with the right phone call, or just a word in someone's ear. I wondered how far he would go with that…'

She shrugs. 'Well, it wasn't much of a word, as I recall.' She says it through her toast, which takes the edge off it sounding like the confession it is. 'He just asked me to let you do the talking, and make sure I sounded impressed.' She hasn't moved her eyes from his. 'If you knew something was up, why didn't you say?'

He smiles. 'Well, things happened, didn't they? I didn't want to ruin things. And then, the way we ended up wasn't the way we began.'

She laughs at that. 'Not even the way we ended up was the way we ended up.'

The next couple of hours go by with deadly swiftness. The final rush of preparation: washing, dressing, checking bags. Then April is driving them in the hire car through mild traffic that keeps threatening to thicken. The car is returned to its depot, there's a perfunctory domestic check-in, and then they're sitting on a bench by the departure gate, and there's practically no time left.

Jim is suddenly resentful of everything around them. The rumbling carts, the tannoy announcements, other passengers' chatter: all of it seems like an inexcusable intrusion. He doesn't know what to say, and it seems she doesn't either. Then she asks, 'When are you coming to visit?'

'Soon,' he says.

She shakes her head, as though that's no answer. Which it isn't. 'I'll show you those redwoods.'

'I've seen them. I was at that conference, remember?'

'Yeah, but it wasn't me showing you, was it? It was some floozy whose name you can't even remember.' She drops her head onto his shoulder and leans into him. 'There's got to be a difference, don't you agree?'

'Oh, yes,' he says. 'I do.'

He can't see her eyes, but he's thinking about them. During that other summer, they'd seemed like touchstones to a truth to which he didn't have access. They'd mocked his own idea of truth, had made it seem inadequate. That was the opposite effect to the one Douglas had counted on, but it proved just as effective. It wasn't Jim's pride that April had appealed to at all.

But now he wonders if there's something else in that dazzling glare. He thinks it might be regret – but what could she have had to regret in those days? It's something else, but he can't grasp what.

When the announcement comes, they stand and kiss for a long time. The way teenagers kiss: as though nothing and nobody else in the world exists.

'I've got your number,' she says, 'and you've got mine. And there's email, and Skype, and Facebook. We're not going to be able to move for each other's company from now on. You know that, right?'

'I do.'

'But I'm going to want real-world, face-to-face time with you, too. I'm being serious now – do you understand?'

'Yes, yes,' he says, 'I do.'

'Look—' and he looks at her, and those eyes seem to subsume him, take him into their version of what truth is, '—I know you're not going to leave the Loch Ness Monster for me. I'm just the bit on the side, and that's just fine. You know what? You're not my monster either.'

He knew she would do this to him – leave him laughing, despite how he feels. 'I will visit,' he says. 'Soon, I promise. But I've only just begun to make things right here.' He was thinking that he had a vote to cast, at the very least. 'I can do both, can't I?'

She holds the backs of her fingers to his cheek, above his beard, so that he can feel the tingling coolness of her nails. 'Oh, you can always do both,' she says. Then she leaves him, passing through the glass doors, and he keeps watching until there's nothing left to see.

Acknowledgements

Thanks first to the head of Unbound Digital, Xander Cansell, who patiently guided me through a very particular publishing process, and to my editors, Craig Taylor and Andrew Chapman, who were just as patient and who taught me much about my capabilities. Early readers helped keep me headed in the right direction – thanks to Emily Bryan, Bob Edwards, Tom Evershed, Elizabeth Klett, and Emily Sheriff. I also benefited from feedback left by some of the 300 readers who subscribed to *The Continuity Girl* on The Pigeonhole. Thanks to all of them, and to Rebecca Stacey for supervising the serialisation. The cover was designed by Mark Ecob, and I am grateful to him for suggesting a level of wit that I hope is reflective of the novel itself.

I was fortunate in finding support for my pitch to Unbound and the subsequent crowdfunding campaign from two prominent fans of *The Private Life of Sherlock Holmes*: the novelist Jonathan Coe and the novelist and film critic Kim Newman. Adrian Shine of the Loch Ness and Loch Morar Project not only granted me an interview about his 40-year career assessing evidence for the Loch Ness Monster, but also volunteered to check my science. Paul Diamond, the screenwriting son of Billy Wilder's writing partner, I.A.L. Diamond, fulfilled a similar duty with regards to my depiction of film set practices in the summer of 1969. All extant mistakes in both cases are my own. A Twitter encounter with Lindsay McPhee led to an interview with her father, Robert McPhee, who was an extra on the film. Thanks also to Tony Lindsell, Alex Breeze, Charlotte Walters, and Michael McEntee for their help in promoting the book.

Many aspiring authors belong to a writing group, and I've been lucky enough to belong to two. One is the Facebook group to which all Unbound writers are invited, and which is full of wisdom and reassurance. The other is Leamington Writers, run by

Stephen Calcutt. Not a single comment made about my writing by members of the group has gone unheeded.

The Continuity Girl was inspired by a great Billy Wilder film – but it is also the bi-product of a honeymoon spent in the Highlands. I suppose it was inevitable that a story begun during that week would end up a romantic one. My wife and I developed my initial idea in conversations over the next couple of years, and then made separate attempts to complete the same story in different forms. I chose the novel. As in so much else, it's to Heather I owe most thanks.

The best books I read in preparation for writing gave a sense of the times, as well as furnishing facts. Special mention should be made of *Knight Errant* (Robert Stephens), *Tall, Dark and Gruesome* (Christopher Lee), *Billy Wilder: Interviews* (ed. Robert Horton), and *On Sunset Boulevard: The Life and Times of Billy Wilder* (Ed Sikov). Again, remaining untruths are the result of either a stubborn ignorance on my part or myto an application of poetic licence. I should acknowledge here that the real continuity supervisor on *The Private Life of Sherlock Holmes* was Elaine Schreyeck, a formidable figure known in the industry as 'the Duchess', who also worked on many of the films listed in Chapter 13. I recommend you look her up on IMDB.

Of course, none of these hundreds of thousands of wordsthis would have been written without the pairing of Billy Wilder and I.A.L. Diamond. All of us owe them a debt of thanks.

Patrons

Thomas Ainge
Lorraine Ashley
Darren Ballard
Jason Ballinger
Sarah Barnard
Kathryn Bates
Lauren Bennett
Josh Boxall
June Boyd
M R Brend
Gemma Brooks
Hannah Buchanan
Christine Burns
Alexandra Buttery
John Byrne
Caroline Cakebread
Sue Campayne
Paul Carroll
Aaron Cassidy
Peter Claisse
Harriet Cunningham
Paul Diamond
Todd Everett
Matthew Flynn
Lucy Frank
Lucy Gardner
Adam Gibson
Shona Groat
Gemma Hathaway-Taylor
E O Higgins
Charley Hinds
Mary Horlock

Melanie Horner
Anne & John Jenkins
Joanna Jones
Matthew Kalloor
Martin Keady
Robert Kelly
Becky Kimberley
Gillian Kincaid
Shona Kinsella
Julia Kite
Ewan Lawrie
Simon Leake
Adam Lloyd
Paul Main
Adele Mansell
Amelia Marriette
Peter Marshall
Jessica Martin
Jason Maycock
Jess McAlister
Linda McCann
David McDermott
Martine McDonagh
Daniel McGachey
Rex McGee
Jonathan Melville
Sarah Menary
Marian Mestanek
Simon Miller
Ivy Ngeow
Karen Parr
Toby Patterson
Philippa Perry-French
Janet Powell
Rhiannon Pursall
Craig Quinney

Helen Randle
Morven Reid
Anna Renton-Green
Bastian Roeder
Jane Rogers
Dean Ryan
Robert Ryan
Clare Samson
Adam Sear
Alan Searl
Keith Sequeira
Laurence Settle
David Shaw
Ed Sikov
Wendy Silvester
Sheila Smith
Suzanne Spridgeon
Emily Stephenson
Tabatha Stirling
Elisabetta Tarantino
Francesca Tondi
Rebecca Tonks
Rob Tranter
Finlay Turner-Berry
Nathan Wade
Natalie de Weerd
Matthew West
Flora Wilson
Rebecca de Winter
Gretchen Woelfle
Juanjo
Cornelia